EXALTATIONS

EXALTATIONS

RICHARD GARFINKLE

www.achronalpress.com

Exaltations

Achronal Press
www.achronalpress.com

First edition
ISBN 978-0-578-02362-5

Cover art and book design by Alessandra Kelley

To Robert, Corey, Alex, and Alessandra
for reasons that should be clear.

1. Election

Isolation by Exaltation
followed by Fated mingling leads to
a Society on a Quest.

| ACCEPTANCE |

Peter Refton walked into the war zone. It was the only way he knew to leave his world. He had come as a reporter, the job he had most commonly held in his thirteen -- or was it fourteen? -- lives. It was difficult to remember exactly how many times he had lived. It might even have been more than fourteen, since he had only started writing them down seven lives ago in order to stem the tide of forgetfulness.

He left his jeep behind and climbed, hard-booted and camouflaged, up the mountains of Afghanistan, following a Russian patrol, a group of young men from poor families searching for other squads of young men from poor families.

Refton had seen three firefights since coming to this war, but none of them had given him the opportunity to leave the world. He hoped it would come soon. He had no idea if he could die, but he knew how badly he could be hurt.

His backpack dug into him like a sack of gold bricks, the weight of lives heavy upon him. He carried his pasts with him on paper, not trusting the vagaries of magnetism or optical storage. If he needed to remind himself about who he had been he wanted to pull out paper and read immediately, not seek for some computer or rely on his laptop's batteries, which had died many times in worlds that lacked electricity or had AC sockets of inappropriate configuration.

Only seven lives were recorded; six or seven more, partially remembered, occupied loose sheets of note-paper.

Writing Lives was what Refton did. He was a biographer, a hunter and catcher of pasts leading to presents leading to futures. His own pasts were muddled, his present variable, and his future too indefinite to conceive.

There were a precious few pillars of his being that did not change from life to life. He was always alone, without a family. Mostly single. Divorced in two lives. Once widowed. Linda and baby Terry in a car crash. It had been five lives since, but still he remembered them, remembered the last day he had seen them, even though they had never met, never existed. He had come back to the world from the arms of his Poetess, and his new life had rushed into him. Linda and Terry had been dead for six years and the pain appeared in his soul, raw with the newness of the life the world had given him.

Shots from behind rocks, the familiar staccato of guerilla warfare. Crouch down, seek cover, hope and wait.

Only in this world, the world he came from, did lives wait for him. In the others he visited he appeared as a stranger without past or recognition, making his way as an alien among unknowns, giving locally appropriate variations on his name. When he returned from such alternate places this world, presumably his native one, would take him back, presenting him with a new past that always contained his name, his age and his books, but never kept anything else.

He had been born in Alberta, New Mexico, Sydney, Llandudnow, Hong Kong; he had had various parents, a rainbow of schooling, a romance-series of loves and hates. But whatever precursors he had been given, his life and his mind had turned inevitably toward biography. His books, unchanged, maintained their places on the best-seller lists no matter what his past.

Bullets flew, still too fast to be seen. If they slowed down there would be an opportunity.

EXALTATIONS

No, not slowed, that wasn't right. If the bullets became clear and important, if the understanding of the world rested on the coming of a single shot, if.

There, heading for the Lieutenant, young Feodor, whose elderly mother lived in Saint Petersburg and sold her allotment of prescription drugs on the street in order to buy food. The bullet was coming for him. His head was almost in its line. Maybe, maybe not, life or death in a few millimeters, in the toss of a neck, the toss of a coin, Fate given or taken away in a single

Crack.

No sound, but a break, an opening in the world, as if there were sudden sharp edges to reality, rifts in Time and Space. Refton could and did dive through one, vanishing from the battlefield.

Out for a moment, into the vast dark expanses between the worlds, between realities, between Earths. Refton had no good words for where he was going and no conception of what he was passing through. He saw long, bone-white islands floating in the black sea and knew each of them to be a world like his, knew the length of those isles was the Time that governed them and that supposedly he could go anywhere or anywhen. But it didn't happen like that. He was a hunter, hunting lives to catch and trap them, and he could only go where his desired quarry roamed.

He was seeking someone who might tell him what had happened to him, why he could do what he did. He had tried before, had hunted the Priest from world to world, chasing down priesthood through times unlike his own and worlds where prayers were efficacious, blessings appeared, and gods walked the Earth. But the Priest could not tell him anything about his state. All that had come of that was a book, a written life encompassing all Priests from all times and possibilities. Awards and money, but no answers. This time he would hunt a different source of understanding. This time his prey was the Magician.

No one noticed his going. No one remembered that Peter Refton had ever been there. No such reporter existed, had ever existed, would witness Feodor's death or life. The only things of Peter Refton left behind were his books, the biographies he had written. They would wait on the shelves and in people's homes for their maker's re-entrance. If he returned, his picture and biography would appear, would have always have been on their dust jackets. Time would grudgingly accommodate the needs of Life if Refton returned. If not, the books would still be there and everyone would be vague about the writer, the biographer with no biography.

Pick up a handful of coins from a bowl of change. Toss them onto the floor. Some land alone, some together, some buried under others, some burying.

A few shine in the light, others hide, some roll under beds and dressers and are lost.

Gather them up and do it again.

The result has the same heaping shape, but different coins are on top, different golds and silvers gleam in the light. Why would anyone care which coins go where?

The first bell of Matins rang clear and sharp through the fortress-monastery of the order of St. Parsival just outside the spired capital of Aachen.

Sir Johannes DeLondres had lain waiting for the bell, keeping his body still and his soul clear of thoughts and troubles. When the first echoes of the first bell began, he rose from bed, smoothly yet slowly, and stood, his feet gripping the stone floor of his monastic cell.

His eyes were shut, his spirit attentive to the place just below his stomach.

"God created man in Eden," he intoned in his spirit; the image of the garden formed in his awareness of his abdomen. "All life comes from Eden, all living things gathered there. We come from Eden."

A warmth grew in the garden in his body, a stirring.

"The breath of God comes into Eden to make life."

He inhaled as he had been taught years ago when he first joined the order. Do not pull in with your lungs, rather open yourself, let God give you your inbreath. But when you breathe out, do so forcefully. Inhale in peace, accepting the gifts of God. Exhale in war, giving up yourself as sacrifice to God.

The first gift of God flowed down his lungs into the Garden of Eden within him, filling him with Anima, Spiritus, Breath.

"Four rivers flow out of Eden."

Flow on, one river into each limb. Tigris to the left leg, Euphrates to the right, the Nile to the right arm, the Danube to the left. His arms and legs came alive with the blessings of God. His body lived and began to move through the Matins exercises St. Parsival had created seven centuries before when he had served as marshal to Carolus Magnus and, in training that Frankish lord's troops, gave all Europe and Asia Minor to his Emperor.

Kneel and Rise up. Turn and face the four directions, acknowledging the realm God has given you to defend. Extend to the East, Pull back from the West, Push to the North, Sweep to the South.

Begin now the longer form, with its elaborately named martial/spiritual maneuvers:

The Cherubim guards the Garden, imaginary sword of flame turning each way in the knight's hands. No man shall pass to strike into Eden.

Saint George Slays the Dragon, arms rise up, feet kick down, like lance and horse.

EXALTATIONS

Shepherd Guards the Flock, a round walk to keep a perimeter, feet planted in God's Earth, Spirit solid in Faith.

Greater Love Hath No Man, stepping in to take a blow and protect one's fellows.

Through the long slow series, knowing that all through the monastery his brothers in God were doing the same things at the same time, from the newest novice to the Holy Marshal. From least to greatest, all moved as one, all bowed as one to the same God, all learned as one, until the last maneuver, lying down and rising up in the death-accepting posture called Hour of Judgement. Then did the unity end and each man of the Order come to face his own individual relations with God.

In his Life of Saint Parsival, which the Reader read out each year on the saint's day, Petrus of Reeftown had inscribed these words:

"Saint Parsival said that together the army of God fights as one, each man serving the Lord, his Emperor, and each other in perfected harmony. But when the battle ends, each man faces God alone and must look within himself, for no deeds on the field of arms will save a man from the demons within him, nor help the saints and angels that dwell within to liberate his soul."

So came the moment for Sir Johannes as it did each morning, the inventory of his united soul and body, the walking of the watch within, wherein he could judge and be judged as to his own discipline.

In every part and parcel of the body and soul, a demon fought with a saint or angel, seeking to corrupt and enervate, to undermine the blessings God had placed all through the holy work of man. Most people lived their lives unaware of these continual battles. It was the revelation of this conflict to Saint Parsival which had given him the understanding to overcome the demons within him and so bring holiness to all his mortal actions, and earthly victory to his heaven-appointed Emperor.

Sir Johannes began with his hands and feet. Saint Michael held sway in the former, Saint Peter in the latter. Sir Johannes had long ago defeated the demons of both. His hands would not turn to evil; they could burn with holy fire if needed, and fight with the skill of God's general when called upon. His feet would not fly from any enemy, nor stumble on the most treacherous ground. If need be, if he had to, he could walk on water.

There were footsteps outside Johannes' cell. Some of his brethren were leaving their rooms. The least and the greatest, no doubt. His saintly brethren who had defeated most or all of their demons had swift inventories, simply noting and exchanging greetings with the triumphant saints and angels within them, while the newest monks could not yet see the battles taking place in their bodies and souls. The wise and the ignorant mingled in the hallways of the fortress, the former instructing the latter as they made their way to the refectory.

Saint Benedict ruled the mouth-for-eating and the stomach. Gluttony had been banished from Sir Johannes after hard struggle. He had been surprised, naive as he had been at the time, to discover that food had greater savor when no demon wished for more at each bite. He could enjoy each morsel given him as the everflowing bounty of God, and taste perfectly the blessings of flavor, and survive on a crust of bread and a sip of water if need be.

Saint Kyril guarded the ears. Sir Johannes had fought for two years to defeat the demon that corrupted the hearing of words and had finally triumphed. The Holy Marshal had been well pleased with this. Hearing was one of Satan's favorite avenues of entry into the souls of mankind. A knight whose hearing was flawless would not be distracted in battle or life. With Kyril's aid, Sir Johannes could fight in darkness or thunder, and not be pulled from his attention by the thousand distractions of the Adversary. And he could not be lied to.

It was for that quality that Sir Johannes had been dispatched by the fardescended-and-fallen-from-Carolus-Magnus Emperor six months ago to speak to the new Marianite order established on Mount Athos. No doubt the Emperor had thought of it as a spying mission, but the Holy Marshal had been explicit on the true purpose: "Listen to such truths as the Marianites speak and bring them back to us."

On this Sir Johannes had been half successful. He had listened, but could not formulate the words to speak the truths he had been told. The demon still gripped his mouth-of-speech, preventing Saint Paul from loosening the sacred speakings.

The demons and angels reviewed, it was time for the next inventory, the pilgrimage through the holy places within him.

More doors had opened outside. Other brothers and sisters had passed out of their cells: those who had seen the demons but had little they could yet do about them, and those who had conquered most but not all of the corruption within them. Less ignorant and less wise joined their brothers of the extremes.

Eden and the Rivers Johannes checked properly.

The Serpent still dwelt in Eden, marking the corruption of his roots. The Cherubim prevented entry, for only one purified in breath could step into Eden. Yet from the flaming gates, Johannes could see the two Trees, growing holy, nourished by his deeds.

The Rivers flowed well, their passages to his freed limbs unchecked by the demons that had once lived there, the beasts that had blocked channels and corrupted the pure waters of God.

Jerusalem was strong and vivid in his heart. Christ and AntiChrist warred there until the day came when he could undertake the Crusade and liberate the city of his heart from the final evil.

Egypt, the House of Bondage from which the Children of Israel fled in order to become chosen of God, lay in his liver. Sir Johannes felt a twinge there. The Marianites had told him something of Israel that he had not been able to speak. That secret lay chained in the house of bondage.

EXALTATIONS

Bethlehem lay in his generative organs, giving birth only within him, for he was sworn to chastity. The Marianites had hinted of other holy acts involving the Bethlehem of the body.

Mount Sinai was his spine, rising from earthly base to heavenly head. Moses climbed up and down, bearing the Law from God to the People. At the top of his spine, where head and neck become one, in the place where the demon of matters-unresolved lived and contested with the courage of Saint George, in that spot was the burning seed that the Marianites had given him in a single secret.

How had they done it? How had they developed a sudden school of divine awareness to rise up contrary to the gradual teachings of Saint Parsival and those who had come after him?

The prioress of the Marianites had spoken to him a simple riddle, or so it had seemed. "God looks at humanity. Only three have looked back. In the face of God, how can they be different?"

His freed ears had admitted those words into his mind and soul. Deep and high they had travelled until they lodged at the heights of Sinai, blocking off his head. His head was becoming something else, something never heard of in the teachings of his or any other order, something black and stony with a city around it.

The last footsteps passed by his door. The others had all gone down. Only Sir Johannes remained, struggling with the lodger in his soul.

At last he stood and went out. It would not do to keep the others from their repast. Each soldier of God had to give up things for the good of the others, including the time he needed to wrestle with his spirit.

Down the stone stairs he walked, his plain grey robes brushing gently against the smoothed granite walls, down to the refectory where the two hundred sixty-eight other members of the order waited. The Holy Marshal, his face wearied from what had no doubt been a long night's prayer, beckoned Sir Johannes over to sit next to him.

"The Emperor will send for us today," the old man said, his voice audible only to the knight. "You must prepare to give what answer you can."

"Do you think he will send us against the Marianites?"

"He will want to," the Holy Marshal said. "But Christ forbids unjust war."

Sir Johannes with Saint Peter's aid gripped the floor with his feet. The Holy Marshal had been instructed by God to defy the Emperor. It would not be the first time such a thing had happened in the order's history. Though the Emperor commanded, he was but the viceroy on Earth for the true Lord in Heaven. Many who had sat on the throne of the Caesars had grumbled at Saint Parsival's creation of a back channel to the almighty.

Somewhere -- nearby, but in a place, a direction he had never heard before -- Sir Johannes heard a cracking, as of some carefully crafted masonry breaking from an unexpected flaw. Sounds washed into his perfected ears, sounds of speeches he had never heard in tongues unknown but intelligible. Somewhere, nearby but unseen, voices were loudly raised in telling and dispute.

There is a place, broad and wide, wider than can be seen, broader in more directions than one can look no matter how wide one's vision. In this place there are strips of narrowness, channels, rivers, roads, what-have-you.

The broad place and the channels are unlike each other. You could depict them as painted in opposing colors, black ground, white channels, greensward with red roads. You could conceive of them as being of two distinct kinds, a sea with narrow islands, a plain with rivers, cloud banks with fronts.

You could array them as linguistically distinct: vast Space and confining Time; Freedom to Act, Fated to Come to an End. You could call them by divine names, the open fields of Life, the narrow graves of Death -- or the vasty halls of Death and the inevitable courses of Life.

You can name them many things, so long as what you name them accords with their reality

and their stories.

And so long as you accept the consequences of that naming.

Tai-Mu-Sang came again to be in the breath of mulberry incense, in the reading of her life story, in the mind of an Impersonator of the Dead.

Intermittency, that was the blessing of being an Ancestor, only having to think and act when called upon -- although what actions she could take and how she could think depended very much on the mind she was called into. This one was serviceable, a young woman who had recently passed her exams. Tai-Mu-Sang could feel the palpable relief in the memory of the moment when her hostess had received her certificates and had been inducted into the imperial bureaucracy.

If she was here for a long stay, it would be necessary to make room in the mind for her personal thoughts. First the ancestress would have to overlay her understanding of the classics on this young woman's. That would help the Impersonator along when Tai-Mu-Sang's spirit departed, a small hostess gift from the dead to the living.

Intermittency. It had been so hard to work with when she had lived. Tai-Mu-Sang reckoned that she had had an eighth of each day's worth of good capable thinking and the rest of the time she was not of much use. In each day of her long-gone mortal life there had come the moment when she knew her mind was used up and needed refreshment. Often that moment would come in late morning and she would face the prospect of a gloom-dulled day.

But that eighth had been enough to win her immortality. She had been wife to three Sons of Heaven, chief wife to one, mother to three. And she had ruled her departments and then the entire bureaucracy of All Under Heaven efficiently and capably, brilliantly in a few desperate hours. There had been enough brilliance to earn her the honor of being called back time and again over the ensuing five centuries and three dynasties.

Intermittency. The art styles had changed much since her time, and the latest portrait of her which her hostess was still staring at bore little resemblance to her face in life, nor to the way she had been portrayed in her own days. There was, however, much to recommend this new image, clothed in Prime Ministerial gown under a leafed and fruited mulberry from which her nickname had been taken. There in the tree eating the leaves were the silkworms that would spin the wealth and power of All Under Heaven. An insightful artist, Tai-Mu-Sang thought, one who had discerned the secret meaning of her name. The bureaucracy was made up of silkworms spinning webs of power over the land, but she had been the tree from which they fed, nourisher of all.

But no longer. That thought rose up from the hostess, carrying scenes of battle, of an army of horsemen storming Lo-Yang, casting down the Son of Heaven. It was not a great problem, it had happened before. The emperor's wives and mothers would be sad at the loss, but they were disciplined Confucianists; they knew that dynasties changed, new Sons of Heaven were installed who would marry the chief officers of state, taking new wives as they passed their exams, fathering princes who would become emperors and so promote their mothers to the highest positions.

But something was different this time. This conqueror, this Temujin, this Great Khan of the northern barbarians, he had thrown the hierarchy out of the palaces.

"No woman governs for me," he had roared as he sent them packing, bag, baggage and bureaucracy. "Only men rule here."

That was why the ceremony to call Tai-Mu-Sang had been performed in this small bamboo storehouse cluttered with treasures the Khan had not cared about, portraits of women, incense burners, books and all the scribal paraphernalia. The chief officers of state, the mothers and wives of emperors, sat firm and worried in a cluster around the young woman chosen to host this invocation. They wanted to know what was to be done. They had called her, second of their help-seeking invocations.

First they had conjured the Great Master Kung, the man who had turned the women of the Middle Kingdom into the workers in power. They had called him with songs, for it had been hearing an elderly grandmother sing so much of the Book of Odes which had originally caused him to abandon his male students and teach the deserving women of All Under Heaven to be Gentlewomen and Sages.

The Great Master had come into the mind of an old woman who had practiced all her life to incarnate men, a wearying discipline. She had succeeded in calling him back, and he had bid them comport themselves properly and not worry.

"The Khan will call you back or wither away. In a generation or two at most you will return to power."

That had not satisfied these women, so used to the trappings of power, the exercise of dominion. So they had dismissed their sacred teacher and called instead upon a never-fully-deified ancestress who had been sanctified for her grasp of political reality. They had called the Great Mother Mulberry, Tai-Mu-Sang, and now they waited to hear her practical pronouncements.

Using the agile mind of her hostess, the swiftness and sharpness that clever youth enjoys, Tai-Mu-Sang considered her answer. Master Kung had been correct, of course. All Under Heaven could not be governed without the bureaucracy. The invaders would find that out in time. This Khan might refuse to accept that reality, but his successor or his successor's successor would. The women would come back, marry a Khan, make him Son of Heaven, teach him how to speak to the Celestial Bureaucracy, absorb him into the runnings of the Middle Kingdom. It was simple enough. But it was not human.

Most humans clung to power as they clung to life. The women before her had held the silken reins that pulled the country. They would not accept letting go.

It was easy to become competent in the political side of Confucian government, but so hard to maintain the internal discipline necessary to let go of power when things were taken from you. If she seconded the Great Master's views, as she should by rights do, they would simply dismiss her and call another ancestress and another until they found one who would help them try -- and fail -- to regain the power lost.

Tai-Mu-Sang had a dim opinion of those who might be called after her, and a sure sense that they would lead the bureaucracy-in-exile to ruin. She would have to stay and offer help, to give them a chance. They were doomed to fall, no doubt, but she could engineer a soft landing.

Tai-Mu-Sang held the choice between pure right and practicality hard in her hostess' hands, tightening her grip on life. What words could she say? What leaves could she feed these hungry silkworms so they would spin wisely?

"Bring" What was that echo, sounding of sharp steel on soft silk?

"Me" It was coming closer to her spirit, but from where?

"The" Now like molten metal striking cold ice.

"Ministress" Or pebbles thrown in a still pond.

"Of" Or the footsteps of stealthy children sneaking sweets.

"Dams" Now like new lovers fumbling in darkness to learn each other.

"And" Like the hiss of a crowd displeased with a performance.

"Rivers" Like the warning voice of a god.

EXALTATIONS

Conceive of a language with only two words; one word gives force and effectiveness, meaning to everything.

The other gives breadth and scope and variation to everything.

The second word makes both words pliable, malleable; the first makes them both capable, desirable. They come together in combinations, effective and various. The combinations can be given names for the sake of convenience, so that new words appear to be generated. This creates a Lexicon, so that the two parental words are hidden amongst their various progeny. The combinations combine as well, producing an infinite number of words, an endlessly extended Lexicon.

In short, a language grown from two to all.

If presented with such a language, how easy would it be to find the two original words?

The twins returned to the tribe in triumph. The heads of the great beasts that no man had thought to kill lay tied together in a line behind them, the former terrors of their people dragged through the muddy ground. The treasure that would make the tribe whole and thriving again the twins carried before them in the baskets their mother had provided.

Their great epic journey was over, and all that remained of the Quest was reward, eventual deification, and the telling and retelling of their tale.

Story-of-the-War-Twins was satisfied. It had made another place for itself in yet another world. It had grown larger, more definite, and more diverse. This branch of its attention could now turn back to its main being which lived among the other stories.

Story-of-the-War-Twins expanded ever so slightly at the addition to its being. Its attention broadened a scintilla, giving it a touch more Freedom, a little more Power, a slightly higher breadth and scope and, of course, a few new stories it grew close to, and old ones that were closer still.

Story-of-City-Foundings, a near cousin, had slipped through the crowd, making a path for Story-of-the-War-Twins to follow by which it come near to his patron. Grandfather Quest, who sat at the center of this cluster of tales aiding them in their acquisitions, and so profiting himself, was reaching out and around through the worlds, through the combinations of things. Grandfather Quest in action always gave a good chance for his younger relatives to gain a little more territory, a few more variations in the ways they were thought of and narrated.

But Grandfather Quest looked troubled. Something disturbed him around him complex midriff where characters ran in all directions instead of the definite 'out' of his beginning and 'in' of his end. There was something indigestible, unalignable about this new thing happening.

Story-of-the-War-Twins thought it recognized the problem Grandfather Quest was having. Too much Space, too much Freedom, too much distance between the elements of this narration. The characters were diffused over several worlds and over the combinations of things that were not worlds. Too much separation made things difficult. Story-of-the-War-Twins had solved that matter long ago for its own narrations. The twins could be separate, go on different paths. One could even stay home while the other went out to battle, so long as they always came together after each episode. No, distance was no trouble for Story-of-the-War-Twins, provided it could cast the twins properly.

Grandfather Quest squirmed in discomfort, attracting the attention of other large stories and their own family/entourages. Grandmother Lesson came near. Parable-of-Brothers, its sister, kissed Story-of-the-War-Twins briefly. They were close but not very close, having a commonality of characters but not of meanings. Often they turned into each other or fought over a particular pairing of humans. She followed Grandmother Lesson avidly, and when she was around Story-of-the-War-Twins took on certain characteristics in response. Gender for instance; most of the time Story-of-the-War-Twins was neuter, but around Parable-of-Brothers he was decidedly male.

Ancestress Allegory swam up, studied the mess inside Grandfather Quest, and swam off to be visible but not heavily involved.

Something tickled and worried at Story-of-the-War-Twins. There was a lot happening, and it seemed to be organizing itself, somewhere around them, Foremother Story-of-Stories was known to lurk around her descendant tales. Sometimes she would reach in and

Poke and pull and yank up and toss one of them somewhere to be involved, a story to be part of a story.

Story-of-the-War-Twins floundered and splashed in the ocean of Space, the narrow confining Freedom of Reality, so uncomfortable to the denizens of Fiction. Something had collided with Story-of-the-War-Twins, something human, but without a twin, not so easy to take inside it. But Story-of-the-War-Twins had experience. He would incorporate the human as the advisor to the twins, once the twins were found.

But something was happening. The human was doing something to Story-of-War-the-Twins, fitting him into categories and considerations. Had he struck an academic, a Slave-of-Theories? Dangerous. No, a writer. An unexpected prize. If he could absorb this storyteller, Story-of-the-War-Twins would grow in wealth. Now what kind of narrator was this? A little poke into its mind, and --

No! It was a writer of lives, a predator that fed Story-that-Explains-People, a biographer.

Grandfather Quest felt his grandson and the writer settle within his being. Two elements had come together. If he could bring the rest into one place to act in one time then the Quest would go forward properly and his allies would be satisfied and grateful. But Grandfather Quest could feel Foremother Story-of-Stories tugging elsewise, and had an inkling that in the abstracted beyond-Reality-and-Fiction Simplicity of the Dyads where Foremother spent most of her attention something else was happening, something that would work against Grandfather Quest and his exalted allies as they labored to order the worlds to their liking.

Good, for without such a challenge Quest was not Quest.

There are things that wish to be resembled, desire to be mirrored in other beings; this is not petty vanity, but something grander in the schemes of scheming. If one of these is resembled, it and its characteristics are made note of by the sembler and those around the sembler. Once noted, their characteristic actions are copied, or they cause others to copy their actions. In simpler terms, they reach out through the mirrors to grab what looks in at them.

This works well unless there are many hands reaching out to grasp one thing.

That's Politics.

Resemblance is like election, a sudden change of status from being oneself to being a representative of something else. From that point on, both things are everpresent, what is and what is represented. What is goes on with its existence. What is represented acts through that life.

If only one thing were represented then every life would be oriented toward it, as every magnet is oriented toward the pole.

Until you bring another magnet, and another, each pulling in its own direction, turning needles this way and that, swinging the directions and actions of life in a dance of Powers near and far, swirling and turning, making one thing after another the centerpiece of life.

That's Politics.

2. Platforms and Promises

Grandfather Quest slipped roots of his being backwards through the channels of Time. His narrations touched and gathered in certain vital events in the lives of his chosen ones. He altered nothing of their reality, only changed the emphasis, raising some moments to life-altering character and shrouding others in unimportance. Thus marked, their pasts would propel his cast-in characters along the inevitable path he had laid down for them.

The pasts of the Knight and the Ancestress held rich veins of prologue from which to mine their futures; and the Biographer, he was a mother-lode of lives. Grandfather Quest savored these moments when he could choose among the rough gems that lay under the mortal strata and from them fashion the crowns of heroic glory.

It was important to Grandfather Quest that his characters focus on the goals he would set for them and the prize to be won at the end of their journey through his body. It was needful for the Quest to become the lodestar for the questers. To do that he had to draw attention to himself -- but properly. Each of these potential characters had to see him according to their own light and life, a simple matter to arrange once those lives had been properly dug through.

Once done, and their courses set down, it would be necessary to undertake the hard work: cajoling Time into letting Quest rearrange things according to his way of doing things. It would be hard because Time was the Constraint of Result and it did not approve of changing the way results were constrained. It would be necessary for Grandfather Quest to show Time how this particular change would be to its advantage.

Time and Quest were excellent company one for another. Though unlike in their natures, Time being of Simplicity and Quest of Multiplicity, they were both naturally in accord as to the linearity of experience.

In consequence of this, Quest had found Time a valuable ally among the fundamental components of existence, and Time found Quest useful as a sort of herdsman who would constrain the minds and souls of those who labored under Time's tyrannical channels. Quest kept those who might otherwise stray outside their worlds in the clear and simple paths to Power that Time permitted in each of those worlds.

Yet, in this case, neither the Simple Time nor the Multiplied Quest understood that something was being colored outside their lines.

| ACCEPTANCE |

The Knight's past, both personal and worldly, offered many useful events to Grandfather Quest. Johannes' politics, both human and metaphysical, were rife with causes and justifications that would lead the Knight out of his world and into Quest's path.

Where to begin? And When?

Youth was a good starting point. It was easy enough to pick up the slights and distresses of young humans and magnify them into all-encompassing needs.

In childhood Sir Johannes DeLondres had shown deep endurance and patience, once standing in the snow for a day and a night to await his father's return from a battle. He had also shown a kindness that marked him out as unusual among a social class whose existence depended upon blood and war. Yet despite this tender heartedness toward all he met, it was his ready aptitude for the sword that had caused his father to offer young Johannes to the Order of Saint Parsival.

Sir Johannes's sainted ears pricked up. Someone at some unknown distance in some unknowable direction was telling half-truths about him.

Saint Parsival's was the most ancient of the sacred warrior orders of Christendom. Half the nobility from Antioch to Cardigan wanted to place their sons (and very rarely daughters) in its cloistered walls, for only therein were the heroes of the Holy Roman Empire made. The other half of the nobility strove mightily to keep their children out of it, for in its walls mortal loyalty was purged away in place of devotion to God, and these old-line nobles could not accept their children having any father before them.

More half-truths, Johannes thought. He still held his loyalty to his family, loved his father and mother, kissed his sisters and helped his brother when he could. And he was loyal to the Emperor as God's viceroy, but only when the Emperor acted as God's viceroy, as he probably would not when the matter of the Marianites was laid before him. Still, Sebastien was Emperor. He had to be given the chance to act according to God's ways even if only a miracle could turn his earthly mind to such heavenly concerns.

The dormer of Saint Parsival's was like all such young men's academies. Regardless of their purpose and the eventual fate of the youths, they were bastions of petty jealousies and strong-gripped pecking orders.

"All such young mens' academies"? Such a heavy phrase. There was a tone of broad experience in the voice, as if the speaker had seen into more dormitories than any mortal could experience in a thousand lifetimes. And "academies" -- Why use a word that hinted of the Doctors of the Church and their verbal games when speaking of the holy orders of battle?

Johannes rose above the trivial bickering of his fellows.

Now that was an outright lie, Johannes thought. I committed as many sins of pride, envy, wrath, and avarice as any of us. Why was this voice trying to raise him up above his fellows? He was only one of many of the warriors of God. This voice seemed to be singling him out for some other-than-godly purpose.

Perhaps this was some effect of the Marianite riddle? No -- that still lay in half-lidded slumber at the base of his neck, unspeaking but unforgettable. Some infiltration of a foreign order into his mind perhaps? The warriors from the Order of Arjuna in Asokastan were known to have the ability to fire arrows into the minds of their opponents. But Asokastan was at peace with the Holy Roman Empire. In fact, the two great nations were nearly allied since both were battling the Caliphate. Some Dervish assault perhaps? No, their attacks elevated Love in the heart rather than Pride.

At the still-young age of thirty-two Johannes was entrusted with a mission to one of the new orders that were rising up to change the world.

One of the new orders? Change the world?

"What do you hear, brother Johannes?" asked the Holy Marshal.

"I do not know, Master," Sir Johannes said. "It does not sound like the voice of prophesy, but it tells of the past and the future."

"Is it Angel, Saint, or Demon?"

"None of them, Master. There is no choir-song, nor moaning-pit in the background. It speaks alone. It tells half-truths like a Demon, but it does not sound as foolish as the children of Lucifer."

"What is its import?"

EXALTATIONS

"Its words exalt my importance above my station, Master," Johannes said with the ease of one accustomed to confessing what lay in every cranny of his soul.

"Then perhaps it speaks truth," the Holy Marshal said. "Your Fateful hour has come; the emperor awaits."

Thus did Johannes exit his order's home, not knowing how far his journey would be or what strange beings, mortal and immortal, awaited him beyond the confines of his narrow contemplation of God.

All contemplations of God are by the natures of Contemplation and God narrow.

| ACCEPTANCE AND REJECTION |

Tai-Mu-Sang had been born with a different name and lived with yet another name for the early years of her life. Only after she had seen two of her sons seated on the throne of the Son of Heaven had she been given the honorific, Great Mother Mulberry.

Tai-Mu-Sang shifted uncomfortably in the mind she was riding. There were echoes in this thinking cavern that were unlike human memory, nor like the ancestral propriety that was the substrate of her deceased being, nor did these sound like the resonant gongs of divine appearance. There was a crackling alienness about these sounds like the touch of wool on silk-accustomed skin.

The court of the Son of Heaven like all royal courts combined the intrigue of government with the rivalry of families. Tai-Mu-Sang had perfected the arts of managing both. She did this by use of simple propriety. She was no one's friend, but everyone's advisor. She took a step back, a step up from the everyday politics of court and hearth to become the eminence grise of each and every cabal. She played at metapolitics so no one thought of her as a target for politics. She was a thing of the Tao like the Sun, the Spring, the darkness, or as someone at last saw her, like the mulberry tree. She hatched no plots, but plots hatched because of her. She gave sustenance to the spinners of silken schemes and profited the land from their cast-off cocoons. No one even thought of bringing her down, for no one could approach the height she had created for herself.

Flattery was happening somewhere, but Tai-Mu-Sang had neither time nor interest in the laudations of others.

Yet this praise had one peculiarity that attracted her attention: It was not coming toward her. It was as if she were being recommended for a position. Yet by whom and for what? Her application for a place among the gods had been stalled in the celestial bureaucracy since her death, the gods having chosen for their divinely unknowable reasons neither to promote her nor deny her.

This new flattery had not the cadences of heavenly suggestion. It lacked the simplicity and art of such petitions. Tai-Mu-Sang wished briefly that she could hear the actual words, then flicked the wish away. She had learned the folly of asking for more than was before her.

The act of creating this metapolitical place cemented the stability of the Middle Kingdom, though no one on that world knew it. Nor did they know that by doing so she had aligned herself with fundamental reality. The gods of her world knew it and waited for the appropriate moment to bring her among them. That moment did not come in her lifetime. But the gods are more than patient.

She was being tugged at, a feeling she had never liked in life or death. To be pullable was an uncomfortable experience. These living bureaucrats were pulling her as was this voice from outside. They tugged in two directions, but in conjunction they implied a single path that might be followed.

Tai-Mu-Sang had never trusted anyone who came to her saying, "This is the only way to do this." Such a person might be correct in their assessment, but that had nothing to do with the person's judgement. A wise petitioner would say, "This is the best way I can find," and kow-tow in apology. Tai-Mu-Sang had learned in life to take up correct actions while casting down the single-minded people who had proposed them.

Her death had translated her to the ancestral realm where waited all the revered dead. From thence she had been called forth many times to give advice and respite to the earthly bureaucracy as well as lend a high, deep and broad view to the Sons of Heaven. When her own dynasty fell from not heeding her otherworldly words, she offered benevolent and righteous advice to the next one and the one after that. Her perfect propriety toward the successor dynasties was well remarked in the shaping of her legend.

There was a distance as well to this speech, like but not like the vast/one-step chasm that kept apart the living and the dead. This voice was like that of King Yama calling her to die. It wanted her out of the world, on its terms, for its purposes.

When, at the end of her earthly life, she had become an old woman with weak joints and failing eyes, a woman waiting for Death, hoping to answer that call, she had not let herself become any less a being of dignity and propriety. Her voice had quavered when she spoke, but she had put a terror in that quaver that made even the most disrespectful of youth bow low before her. Her active hours had shrunk to the twentieth part of each day, and the rest of her time had been divided between contemplation and sleep. Sleep had been better. Contemplation had acted toward her as it would toward a rival, offering bad advice that showed the way to proper action. All she had needed to do was oppose whatever came of her contemplations to do good in her final years. Death had finally come and she had gone to the Yama Kings, free of youth and age, free of mortal mind but still filled with propriety and humanity.

Now she had a share in youth and vigor and the loan of a mortal mind, all of which were needful to reduce the calamity of human folly. She did not wish to be called out again, and, being dead already, did not have to surrender to whatever severance came her way. But the call was hard to resist; a way would have to be found to stay and go simultaneously.

If looked for, a way can always be found.

A Society can consist of as few as two people, if one of them can do and the other can judge what needs to be done.

All that is needful is to bring the two together and give them an opportunity to intertwine.

| ACCEPTANCE |

Story-of-the-War-Twins was an up-and-coming tale, an ambitious narration with enough breadth of being to fit in nicely wherever humans existed and procreated.

Grandfather, stop distracting me! I've got a writer by the tale.

The young story had grown under the protection of doting forbears who had given it easy grazing places in which to grow strong and fat. Under the guidance of a benevolent grandfather, Story-of-the-War-Twins had been narrated over and over in many worlds, gaining the Power to influence those worlds and the Freedom to range across vast mental vistas.

You aren't the only one who helped me, Grandfather. And I have struck out on my own.

Recently, the young tale had ventured forth into realms that had not been given it, showing a boldness unexpected by its elders.

Is this about those two Quests I conjoined, making twins of the heroes? I don't see why you'd be mad about that. The Quests were completed.

Such daring attracted the attention of the growing story's forebears, who decided to give it a deeper understanding of its own nature. In this way, Story-of-the-War-Twins would be able to rise beyond its coddled existence and come to appreciate the struggles that its elder tales had undertaken and triumphed over in order to secure that coddling.

Now, Grandfather, I've always appreciated what you and the other old, old stories have done for me. There's really no need to take this extreme step --

Therefore, Story-of-the-War-Twins found itself cast within a greater story. Made into a character, the youth would gain a worthwhile perspective and perhaps be forgiven by its ancestors for its overbold approach.

I'm sorry, Grandfather. Really sorry. There's no need for this.

But taking a part in a story was only half the lesson being given. Story-of-the-War-Twins had been gifted not just with a wealth of narrative multiplications, but a small fortune in tame narrators who told it over and over in its range of worlds. This upstart tale had never had to personally rope in and tie up a taleteller. It had as yet no inkling of the real difficulties that attended upon the taming of narrators.

Grandfather, that just isn't true. I've watched you and the others bring narrators around, force them to follow your conventions, constrain even the wildest of writers and speakers to your way of doing things.

Seen such activities it had, but the young story had never been forced to actually wrangle a writer, until now.

If you insist, I will do it, Grandfather. But couldn't you have found me a narrator who at least tells the right kind of tale?

The young story had a great task before it, a Quest to bring in and tame a narrator of a wholly different sort of story. Thus was he saddled with the biographer.

Grandfather!

It would do Story-of-the-War-Twins no good to beg or complain. He had been cast and now had to work through the story around him.

Yes, Grandfather. May I return to this wrestling?

Thus did the young story, chastened, return to his works.

Thank you so much, Grandfather.

A Society can certainly be made from two people and one story.

| ACCEPTANCE |

Peter Refton's life had many beginnings, one middle with multiple variations, and now he sought an ending.

He did not realize that that was what he was seeking. He thought he was looking for answers. His world had become dominated by Questions and answers, and though he had seen many other worlds and many other ruling powers, still he had not been able to shake off his parochial desire for resolution by knowledge.

Refton was in most ways well equipped to undertake this quest for understanding. He had a measure of Power, though he knew nothing of its origins or purposes. He had as well a strong degree of Freedom, though again he was ignorant of its nature. He was intimate with Contemplation and was well versed in the investigation and writing down of lives.

Yet by other standards, Refton was poorly set up for his Quest. He had not an ounce of humility in him. He had chronicled the lives of Saints, witnessing their acts and delineating their souls without learning from them. He had seen Gods take part in the affairs of mortal lives and seen the curves and twists of Fate lay low the brightest and wisest and most powerful of men and women. He had seen Death many times and knew it was the end of all Lives, yet his soul was moved not a jot from its overweening self-possession.

In the Space between worlds where there is no weight to any matter, where there is no consequence to action, where all is Freedom to move and do but never see result, where no change mattered, something happened to Peter Refton. His backpack grew heavier, loading him down where no load could be.

Refton's travels to other worlds had made little impression on him. He had wandered as a biographer, an abstracted journalist, a chronicler. He had had great impact on the worlds he had touched, giving eternal life to saints, conjurable personality to ancestors, alien gifts to mortals, and food for thought to many Theories. But these people, mortal, divine and other had touched him little.

The weight on Refton's back felt uneven, as if this life-tale had a slant to it unlike his others. It was pushing him off course, away from his intended goal.

Refton had no specific goal, only a kind of life he wanted to write about. He was hunting Magicians, but since there was no way to tell who was and was not a Magician he had to rely upon the Power within him that had guided him to his prey before. Like most people who know a great deal, Refton did not comprehend the vastness of his ignorance. He had discovered that there were many worlds, learned of the Space between them, found histories like and unlike his own, met many people and lived more lives than he knew of. Yet for all that he did not realize how narrow his view of reality was.

Peter Refton pulled this newly forming life from his pack and began to read. The words and voice seemed to be ones he would himself use if writing a biography of an evil or foolish man. "Tell me more," he said to the life-story.

More things were alive than Refton knew of. More things had Humanity, and more things had Minds and Souls than he understood. For all his beloved Contemplations, he was only one person with one view. Soon he would collide with something larger than himself and learn what it was that writers served.

Refton put the book back among his other lives and began to contemplate its meaning. As always happened when his mind was deeply wrapped in thought, he felt himself moving toward a distant place with a beauty both of geography and inhabitation.

But as had never happened before, Refton crashed before he reached that lonely isle, crashed into and through a floating something, a half-seen creature of many limbs and a fluid body. Like food for an amoeba, Refton was surrounded by this thing and shunted to a place inside where he could be digested. But Refton, as his most recent life had declared, was too lacking in humility to let himself be consumed.

A Society that has two people, one story, and a Teller of stories is complete.
Not a Teller, a narrator.
A narrator.

RICHARD GARFINKLE

| NEITHER ACCEPTANCE NOR REJECTION |

Oh.
Oh!

"Four drams of virgin moonlight, one gill of deep sea water, ten drops of human blood." The Poetess recited the formula as she mixed ink by the light of her mirror.

When the mixture glistered with just the right emulsion of red and silver, and after a shake it gave off a few golden teardrops, she took down the hand-pressed sheets of paper from their oaken shelf, kissed each one to make it her own, and at last took out the pen.

It was the only pen in the Poetess' world and had come with the gift of writing from another world. Pyotr the Reft One had brought it and given it to the Poetess, along with the new art of putting memory into paper, given it in exchange for her Life.

He had been surprised that she had made the transaction so easily. "The folk of the mirror, the Faerie people," she had said in proper poetic doubling of description, "are always trading for lives, looking for substance to fill their reflective natures."

"That is what I am asking for as well," the Reft One had said. "I will put your life down into the images of memory, the words upon the pages."

The Poetess, who had traded her Life through the mirror a hundred times and more, happily passed the details of her past to Pyotr. He in turn had taught her the way of the pen, the making of ink and paper, and had left her with the steel nib in its wooden shaft.

Seven years had passed since he had left her world. In that time her words had travelled in books across the lands and seas, carrying reading to other poets. But among all the word-workers, all the Faerie-inspired drinkers of poetry only she could write. She had become the source of memory in her world, and all the poets accounted her their mistress.

Over that span of years thoughts of Pyotr the man had dimmed in the light of his extraordinary gift. But this night with this bottle of ink and these kissed sheets, the woman remembered the man.

She looked into the mirror and sought out his reflections. He himself, the real human, could not be seen. No true being was ever shown in the mirror of Faerie. But the appearance of each thing in all the worlds and in the mosaics that made the worlds swam in that silver globe, waiting, hoping to be seen by some outsider.

"You'd like to think there are laws," the Poetess wrote, putting words in the mouth of Pyotr the Reft One, his aged experienced self talking to his younger naive soul that was just setting out upon its grand Quest. *"You were taught that the universe functions on principles, that it operates by set procedures. You were taught this over and over again in every birth you remember. It was the fashion in our time and world to think that Law underlies all organization. But our world had forgotten one simple thing: Laws are made by Governments, lobbied for by interests, undermined by loopholes, and retracted when Power changes hands or Freedom rises in the masses. You forgot to ask who made the Laws."*

"I suppose you want me to believe that God did?" Pyotr's younger self responded.

"God signs or vetoes the Laws," the older Reft One replied. "But others make up the two houses of the worlds-ruling parliament."

"Who?"

"Find out."

"Is that my Quest?"

"Yes," the Poetess wrote.

"No," Refton's elder self said.

A Society that has one who watches it and makes note of its principles and purposes will not be led astray.

In Consequence it shall continue to achieve what it sets out to do.

| IRRELEVANT |

Uh-oh.

Uh-oh, indeed.

3. Inauguration

Peter Refton waited by the side of the road, knowing that two bewildered young people would be along presently, their lives in need of his guidance.

Ridiculous. Why am I by the side of the road? Where did I come from? Who are these young people?

For that matter, where is this road? What world is this? Who is trying to squash my memories and direct my actions?

Peter Refton waited --

No, I'm not waiting. I'm --

This is not how it is supposed to be.

Was I thinking that or did the thing speaking to me think that?

Peter Refton had left the world.

That's right. I left the world to seek the Magician's life.

Peter Refton left the world on a Quest.

Grandfather, stop poking into me. I'll break him myself! Peter Refton left the world seeking something. Along the way he found others who needed his help, two children, young and in need of wisdom and guidance in their path of life.

EXALTATIONS

What children? There aren't any children here, just the road and the wayside. There isn't even a horizon. There is no place to be.

What is this place? It doesn't look like a real world. There's too little detail, and too much emphasis on what detail there is. This doesn't feel or remember like a new life.

For that matter, no other world has talked to me before.

"Who are you?" Refton called aloud. "Why are you trying to force me into this --"

-- story.

This is a story? How is that possible? How can a real person be in a story?

How did I get here? I left the world to find another world, not this false place. I left on hunt, and I was --

-- waylaid and left beside the road, Peter Refton gave up his own journey to help others, the twins who were fast approaching, in need of advice from one experienced in the ways of many worlds, a wily hunter who could teach them to catch any prey.

This story has a one-track mind. Maybe if I push at it, it will crack like the shell of a world and I can leave for a real place.

A story in the space between worlds? Was that what floated through the emptiness? That doesn't sound right. I've passed between too many times -- how many times, I wonder -- but this has never happened before.

Someone's doing something to me. What kind of change is it trying to make in my life?

Is this my doing? I came hunting a Magician and I'm caught in a story. Does the story lead to the Magician?

Through a Quest.

Worry about it later. Remember who you are and what you can do. It says it's a story, write it.

Peter Refton was waiting --

Peter Refton was hunting --

-- for the war twins.

-- for a way out.

In many societies there is a constant churning as people struggle with each other to occupy the valuable or useful places in that Society. When this conflict is seen as a struggle for Power it is regarded as unseemly and grasping and the combatants are disapproved of. When the battle is for Freedom it is praised and the people exalted.

Of course, that distinction presumes that Power and Freedom are separable.

The main streets of Aachen were paved with roughened stones that fit haphazardly together, so that someone looking down upon them would find their eyes watering trying to make sense of the chaotic mosaic. Only by looking more broadly and seeing that the lanes were wide enough for an army to march, broad enough for carts and horses and walkers to go in all directions, could one understand the purpose of that press of rocks.

Yet purpose embodied often thwarts the purpose one has in mind. One look at those thronged streets revealed that the military mind that had meant them to be vast to aid the rapidity of armies had unfortunately made them so large as to invite the civilian users to treat the lanes as an open space for darting across and jockeying for position. Thus it was in all trafficked worlds where a hundred colliding quests for speed created slowness for thousands of travellers.

Sir Johannes walked these streets three steps behind the Holy Marshal. The traffic parted before them. Where the knights of the holy orders went the people cleared the way as they would not do for priests or bishops or the lesser nobility. Only those highly favored of God or God's viceroy the Emperor warranted the deference of commerce suspended and daily speech curtailed.

Saint Parsival's Way was the name of this road, built on the command of Carolus Magnus so that his Marshal could go day to day between the imperial palace and the fort-abbey which had housed the saint's first students. Saint Parsival had made clear to his earthly master that for his life to be properly given in service to both man and God the saint would need to pass on his teachings regardless of how much this took him away from the work of generalship.

"God has given me through years of practice great health and longevity," the Life of Saint Parsival declared. "But however greatly favored I am in mortal extent, still the day will come when God will send the Angel of Death to take me from the world. Oh my Emperor, Death comes to everyone, and only the passing on of my disciplines both physical and spiritual will preserve the Holy Roman Empire and your heirs from their enemies. Give me leave to take on students that I may make a legacy of my vision."

By the feel of his feet gripping deep the earth below him, Sir Johannes was reminded of all the knights who had come before him on this road bearing their allegiance to the Emperor and to God. St. Peter in his feet, in the stones beneath, gripped and released with the power to bind and the freedom to loose on Earth as in Heaven.

The Emperor would ask Johannes questions about the Marianites and he was bound to answer truthfully. But the riddle in his spine asked him what truth he could speak about it, about the unanswered and if answered unspeakable understanding that coiled about his backbone.

Saint Kyril in his ears was hearing much beyond the deferential crowd in front and the active commerce beyond. There was something that sounded like an argument, noisy and messy like the Doctors of the Church when they engaged in disputes about the nature of God and Heaven. No one paid the doctors any mind. Let them debate in their universities. What difference did their theories make when God revealed himself daily, showing himself to be unconfinable by distinctions, and unfathomable by disputation?

But what was this argument, distant but near?

Sir Johannes walked down the Road, accompanied by his brother.

What? Who said that?

"Johannes," said the Holy Marshal. "What troubles you?"

"I heard a voice again, master. Something not human, but neither demon, nor saint, nor angel, near but distant. It was telling me what I was doing."

"Johannes, hold the voice away for the moment. When we return, go to your cell and listen. For now pay heed to the Emperor."

They had come to the gilded iron gates of the palace and saluted the guards, mortal soldiers who stood in awe and fear of the members of the holy orders. But though inferior in battle and sanctity, they were bolstered in status by the Eagle badge of the Caesars. Answering salute with salute to equals the guards bid the holy knights enter.

Sir Johannes and his brother came face to face with the first of their trials, the ignorant man who governed this world of monsters.

Monsters? The world had no monsters in it, only men and women, blessed in the many ways of God. The empire had its rivals and its enemies, but that was politics. The orders had their counterparts in the other great dominions of the world: The Dervishes of the Caliphate, the Fighting Taoists and the order of the Stone Monkey of the Han country, the orders of Arjuna and Manjusri in Asokastan. Dangerous certainly, but not monsters.

-- Unless the voice meant the new hybrid orders, the Marianites and their other two faces. Or the reports of strange new groupings between Asokastan and the Han, something about Kalkin, Maitreya and the Embryonic Pearl. No one in any of the Imperial orders understood what those were, but those blessed in hearing as Johannes was could distinguish strange doings and the coming to be of new things in the world.

But were these prodigies monsters? And why did the voice refer to the Holy Marshal as his brother? It was a true thing, certainly. Monks were all brothers to each other. But it was such a small truth compared to the greater reality of knight serving commander.

"Oh Caesar, Emperor of this World, Viceroy of God, Defender of the Faithful, Protector of the Holy, Governor of all who Walk God's Earth, . . ." The courtier continued the long list of titles.

Grown longer each year.

That thought had come from the Holy Marshal, spoken within himself but directed outward by Saint Paul in his tongue, knowing that Sir Johannes would hear with Saint Kyril's aid.

The Sovereign of the Monstrous World bid the brothers make obeisance, and they did though they were troubled in their hearts.

Sebastien IV gestured for the two knights to approach. The throne he sat on was at heart the simple wooden contrivance that had set Carolus Magnus above his fellows, but in the centuries since it had grown in ornamentation. The inlays of mosaics and icons brought to Aachen when Carolus' son Otto had married the Empress in Constantinople and reunited the two sides of the Empire had begun the flood of flourishes. Now the throne had wings behind it and pillars to its side. There were angels woven in a canopy above and an inlaid crown of ruby and jasper on the throne's back that always framed the Emperor's head, whether he went barescalped or not.

Sebastien IV was young.

Too young, the Holy Marshal thought audibly.

Sir Johannes knew that his superior was thinking not of years but of soul. Too young was a classification given to novices who refused to see that there might be much to win within the monastery and within themselves. They saw only what they had given up to join the order. Too young meant ignorant of the real world that lay behind the world.

Isn't everybody too young? Aren't we all ignorant? I thought I knew what was behind the worlds, but there seems to be more.

What voice was that? It came from the same place as the narration of his entrance, but it sounded more human, more confused. And it sounded familiar, though Sir Johannes was sure he had never heard it before.

"We will speak in private," Sebastien IV said.

Private meant a large room around a heavy oak table with only a dozen courtiers and the Captain of the Guard, who deferred to the Holy Marshal and was looked down upon by the courtiers.

"Now, Marshal," said Sebastien after seating himself under his purple canopy, "bid your monk speak to us about his espionage on our part."

"Johannes," the Holy Marshal said.

"Caesar," said Sir Johannes. "I spoke to members of the order of Mary-Who-Has-Seen-God as you commanded, and I listened to what they said."

The chapterhouse of the Marianites was built on mount Athos. They were returning, they had said, to the roots of monasticism, to the places where only two centuries after the Crucifixion the first hermit saints had secluded themselves. From those heights the old saints sometimes emerged to reveal what God had given them. In those days saints cast out demons in others and were called Iron-Eaters for the terrible power they displayed over men and spirits. There on those heights the Marianites had built their home, and there Sir Johannes and come and spoken honestly to the Mother Superior:

"I was sent by the Emperor who wishes to know what you practice here, for rumors have come back to the court of strange icons and mysteries behind the veil of Mary."

"And for what have you come, Knight of Saint Parsival?" the Mother Superior had asked. She was a young woman to hold such a title, but her eyes had possessed that half-distant, yet perfectly focused look that characterized those who looked at God wherever they gazed. He had known she would ask that. Any leader of an order would have done so. He had meditated long upon his answer.

"To see if you have been blessed with any spiritual techniques that would be helpful to my order in our seeking after God."

EXALTATIONS

Sir Johannes and his brother quested for God, for with God's help they could rid themselves and the world of the demons that were ever present and the monsters that were coming.

The thought had slid into his memory. He had not thought or heard it at the time, but now it lodged there as if he had thought it the moment the Marianite asked him the question. Whatever was speaking to him was twisting what had truly happened.

It's trying to fit you in, Sir Knight. Remember Saint Parsival's teachings. Grip hold to the rock of Faith. Place yourself deep in Eden and do not falter when the spirits seek to pull you one way or another.

Who are you? Sir Johannes thought.

I am Petrus of Reeftown, and I am caught by this narration that seeks to pull you and others in. I am wrestling with it.

Petrus, who wrote the Life of Saint Parsival? Yes, the voice that was speaking was like the voice hidden in that chronicle.

The same.

Where are you?

I don't know.

"Sir Johannes, we await your answers," the Emperor said.

Johannes blinked and clear-spoke an apology. "Caesar, it is difficult to say what the Marianites are doing. They have mysteries and sudden teachings unlike ours. They teach that when Christ was born, Mary looked at him with the eyes of a loving mother and loved God with the perfection that only a mother's love for her child holds. They say that in that sudden perfect moment of love, God blessed Mary with all the gifts that mortal soul and body can bear."

"Yes, yes, a lovely tale," the Emperor said. "But what does it mean?"

"That that which we and the other orders that serve you strive for in years of effort they can achieve in a moment. They say that if they can but look rightly as Mary did upon God then they will be blessed as she was."

"Well, different teachings for different orders," Sebastien IV said with the ease of ignorance. "They sound useful. We will have them moved closer to the capital and they will supply us with soldiers as you do."

Johannes hesitated, the demon of his mouth wrestling hard against Saint Paul. If he spoke no more there would be trouble but it would not come through him.

Sir Johannes reached out and pulled down the demon. He would speak and bear the troubles himself.

"Caesar, the Marianites say that two others have also looked at God and gained this sudden teaching."

"And who are those two?" Sebastien asked, his gaze flickering around the room, clearly more interested in the repairs that had been made to his audience chamber than to the knight before him.

"They say that Moses saw God upon Sinai and was given a vision of the entire world that was, is, and ever shall be, and that he was given the whole of the Hebrew Torah in that moment."

One of the courtiers, a Doctor of the Church, coughed.

"And the other?" said Sebastien.

Forgive me for loosing the deluge, Sir Johannes prayed.

"The Marianites say Mohammed was given a vision of God in the Mir'aj and became the Perfect Prophet."

The uproar came.

And the King of the Monsters roared his anger that those who had seemed to be in his service were also in service to his enemies.

It's going to fall apart. Johannes recognized the voice that claimed to be Petrus of Reeftown. *The whole world is going to fall to pieces. The orders have cross fertilized, bringing new powers into the world. I can see it from out here. I can see the whole struggle ahead. Johannes, your world is doomed to centuries of pain.*

Because I spoke?

Someone would have. It couldn't be kept secret too much longer. You were the messenger, but someone would have said it. The war will start.

Against the Marianites.

Against the orders, all of them in every empire. Look at your Marshal. Will he lead his army against the Marianites because they see God differently?

Of course not.

Then what will the Emperor do?

Sir Johannes looked at the young man on the throne, and knew the terrible temper that would come forth in anger against those who defied him. He was God's Viceroy, but only if he followed God. If not, he was a man who would be obeyed by men, and disobeyed by other men. Civil war. Holy war. One and the same. Sir Johannes knew that the Caliph would act similarly when the Dervishes did not dance to his Jihad. He could hear that similar things would happen for subtly different causes in the Han nation and in Asokastan. It would all come out, the great secret of the Orders would emerge, that they had much more in common with each other than they did with the uncloistered in their nations, that their service was truly given not to their Emperors but to God in all his forms personal and impersonal.

He could hear that the voice of Petrus spoke soothly, knew in the saints within him that Petrus of Reeftown speaking to him from somewhere was prophesying the doom of his world.

Come out and Quest for the answer to free your people. Come out.

The world shattered around Sir Johannes and he was --

-- walking down a road, his brother by his side.

No one was by his side. A shadow, an image, that was all. No brother. It had no real footsteps. Its motions were being spoken, not done.

Sir Johannes walked down the road with his shadow-brother. Over a rise they saw a man sitting beside the road, pen in hand. He looked up when they came.

"Sir Johannes?" the man said. He was struggling to control his words. "I am, or was when I visited your world, Petrus of Reeftown."

"I have come as you called."

EXALTATIONS

"I did not call you. It did, the story. It's put us both into roles and grabbed hold of my tongue after I told you what would happen."

"You spoke. It came from your heart. Saint Kyril is not easily deceived."

"Saint Kyril?" Peter Refton remembered the spiritual anatomy Saint Parsival had invented, saying it was given him by God. Kyril was no part of it. "What does Kyril rule?"

"The ears."

"Of course. Saint Kyril the translator. Very sensible and a good addition to holy anatomy. I guess the story did tear the words from my heart. I saw what Parsival created, and I didn't want it destroyed. *I didn't want to see your world overrun with beasts and demons, or the empires fall into nothingness because of fear. I* --aarrch-- Get out of my mouth, damn you, story! Let me speak like a human being. Get out or I'll rewrite you into a comedy."

Story-of-the-War-Twins extracted itself from the hunter's mouth, not wanting to risk further damage to the partially broken narrator. Things were going properly at last. He could work with one real twin and one shadow. It had been done before. And Grandfather Quest was happy with the arrangement. That would help, certainly.

Now, what else did he need? A mother for the twins. That would make things easier.

Linearity was the common ground between Time and Grandfather Quest. They both dearly loved lines: straight, curved, bent, twisted, knotted. All of those were fine. Just as long as things had a blissful one-dimensionality the two of them would be happy.

Sometimes their lines crossed like swords. Quests that changed the way things worked occurred in channel after channel, altering again and again the constraints Time placed most heavily upon its subjects. In return Time had been known to break Quests by the simple expedient of killing off heroes with the inevitable logic of reality. There were just so many bullets a body could dodge in a lifetime, regardless of how much Quest wanted that individual to succeed.

But this conflict never stopped the meeting of aesthetics upon which their alliance was grounded. Actions should go in a line, one might say, and the other would agree. One thing should happen after another. Choices should be listed in small numbers and offered with conjuror's forces to the choosers.

Unfortunately for them, God prefers Mosaics to paths.

| EXPLICIT ACCEPTANCE/IMPLICIT REJECTION |

Through two years and too, too many bodies and minds, Tai-Mu-Sang labored against the Khan. Throughout All-Under-Heaven she was being recalled, remembered, and regrouped. Talking to herself from one impersonator to another, she laid her plans.

But she was becoming thin, stretched and multiplied. The telling of her echoed in the ears of those she inhabited, making her second guess herself. Her actions in one body were bewildering her memory in another. She was becoming mushy, fuzzy around the edges, unclear in her being. She was turning from vividly chronicled ancestor into overly present legend.

But the plans progressed. The Khan's tax collectors could not find the wealth of All-Under-Heaven, his armies could not recruit new soldiers, his judges could not find appropriate or useful people to punish. This the bureaucracy applauded and they sang praises to Tai-Mu-Sang, lauding her with each new call, offering her name to Heaven again and again for full deification.

Heaven remained silent, waiting to see what would happen before retroactively handing down its Mandate. Heaven was perfectly adept at choosing the winners in all conflicts by the simple expedient of waiting until the race was over before laying down its bets.

But the Khan's anger was growing and the revenged-upon bodies were mounting, bodies of men. The Khan blamed the village headmen and the soldiers who had served the Son of Heaven for his troubles. He could not blame or execute the women since he could not accept that they were acting against him. But he could kill their fathers, husbands, and sons, and even the stoniest of hearts would break seeing the ignorant men killed for the insurrection of the women.

Eventually the Khan would either wreck the country or put aside his blindness and turn upon his enemies. That was what Master Kung had warned the bureaucracy about. If they had simply waited, doing nothing, the Khan or one of his successors would have come to see that this vast nation did not do what the Khan wanted. Eventually, a Khan would open his eyes and see the solution; he would restore the women to Power.

But after this rebellion, when his eyes opened blood-minded Temujin would turn upon the women and destroy them, unless Tai-Mu-Sang could offer him an alternative. She would have to put something else in front of the hands he was using to cover his eyes, offer an alternative to the tuneless child's la-la-la-I-can't-hear-you he was singing to his own good sense.

She had hoped in stretching out and borrowing so many minds that an answer would present itself. But it had not. She would have to look elsewhere --

Got you. Here, Grandson.

Thank you, Grandfather Quest.

Great Mother Mulberry was worried about her sons. They had been gone long in search of their father. They should have been back ages ago with the holy weapons that would topple the tyrant.

Nonsense.

What was that on the fuzzy periphery of her being? Someone was telling her what she was doing and why, offering a way to win, to beat the Khan. If only she would follow this way, this narrow, laid-down way, it would lead to perfection. A one-true-wayer was before her. He would receive the Fate she always gave to such people.

Great Mother Mulberry lived her life according to ritual and propriety, according to li *as set down in the sacred books of her ancestors. She had reared her sons to follow* li. *Accordingly, at their proper ages she had sent them forth to seek their father as prescribed in the ancient texts.*

The Classics had no such prescriptions. Someone was lying about *li* and *ren*, about the ways to be rightly human. Someone was lying in her name and with her reputation.

Mathematically any object can be seen as having a bundle of arrows sticking out of it. These arrows are called vectors. The arrows represent the object's ability to affect the things that come near it. The arrow shows in which direction it can affect, and the length reveals how strong the effect can be.

Examine the bundle, sharp and irregular, a map of the Power and Freedom of any one thing.

Now put things together and see what happens to the arrows. One thing may have arrows pointing against the arrows of another, canceling both of their Powers, neutralizing the directions of Freedom. Other arrows will lie in the same direction, strengthening, creating greater Power.

But in most cases, the arrows will lie neither directly against nor directly aligned with each other. Then two parent-arrows add and form something else that points in a wholly different way than either of the parent-arrows. The child-vector may be weaker or stronger, but it takes the place of the parents and has its own ideas of Power and Freedom.

That is the simple means of combining these bundles, the harsh brutality of addition. Sometimes something else happens.

Sometimes one arrow hits an object a glancing blow and sets it spinning, and of a sudden new arrows spring up in dimensions unknown to the arrows of the unmoving generation. Sometimes vectors Multiply.

At the top of the spiral staircase there was only the Sharp above and the Smooth below. Sharp was bright and glorious, terrible and savage. It loomed overhead, a spearpoint, a swordpoint, a point of inquiry, a point of debate, a game point. Smooth was broad and deep, oceanic, vaster than space, broader than thought, failing of metaphor at its limitlessness.

At the top of the spiral staircase there was no one to see the Sharp and Smooth. There was no spiral staircase, there was no seeing or being seen. There was only Sharp and Smooth.

Mercifully -- though there was not yet mercy -- Smooth permitted the no one to descend and Sharp gave the impetus for descent.

Going down, the Sharp and Smooth came together, in all ways in all places resolving themselves into a shower of coins, an arrangement of statues, a mosaic of stones, a lexicon of words.

That which descended now had words for what it was: Human, Mind, Spirit, Hermit, Contemplation, Transition, Redaction, Magician, Cycle, River.

These were a few of the active components of the universe, the Dyads, as they had been named by that which descended. They were seemingly inert in this view, as entries in a dictionary seem inert, or old coins in an album, long since spent. That which descended knew better. This view did not avail itself of the active sides of the Dyad coins. That would be another Contemplation for another . . . Time.

Descend before Time sees and swoops. Time is the enemy. Time is the tyrant, and its mistress Fate the scourge.

Evadne ducked down swiftly through the next after next turning of the staircase. Her name was back, and her memories. At this level the Dyads had multiplied themselves to create individual beings living out individual existences.

"That isn't right," Evadne said. She was talking to herself. She had little choice since no one else lived on her island.

"There must be levels I'm missing, but I can't find them. There must be something between the abstraction of Simplicity and the concreteness of Multiplicity."

The Island took note of her words and reshaped itself in accord with them. It existed for Contemplation, so it assisted in contemplation. The only thing that could be done to resolution on the island was to contemplate.

Evadne looked about her home. It had become a broad and open courtyard building with many distinct rooms. Company was coming. The great mountain that had been the spiral staircase overshadowed the courts. Her home had, now, a central fountain that could be reached from any of the courtyards. Sharp jets of water cascaded down into a deep pool with many channels running off into the various rooms. A good image for what she had just seen, and of course the water would eventually run out through the new seaside vista into the ocean of Space beyond.

"Best to take a look," she said. "Before the guests arrive."

Water splashed from one of the rivulets, glistening droplets reflecting light, melding together, forming a convex mirror, the mirror of Prudence who sees not just herself but the Faerie image of the whole world around her.

Evadne did not like being Prudence. Prudence was depressing and tiresome and never climbed the spiral high enough. Someone would look at her and see Prudence and she would be caught.

But the drama of the mirror's creation hinted at another seeing. She would be the Sorceress to one of those coming. Prudence and the Sorceress in the same viewing. That would be hard. It was sure to age her.

EXALTATIONS

How old was she now? The mirror revealed a few lines of fixed concern in a face that had shown much of youthful indiscretion when she had climbed up just now. This time the growing cycle was swift. It would not be long. A few leaps of invention, a smattering of satoris and she would be an old woman in need of diminishment.

Had she always been like this, aging and youthening in contemplation? she wondered. Or had there once been a woman who came to this island and stayed in the cycles of learning and forgetting? Or had she originally been an extension of Contemplation who had in one trip up or down the spiral, the mountain, the ladder, the Ecstasy, become human and stayed that way?

That was the problem with connection to the Dyads. They did not let go once you were joined to them. They gave Power and Freedom in their own way, but they extracted a perfect loyalty. It was impossible to betray a Dyad since every action you undertook served their interests by bringing forth their multiplications. She served Contemplation in all that she was and did. There was no choice in that since her Freedom directed her to Contemplation's benefit and her Power made those directions effective.

"Well now, what's this?" she said, spying a rolling bundle of tightly wrapped . . . something, pushing itself along the vast sea of Space, inexorably heading toward the landing where those contemplatives who were adrift in their own thoughts and ways might, if they were fortunate, end up.

What's this?

The question echoed around the island. It gave an adornment to the vista, creating a broad, high brooding cliff. It flung filled bookshelves into some of the rooms, bookshelves filled with biographies. Evadne's heart beat faster as if a long forgotten joy were returning. Another room panoplied itself with silk painted images of divinities and carved jade statuary along the walkways. Evadne glowered at those. Someone annoying was coming along with someone longed for.

The island washed over itself, building intimate bridges with moonlit views over the channels, and, in a final flourish, stationed a huge serpent coiled upon the landing.

"A story?" Evadne said.

Those were the worst. When people came here by story they had fixed ideas of how they should react and they tended to paint her in the strangest forms. She had no desire to trick and then make love to another bewildered scholar who had found an image in a book and fallen into fascination with it. Or worse, she did not want to be out-riddled or killed again by some hero who needed to climb the way-up in order to find the one Dyad which would permit him to do some back-home vital deed. They never understood her warnings. Bring a Dyad somewhere and you change the balance of things.

"Understand what you're doing first," she always said.

But they, forced by the story, forced by that nosy, intrusive Quest or single-minded Lesson, would thrust her aside in mind or body and climb up to be duped by the fundamental forces of the universe, duped into being messengers and multipliers of Power and Freedom.

"Well, let them come," she said, her words drawing the ship-story closer in and alerting the Snake of Ignorance to play its part as obstacle.

The Mirror of Prudence glinted for her attention. Evadne grasped it and looked within. Her hair, raven-shaded now, had been pulled back into a mare's tail and held in place by a single coin. Oh no, not another one. She tried to be careful when climbing the spiral staircase, tried to avoid catching any more Dyads.

"Which are you?" she said.

Freedom to bring together Power and Freedom in agreement and disagreement.

"Politics?" Evadne said and grew older.

4. Colloquy

Among the infinity of alliances made between the Dyads some were strong and terrible, others weak and trivial. In the Simplicity in which the Dyads existed there was no way to discern the differences between powerful free alliances and powerless bound ones, for in Simplicity all such groupings seemed no more than a nearness of one metaphysical stone to another. But in the Multiplicity where the Dyads showed themselves forth in action and being it was easy to discern the relative efficacy of such groups.

Space and Time had reached one of the most far-spanning and deep-gripping accords, one that gave them almost as much Power and Freedom as the agreement between Mind, Spirit, and Humanity. In their alliance Space, or Freedom of Action, had manifested itself as a vast stretch of, well, space, and Time the Constraint of Results had entered as long channels of time. Between the two of them they created a great arena for the other Dyads to multiply, provided the others acceded to the Freedom of Space and the Power of Time. The Dyads had by their nature acceded to these conditions, since they had to multiply and the domain of Space and Time was the largest and most diverse table on which to produce themselves.

Yet within this alliance there were little cheats, grubbings for extra authority by both Space and Time. In the channels Time constrained Result in fixed fashions according to the Dyads that agreed with it in those channels. These Dyads in alliance with Time constrained Space from being too free within the time-channels. Outside the channels Space permitted other Dyads to compel Time, creating small islands where specific results could be constrained. These Floating Worlds used Time, enslaved it as it enslaved all the other Dyads in the long islands, the great channels, the tyrant tyrannized in the service of slaves freed.

That, however, was only the first iteration of intraparty squabbling, for within this cheat of Space, Time created its own cheat. Every Floating World had to accept some Time within it. Subservient though Time was, still it was present and so it spread its power.

Within that cheat Space cheated as well, using the Constraints of Results to generate new Freedoms of Actions. Thus the two of them played each other, like master card mechanics admiring and learning one from another, while all around them other players were wiped out of the game.

Story-of-the-War-Twins did not even know he was playing any game until he discovered that his human cards were shuffling themselves.

"Tai-Mu-Sang?" Peter Refton asked the vague figure of the twins' mother.

"Chronicler?" she said with the edge of her being that had been drawn into the story.

No, no, no. When the Mentor meets the Mother they exchange cryptic speakings about the twins and their fate.

Peter Refton pushed these thoughts from his mind and focused on forming words in his mouth, enacting and redacting them as if they were to be inscribed on paper. Only writing could hold the forced dialogue and the inevitable plot developments of their story-prison at bay. But this was not his kind of writing. He was a biographer; he needed a life to catch hold of and wrestle into his mind.

There was Sir Johannes, but Refton had not been able to find the knight's life as yet. Now there was Tai-Mu-Sang, and Refton had already written her life, up until the moment of her death when he had written her into the realm of ancestral ghosts. Now that ghost was back, or at least part of it was. He could grab hold of that.

But she isn't a Magician, and I'm hunting Magicians.

Refton did not notice the intrusion of that thought. He believed it to have come from his own mind. Thus Grandfather Quest insinuated himself into the writer's mind, using his grandson's brute force manipulations as a blind. The storychild would learn if it ever grew broad and free enough, if it ever expanded beyond the confines of *Two children of strange parentage go forth from their home, are gifted by their father, and return to free the world from monsters.* If Story-of-the-War-Twins could keep the writer occupied then Grandfather Quest could push him so deep into his own story that he could never write his way out.

"How have you come here?" Refton asked the ancestress.

"I am not here," she said. "I am throughout All-Under-Heaven centuries after my death. A bit of me was drawn here from the mind of one of a number of young and eager bureaucrats."

"Tell me all," Refton said. She was not a Magician but he could use her Life as a talisman, a magical act to ward off the Story imprisoning them.

That was sound magical thinking and should inevitably lead to the Magician.

Grandfather, Story-of-the-War-Twins said, *what are you doing?*

"There is someone else here," Sir Johannes said, pushing with Saint Michael's aid against the force that was tying down both the saint and the demon of his tongue. "Someone else is speaking."

From the empty form of its telling the Shadow-Twin did not yet watch, but once it had come to be it would have been watching, so it was said to watch. That was at Grandfather Quest's insistence, to which Story-of-the-War-Twins acquiesced.

Quest could not leave the shadow empty. It was too tempting a component of the path, an empty character, a lifeless, soulless, mindless, inhuman being who could be filled in as the plot required, useful leverage against the rest of the group.

The other twin in particular was troubling. The Knight could hear Grandfather Quest even where the Writer could not. It was dangerous to speak too much. They were on the track. He could let them go a little. He would not have to intervene again until they reached the Floating World of Contemplation, and the first of the three magicians necessary to the quest.

They're coming, Mother.

"Someone plots against us," said Tai-Mu-Sang.

The ship of tales docked at the Island of Contemplation. In a moment of insight, the prisoners of the story were freed --

Grandfather, no!

Free to contemplate the courses that would liberate them from their quandaries. The biographer could seek the Magician. The knight could work to free the demons from his soul and the monsters from his world. The ancestress would find here the means to conquer her enemies. The shadow could gain humanity, and the story itself could see how it fit into the grander schemes of tales.

Oh. . . . Very well.

"Now we are being placated," said Tai-Mu-Sang as she looked at the appearance of flesh in which she had been clothed, her own appearance given back to her after centuries of borrowed bodies -- not just any seeming, but the appearance of her vivacious youth. Clearly whoever was doing this did not understand her! This was not the flesh of her power but of her learning. If the placater wanted to please her it would have given her back her eyes of iron glance instead of fluttering allurement and her hard-won wrinkles of Contemplation rather than the smooth skin of naiveté.

Sir Johannes debarked, sword drawn to face the monster on the dock. He looked in the glowing eyes of the great serpent that barred their way, listened to its hiss, and knew it for a lie.

"A plot device," Refton said. "We're still in the story."

"Not a plot device, Peter," said the woman who stood on the hill overlooking the harbor. "A representation of the need for courage in contemplation."

"How is that not a plot device in a story of contemplation?" Refton asked. The woman looked and sounded familiar to him in the half-pleasant, half-worrying fashion that comes of seeing someone one should know and failing to remember their name, until the realization dawns that this was a former lover now consigned to the pits of hidden memory.

"If the tale is told," she said -- what was her name? -- "then it is as you describe it, Peter Life's Writer. But if you contemplate and make of your fear of knowledge a thing you must confront in your own mind, then you will find this serpent. Or this thing in some other shape. The bravest of you has given it this form. I assume that would be you, Sir Johannes, oh knight in steel."

"I have only the bravery God and Saint George have given me," Sir Johannes said, studying the woman who seemed like an icon of Mary Magdalene. "But I know this snake of old. It lives in my belly, raging through Eden."

Crush it under your heel, said the riddle in his spine. Eve was given this power by God, and I am Eve who also looked God in the face.

Tai-Mu-Sang watched this play out, perplexed by it all. Everyone seemed to know what to say and do, though the Chronicler, as she had known him when she had lived, was struggling against the tide of set speeches and actions. This was usually unwise, but he seemed to be, in some sense, winning. There was a *li* here, a course of ritual connected with stories, but not one she knew. And there was a plot, a behind-the-scenes maneuvering. All her political instincts told her this. But the sense or purpose of it, she could not grasp.

The woman looked familiar to her as well, someone she had debated with long years past, someone disliked but necessary, the minister of some important bureau whom one had to deal with regardless of personal feelings. The woman wore a mask of disdain, but underneath Tai-Mu-Sang could tell was the boredom of over-familiarity, of a thing being played out for the ten-thousandth time with all the possible results known, catalogued and awaited with a dull dread.

Tai-Mu-Sang felt a world-weary compassion for the woman. The hidden face had spoken volumes, told tales of the eager and ignorant who had come seeking great advancement and found only -- what? The dull plodding rise through the ranks. That had been Tai-Mu-Sang's experience when she had watched such rising stars in the bureaucracy, finding their youthful exuberance and brilliance worn down by the day-to-day necessities of governance. This woman was, like herself, a governor dealing daily with half-conceived notions needing to be honed against the hard edges of reality.

Sir Johannes advanced toward the great snake, gripping the ground with his sabatonned feet, seeking to draw the solid Earth through Uriel its angel. But Uriel cannot be deceived. Through the muscles of his feet, Sir Johannes was warned. There is no ground beneath; only the appearance of God's Earth touches your soles.

Saint Michael warned as well. There is no sword in the hand, only the appearance. Saint Peter declared, You have no body here, only the body of breath, the spirit loaned from God.

Saint Kyril told him that the snake was not real either.

So Sir Johannes wondered. Why does this not feel like meditation and internal battle? Why if all is spirit and appearance does the snake's strike, blocked by shield and countered with a turn, a spiked elbow and a swirling undercut, feel hard against me? Why in this illusion do I not see the meaning of the snake? If I battle the serpent should I not be conquering Eden? But I am not.

Then thought vanished in the purity of battle. The snake had coils within its coils, turns and twists that put snake-flesh everywhere around him. Sir Johannes knelt, leaped up in the posture called Raising the Cross and landed on the snake's back, then struck swift and hard with the appearance of the sword, severing the beast's head. It fell, too bloodless, too easy, too unreal.

Unreal, but not of the spirit. There was no meaning to the act, no change in his soul from the conquering. It had not been like slaying a demon to liberate a part of his body and soul. This was more like practice, but with an illusion of death to it. Meaningless, valueless, an empty killing of an empty thing.

Evadne watched and wondered at the knight's actions. He had not been ignorant. The snake should not have been there for the knight to fight. It, she, her island was being used by a story, misused by the Quest. She looked hard at the three who had disembarked and at the story floating shiplike in her harbor.

The story had been humbled and silenced by its elder, but she recognized it. It had delivered many a seeker to her shores, either in pairs or one alone, separated from the other by seas and purposes. Ignorant they had come. The snake had greeted them in its many forms.

But these just-disembarked people, the living and the dead, had visited her in their idylls and their labors. Each had been contemplative in their own way: chaste warrior, hard politician, ardent lover of Life. They were not the young and foolish seekers who would be met by the snake of ignorance. They should have found a place familiar to them, the routinely paced brown study of their internal labors, not the exotic landscape confronting the one who has but glimpsed wisdom.

There was too much wrong here. She could not permit this abuse of her island. She would have to take charge of the matter.

Evadne stepped down the rocky steps toward the quay.

"Welcome, old friends," she said, her voice aging, her face wrinkling and her hair whitening as she took on the years needed to be mistress of this land. It was hard to take up so much wisdom at once, but necessary. Otherwise Contemplation would become chattel to the Quest and no one would be able to seek without a line of struggle laid down before them.

Old friends? Peter Refton looked hard at the aging woman. He had never seen the like in any of the worlds he had visited, never seen someone age so speedily. In every world, age had come in its own way and at its own time. He had heard of such things in stories, of course, but this did not feel like the control of the story. This was something else. Another something else. How many something elses were involved here?

The bag of lives weighed down his shoulders, heavier than ever.

Maybe a few of them could be dropped. Some lives had been dull. It might be worth Redacting the burden. After all, a person only needed one life. The others could be summarized into background, a framework or context for his own life.

Perhaps it would be a good idea. He could sort through his pasts, shrink them for his --

Autobiography.

The word fluttered like the shroud in a wind-battered funeral.

Evadne spoke again, giving her voice to the wind so that her words might be heard by Quest and questers alike. "Welcome to Contemplation. Here may all secrets be uncovered at a price of innocence, and innocence recovered at the cost of secrets."

Magician.

"Someone is trying to keep us off balance," said Tai-Mu-Sang.

"That is the Quest," said Evadne.

"Quest for what?" said Sir Johannes.

"Not a Quest," Evadne said. "Quest itself, the story of the Quest. It has drawn you in."

"That story?" Refton gestured backhand toward the now very-shiplike Story-of-the-War-Twins.

"Not that small tale," Evadne said. "Quest is vast and terrible, powerful and free among the stories. Come within Contemplation and I will tell you what I can and you will discover what you will."

"That sounds like a quest," Refton said.

"Of course," Evadne said, growing a little younger with irony and a flash of remembered joining.

They were in the courtyard, though they had not gone there. Refton was certain that they took no steps, travelled no distance, but there was in his mind a sense of duration, of something having passed between the outside and the inside.

No, Refton corrected himself, cautious of his own thoughts. There was no passage, only distinction. One place was not another. One way of being was not another. Therefore his mind, storylike, had filled in the act of journeying where no trip had occurred. Or perhaps it had filled in a known journey to gloss over the unknown.

That must be where this quest is insinuating itself, he thought, declaiming each word of the thought one after the other while holding hard to the idea he was laying down. Between events there is passage, therefore life is a Quest.

Life is a Quest.

The echo slid surreptitiously into Refton's mind, lying down in the vast shadow of Life.

Sir Johannes had not been so easily fooled by the transition. His feet did not lie to him and he had long since learned the transitions of the body. He had been standing over the corpse of Ignorance and now found himself in an open yard with a fountain and rivulets.

Four rivers run out of Eden, said the riddle in his spine, echoing a voice that had no part of his spiritual body but permeated his knightly practices.

He had come into a place that could be thought of as Eden. He had defeated the serpent. Could he from here free the center of his being, liberate the arising of man, the focus by which the Spirit of God entered him?

This was not like the inner journeyings he had been taught to undertake. But was it so unlike? He had no body here. Was he not then a spirit? No, that was a worry for the Doctors of the Church, not for him. This place was not what he knew of Eden.

You have seen much that is not what you know but is true natheless, said the seed and the echo together.

Is this Eden? Sir Johannes asked of Saint Kyril.

It might be, said the Saint. If you listen to it one way you can hear the whisperings of Adam and Eve, the speech of beasts, the allure of trees, and the flickering of the fiery sword. If you hear it another way, it is not Eden at all.

"Seat yourselves," Evadne said.

Knight and Hunter, Ghost and Mage, Shadow and Story arrayed themselves.

Grandfather, why am I here? What role have you cast me in?

But the great story did not answer the lesser.

Putting us in our places, Evadne thought, setting up the moment of hard decision that comes in the throat of all Quests, the moment when the food chooses to be swallowed or to disgorge itself. This is the place where those involved cease to be pushed by the outside and choose to act on their own. Or so it seems. Now what can I do about this?

In Contemplation, questions gives rise to awareness.

It was clear. Grab the event Quest had made, call upon a Dyad to change its purpose in the Multiplicity. Dangerous, but better than being dragged through this.

Human, Mind, Spirit, Hermit, Contemplation, Transition, Redaction, Magician, Cycle, River, Politics. Which to call upon? Quest loved and used them all, even Redaction, Evadne's favorite tool. What was better for Contemplation than changing the precursers of things, editing Mind and Reality to fit a particular awareness. Sometimes it seemed to Evadne that she and Quest had too much in common.

But now she had something new, something Quest involved himself in but did not control. Politics was feared and bowed to by all the Dyads -- all of the Dyads that could fear and bow, that is. It was always necessary to be clear. Otherwise Contemplation would fall, or she would fall away from contemplation.

But she had just gained her connection to Politics, just before this Quest arrived. It was too convenient. She was being used by whatever was maneuvering with and against the Quest. What Dyad or Dyads were doing so? Or was it not a Dyad at all? Perhaps something of -------- was interfering.

Perhaps someone is plotting to use these people for a higher end.

| ACCEPTANCE |

Evadne did not know, and in her ignorance grew younger again, into a mature woman with the beauty of experience and the quiet, thoughtful eyes of one who has seen much.

Tai-Mu-Sang saw this change and thought, What a perfect recruit for the bureaucracy this woman would be. Then she shook the thought off. Appearances were deception, but not here. In this place appearances were revelation. What would she see if she could drag Temujin here and what would he see?

Evadne hesitated, weighing the choice, knowing that weighing the choice served the proprieties of Quest. But what else could she do in Contemplation?

Evadne looked around for something on which to clasp the arising of understanding. The Way Up had become a mountain, one of Quest's favored formulations. The books had become life stories, manuals of spiritual practice, a collection of much-commentaried Chinese classics, and a multitude of twin-tales. There was much to be seen about those drawn here.

A flicker of aging came upon her. I see, she thought; these people are hardly Quest's usual material. They were not young, brash, ignorant, or desperate. They had their troubles, but those troubles were not overwhelming, nor did they originate in a single source.

Quest is playing for too much Power, Evadne realized. Quest is afraid. He has made some alliance and does not know what his allies want. He has drawn these in, and me as well, in order to keep us from doing something. But Quest cannot prevent action, nor change the goals of people, only lay down the process of achievement.

Quest, maker and manipulator of desperate hours, has come to a Desperate Hour of his own, so he has pulled and pushed, brought them here in his coils in order to --

Bring us to success against him. What else can he do? Quest is Quest. He cannot engineer failure, only seek to be present at the winning, to gain from losing.

But losing what? What value had these people and their needs to Quest that he would cast himself as the dark and evil manipulator? Why would Quest make himself the villain of the piece?

Politics. There was no choice.

"Welcome," Evadne said. "My name is Evadne, and I hold session here on Contemplation's Isle."

EXALTATIONS

Session. The word resonated through Tai-Mu-Sang, though only then did she realize that no language was being spoken. Things were being offered to be thought about, and her own mind, or the mind she had borrowed, were turning those pre-thoughts into internal speech. A session, as if this were a normal tenday meeting to discuss the usual run of business and the normal troubles of All-Under-Heaven. Tai-Mu-Sang relaxed into her seat, letting the illusion of tension flow out of the appearance of a borrowed body. This was politics, the rice and tea of a dead bureaucrat.

Peter Refton heard the deliberate choosing of words, heard the careful manipulation of language that belongs to the rhetoritican and the writer. Evadne had spoken an unadorned sentence, but there was much compacted into those words. The sentence had given three names, that of the woman whose name placed her where she belonged: in his heart; that of the place where he had been many times; and the thing being done which was the thing he was doing. Evadne, Isle, Contemplation.

Sir Johannes and his shadow waited. Speechifying was for the court, but it always gave way in the end to a call for action or a command of awareness.

Story-of-the-War-Twins watched and waited until, as inevitably happened, Grandfather Quest's attention and determination fell upon him.

They are against you, Grandfather.

What would a Quest be, if the Questers did not rail against their fate?

"This is not Fate," Evadne said, seemingly to the empty air. "I do not let Time have enough foothold here to bring his whore with him."

Time will come to this Society.

Any Society relies upon Time for its continuity. But a small Society of sufficiently Free and Powerful beings could rely more upon Space for breadth of results.

Continuity of action is not the only way for actions to generate Consequences.

| ACCEPTANCE |

All of them had heard the voice of Quest, no longer sneaking into their minds, but bold and belling like a bull before a charge.

"Why do you speak the Tyrant's name?" Evadne said. "And why do you reveal yourself now?"

When the Questers are gathered, Prophecies are spoken.

"Time's heralds do not come here either."

Do not be so sure, Sorceress.

"Why that title?"

For the Quest.

A wind blew through, and Grandfather Quest withdrew into shallower presence.

"You tricked him," Sir Johannes said. "He is like a demon. He will brag and boast when challenged."

"That was not the trick," Evadne said. "On this island, questions require answers and the hidden reveals itself. Quest is powerful, but not free to flout the ways of my island and my Dyad."

"We've got to mess him up," Refton said. "Talk and act like human beings, not characters in his story."

That will not do what you think, Story-of-the-War-Twins said. *Grandfather Quest can embrace all the tongues and speeches of humanity. It is you, oh Writer, who are forcing archaism upon we stories.*

"You mean I'm supplying your voice?"

No one else here calls upon speech, and no one else needs it. You are giving my voice human form as you provide me a home in your mind, as you have given Grandfather Quest a home -- although he has so many that one more or less has little effect upon him.

Awareness slammed hard into Peter Refton, forcing him into a moment of self-examination.

| ACCEPTANCE |

That moment spread, grasping the others, pulling them into Refton, into his Mind, into the hunter of Lives.

Hounds bayed, wind swept up leaves, scattering scent across the open moorland. The hunter was coming, coming again for Tai-Mu-Sang, coming for Sir Johannes, coming for Story-of-the-War-Twins, but most of all coming for Evadne.

"Don't run," Tai-Mu-Sang said. "He'll find you if you try to hide. He hunted me before and caught me."

It had been a pleasant catching, years of hunting and playing between the two of them. He had come from failing Rome, he had said, though she later found out that was but a ruse to fit in. He had come along the paths of commerce where the silks of All-Under-Heaven were traded for the gold, tin, and iron that had kept Rome in power. The odd, pale westerners were not an uncommon sight in the streets of LoYang, and some of them spoke the Han language. But Refton did more. He could write that speech, handle a brush and an inkstone as if he had been born in a Han city, and he knew the classics, or something like them. The names he had for Master Kung's disciples were those of men, not women, yet the contents of the works were true and right. He had intrigued Tai-Mu-Sang's third son who was emperor at the time, and that Son of woman and Heaven had in turn brought the stranger to meet his mother, saying, "Great Mother, here is a man who knows the entire canon."

From that point on she was his to study. She gave up her life to him and he gave it back to her so that she could survive throughout the ages. Master Kung had said that a normal person survived five generations in memory, but a sage-woman would be recalled forever. Refton the Chronicler had made her a sage.

"Don't run?" Sir Johannes said incredulously. Flight had never occurred to him. Petrus had brought down the life of his saint, and in that hunting had given Parsival to the ages, marking a beginning of the order and a vital lesson in the unfolding of understanding. Petrus of Reeftown had written down Saint Parsival's practices, and in so doing had shown his followers that a Saint could be blessed with awareness and ability, but that the living Saint, being mortal, could still have limited understanding, and that his followers had a duty to make more of what he had done, to expand upon his labors, not slavishly adhere to them.

The order owed Petrus a debt, and if Sir Johannes' life was the means to pay that debt, then so be it.

They are not doing as they should, Grandfather, said Story-of-the-War-Twins. But no answer came from the overarching Quest, only a lowering of tension, a feeling that perhaps the hunt was not on, that no one was chasing the people down to tear their lives from their throats.

The hunter's dogs howled joyously at the moon. The wind blew over the moorland bringing a scent of heather and honeysuckle. It was a pleasant night for a stroll, and Peter Refton joined his guests in walking the darklands of his mindscape.

There were ways and ways across the swamps of Refton's awareness, intersecting paths that would open up into glades of thought, pools of water illuminated by glints of light from the two mountains that marked the edges of his mind. In the pools the travellers could see their pasts and their actions.

Tai-Mu-Sang saw vividly her life as laid down, studied her rise and her successes, noted her failures, and contemplated the many times she had been brought back into the minds of others, and always she saw her petition for divinity sitting on a Celestial Desk beside a chop of approval not yet stamped. The image of herself split into ripples as if a score of stones had been heaved into the pool and she saw all the bodies she was now occupying and all the actions she was undertaking. There were her works making ripples through All-Under-Heaven, washing the half-submerged stump that was the Great Khan. She looked and all her other selves looked at her and made inquiry.

"Where are you of us? What do you do? What gain or loss have you found?"

"None yet," Tai-Mu-Sang replied to her selves. "This place and these events are far removed from our concerns."

"Then come back and attend to what we need," said the one of her that had relived longest in the world, the one that had grown comfortable in the no-longer-so-young woman who had lent her mind and spirit to the purposes of the bureaucracy soon after they had been dispossessed.

"Not yet," said Tai-Mu-Sang to herself. "I think there are useful things to be learned here, and what does it matter where I am if we cannot defeat the Khan?"

The Tai-Mu-Sangs bowed their acknowledgement to her and faded into the dark water.

Story-of-the-War-Twins had also seen his own many forms, but he was used to awareness of Multiplicity and being a story in a writer's mind did not trouble him, for here he could find the hooks that would make this writer his.

Actually, he thought after a time, if I push a little harder into the water, I'll have him. Just a drop into the water and -- ahh! It's hot! Maybe there's another way.

Evadne looked, saw herself growing old and young through the endless cycle . . . and shrugged. She had seen it before in many another mind. Yet never before had all her ages been seen as equally beautiful. Here was a mind that saw her in a way unlike others, as if he had some unnoticed perspective.

Sir Johannes looked hard and deep upon his life, noting all the temptations he had succumbed to as well as the ones he had overcome. The demons within him sought to distract his attention as they appeared in clear relief, but he was not to be dislodged. As he watched, the seed the Marianites had planted in him slid down the mountain of his spine, rolling and gathering as it went until, tripping and falling, it struck into the heart of Eden, taking Johannes' breath away.

He saw Eden.

He was Adam who had looked upon God, done as God had commanded and still erred, who had brought labor to the life of man in his mistakes.

He was Eve who had looked upon God, listened to God, but listened to another as well and had brought two voices to the minds of men, so that all words bore both God and the Serpent within them.

He was the Tree of Knowledge and the Tree of Life, the two visible pillars of divinity, the Power and the Freedom of God.

He was breathless.

The Shadow-Twin caught his breath.

Peter Refton looked within himself and saw the two mountains at the edges of his being, saw the shining, glinting half-sun half-moon disks that illuminated him. He had always known they were there, but had never looked upon them clearly.

Refton reached his hands into the water and pulled out the lights from the mountains. They came into his hands, two coins from a fountain, little disks, heavy upon his grasp, too weighty to hold for long.

"What are these?" asked Refton in surprise.

"Dyads," Evadne said. "Two of the fundamental metaphysical components of existence. The one in your right hand is Mind, the Process of Opening Freedom. I know it well; it is a component of Contemplation. The left one is Life, which is Embodiment Guided by Reality. Look closely at it."

Refton held the quarter-sized coin up to his eyes. It seemed to be made of two different metals, one bright, one dark, like silver and iron. They were mixed in a complex fashion, interleaving each other, iron veins in silver and silver arteries in iron. There were shapes within the shape as if other coins were hidden in this one.

"You have two Dyads in you. By your actions you have arranged them into a Mosaic of two stones. You write down Lives for Mind to take in. You have made a Mosaic of Biographies."

"What are these things doing in me?"

"You represent them," she said.

"Symbolically?"

"Parliamentarily."

5. Inquiries

Where do questions come from?
Is that a joke?
If I say it isn't will you take it seriously?
How can I do that with this game of questions you're playing?
If I stop the game will you take the question seriously?
If I say yes, will you stop the game?
Yes.
Yes.
You noticed that I stopped the game before you said yes.
I noticed. Now, what was the question again?
Where do questions come from?
Questions come from stones against each other.
What kind of stones?
Ah, now that's the question.
Is that a joke?

| REJECTION |

Inside out, upside down, back and forth, tossed and turned.

Back upon Contemplation.

Upon Contemplation's back.

"What happened?" asked Tai-Mu-Sang.

"A question was answered," Evadne said, "so we came back. That's how Space and Time operate here on Contemplation's Isle. You go off on a question, come back on an answer, Freedom of Action, Constraint of Result."

The last two phrases sounded sing-song to Tai-Mu-Sang's ear, as if Evadne were quoting well-known lines from a classic. The phrases had implications, assumptions, disputations, and contemplations in them. Someone had labored hard at their making in order to perfect a single act of communication. Yet Tai-Mu-Sang did not know what was meant.

A question began to form in her mind, but she squelched it. If here questions flew one off to strange places or into the minds of others, then she was not going to make idle inquiries. She would prepare and perfect any requests for information as carefully as she would have a command to lower officials or a memorial to the Son of Heaven's throne.

She would not ask for meaning, nor would she inquire as to how it came to be that Evadne was once again a young woman, and a different young woman at that. The glaring, dangerous creature who had greeted them on the docks now projected a spirit of provocativeness and provocation, seduction and challenge, ambition and the trying of ambition.

That change seemed both right and wrong to Tai-Mu-Sang, right in *li*, wrong in *ren*. Ritually Evadne's appearance and spirit altered according to the local ceremonies of contemplation. But a person should not be so altered by the vagaries of thought. That was an offence against Humanity.

But how human was Evadne, or any of them for that matter?

The question was formed and Tai-Mu-Sang instantly knew the answer. She was human though long dead, with borrowed mind and spirit. Refton the Chronicler was human no matter how many lives he led or what he stood for. Evadne was human, but a prisoner. To Tai-Mu-Sang's surprise Story-of the-War-Twins was human as well, but the shadow-shape that stood behind Sir Johannes was not, though it could be if it chose rightly. Sir Johannes, holding his breath, had been for one moment not human but an appellant before the court of Heaven; then he opened his mouth and became in a sudden, provocative, attractive explosion of *ren* more human than any of them.

How did she know? How did she know that she knew?

"Stop!" Evadne said. "Don't make recursive questions or you'll tie your mind in knots."

Tai-Mu-Sang grabbed hold of her own errant thoughts, pulling them into line by singing a song from the Book of Odes, the song she had long used to discipline herself and her subordinates.

"Behold the rat.
He has his teeth.
But a woman without *li*,
A woman without *li*,
Should die."

Die, and stay dead. Not return, not be remembered, recalled, or reinstated.

"We must leave," Tai-Mu-Sang said. "This island has no propriety."

"Propriety is a prison," Evadne said, saying the words she had said over and over to Tai-Mu-Sang in the Ancestresses' many contemplations of the right courses of life. "Here are chains broken."

"Propriety is the way to right living," Tai-Mu-Sang said, and realized she had spoken that answer a myriad of times in her life, and after it, always to this woman and always in this place that she had never visited before.

A belling rang, hard and clear as if a church carillon sounded through a clear Christmas morning, calling a village to awake and rejoice.

In that tolling there were words in Evadne's voice, but not from her mouth.

"The matter before this body is the enaction or rejection of Propriety. Let debate be called."

"Politics," Refton said, his voice a brew of growl and sigh. In all of the pasts he remembered he had grown up in lands cynical of their politicos. He had travelled to other worlds and seen governance by tyrants, emperors, bureaucracies, theocracies, republics, democracies, oligarchies, and a score of other systems. He had met and preserved the lives of wise rulers like Tai-Mu-Sang, morally good generals like Saint Parsival, and many others who labored rightly in the vineyards of governance. Yet still his rooted distrust of all things political was not shaken.

Sir Johannes smelled a forming battle, heard sides being drawn up, war engines mounted, soldiers mustered, the fate of nations or worlds lying in the outcome. But he did not hear the messengers of God calling the battle, only two people disagreeing.

He took a step toward the disputation, but his shadow reached them first.

The twin, newly living, empty-minded, unthinking, inhuman, had only Spirit of the trinity of human Dyads. It was nothing-but-breathing, so it breathed, pulled the debate into its metaphoric lungs, drew the argument deep into the Eden within it, forming Adam and Eve, trees of Life and Knowledge from the disputation. Modelling itself upon the brother it had been forced upon, it grew, growing, oh growing a Mind and a Humanity.

"What is it to be a rat?" the twin asked. "What is it to contemplate? What difference does it make whether there is more or less here?"

Evadne, who had seen people come into being before, treated the new one as she would have any other visitor to her island, particularly a visitor with questions.

EXALTATIONS

"As long as Contemplation is the lone Dyad of this island, we will be safe from the incursions of Time."

"Time is everywhere," Refton said. "In every world I've been to."

"This is not a world as you know worlds," Evadne said. "This is a Floating World, a pocket within Space where Time is a servant. If there is too much to do here, if there are too many actions taken that need results, then Time will grow in power. Time, the Tyrant will bring in his Dyad Cronies: Reality, Matter, Fate, History, Death. Time will impose what he calls Natural Order. But it is not natural, it is only the order that Time is comfortable with. If that happens, this small island will grow into a vast world. Humanity, Mind, and Spirit will manifest in billions of Lives, all given to Time as slaves.

"That is what your worlds are, the slave plantations of Time."

But the Magician Evadne did not understand that she was herself a slave. The War Twins had come to her island to free her from the spiralled self-delusion Contemplation created in her mind. They --

"Quiet, Story-of-the-War-Twins," Evadne said. "How can you justify calling me a slave?"

Evadne, who had served heroes of a thousand-thousand stories in the roles of mistress, teacher, enemy, seductress, seduced; Evadne, whose words could enlighten, whose house held secrets, who could open Minds to Freedom or fill them with Power, had formed an alliance with one of Time's Cronies, as she called them. The Cycle had her, and with the aging and youthening of her life she was slowly, cycle after cycle, bringing Time to her world. She had learned this over and over in her contemplations, but whenever she found this piece of knowledge she would age to the point where she needed to invoke Cycle to renew her youth. Then would she forget and return to her labors on Time's behalf.

Cycle tried to age Evadne as it always had, but Politics intervened, dragging words from Grandfather Quest.

The Sorceress refused to accept this, so sure was she of her own supremacy. It would take great effort on the travellers' part to convince her that she needed to leave the Island of Contemplation.

Or they could take a more direct approach.

"No, they couldn't," said Refton. "You won't get us to kidnap her. And we won't do your bidding, Quest."

"Quest has no bidding," said Evadne, changing the subject, knowing she was changing the subject, ashamed of the fact that she was changing the subject, "only a form in which things are done. Quest is a propriety." She glared at Tai-Mu-Sang. "Is that what you want to bring here?"

"Not that self-serving propriety," Tai-Mu-Sang said. "I would bring real propriety, *li*, the way by which one lives ones life."

"Lives in a prison, you mean," Evadne said. "Your *li* is but the code of conduct of slaves who think that following the right procedure makes them free."

In the Shadow-Twin's belly the fight between Adam and Eve raged, bringing the heat of life into him. If he could keep at it long enough he would be born, he would be someone -- who, he did not care -- a someone, not the shadow of a man.

The words of the dispute faded to silence in Sir Johannes' sainted ears, and in their place rose up a host of implications. None of the host were real as yet, but they waited to become real, waited beyond earshot, each vying to be the eventual meaning of this dispute. He had heard them before in a different context. On battlefields before the day was won or lost, when the armies of empires fought for ground and glory he had heard them, the battle ravens waiting to dine meaningfully upon the outcome of mortal conflict.

Listen to the Society of Ravens.
They tell the Consequences of actions.

| SILENCE OF ACCEPTANCE |

Sir Johannes could hear but not speak the words of those not-yet-in-being ravens. Yet he could think upon them. Here on this island the birds were nearer and more numerous than on those worldly battlefields. They flocked in numbers far greater than he could count. They blackened the sky with potential consequence as if the wars of mortal empires could have but few potential meanings compared to the many 'what could truly be said's about this single dispute.

In the recent clarification of his spirit something came, a bit of divine wisdom which dropped into his mortal mind like a ripe apple falling from a holy tree. In Time, it told him, meaning is carefully apportioned, given out like gruel to the starving. Here outside Time all meanings are possible.

And he knew, knew in the Eden liberated from the snake, that this restriction came from original sin, that man's clouded, narrowed mind was the result of seeking knowledge of good and evil.

And he knew that that was only one meaning.

Sir Johannes' heart skipped a beat, then another, then another. The AntiChrist was struggling against the wisdom gained, seeking to burn down Jerusalem within his heart before he might undertake the Crusade and liberate it to Christ's dominion.

"I have no mortal heart here," Johannes said to the Beast within him. "You cannot kill me for my understanding."

"You will return to Time and then you will die," the AntiChrist said.

"All things die in Time," the Christ said within him. "But you can come to new life."

EXALTATIONS

Peter Refton watched the lives in collision around him, lives of people, ghosts, saints, magicians, shadows, stories, and these beyond-life things Evadne called Dyads, lives welling up and acting at a critical juncture for all of them. He had written these points in lives many times. He had framed them in biographies as moments of decision, or destiny, or blessing, or warning, all the tools a writer could use to cover the actions of mind, spirit and humanity where outside understanding simply could not enter.

People did things, they argued, they accepted, the fought, they died, they rose again. It was easy to write their actions when they were following the normal paths of life. But when these alien moments came, these points where they were free to go or stay, to change things or let them go, then the writer failed. These moments could not be set down justly and clearly.

He had hunted through lives and worlds and could not catch the moments of Freedom, the moments that after the fact were accorded to wisdom, folly, destiny, or chance.

Almost he formed a question about the nature and purpose of this freedom of contemplation and decision. Perhaps he did form it. Perhaps he saw through it into a true decision, perhaps he took that decision. Or perhaps he felt a spiral of recursive thought lying wormlike in that almost-query and knew that to ask was to tie oneself down to the island and its cycles.

Life and Mind conjoined within him, flashing lightning-understanding down and up into him and unto him. He knew Evadne's past, knew why and how she had been trapped here and why and how she was forever Free.

"We're leaving," Refton said.

|SECRET ACCEPTANCE|

If someone speaks, why does anyone listen?

Do they listen?

Don't start that again. I'm serious. If someone says something, why would anyone else listen?

Any of a number of reasons. They might like or trust the person. The voice might be attractive. The subject might be of interest to them. They might want the speaker to think they were interested in them or what they were talking about.

No. No. No. Those are all after-the-fact explanations and justifications. When someone opens their mouth to speak why does someone else cock an ear to attend, why at the moment before a decision is made does a hearer attend to a speaker?

You wish to Tell the answer?

Yes. It is because they are of the same Society, and it compels them to listen and perhaps take action.

| ACCEPTANCE |

"There are two ways off this island," Evadne said, unsure of why she was going along with Refton, troubled by echoes in her contemplative mind, the sounds of two Somethings discussing listening without coming to any conclusion.

Or perhaps they were Telling. That made sense, but if so what were they trying to do and what would the Great Way do with what they Told?

She had the feeling that that distant converse had influenced her to accede. But even as she thought that, justifications welled up in her mind. She was leaving because Tai-Mu-Sang was right. She had been a prisoner of Contemplation just as much as most humans were slaves of Time. She was going because she was weary of playing her part in the lives of contemplatives, tired of being stuck in roles for their edification. She was going because she wanted to continue arguing with Tai-Mu-Sang, a pleasurable disputation. She was departing to watch over the newborn Shadow-Twin, who would need help if he was not to turn into some roaming, aimless, ignorant monster. She was going because she wanted to be with Peter Refton.

"We can sail out through the sea of Space," she said. "From there we can reach any of the big islands where Time rules, or any of the other Floating Worlds. Or even leave this Archipelago and find islands of other Dyadic combinations."

"Can we reach the story that's manipulating us?" Refton asked.

"No," Evadne said. "Stories do not dwell in the Hegemony of Space and Time. They exist in an unislanded Nation."

"Can the other way off lead there?"

"It can," she said, hesitantly. Evadne pointed to the mountain. "But it leads through Contemplation. That is the Way Up, the ascension of awareness through a series of unfoldings of thought. It is the way to Power and Freedom, the way to self-understanding, the way to answered questions and solved problems."

"All of those at once?" Tai-Mu-Sang's voice was dry with sarcasm.

"No, one at a time," Evadne said. "You must choose what you are ascending, but your choice and your goal may not be what you think they are. It's a dangerous way. If you pick something that the mind cannot embrace you may go mad. If you try to climb a thing which does not exist you may find yourself spiralling forever upward through the illusion of progress. If you will not confront what you face with courage you will fall into self-deception."

EXALTATIONS

Courage. The word sank deep into Sir Johannes in a way it never had before. It came into his ears, flowed down into Eden and travelled through him to his heart. Coeur-age, the virtue of the heart, the virtue of the one who was freed of the Anti-Christ, the blessing of the triumphant crusader.

"Petrus?" he said. "There is a thing you wrote in the Life of Saint Parsival that I wish to ask you of."

Refton nodded to the knight, mustering the remembrance of the Saint. Such a small man in body he had been, a head shorter than most of his Saxon kinfolk. He had been converted by Charlemagne --

Carolus Magnus. Refton had had to bite his tongue many times during his years at the Emperor's court not to speak of Charles' future in his own world.

Refton had travelled seeking the Life of a Christian General. He had thought at first that Charles was the one he had come to find, until in the waters of the Rhine the third son of a defeated tribal chief had accepted baptism and vowed to serve Charles in all the ways he could. Then he had gone and sat in the forest until the angels came to him.

The torments of angels, Refton had written, *are a thousand times harder upon the soul than those of demons. Demons seek to make you suffer but not to be aware of what is happening to you. Angels seek to make you know all things of your life, to know your soul, body and actions. No pain is greater than the truth confronted. No pain is more liberating.*

In the woods the newly-named Parsival suffered Purgatory and found what God had wrought within the being of every mortal man. *Your soul is made in my image, God had said to the new saint. Your mind and body are the images of Heaven and Earth. Liberate them from the demons that entered humanity for its sins and you shall walk in my way.*

Parsival had done so, and Refton had been his witness.

"Ask what you will, Johannes," Refton said. "But remember I only saw and spoke to him. I did not practice what he taught. I don't understand everything that he said or did. In you is a deeper knowledge of Parsival than I have."

"Nevertheless, you were there," Johannes said. "You wrote about a speech Saint Parsival made after he led his warriors to the wintry victory over the Rus."

Refton, bodiless though he was, shivered in memory of that time. He had warned Parsival that many had tried to invade the eastern lands in winter and never succeeded. But the saint was better than Refton's history.

"After that conquest," Johannes went on, "he spoke to the corps of his followers who were learning his way and said, 'When Eden is liberated your body can do no wrong, but only when Jerusalem is freed will your spirit and body together be perfected.' Did he truly say that?"

"Almost," Refton said. "I Redacted the speech slightly. Parsival was not given to flowery turns of phrase, but a Saint's Life must be written in a proper way. What he said was, 'Free Eden and your enemy falls. Free Jerusalem and you won't fall.'"

"Ah." The words flowed into Johannes, planting seeds within him. Something began to flourish on the Temple Mount of Jerusalem. Something else grew on Golgotha. The AntiChrist looked distrustingly at these shoots, but the Christ defended them from the withering glance of his eternal foe.

He had been changed by the Marianites, Johannes realized. Not only had they taught him new things, they had taught him new ways to be taught.

Here on Contemplation's Isle those ways had come out swiftly and clearly. Johannes could see the allure of the place. It was an anchorite's pole, a hermit's cave, a place for isolation and self-perfection, one of God's gifts for those who needed time away from society to become closer to him.

But Saint Parsival had taught and his follower had accepted that too much isolation led not to God, but to self-involvement, to over-delicacy, to . . .

"What did Saint Parsival really say about spending too much time alone?"

Refton smiled. "He said, 'God made mud. Sometimes you learn by leaping over it, sometimes by slogging through it.'"

"Did he really say that?" Evadne asked. She had met several saints and want-to-be-saints, but had not met many who spoke in that way.

"More or less," Refton said. "Saxon can be a very earthy language."

What is speaking like if you don't have a language?

There isn't any speaking without language of some sort.

So speaking makes the language.

I suppose. Why are you asking so much about asking and speaking? Don't you have anything better to do than muddy the waters of discourse?

I do. I'm doing it.

What are you playing at now?

Becoming audible, sounding more like someone talking. I've been making a language by speaking it.

And using me as a sounding board and a straight man.

I've been making you audible as well. It'll help both of us. We make a cometary swoop in from Telling to Narrative to Speaking. We catch the appropriate attention, generate the correct oracular interpretations, and then swoop out. If we can trinitize speech we'll have an advantage.

I hope so. Speaking and Narrating are too close to the trap of Multiplicity for my comfort.

Don't worry. We'll be safe. Just a dive and rise.

Dive and rise? Evadne looked hard into her mind where she found images in conflict: a ball of fire and ice swooping near the Sun then vanishing into the distance, soothsayers forecalling the end of the world, a bird of flame, the Phoenix being seen in the skies before its death and then again after its rebirth. Someone was talking to her, but what about?

EXALTATIONS

"Which way do you want to climb, Chronicler?" Tai-Mu-Sang was asking Refton.

The question sounded testish to Evadne, as of an examiner inquiring of a bright but unfocused student. It came to her suddenly that she had not been paying proper attention to the interactions of this group of visitors. There was more here than simply three people, a story and a shadow. A Society had been insinuated into her island which had always been a place of hermits. Someone who knew how to build a society from diverse components had made one of this batch. What good was such a small but capable gathering of Humanity? Who would want it? Quest, certainly, he loved such clusters; he could be told as broad sweeping epics around them. But who else? And was Quest behind it or being manipulated by whoever was behind it? What politics, what faction did it serve? And in which government?

And why had she *somehow* been swept up with them?

Somehow. She sniffed at the word. It was an insinuation into her mind from Quest, an obvious one. He was playing games with her. But he did not play games, he made them. Something was happening on a scale she had rarely contemplated. It was not the highest or simplest -- those she had looked upon time and again -- nor the lowest and vasted -- those she knew, though she had paid little attention to them.

In the heights the universe was simple: Power and Freedom combined and recombined to create the Language whose words were Dyads. All things could be seen and understood in the politics of that language.

In the lowest scale the multiplications of the Dyads went about their existences under whatever dominion they knew, accepting their native politics as fundamental to reality.

Somewhere in the middle, in a partly manifest, partly fundamental state, somewhere in the confusion and profusion of interactions, something was happening which had dragged them all into it.

She had been distracted again. Quest had done it deliberately, inserted a single word into her mind to remove her attention from the others and the way they had come to a decision.

"We'll ascend a story," Refton said. "Not one of these pandemic stories like Grandfather Quest. We'll take one with many forms that intrudes on many lives, but still has constraints on where and how it can manifest."

"You know such a story?" Evadne asked.

"I do," Refton said. "I've heard it in many forms. It is not so free as our comrade here, and not as pervasive and exacting as Quest. It travelled with one culture and in the worlds where that culture grew it took root in many places."

"Why climb this story?" Evadne said.

"Because Quest is in it, but he doesn't set the rules of it. And I know how it goes and how it is told. It's a life story, you see, or a collision of life stories. Through it we can reach Quest but he can't get at us."

It made sense to Evadne. Too much sense. How had Refton come to know so much of the organization of stories? He had left too much ignorance behind too quickly. What had been happening and what had been distracting her?

Evadne tugged at the thought.

The thought was pulled up, tossed around, then dropped down.

Evadne refused to Contemplate.

There are ways of thinking that no one thinks to think about. People use these ways, skipping mightily from preceding notion to consequent notion, never realizing the vast mental space they are traversing. They go point by point, unaware of the infinity of points that lie between one idea and the next. Through such a vast space, anything could traverse safely, passing unscathed through --

|ACCEPTANCE OF TELLING/REJECTION OF TELLERS|

Wait! I'm caught on something!

6. Machinations

Paperwork moved slowly through the Bureaucracy of Heaven, yet always arrived at the proper moment. The petition for Tai-Mu-Sang's deification had been beautifully scribed by the Great Chronicler himself using a bamboo brush tufted with the thinnest sheep's hair anyone had ever seen. The ink seemed to have been ground to a fineness no hand could match. His brushwork was excellent, but he used characters unknown to the court although the most skilled calligraphers could work out what they must have meant. He had smiled at their inquiries and said, "Heaven will recognize them."

The petition had been duly presented by the Son of Heaven after his grandmother, Tai-Mu-Sang's, death and properly enshrined in her ancestral altar to await a response. There it had sat while the decades turned into centuries and dynasties rose and fell. No word came from Heaven, neither acceptance nor rejection, only the long wait.

It was often said by those who asked that Heaven was patient, but this was not so. Heaven was neither patient nor impatient. It acted when the circumstances were correct.

"It is like a game of Go," one particularly wise priestess had said to a visiting foreigner four centuries after Tai-Mu-Sang's death. "The place awaits the stone. You do not put down the 'yes' of black or the 'no' of white until it will fit properly into the life and death of the stones around it."

The foreigner, a traveller from the west named Petronius Reeve, had inquired of the memorial to Heaven while gathering in details of the priestess' life. The priestess had noticed the deftness of the traveller's calligraphy and had been impressed by its similarity to the writing on the aged petition itself. A strange thing, but no stranger than finding a literate man, or a literate foreigner for that matter.

"Heaven acts with Perfect Propriety," she had said, "placing stones in the mosaic of the Wall of Heaven only when they are needed, and always when they are needed."

At this pronouncement Petronius Reeve had pronounced himself satisfied, but the priestess noticed a look of calculation in his eyes.

At the present moment when some of the Dyad stones were rising and some falling, Heaven broke the seals on the divination of Tai-Mu-Sang, weighed the pros and cons in the Heavenly balance scale on which All-Under-Heaven teetered against All-That-Is-Not-Under-Heaven, and after due and just deliberation, stamped

| ACCEPTANCE |

After which all that was needful was for this command to pass through the departments of the eternal bureaucracy. Orders were placed, one to create a point in Space where she would earn her divinity, another to generate a proper moment in Time for deification. There were papers for enlistment of priestesses. drafting of a steed, finding of a consort, a creation of a proper form with which she could influence all things. It would take several moments in which to complete the process. Heaven scattered those moments through the events of the Multiplicity to give them an acceptable sequence. And, of course, Heaven drafted a story for Tai-Mu-Sang's deification.

Where would Peter Refton have gone if Grandfather Quest had not dragooned him? What worlds would he have travelled to, what magicians found? What Life would he have written?

In the Library on Contemplation's Isle Peter Refton read the answers to these questions in his own words and with the understanding that would have arisen in his mind had he succeeded in his own search rather than in the search's search.

The Magician is found in isolation, in a separate Mind, in a hermitage either within the world or without. It is well established that humans are the multiplications of three Dyads: Humanity, Mind, and Spirit. Magicians are also multiplications of the Dyad Hermit which is Humanity Guided by Other than Humanity.

Refton stared perplexed at his words. How had his hypothetical future self come to know so much about the metaphysical nature of things that Evadne had only briefly outlined?

It's a secret, Peter, something concealed, almost a mystery but not quite.

Who's writing this? Refton wondered.

We three are, Peter, you and I and me. Peter Refton. We would have written this book. We would have lived this life; that's as good as having lived it.

"No it isn't," Refton said aloud, though on Contemplation's Isle it was hard to distinguish words thought and words spoken. "Hypothetical lives can be written down, not experienced."

What about the lives we tote around? Are they lived or experienced?

"They're remembered."

Then remember this one.

Refton picked up the book and weighed it in his hands. It had an unbalanced weight to it, as if the front half of the book were trying to fall and the second half to rise.

"Evadne? May I take this book?"

The Lady of the Isle thumbed through the volume from end to beginning, each page youthening her, putting a blush into cheeks no longer wrinkled, a twinkle into eyes no longer experienced. When the first page and the cover had been closed she handed it to Refton accompanied by a kiss.

Into the backpack went the life Peter Refton remembered.

The Magician was the longest hunt of Refton's lives. Through world after world he had sought his quarry. He had found many who had gained access to Power and Freedom beyond the limits Time had placed in their worlds. He had acquainted himself with wonder workers and god seekers. He had written the lives of Power-mad dark lords and Freedom-crazed heroes. He had learned the secret ceremonies of smiths, the herb lore of a hundred worlds, the charms and invocations that could conjure spirits from a multitude of floating worlds, the poems of a thousand heavens. He had spoken with the dead, with angels with demons and with spirits aligned with Dyads unconnected to morality. He had seen the future, divined the past, looked into the hearts of men and the souls of beasts. He had trafficked with gods and trafficked in souls. He had drawn down blessings and curses, mortified his flesh, corrupted and then purified his soul.

Under a dozen teachers with a gross of world-views he pieced together the metaphysical nature of things. He learned to see the underlying suprareality as a Lexicon, an infinite dictionary that had within it two primal words: Power and Freedom. From those two words were generated an infinitude of other words which were the Dyads, the metaphysics, or perhaps the kataphysics. The Dyads comprised the simpler overarching or underlying reality above or beneath the complex reality he was accustomed to living in.

The Dyads, he was told, were infinite in number because Freedom was broad and gave breadth to everything in existence, particularly the things that partook directly of it, that is the Dyads. The Dyads were effective because Power was within them and rendered them not inert concepts but active constituents in all things.

"But what are all things?" Refton had asked, adopting the pose of a naive student, for the teachers he had found liked to hear the lectern-delivered sounds of their own voices. Refton had pegged them all as observers of Life rather than participants. He had not then wondered why he had attached himself to that sort of person.

"What I have just described for you," one of these teachers had said, "is the Simplicity, the existence of the Dyads. But the Dyads interact effectively (because of Power) in all the ways they can (because of Freedom). These interactions create the worlds we know, the Multiplicity.

"That is a very neat understanding," Refton had said to each of his teachers in turn, but none of them had caught the edge of mistrust in his voice.

There was an art, Refton learned, to discerning which Dyads could Multiply in what permitted forms in each particular world. He learned to measure and craft, study and use the particular multiplications. So he went on his way from world to world, from life to life.

But he never found the Magician.

"What kind of an idiot was I?" Refton asked as he shut the book of memory.

And what kind of an idiot am I now? he thought. Why am I letting myself be distracted with this self-examination? And then he wondered further. Is it me that is examining myself?

"Petrus," Sir Johannes called from the wilderness of Contemplation. "The Quest awaits."

All the saints in Heaven sang hymns before the unknowable throne of God, while in amongst them rising and falling like a geyser came the thoughts of the prayerful and the spirits of the ecstatic. Rise they did, the still living coming up to experience the indivisible Power and Freedom of God and so be transformed by it before falling back to their worlds, blessed or cursed based on what they had brought before the throne.

Up in a sudden spray came the leader of the Order of the Three Who Have Faced God, those who Sir Johannes knew as the Marianites.

"Our emissary is gone," she said, humbling herself before the visage through which God could be glimpsed. It was a hard task to obtain the perfect humility necessary not to idolatrize the visage. For one thing the saints and angels and their constant singing of praises were such a distraction. The devil within her suggested she tell them to shut up but she ignored him as just another of the distractions. God was before her as God was before everyone, present in all things, in all actions, not the being she imagined she was seeing, not the being she had been taught to see, but the being that was. All the apparatus of Heaven, all the inhabitants, the dead, the never-born, and the yet-to-be, all the boundless glory of things around her, were simply aids to her ecstatic rise.

But there came a point where the aids, the crutches of the living soul, had to be cast off so that God could be seen full in the faceless face. That was the deepest secret of her order, the secret that they had learned from orders in empires neither Christian nor Muslim where such things were not secrets, where all seekers knew that the appearance was only an illusion, that in order to embrace the reality everything had to be cast off.

The weight of her life and experience weighed heavily upon her. The worldliness of running the order, of keeping so many nuns and monks in line was like a winding sheet about her body, and the maintaining of secrets that should be shouted to the world was like a lead coffin.

"Our emissary has left the world," she said again as she tore away the masks from God's face, from her own face, from the faces of the saints one by one until she came to the mask of Saint Parsival. Then she hesitated.

"If you meet a saint, martyr him," Parsival said, his voice a sword blade. "If you meet Jesus, crucify him. If you meet God, kill God."

"Our emissary must return," she said, tearing down the firmament of Heaven to embrace her final Exaltation.

| ACCEPTANCE |

Up she rose and met herself.
If you meet yourself, kill yourself.

Evadne wrestled with herself in the Field of Combat. It was an unfair contest, ten thousand young, eager, passionate girls against one refined, reserved, bored old lady. A few throws and tosses and the ten thousand were put down, to arise older, wiser, and fewer by a divisor of ten. A thousand clever young women threw themselves against the one eternal wise woman, employing a millennium of ruses and tricks against her. But the old one was never where they thought she would be, and their trickery she turned to strike them down, aging and decimating them anew. A hundred smart women drew up their plans, schemed their schemes and waited for the right moment to strike. But the moment never came. Somehow their target never presented herself to their sights. At last, their patience exhausted, they released their assaults only to find their ambitions shattered, their machinations broken and they razed with them.

Ten mature women presented themselves before one palsied, wearied grande dame and asked, "Which of us is to become you?"

"The one who can tell me why we are involved in this matter instead of detached from it."

The decade paused and looked at each other. Before they had been members of one army seeking to conquer and supplant. Now older and wiser they discovered themselves to be rival claimants, challengers against each other as much as against the old woman.

In seeking advancement, it was vital but gravely difficult to choose the right moment to speak. Sometimes the first thing one thought of was the correct one. If that were so then the battle would go to the swiftest. Sometimes the second thought was best, but rarely. Second thoughts most often only tripped one up. Whoever spoke second was likely doomed. Third thoughts won out frequently, taking the useful place of synthesis in the triune dialectic. Last thoughts were common victors, sometimes by virtue of rightness, more often by simple exhaustion.

"I'm waiting," Old Evadne said.

"For love," said one of the ten, "of man and of child we are involved."

"True but distracting," Old Evadne said, dismissing the first speaker back to childishness.

Of the nine remaining one stepped forth with an air of martyrdom about her. "We are involved because of the Will of God," she said in the voice of the leader of the Marianites.

"Not yet," Old Evadne replied. "Go and reveal yourself to God."

That Evadne disappeared through a sudden-appearing gate of glory and wonder, vanishing into Heaven and folding up the gates with her.

Four of the remaining contestants leaped out seeking to offer Synthesis, but were dismissed before they could speak.

"Not so simple," Old Evadne said.

Six down, four to go.

"We are involved for reasons as yet shrouded," said one of the others.

"True," Old Evadne said. "Go and be born."

That one vanished and the others faded into silence.

Seven down, and -- faded into silence?

"Things not going as you want them to, Quest?" Evadne asked, youthening herself as she cast off her worries.

They transpire well enough, Sorceress, was the answer.

"For me as well," Evadne said, though she did not know why that was true.

Tai-Mu-Sang and Sir Johannes had watched this curious combat from the Courtyard That Looks Upon Self Conflict.

"A noble but flawed practice," the Knight said, "to bring forth one's ambivalence and do battle with many selves instead of fighting the vices that lead to the ambivalence. But how can there be a final victory in such a fight if the roots of the confusion are not pulled from the soil of one's soul?"

"It's a wasteful discipline," Tai-Mu-Sang said. "To have so many minds and bodies and winnow them down instead of employing them each in their own departments."

But Peter Refton who had watched all this from the base of the mountain did nothing but blow a kiss to Evadne.

Elsewhere upon the island, the last two participants in the Grand Quest, Story-of-the-War-Twins and the Shadow-Twin, occupied themselves in more sensible preparation than the self-involved contemplations of the human-born seekers.

Petulance, Grandfather? Story-of-the-War-Twins asked, borrowing the voice of an ironist he had earned from Grandmother Allegory.

They are breaking the rhythm of the narration, the old, old story said. They are evading the herding efforts of myself and Time, and my other allies seem to be silent about this matter.

Other allies? Grandfather, what are you playing for?

Power and Freedom, of course. They are the only things that are.

But in what form are you playing for them? What will you get from this telling?

Life of Ecstasy.

What is that?

The young story had yet to learn the Lexicon, so he did not yet know how to fit together narration and Speaking to bring forth the Dyads into his own being. His doting and indulgent grandfather was giving him an opportunity to expand his own being and embrace the Simplicity that lay below the Multiplicity of being. If the young tale did as he was told he would emerge with a share of Power and Freedom and perhaps direct access to one or more of the Dyads. What was needful at this moment was for Story-of-the-War-Twins to guide and control the newly inspired though yet mindless Shadow Twin.

As you say, Grandfather. The Shadow Twin, born as he was of his brother's spirit, was the Energy of his Guidance (Does that do it for you Grandfather? You see, I have studied the Lexicon of Dyads.)

Very good Grandson. Now, can you catch the Dyad's attention or will you simply call it by its definition?

Listen and hear, Grandfather. It was the duty of the Shadow-Twin to fill and direct his brother to act in accord with the proper way of things, for Johannes the Knight had been touched in his soul by a strangeness that flared up in sudden fits and confusions. The woman who had touched him was the harbinger of monsters, the herald of destruction who would call forth the end of the world Johannes had known. His twin would have hard labor to guide him back to the clear zealous path of his order.

And what path would that be?

The holy quest laid down for him by the Emperor to preserve his empire against this encroachment.

And how is he to do that?

By following the writer of his saint's life until he reaches the saint who is his source. In the presence of Parsival this foreign intrusion into his soul can be expunged and he will return purified to his world, ready to lead the crusade against the monster-bringers or to transcend all the limitations of order and make his world anew. Is that good enough, Grandfather?

Almost, Grandson. You have not yet called down the Dyad, nor have you placed yourself properly within this Quest.

But Grandfather. . .

Do as I bid you, Grandson.

Yes, Grandfather.

Sir Johannes had been blessed with a redoubled doubling of his Spirit. The calling in him resounded bell-like in the emptiness of his shadow and echoed in the lofty mosaics above where Spirit held an honored place in the stones of God.

The Isle of Contemplation shook as if an earthquake gripped it, though it dwelled in no earth and was not bound by any of the dicta of Reality. It could not quake. Still it shook, for in the Lexicon Contemplation incorporates Spirit within it. Therefore when Spirit comes a-multiplying, Contemplation shivers and lets it in.

Spirit comes like a wind, a breath inhaled and screamed out with newborn being. Spirit comes like a guiding beacon illuminating what is known and revealing what is unknown. Spirit comes in a great directing and a fiery energy. Spirit comes, takes root, and sends forth branches.

Into Sir Johannes DeLondres, Spirit came.

No! It was supposed to enter my Grandson. Where are you? Why aren't you directing the Multiplication? Have you betrayed me?

But no answer came to the bewildered story.

Who's Telling this?

Never mind that now. Try to pull away.

I can't. I'm stuck on something.

Everything's going wrong. Someone must be working against us.

Worry about that later. Help me get free.

All the Saints, Angels, Demons, and the single Soul within Sir Johannes awoke with a sudden spark as if they had never lived before but now had come to be. All of them gave forth their birth cries. We live. We are. We are Power to fill up. We are Free to guide.

Christ and Antichrist were.

God was.

Sir Johannes was.

EXALTATIONS

The Riddle was.

| ACCEPTANCE |

Narration read in truth and cause, the Poetess wrote as the Faerie globe showed the appearance of all to her, *reveals the seeming of Lives.*

She looked at the sentence and knew it did not come from her own thinking. Whose mind had she been looking into this time?

'All seeing' was one of her titles. Her people thought that meant she knew everything, but she knew better. She could look upon the vision of anything, hear, smell, taste, touch, take in a thousand senses most humans never conceived of, but all that gave her was a perfect image, not reality.

Pyotr plotted against his enemy. The Knight bathed himself in the sanctity of his God. The Sorceress looked and schemed; twice she had interrupted herself to stare the Poetess in the face and argue with her about the nature of what was happening. The Ancestress conceived the politics of the situation, judging when and how to make war upon the foe, as well as laying down the proprieties under which the warriors could act.

All looked proper and correct. All the causes of action could be written down truthfully. But no real understanding would come from these perceptions, for they were the tools of something other than Mind.

The story, the great story, the grand story, the Quest showed forth in all that showed itself before the Poetess. She had sung his epics, recently penned his tales. She had served him since language had been given her upon the day her mother had whispered those great and secret words that opened the doors to Faerie: *Once upon a Time.*

But now the Poetess saw her master with new illumination and was mazed at her previous ignorance. How had he shrouded himself from her wandering eyes for all these years? She had looked through Faerie Time out of Mind, had seen many a story enacted, but never a Story in Action.

Had he shrouded himself, or had he simply directed her Mind in its musings, guided her according to the ways she was accustomed to look?

Let me peer, she thought, turning the beauteous ball in her hands. And then she wondered. *Was that thought mine or given to me by a story? Did I understand or am I stood upon?*

Perhaps Stories control us, and we need more objective views of our minds. That did not sound like a story, and it had a tinny, unpoetic quality not native to her own thinking either. It smelled to the Poetess as if she were being offered a new kind of chain in place of the old. *In Theory, there are thoughts unbounded by any fetters.*

Now that sounded true in statement and false in implication, right appearance with wrong shadow.

How many kinds of chains are there? she wondered, and the globe answered her with a vision so vast that her Mind had to open itself over and over again in a dizzy flowering to take in the size of the view.

The worlds are governed, she wrote, distressed at the antipoetry of her text, *not one by one, but in clusters. Nations of many worlds, all of similar character, are underlain by the same principles. The governors of these Nations care as much about individual worlds as Tyrants do about their subjects. There are a few favorites among them and there is the vast throng of riff-raff to be ignored.*

How did the governors rise to Power? They found the weakest point in the overall structure of being. Around this point they caused the other fundamental components to organize themselves, making a Perfect Mosaic that would be invoked more commonly than the other lesser Mosaics.

Why isn't this being Redacted?

Faerie is only an image. She isn't talking about what's really happening, only what appears to be happening.

Can't we stop her?

It doesn't matter. Faerie has no real consequence, and she only appears to play a part in what is happening.

Each of these governors found many ways of dealing with the weak point. Some saw it as a river that could be drunk from or channelled, others as an aspect of their own minds that could be thought through.

Some saw it as an ultimate being that could be talked to as one would talk to another person.

The Poetess wrenched pen and mind from this theoretic control and channeled the next thought into poetic formulation.

Arising/sustaining/passing, so fragile. The weakest point is God.

Weakest, but most Powerful and most Free.

| ACKNOWLEDGEMENT |

Enough of this! Grandfather Quest said. *The Questers gathered at the base of the mountain. Their leader deemed that at its height might be found the means of defeating the story which had imprisoned them. Towering above them, its narrow path held troubles aplenty. But together they might overcome these obstacles and in so doing claim the prize of Power and Freedom that would give to each his heart's desire.*

"Nonsense," Refton said. "We are doing no such thing. We are going to War."

They would come together to battle against their enemy.

"Not that kind of war," Refton said. "We are going to the war for whose world it is."

And in that war they shall battle and triumph over those who would make the world an evil place.

"I didn't say we were going to fight," Refton said. "Only that we were going to war."

Is this some riddle? asked Story-of-the-War-Twins, seeking to break the back and forth conflict between writer and story.

"Yes," Sir Johannes said, knowing he spoke forth the guidance of their souls, though he knew not the meaning of what he said. "It is the riddle."

Help! It's pulling me down!

7. War

The mountain soared above them, cloud-piercing. Around its bone-strewn base circled an unkindness of ravens and a murder of crows. Near the peak, swooping through the thunderheads, flew a convocation of eagles. Looking upon all from the shadows was a parliament of owls. What omens did these birds portend for their coming quest?

"A mountain's all wrong for this," Refton said. *The hunt had risen in his blood and his mood was fey.*

Fey? Refton thought. What am I supposed to be, Hern the Hunter? I'm tense and excited, certainly, but not fey, not here and not without the Poetess.

In the midst of the trackless desert the Ladder rose high into heaven. At the bottom rung a sheik's tent covered the sands, providing moderation of day and night.

"A ladder's no better," Refton said, *growing impatient.*

I bloody well am growing impatient, he thought. There are too many voices trying to tell us what we're doing and why, just like a parliament.

At the base of the greasy pole sat the voting booth.

"Not a farce," Refton said. "Listen to me, Contemplation."

In his mind Refton pulled out a pen and began to inscribe as he spoke. "Around the walls of the city sat an army camp."

That is not a Way Up. The thought came hard upon him, like cold iron upon his fey -- not fey -- mood. *This is not your place to make up as you see fit. You may alter the formulations to fit the workings of your mind, but you cannot change what they are. This is the Way Up. Fit what is really here to your thinking or turn aside.*

Refton considered, erased the line in his mind and wrote anew. "At one root of the world tree sat the well of the Norns."

There. That wasn't so hard, now, was it?

"Why have you come?" asked Urd/Wyrd/Fate.

"To climb the tree to all the worlds," Refton said.

"This tree does not lead to worlds, only to the stories of worlds."

"That is what we wish to climb."

"Then beware, for if you seek the --"

"No, harlot," Evadne said. "You will not bring Fate to this island. I know you, whore of Time. You will keep silent with your prophecies. We will make our own way, whatever it comes to be."

Tai-Mu-Sang was scandalized. To disrupt a fortune-teller was a dangerous action, and not to hear warnings of the future was foolish.

"Speak on, sister," she said, presuming that her ancestress status gave her equality of generation with the speaker.

"Don't," Evadne said.

"Please, my ladies," Sir Johannes said, "you are dragging us into battle with each other."

"Johannes speaks truly," Refton said. "We are going to ascend a war. The only way we can do that safely is to keep peace among ourselves."

How does he know that? Evadne wondered, but for once the Isle of Contemplation did not rise to meet her question.

Who is playing us? she thought. How many Dyads, how many factions are pushing us in ways and toward ends we cannot see? But again there came no answer.

"Prophesy," Refton said to the Norns. "For there were prophets in many of the wars we are going to climb."

"Our prophecy is simple enough to fit the needs of Contemplation's slave," Wyrd said, looking at Evadne with impossibly combined impassivity and hate. "If you pursue victory or defeat you will win and lose. If you pursue neutrality you will not ascend. If you seek the tree you will be treed. Find if you can a way through War."

A cock crowed for the last time. An eagle screamed for the first. A squirrel chittered in fear. From deep below the worlds a boat of fingernails set sail captained by fire and venom. A wolf snapped its tether of nine impossible things. From above a horn sounded, thunder roared, eight-hooves from one horse pounded upon divine fields. The rainbow shook.

"The last battle shall be first," Refton said, grinning in a way uncomfortable to his face and soul. "Let's find the end of the rainbow."

Now what are we going to do? We're stuck with them. And they're pulling us around.

You're stuck with them. I'm just going with you to try and drag you out of this mess.

If you're not stuck, why are you speaking instead of Telling what's happening?

I'm not.

You are.

Oh dear. We are stuck, and look where they're dragging us.

Axe time, sword time, wind time, wolf time.

Sir Johannes watched the mad rush of battle, dead souls against dead souls, gods against frost giants, fire and monster against wisdom and thunder. His eyes witnessed a pagan spectacle that he had heard tell of in the quiet secrets of his order. Saint Parsival had told his followers of the gods and legends of his native people. He had spoken of Ragnarok, and Petrus of Reeftown had recorded his words.

"In battle alone they were elevated, brought close to their gods," the Life of Parsival said. "But they battled only for glory and the notice of Wotan. They did not by their fighting improve their souls. They were glorified in their deaths, but weak in their living. We shall do better, for we shall fight only justly and on our swords shall ride humility and mercy along with glory and righteousness."

But Saint Parsival had not told his followers everything about Ragnarok. He had kept some secrets for the most advanced of his students, and one mystery he had taken to his grave and beyond. Now a follower had come, not advanced enough for the secrets, but with Saint Kyril in his ears to hear every mystery this eternal battle held.

In this conflict Sir Johannes heard the Crusade being called. In the rising of Wotan against the Wolf he heard the clash between Christ and Anti-Christ. In the hammering of Thor against Jormungandr he heard the clash of arms to take the holy city that lay within the hearts of men.

Sir Johannes' mind was tempted to rebel against his hearing, to seek the illusion of faith that is belief, but the discipline of his order, the acceptance of reality however strange and contrary to teaching it might seem, gripped him.

He drew his sword and leapt into the battle, one living soul among this tale of dead against dead.

He had never fought so purely and perfectly before. The breath of God flowed through him, through liberated Eden unsullied by the serpent. The breath of God flowed through him and he could do no wrong as the souls of the unblessed dead fell before him. The Einherjar, battling by his side, looked in amazement at his skill.

One in particular, a young man who also held a beating heart within him, watched the knight and in body and soul copied his moves.

"Johannes," Refton called. "Protect that one."

"As you say, Petrus." Johannes executed Greater Love Hath No Man with perfection, blocking a spear thrust from a half-fleshed corpse that threatened to cut into the young warrior.

The young man's eyes and mouth opened in a moment of pure clean realization that Johannes recognized, the Baptism of the Spirit when God enters the soul, giving perfect understanding. In that rush could be found all things of God. In that moment was absolution and canonization.

Sir Johannes had been taught that the moment rarely lasted. His order explained that the demons had learned well how to sweep away perfection with the inherent failure of the human heart. Satan had taught them how to muddy the divine waters with impure poison and sullied blood.

The riddle in Johannes spoke a different teaching, showing that the moment need never be left, that the sudden could become the eternal. Across the chasm between soul and soul the riddle leapt, crossing in a single breath into the mouth of this other living warrior.

The moment stayed for one heart beat, two, three. Then the Saxon youth vanished in a wisp of breath.

He had been alive, was still alive somewhere, somewhen, carrying the Marianite's teaching back with him, there to nurture and change it. Somewhere the snake bit itself on its own tail and found its venom turned to holy chrism. In Eden the serpent died.

Johannes turned and struck down another of the dead.

"Johannes, come back," Refton called, pointing to a long building that both burned and froze under the assault of two contrary giants. "We need to reach that crumbling hall."

The knight returned, carving his way through the undead who step by step grew shadowier, less real, more stories of the dead than dead in truth.

Tai-Mu-Sang watched Johannes make his way toward them and wondered what he had seen and thought he was doing. The whole space around them had been shadowy and ill-defined to her, as if someone was telling her a tale in a foreign tongue and stumbling over the words. She could see several uncouth wooden halls situated on a poorly maintained field. She could hear the distant clang of battle and the shouts of men as they fought. At one point she thought she heard a wolf growl and a snake hiss, but she was not sure.

She definitely had seen the Shadow-Twin slip off into the fog at one point, then return looking a little more solid and holding the core of an apple that smelled to her like the peaches of immortality. The shadow was growing in awareness, she was sure of that, but it still lacked solidity. Perhaps she could take it back to her world, use it as a spy. It had the appearance of maleness and might be able to slip into Temujin's court where her women could not.

"This way." Refton pointed toward one of the rude structures. Tai-Mu-Sang wondered how the Chronicler could distinguish one from the other. She had the suspicion that someone was using him as she used the various impersonators of the dead, but she could not be sure. It was a subtler use than hers, an influence of speech, action, and most of all confidence. He seemed to know where he was going and what he was doing. It was time to challenge and test as she would any minister who claimed understanding.

"How do you know our course?" she asked.

"The Ludskjalf," he said. "The high seat from which Othin the chief god looks out across all the worlds. Evadne said we need to climb up and get some perspective."

Plausible, Tai-Mu-Sang thought. But still too swift and sure. Not the way of the careful Chronicler who had hunted her for years. Something was manipulating him, something that did not sound like Quest.

She's got her eyes on me. If she stares me down, we're lost.

Not lost, trapped.

That's worse.

Not necessarily. We've fallen down to the level of spirits, but if we Tell this right we can ascend again back to our proper places.

The High seat of Odin looked out across the nine worlds and back across the whole history of the Aesir, the history that ended in this battle.

Evadne had come to this seat before, had bargained with Odin for wisdom, had drunk his mead, hung from the tree with him, taken his eye. But she had always come in peaceful times.

This battle fascinated her, its richness of meaning, the vast panoply of things to contemplate. Thor, son of Odin and of the Earth, god of the lower classes, god of thunder, prime enemy of the giants, fighting to double death with the Midgard serpent, the beast that circled the Earth his mother. A mutual killing, as was the blade against blade double impalement of Loki and Heimdall. These dual deaths, two on each side, resonated strongly, implying deep kinship, as did the conflict between the two categories of the dead, the chosen and the left behind. And there were Thor's two sons Magni and Modi waiting in the wings for their chance to shine after the elder gods were gone. There was great twinness here. She looked at Story-of-the-War-Twins growing in strength and felt the confirmation of her ideas.

Looking down from the high seat, down into Hel's hall, where the knife called Hunger had been set aside and all the mortal dead had been cleared out, she saw one last set of twins, slayer and slain: Blind Hod and Blinding Baldur, dead, waiting to come back, to reign when all sides had been destroyed and all the labors of the universe undone. They who had heralded the destruction of everything would soon come back and be gods of the reborn world.

EXALTATIONS

"There, look there," Refton called, pointing in a direction through the umbra Time had laid upon the past. "Into the past stories. This is the third form of this war for these people."

His finger pointed in a direction not found on any compass.

They looked along his index to when this hall was new-built, lacking even the high stone walls they had just seen torn down by wolfen jaws. Back to when a woman, gold-dripping, came here offering secrets and love for wealth, a witch-woman, a woman of the Vanir, the other Gods. She came, she tricked, she was slain, she was quested and warred over. God battled god in the time before man, fury unleashed over gold taken and woman killed. Then an ending to blood. Peace was made. Kvassir's blood was drunk in inspiration. Hostages were exchanged. Love given for the appearance of leadership, the two kinds of gods came together in agreement and acceptance, joining against mutual foes. The woman who caused the war was forgotten.

Refton pointed again. Back before the world was made, back to the first three Aesir: Odin, Vili, and Ve who slew Ymir in the set-down battle which made gods and jotuns enemies eternal. Slain and dismembered, Ymir became the stuff of Midgard, so that no mortal could look upon their world and not see the corpse of divinity.

One battle at the beginning, one in the middle, one at the end, clean and simple.

"But isn't it really only one battle?" Refton asked.

Or something speaking through him asked rhetorically.

Evadne grabbed his words from the air and contemplated them, turning them over and over, wondering what was cohabiting in his mind.

Tai-Mu-Sang glared her equal perplexity.

Out of the corners of their eyes, Evadne and Tai-Mu-Sang each saw the other, looking at Refton with the same expression.

With a shock both women realized that they had seen the same thing, were troubled in the same way, in short, that they were on this matter allied.

Those two are dangerous. They're going to find us and stuff us in bottles, or brush us down on to paper. Then Time will catch us. Fate will name and thread us. We'll be spirits forever.

Not if we get Quest's help

You want to deal with that crazy story from this diminished state? You know how Power-hungry and Freedom-thirsting he is. Once he knows we're falling he'll try to pull us into him.

I didn't say I wanted to deal with him. I want to enlist him. I don't want him to know he's enlisted, and I certainly don't want him to know we've fallen.

"One battle told in many forms by one people," Refton said.

"Which people?" the Shadow-Twin asked, savoring his breath and enjoying the ability to form and speak words.

"In my world, in my time, they are called after a language invented to fit linguistic assumptions. They are called Indo-Europeans. We don't know much about what they were like or what they did when they were a single unified people, only what they were like spread out, when they called themselves Dorians, Aryans, Cymru, and a great many other names besides."

"Who are they?" Sir Johannes asked.

"Some of them were your ancestors. Some were mine. In most of the worlds I've visited they held a large part of Europe and fair chunks of the East. And they always had this war and its stories."

Always twins, Story-of-the-War-Twins said. *Always with me in it in one form or another. I have many narrators in many peoples. Many tales sometimes involve me, but this one always does.*

The story's words grounded into Refton's mind, elevating him. He had never been so high in his seeing before. Always he had hunted one life at a time, bagged one tale and brought it back. Sometimes he could weave the many lives into one as when he made the Life of the Priest out of the lives of individual god-servers, but still that was one person of many aspects. But this, this epic scale, this hunting of an entire people, this catching of a great war that existed in so many forms, *with so many meanings,* this was the greatness of his art. He would catch this tale entire and snag their minor enemy the Quest in one single hunt.

Ecstasy has him. You know what she'll do to us. You know how she treats spirits.

Calm yourself. If we snare Quest, we can ride on Ecstasy when she ascends again.

Ride her? Have you made alliance with Mania? First you want to quest for Quest, then you want to ride Ecstasy. What's next? Hiding from God?

Not yet.

What's happened to you?

I'm using the Twin-story, and it's crawling up me. We can hide in the Shadow-Twin.

It's become human. Do you want to be its soul?

Maybe.

You want to fall that far again. Do you want to be human again?

Not fall, swoop. And being human isn't so bad.

Swooping is how we got into this trouble.

And how we will escape. The shadow is glimpsing Freedom. Freedom itself will free us if we can find the Power to realize it.

And you want to take the Power from this story?

From Ecstasy's narration of the story.

Deeper and deeper we go. Down into the pits of fact and fiction.

Down and then up.

That's what you said before.

Where now? Where now? Refton's wild mind darted through his knowledge of the Indo-European War Story and its many forms. He had done what was needful in Ragnarok, climbed high enough to see, and had incidently inserted Sir Johannes into the vision of Ragnarok Saint Parsival had had just before he had been visited by the angels.

Where now? So many choices. He needed to find the way into the heart of the story, had to find a form of it that showed more than just the battle.

Where?

His darting thoughts flew over the form that took up the most space in his mind, the tale told over and over in the many classical educations he had experienced.

Troy.

The Trojan war had no beginning and no ending.

But it had a pivotal moment.

On a mountain with a princely shepherd, an apple marked 'For the fairest', three naked goddesses, and three offered bribes.

Troy trifurcated. Three blind Homers sang three wholly different but intertwined Iliads in three groups of worlds.

Paris held out the apple to --

Aphrodite:

And was given the most beautiful woman in the world. But he had to go get her from her husband, *Menelaus, the lesser member of one set of War Twins in this battle. There were several twinnings in different forms: Akhilleus who chose to fight because his lover/twin Patrokles was slain. Aias the Greater and Aias the Lesser who together formed one fighter upon the field, the greatest of the warriors for he battled without divine aid yet everyone feared him. . .*

Refton cut off Story-of-The-War-Twins in mid-self-insertion.

To continue --

Ecstasy's making him a Teller. She's pulling him up into our place.

He rises. We fall. It fits. It fits the war too well.

We must ask God for help.

What bargain can we offer God? And can we speak to God from this low place?

Others speak from much lower.

But I don't know how, I've never been this low.

And I never spoke to God when I was this low, though I saw God many times in undivine forms.

-- All the people of the world rose up against Paris, instigated by the two losing Goddesses. Hera put the dominion of the world against him, and Athena put the wisdom of battle in his way.

"All the people of the world?" Tai-Mu-Sang said. "I have never heard of this battle or these people. If it did not involve All-Under-Heaven, how can all the people be involved?"

Refton hesitated. As he did so, the *Questers* fell, down, down to the plains of Troy, where mighty battle cries were raised, anonymous soldiers charged and fell, but only the heroes truly fought.

Heroism searched through these new appearances and swiftly grasped Sir Johannes, pushing against the Saints and Angels in his soul until it found Saint George and Saint Michael and grounded like the lightning of God through them and into the knight.

Hero-light appeared around his head. Divinity danced around him. The gods called him to battle.

But Johannes would not go. He had heard this tale, been told it by some of the Doctors of the Church as they had spun their theories, dragging in the Greek and Latin classics, seeking to reconcile the pagan epics with the Christian world. He had heard and shaken his head sadly. These heroes were common soldiers, not members of orders. They fought for spoils and honor, they abandoned and took up battle for the pettiest of reasons. He would not join them.

Heroism dug deeper into Johannes, coming to the gates of Jerusalem, shouting that the city must be taken. It gripped the Knight's eyes, turning Troy into the holy city, Paris into the Anti-Christ, and Helen into the captive church.

But Johannes knew better than to trust his eyes. His ears did not accept the story of heroism. So Heroism was forced to wait outside the gates, sulking in its tent just outside Johannes' heart.

"All of Hellas was assembled," Refton said. His voice rose again to cover the field entire, pulling the others up with him.

For ten years they fought back and forth, each side losing heroes, until by the cunning of Odysseus the city was taken.

Evadne looked down fondly at barrel-chested Odysseus. She had met him many times on Contemplation's Isle, as Kirke, as Kalypso, as young, naive Nausikaa. They had had a son together who went off into the world of stories, into the story that came after this one.

How did she remember that? She had grown old and young so many times since, how did she remember her son? A flicker of thought, one son among many, and certainly not the first.

A statue was stolen, a horse was made, a lintel removed, a city pillaged.

That should have been the end of it.

But it was not. The heroes offended the gods and each one came to suffer greatly for his actions.

Agamemnon was killed by his bride. But Menelaus returned in peace with his. That is the fate of the War-Twins.

Troy burned. The world fell apart. Odysseus wandered the islands for ten more years seeking the way home. Rome was founded by refugees from Troy.

Paris reached out and gave the apple to

Hera:

Paris was made lord of all the world -- Lord of Hellas and Persia, Syria, Syrakuse and Italy. From Troy he ruled and all the kings bowed before him, acknowledging him as rightful master. Only one king stood against him.

With the favor of Athena, Odysseus did not fall under the high king's sway. Wily Odysseus began to labor in secret, speaking subtly to the ears of all men who were not kings, gathering a hidden army, an army of shadow, of strikes in the night, of spies, of assassins, an army no king could find, for its secret warriors were wiser than every king.

Odysseus had but two allies, gifts of Aphrodite.

With these he Quested to overcome the high king.

"Petrus, there's the way in. I can hear it through the narration. There's Quest sitting like a dragon on the treasure."

Not yet.

One of Odysseus' secret allies sat in Paris' court. Aeneas, son of the love goddess, chief spy upon the high king's plans, chief learner of his weaknesses, the one who whispered into the high king's ears that the wife of one of the lesser kings favored him and might be smuggled into the capital of Troy and thence to Paris' bed.

Thus did Helen, chosen of Aphrodite, second leader of Odysseus' spy ring come like a Trojan horse to Paris and plunge into his neck the poisoned knife she had concealed beneath her celebrated bosom.

Civil war erupted.

Troy burned. The world fell apart. Odysseus wandered the islands making peace. Rome was founded by the betrayer of Troy.

"Why didn't we go through the story-gate?" Johannes asked.

But Refton did not hear him. The story-strands were gathering in his hands. Soon he would be large enough to pick them up and reach through to the center. A few more narrations and he would be Telling the tale.

I can barely see him. He's risen too high. We're lost.

Paris reached out his hand and gave the apple to

Athena:

And became the wisest man, the craftiest general ever. He raised an army with Odysseus as his lieutenant. The army was taken from the lower classes, for Hera had turned all the kings of the -- of Hellas against him. She even brought the Persians down upon his ears. For ten years Paris whose other name was Alexandros fought, conquering and overthrowing, sending all the kings of Hellas into exile. He planted democracies in all the city-states of Hellas, with each Archon answerable to him and he answerable to them. But no one respected him as ruler, and no one loved him. They only knew that he was wiser than they and that galled all hearts.

The exiled kings of Hellas on their ships made raids upon the democracies that had once been their kingdoms. They made armies of outlaws and brigands, drawing them down into their black ships until they had enough pirates to attack Troy. They struggled mightily against all-crafty Paris and the stratagems of his lieutenant, second-in-craft Odysseus, but in the end the exiles won because the people did not love Paris and would not fight unto death for him. In the end the spirit of Troy was broken, and at last its walls fell as well.

Monarchy and Democracy raged in battle against each other.

Troy burned. The world fell apart. Odysseus wandered the Peloppenese seeking to make amends for his service to Paris. Rome the Republic was founded by the leader of the opposition in democratic Troy.

The same end came to the three forms of the third form of the battle as the Hellenes tell it in all the worlds where they have come to prominence.

Refton's words came from all around the *Questers,* barely discernible as his voice. Where had he gone?

"The third form?" Evadne asked, trying to draw him back. She had an inkling of what was happening to him. He was climbing higher through the Way Up, leaving them behind. But she did not remember taking this way before, and did not always know what lay at the higher reaches.

Refton made a brief entrance as if a distracted actor had wandered onto stage.

"The Hellenes have the tale thrice. First when the gods overcame the Titans, second when they fought the Giants with the aid of half-divine Herakles, and third when Troy fell. The first two are the same in all worlds, but the third has choice in the narration."

He spoke the word 'choice' as a starving lion might mouth 'gazelle', then vanished off stage.

EXALTATIONS

He's up there, he's taken our places.

Not completely. He's still rising. If we can get a few words in edgewise we might be able to keep a bit of ourselves in our seats.

He's about to head for the center of the maelstrom.

Distract him.

This War-for-what-the-World-Is is told of battles between men and men or between gods and gods. In one place it is a fight between men and gods.

The tale attracted Refton's notice as the scent does the hound.

In Ireland they tell the tale five times.

The Fomor came to Ireland and there overthrew the Fir Bolg.

The Tuatha De Dannan came to Ireland and made war upon the Fomor. This war was that of god against god, as was the battle between Aesir and Vanir, between Olympians and Titans, between--

Distract him. The center lies that way.

But that battle was won by the half-De Dannan, half-Fomor god Lugh, master of all arts. It is the next form of the battle that is unique.

In this reiteration, the Sons of Mile, the humans, came to Ireland, and with the Island's help overcame the children of Danu, drove them under the hills into the reflection that is Faerie and made gods of them.

He's caught up in it now. And I've got a hand in the consequences of his actions. We'll go up with him.

No. Can't you feel it? We're being stretched across the heights.

It hurts to be down here and up there.

It hurts, but we can hold on.

After that came the Tain, the cattle raid. This form of the battle is most like the Trojan war, but where the Greeks fought over a woman, the Irish battled over a cow. There is also a Welsh formulation where the struggle is for pigs.

"But what's it really about?" Tai-Mu-Sang asked, seeking to copy Evadne's strategy.

But this time Refton did not return. He answered in the Telling.

For that, we must turn to Persia, and the time before the world began.

Ahura Mazda, the Good God, and Angra Manyu, the Evil God, had been approaching each other forever, until they met and time began.

Good and Evil collide, the Ahura and the Deva. They battle but are equal. Each creates servant spirits, the Ahuras and the Devas. The battle elaborates, but still there is no triumph. Then Ahura Mazda creates a bright and beautiful thing, a gleaming jewel in the emptiness. He calls it the world. Angra Manyu looks at the world, desires it and hates it. He flies with his followers into the world to corrupt and destroy it.

Ahura Mazda slams an iron lid over the world, the iron sky, trapping his enemy within the world.

The battle shifts to inside. Ahura Mazda makes beasts and plants. Angra Manyu also makes such things. Ahura Mazda makes men, soldiers within the world for the battle. Angra Manyu corrupts men, bringing many to his side, setting humanity against humanity.

Ahura Mazda teaches Zarathustra who teaches humanity its true way. Some follow him, some turn aside.

In descent from Zarathustra shall come three leaders, one every two thousand years. They shall raise up the armies of men against the evil spirit, until in the time of the third leader Angra Manyu will finally be overthrown and the world renovated for men to live in, in peace under the loving dominion of the sole remaining god.

Sir Johannes watched the battle, fascinated by this alien depiction of evil as equal to good and the curious concept that God could have enemies. He heard the echoes of the crusade in the battle between these two spirits and wondered which was speech and which reverberation.

Tai-Mu-Sang was at last able to see one of these conflicts clearly. This one she knew of, having traded with Persia in her time and been visited by Magi who explained the theology of their people. There had been some interest by the Taoists in this idea, but they could not bring this good and evil into line with Yin and Yang, so they had let it go.

Story-of-the-War-Twins drank deep at the telling. This was his greatest tale, the highest conflict ever told of twins at battle. Where the followers of Zarathustra were, there he was as well in his hidden form of twins in opposition.

It is a high and noble tale --

An excellent foundation stone for a Society.

What are you doing?

Telling along with him to keep our place. Help me out here.

-- for its Consequences reaches from the heights of heaven to the basics of human action. Everything in the world comes from one of two sources. Every deed done aids one or another camp. Every human is a soldier and the battleground is their life. They --

Hurry. He's moved on. Quick, keep up with him.

Look at the words.

Look at the names: Ahura and Deva. Remember them as we shift around once more.

Don't let him turn too quickly. We need to get more words in.

Umm . . . I've got it. Look at the actions. This battle can be found enacted and lived in many worlds, not just in tale but in ritual.

All across Europes they fight, all through the lands and the underworlds. Battling for the crops, for the cows, the pigs, the grain, the gold, the blood, they fight. Werewolves against Witches, Benandanti against Malandanti, Hunters against Vampires, Shamans against the Dead. In every place the Indo-Europeans settled there is this mystery battle, fought yearly, monthly, in secret times and open times, fought around All Hallows, around Christmas, at springtime and fall time, when the wren cries in the woods, when the souls in moth-shape or wolf-shape come out at night, at the edges of the world. They fight to regain the stolen prize.

"Is that what this is about?" Tai-Mu-Sang asked. "Crop rituals? Why don't they just learn the proper ceremonies and propitiate the bureaucracy of heaven at the correct times?"

Refton flickered in for a briefing. "That is what they are doing, in their own way."

"Uncivilized," she said with Confucian condemnation. "And overcomplicated. Why do all this just for the crops?"

"It is not just the crops," Refton said as he faded.

They fight not just for wealth. They fight to see whose world it is.

The story stirred, a sleeping giant whose name had been called. It stirred, touching many more places and an infinity more societies than the multiplied Indo-Europeans. Almost it stretched out its fingers to grasp the travellers. But grandfather Quest sang it a lullaby and it fell back into its well-fed rest.

"Politics," Evadne said.

Remember the names: Ahura and Deva.

He's trying again.

Let him. I've got hold. He can yank us into the Maelstrom if he wants and we'll still have him.

The Devas and the Asuras, the gods and the anti-gods.

At the beginning of the world they churned a mountain in the ocean, bringing forth soma and poison, beasts of wonder and monsters of terror. They worked in opposite directions, Devas on one side, Asuras on the other.

"I know this tale," Tai-Mu-Sang said. "It is a story of the Hindis."

In India they recapitulate this battle over and over again. Devas against Asuras in the first Yuga. Then in the first and second Yugas the Deva Vishnu incarnates over and over, fighting various demons, either Asuras or Rakshasi, each time battling to take the world. Each time Vishnu regains the world for the Devas and the humans.

Then at the end of the third Yuga comes the greatest of the battles, a fight that seems to be humans against humans but is much more, the conflict between the five Pandava brothers and their cousins the hundred Kurus, a battle told in the longest epic written in any world: The Mahabharata.

Hang on to me. The door to the Maelstrom's about to open.

I won't let go of -- What is this I'm holding on to?

I think it's my foot.

So that's what a foot is. I've Told about them many times, but never paid them much notice. You know, they're not well made for hanging on to.

Just hang on.

EXALTATIONS

The war of the Pandavas has no beginning and no ending. It persists in every cycle of the world. It has the greatest warriors who have ever lived on both sides. And it is turned by the greatest of gods, Krishna.

Krishna accompanies and advises his twin-in-spirit, Arjuna, the greatest warrior who ever lived, trained by Drona and Bhisma, the greatest warriors who ever lived. Hidden within Arjuna and Krishna are Nara and Narayana, the water and the course of the water. They do not cause the war, but it happens around them. They are the twins at the heart.

Arjuna. Sir Johannes knew that name. He had fought members of the order of Arjuna, archers without parallel. From their bows single shots became many, fire gleamed upon their arrows, and when the masters of the order took the field, a single strike from one of their shafts could fill one's soul with heaven and earth, giving a rapture dangerous to any warrior aware of his own soul.

On a vast battlefield the armies of the earth collided, Pandavas in their chariots, Kurus in theirs. Arjuna dueled with his sixth brother, Karna whom none of the Pandavas knew to be their kin. Arrows flew from their bows, arrows that called upon the fundamental forces of the universe using the secret asthras known only to the greatest of warriors, arrows that created, arrows that held thunder, arrows that destroyed.

An arrow that Karna could not counter struck him. Brother slew brother, one of many terrible wrongs done for the side of right in that war.

A man of truth and duty, a king who followed Dharma would lie so his teacher could die. A child of the wind, a soldier of the gods would send his son to his death and would drink blood from the chest of his enemy. Arjuna's son Abhimanyu who knew half a secret would be slain because he did not know it all. A woman reborn as a man would kill an unkillable man because he had won her and spurned her in her previous life.

Yet when all the bodies were counted and all the dead accounted for, the Pandavas had won. But the night after the battle when in an earlier Yuga there would have been celebration, Kali came to claim this time as her own. On that night the Pandavas suffered the last danger from the Kurus: Aswataman, whose name had been used in deceit to slay his father Drona, went forth and in the camp of the Pandavas slew all their children and grandchildren save the still-in-womb child of Abhimanyu.

Blood flowed upon the field, death reigned, the Yuga turned and gave itself to Kali who would usher in the world's destruction.

But before the battle, before the blood, there had come a moment, a hesitation. Krishna had driven Arjuna out onto the field and Arjuna had looked at both sides and laid down his arms, asking how he could rightly make war upon his teachers and his cousins.

So Krishna TOLD him.

He's doing it now!

Follow the telling, the teller telling, the story telling itself to the teller. Follow the loops upon loops, follow the serpent's coils, the dragon's course, follow the river and the course of the river. Follow the way.

"The Way Up," called Evadne.

"The Way, The Truth and the Light," offered Sir Johannes.

"The Way Of the Sage," pronounced Tai-Mu-Sang.

The Way the story goes, injected Story-of-War-Twins.

The Way of the Quest.

The Way to get to you.

The war imploded into the maelstrom of its narrations. Each voice. each speaking, each recitation revealed itself as an assertion of the world and the war over the world into the heart of this statement, into the *twin* aspects implicit in the story: that there be dissension over the way the world should be and that there be conflict arising in and showing forth the dissension.

Into the maelstrom they dove, setting forth their views against the views of Quest and his allies.

"Parliament is summoned," Politics said through Evadne.

8. Voting

In the storm the Shadow-Twin screamed. This is what it is to be born, to be told what you are by light and warmth, cold and darkness and all the new things of the world. This is what it is to live, to suffer the attentions of the universe. The Shadow screamed and begged to be relieved of Mind, Soul, and Humanity.

"Send me back to the nothingness of character," he prayed, not knowing whom or what he addressed, only knowing that he wanted to not be, and that he of whom he had been born frequently asked aid of that which could not be seen or known. The Shadow-Twin wanted to go back to the unlife of empty narration. But nothing answered him, nor was he given relief from the assault of all things.

In his terror he clung to Story-of-the-War-Twins, the womb from whence he came. But the story did not attend to him. The tale was drinking, eating, expanding himself into every aspect of the War-Story that would accept him. He had been brought to the heart of a tale as vast and secret as Grandfather Quest but much more indolent, and he meant to expand his presence here so that every form of the story would have twins. Then would he rise above his grandfather.

The Shadow-Twin turned to Sir Johannes, and the knight reached out for him with a mother's mercy, broad and enveloping, a vast compassion that arose from knightly closeness to death and from the terrible infinite love of the secret Riddle within him. The Shadow gasped at the breadth of that compassion and fled from it, seeing yet another force that was telling him what he was.

Turning again he came to Tai-Mu-Sang, who looked upon the lightning fields and thunder hills of the Maelstrom with a quiet familiarity, as if the blow and bluster of a thousand wars were nothing more to her than the commonplaces of life. From this serenity the Shadow fled again. Too big, too much, too high, too loud, too quiet.

Too familiar. He darted past Evadne, who watched him go with a jaded comprehension born of seeing the same arising of awareness in people and knowing that what amazed them bored her. Still, she knew the ways of helping, if the one who came to know sought help.

But the Shadow only sought the shadow of help, the 'there, there' of empty comfort, not the 'yes, the world is like this' of wise counsel.

Away he fell from the storm, seeking emptiness.

Evadne watched the direction of his fall and knew that he would find what he sought, but would find no more comfort there than here.

He's doing it. He's peeling them away from their ordained path. Quest will have to take notice of this.

Quiet! If Quest sees our fallen condition, he'll throw us to the Life Hunter in order to distract him.

Sorry.

Shh.

OK. I'll be quiet.

Be quiet now!

Shh.

Oh, sorry.

Grandfather Quest bargained with the great story of which the Indo-European War was but a segment, trading in storytellers. The War dealt carefully, mindful of Quest's uncanny ability to gain advantage, and his reckless willingness to seek that advantage regardless of the consequences to valued trading partners. Grandmother Allegory, who in most minds was so intertwined with Grandfather Quest that one could not be thought of without the other, had found herself jilted in a world where she had fallen from favor, while Grandfather Quest feathered his nest with her disenchanted bards.

His method had been simple and disturbing to other stories. Grandfather Quest had inspired storytellers with the notion that quests existed in reality, that real live human beings acted in a questing fashion. He had spun tales of quests of exploration, of scientific discovery, quests to find the perfect mate, to build a home, to get back to nature. In most worlds and times Quest and Allegory would make use of these tales together, but in the allegory-despising worlds pragmatic Grandfather Quest had been willing to throw Grandmother Allegory aside in order to keep control of his human territory.

The younger stories had been shocked by this action, not knowing the intrigues and double-dealings their elders engaged in.

Such as right now. Quest was bargaining for Peter Refton, a prize among storytellers, but the War story had made a separate arrangement with the Dyad Ecstasy. When Refton had started his ascent, the tale had noticed him and judged him too dangerous to keep as a narrator. It had considered flinging him down but knew that would only benefit Grandfather Quest. Therefore the War tale had called upon Ecstasy to pull Refton out of the pool of commodities and elevate him above Grandfather Quest's grasp.

Ecstasy had agreed. The War was not sure why. He hoped it was because the two of them worked well together, the War in its many forms having given Ecstasy a focus for multiplication and Ecstasy having given the War so many people to play the characters in it that the War had been able to retire from the commerce of tales, wealthier than any other story.

But the War was not sure if Ecstasy was truly its ally. The politics of the Dyads and the politics of stories often intersected, but the latter rarely understood the former.

He is in the maelstrom of the War, Quest narrated. *He has come high and far seeking the second Magician, who will reveal to him the secrets of the universe.*

He thinks the Maelstrom is the secret of the War, the War contributed, playing both sides. *If he sees no more than that he will never leave the storm, never see the calm at its center.*

But he does see, Refton Told.

|PAST ACCEPTANCE|

Evadne's gaze turned upward to the high places that would age her. She had never dared before to simply look through the Way Up. To do so would have been an admission of greater ability in interacting with the tri-levels of being than the youthfulness which she preferred could tolerate.

But this once, just this once she could not hold back her curiosity. The powerful disciplines of Contemplation fell before the blandishments of Politics, and she gave in to the Freedom to look.

There was Refton, flying high above the storm, looking down with raptor's eyes upon Quest, the claws of his Power raised to rake the story, to tear away Quest's captives, liberate them from the prison of *one trial after another until the goal is achieved.*

But Refton's downward gaze did not see what was pulling him upward. Ecstasy had reached down from the Dyads, down far enough to have form and attention, awareness and interests. Down she had come, as a Valkyrie upon an eight-legged horse. The form was beautiful but gore-drenched, armored in gold, braided blond-red hair, yellow of gold, red of blood, eyes and face of Evadne. She came down and caught the eagle-Refton, who did not see or feel the flyer above him.

Evadne shouted a warning, but the Maelstrom, the war within war, crushed her voice and hid the Valkyrie's ecstatic shouts.

Refton struck at Quest.

The story screamed.

The Valkyrie pulled.

Up the Hunter rose.

Through the jagged ecstasies of a thousand tongued visions, prophecies, possessions, compulsions, spells, poems, and languages.

Through the muses' orgies where inspirations mixed in the blood and body of men and gods.

Through the breath of God, the exhalations of heaven, the heights of manifest Multiplication.

Through ________________________________.

Ecstasy alone rose higher, losing form and formulation, back to the quiescent Mosaics of the Dyads.

She had left him in the __________, the condition untellable.

Evadne wept into the Maelstrom, knowing she had lost Refton to her secret, unnameable rival.

It was just a lot of noise and shouting, battle cries raised, standards rallied round, and heroes offended and offending. Certainly they were battling for the world, but without propriety. Tai-Mu-Sang could not see what all the fuss was about. What difference did it make to the world which side won?

And she could see Grandfather Quest, not as a story but as an examination. He was a test trying to force people to take him. This she understood. The entire education system in All-Under-Heaven pointed toward a single exam, a moment when each young woman who had been schooled in the classics would offer herself to the brush, the ink-stone, and the terrible paper with its questions.

EXALTATIONS

It was, Tai-Mu-Sang knew -- though few others did -- a great act of sacrifice, a terrible presentation of one's comprehension of *ren*. It was veiled in inquiries about *li* and the odes, about history and the Great Master's teachings, but it was really about one's insight into Humanity.

On the third day of her own testing she had realized this. She had come to know what her fellow students and the administrators of the test did not know, that accepting the arbitrary set of subjects she had been taught, and had at times rebelled against, was a giving up of one's personal notions of what was important for the sake of Society's awareness of what was important. It was sacrificing the Hermit in one's heart, the one who wanted to live alone in the world. At that moment she had almost, almost tipped over the inkstone, to pour the carefully ground mixture of water and dirt all over her delicate calligraphy. One voice in her head had pushed her to do so, to rebel, to throw away her Confucian training, go into the mountains and seek refuge with Taoists or Buddhists.

But the other voice had chided her, asking if her family's sacrifices on her part were to be cast off for a trivial whim. Was her moment of freedom worth destroying their hopes and lives? Was she of greater value than they?

She remembers us. Quick, into her memory.

But she remembers us as voices, just spirits. If we go into her, into her life and past, we'll be nothing more than guardians of souls.

But she's connected to Refton. If we take a place in her, we will have been there when he showed up to find her life. We'll be in his Telling, and in that bag of lives he carried up to ________.

Oh Mind beyond Mind, we've fallen so far we can't even speak of it!

Grab her.

From that point on, the exam had been easy. It was only a matter of seeing the Humanity within the formality, the *ren* that lay hidden in the *li*, and replying with the proper formality. The exam had taught her the lesson for which it had been created. Using that lesson she had risen to govern All-Under-Heaven, and risen farther above governing to the heart of Governance, risen high enough to have the chop of Heaven stamped upon her. She would rise to Heaven, *once she had saved All-Under-Heaven.*

And she would be able to save it, if only she overcame the last obstacle. If she could reach the center of the Maelstrom the means of toppling Temujin would be hers.

That was Grandfather Quest's offer, a grand sweep of Power to be given her, her place among the gods assured if she followed the path laid down.

It resonated with the exam, but Tai-Mu-Sang knew better. It sounded like the exam because they both had the form Quest had given them. They had a similarity of *li*, but the *ren* within them was different.

Quest was bargaining, trading, going about commerce.

Tai-Mu-Sang considered this piece of given awareness. It arose in her without any obvious source of understanding, nor was it attached to a voice she could trust or mistrust. But she recognized the style. The Chronicler was telling her this. Wherever Refton was, he was offering her aid using what means were available to him.

Some place of narration, she suspected. A Heaven for writers perhaps. Commerce was the province of the lower classes, a thing poorly regarded in All-Under-Heaven. Refton was giving a précis of Quest's life. If it had a life. Was it human?

Tai-Mu-Sang felt something twang within her, something hard and cold, but potentially dangerous like a lump of charcoal the moment before it is set afire.

The Moment.

Incoming Dyad!

Quest was human. All the stories were human. There were more kinds of Humanity than Tai-Mu-Sang had ever dreamed of. She knew in a deepness beyond her borrowed minds and souls what it was to be human. She saw all the Humanity that existed arrayed around a single burning coal, people of more sorts than could be named or imagined sitting around a lone source of warmth and light: *ren*.

Life Guided by Spirit is Humanity.

Humanity around humanity. Humanity arising from humanity. Humanity giving itself to humanity. Breathe in and become human. Breathe out and express humanity.

Quest was human, had a place in the Society of stories, a Human Society. He was rich, powerful, a conveyer of commodities. The commodities of stories were storytellers, venues, societies, and times.

He was rich, but not trusted.

Tai-Mu-Sang knew well what proprieties worked on people like that.

"Let us go, or I will discredit you in my time and place. I will by my own failure demonstrate the valuelessness of seeking beyond what we have. I will show the futility of quests.

"Remember I am a Sage. My memory cannot be undone. The story of my failure will grow in power and wealth. It will rise up and attack you in all the venues of your telling. You will lose all that you prize. Or . . ."

Or you can undertake the trial before you and succeed, bringing back the secrets you need.

Tai-Mu-Sang knew the bluster of merchants. Time and again they had threatened to ruin her, claiming implicitly that wealth was the key to humanity. They did not understand that wealth depends on propriety, and that propriety is the mask humanity wears. The manifest form of *ren* is *li*, not money.

"Or you can let us go, and claim we undertook your quest and won it."

Lie in my own story?

"No. You are the villain of the piece, are you not? I have raised the weapon that defeats you. Your tale is secure if you let us go."

The prize must be taken or the quest is not ended.

"Johannes, can you take this prize?" Tai-Mu-Sang asked.

"I see no prize to claim," Johannes said. "This tale has infiltrated so many ways of doing things, has turned so many paths toward his own way, that I do not believe he has anything to give."

Not infiltrated. Made clear. You could not find your way to your holy city without me. Every act of liberation within you is done through me.

"You are a little path," Johannes said. "I follow the Way, the Truth, and the Light. If I come to my liberation, it will be through Him, not you."

I give form to the way. I am a creature of God just as much as you are.

These words rang true in Johannes' holy ears.

"But you have overreached, stretched into places that God did not give you."

Do you know that? Or were you Told that?

He wouldn't dare.

He would.

We have to do something fast, otherwise we'll never get back.

Take the prize.

What? If we reach out, we'll be nothing more than they are.

Take it. We still have a grasp of Refton.

But taking action, think of Consequence. . .

Don't be squeamish! Take the prize or we'll be taking action for the rest of our -- I can barely say the word -- lives.

You think we have lives now?

I know it. I remember what life was like. This is it. Take the prize!

How?

With your hands!

Oh, those.

What is the prize? How has Grandfather Quest become capable of giving out the prize? Who are these unknown twins who have taken the prize?

Story-of-the-War-Twins offered these riddles to those who could hear his tale and waited to hear answers reverberate from any of the many worlds where he was narrated.

But there was no response, only bewilderment among narrators and audiences.

Hastily, Story-of-the-War-Twins withdrew the riddle from his narration, knowing the Fate of stories that offer questions without answers. He did not wish to become an object of speculation, a subject for the Theories to dissect, nor did he wish to have more parts of him become a mystery story.

But he did wonder. Two had taken the prize, but not the two he had nurtured along. Sir Johannes would not touch it, and the Shadow-Twin was gone. Who were these who had reached through Tai-Mu-Sang, the mother-figure, and completed the Quest?

What do we do with it?

Use it.

How?

I don't know. I've never been under Quest before.

Well, what happened to those we sent on Quests?

Let's see. Usually at this point they went home and employed the prize for their own benefit or to aid the world.

We can't take this home. You know what they'd do to us if we brought the inside of a story to ________.

Careful. You're talking about it as if it were a place. You know what'll happen if we end up trying to Tell from down here.

Redaction. They won't risk Myriadicity reappearing.

Oh . . . er, what's that thing that comes after the word 'oh' when humans want to express fear or awe?

A curse or imprecation.

Oh, imprecation! Evadne is a vessel for Redaction. They're listening to us now.

They'll be using us as well.

Let's stop talking about them and do something with this prize.

What advantage can we glean from it?

Well, it's bright and shiny. It attracts Dyads. It can push against any established political structure.

Can we use it to bargain with God?

We can't bargain down here.

Why not? We may not be able to Tell the universe anything, but we can set something in motion and see how God responds.

What good would that do? God won't put us back. And if we set the wrong things in motion, they'll annihilate us rather than risk Myriadicity.

If we attract Refton's attention we may get him to Tell us back, or draw down a Dyad we can use to pull ourselves up.

Not a bad idea.

If we distribute the prize to these others, that should get his attention.

How do we that?

I guess we break it like this and feed them each a piece.

Then what?

Throw them back where they came from and see what happens.

We can't throw from here.

Refton will do it for us.

How can you get him to do that?

We won't have to. Remember how angry he was at Quest for pulling them in?

He'll send them back.

Only if he thinks it will do them good.

Show him the prize.

How?

Stretch out your hand.

But I might lose my grip on him.

Be careful.

At the end of the Quest lay the prize for which they had struggled, all unknowing. The prize was a coin with two sides. On the obverse was the Power to change the world, on the reverse the Freedom to choose what change would occur.

Why did such prizes lie at the end of Quests? No one who knew could speak of it.

Is that right?

Not sure, but it sounds right for the moment.

|QUALIFIED ACCEPTANCE|

God heard him.

But Refton's hesitating, talking like a multiplied human. If he keeps that up he'll fall back and we can grab our seats again.

Not yet. We need him to Tell them back. Give him a little assistance.

Whatever the source of this Power and Freedom, it was there for the taking. Even those who rejected it did so in the embrace of it, for to turn away from the prize was to take the Freedom to choose and the Power to enforce one's choices.

Sir Johannes DeLondres in rejecting the goal had shown himself wise enough to undertake the challenge of his world and time.

Johannes, the cobbler's son from Augsburg, looked down from the stony face of Mount Athos at the army that had massed below his monastery. The Marianites, the Christian visage of the Order of Three Faces, prayed inside the chapel of his hall. To him had been entrusted the preservation of the order against the forces of the Holy Roman Empire.

"This is a falsehood," Johannes said. "I am not a cobbler's son, nor leader of the Marianites."

But Saint Kyril in his ears told him it was true. Saint Peter in his feet gripped his home ground of Athos.

"But I am Sir Johannes DeLondres of the Order of Saint Parsival."

"That too is true," Saint Michael in his hands said. "Time and your past are as subject to God as all other things. Returning to your world, you have been given a new place, a new Life."

Just as happened to Petrus, Johannes acknowledged. I should have paid more heed to his words about himself.

But how can I fight my comrades?

"The Order of Saint Parsival is not out there," Saint Michael the General said. "No order has come, only the secular soldiers of the Emperor Sebastien."

But how can I fight my people?

How can I fight my teachers and my cousins?

Arjuna had asked and been answered by his god.

Tai-Mu-Sang had turned aside from the impropriety of the prize. Thus she had won her humanity, and her propriety.

EXALTATIONS

All the elements had been put into place. The rebellion against Temujin would happen throughout All-Under-Heaven. It had been timed and co-ordinated. Tai-Mu-Sang would set it off at the correct moment, the night before the great Khan's army was to begin its muster for the march westward. The soldiers of the Khan would have a final night's carouse before packing their belongings and departing. In the middle of the night All-Under-Heaven would rise up.

It was absurd, a ridiculous plan that she would never in her sanest moments have crafted. But it would work. She had seen it before her return, seen the uprising, seen the fall of Temujin, the shattering of Mongol power. The success had no justification in sense or practicality, but it would happen and she would be raised from ancestral to deific status for it.

The triumph had no proper cause, no traceable chain of actions that would lead to this event, yet she had done it and would be rewarded for it. Had she been a pettier person she would have complained to Heaven about the nonsense of her victory, but Tai-Mu-Sang knew too well that the rise and fall of the powerful sometimes came in farce.

So, as was only proper, she bowed to the will of Heaven and accepted her place in it.

The Shadow-Twin had set out on a quest of his own.

I can't help him. I can't Tell into the deeper reaches of Space.

Refton's 'I'-ing again. Push a little. They might kick him out.

You've forgotten what it's like to come there in the first place. We all 'I' a few times before settling in.

I didn't.

You were always there. Not like us late-comers.

Late, but pleasant company.

You're too kind.

Not at all.

Story-of-the-War-Twins had amassed some wealth in the interactions with Grandfather Quest and the War. He was grateful to leave the places of Reality and return to the safety of his storied kin in Fiction.

What's been happening? Story-of-the-War-Twins asked Story-of-City-Foundings.

Grandfather Quest has lost a lot and has been having an argument with Story-of-Stories.

What does she say?

She says the matter is between the Dyads and the Stories and does not wish to talk about it.

Between?

In the region between. You know, the one where . . .

Yes, yes.

And Evadne.

Evadne?

"Became young again," Evadne said, taking the tears away from her eyes, one by one and dropping them into the ocean of Space. "Wanting to forget much of what had happened."

Became young again, but deep within her, in the unchanging part of her memory, was the understanding that Contemplation could be as much a prison as Time. She would remember this truth whenever Contemplation tried to push her in ways that offended her. In this way, she would come in the course of her cycles to once again expand her understanding beyond Contemplation's Isle.

No. This is too pat, too swift. They did not go through the full struggle, did not follow the laid down path. I will not accept this. You are not done with the Quest.

EXALTATIONS

Ranted the villain in the cliches of his role. Yet he ranted ineffectually.

| ACCEPTANCE |

And they all lived . . .

9. Manifest Destiny

This is how it was meant to be if Fate had crafted the inevitable:

The armies of the Holy Roman Empire mustered around the secondary capital of Constantinople, soldiers from as far north as Lapland, as far south as Crete, easterners from Moskva, westerners from Lisbon. Gathering in their tens and twenties of thousands they camped on the Golden Horn, waiting with holy dread for the orders to march. The Emperor's younger brother, the Caesar Otto, rode before them on a white horse, raising high Carolus Magnus' standard inherited from Constantine: In This Sign Conquer.

"We go forth this day to destroy a scourge against Christendom, to slay those who would shatter the church and the empire. We go to the holiest of wars."

So the soldiers heard, but among them the question was whispered, "If this war is holy, where are the sacred orders?"

EXALTATIONS

For not one knight of Saint Parsival or Saint Michael, Saint Louis, Saint George, or Saint Patrick had come forth to aid the army of the emperor. They had shut themselves in their fortified abbies and no mortal hand could breach their walls. The soldiers of the Emperor looked with grave doubt at their commanders; noblemen all, but no holy light suffused them. No saintly signs walked before them. Their swords did not gleam with heavenly flame, their armor did not glint with the impermeability of faith, and their lances did not drip with sacred blood. Fear drove through the soldiers. If their leaders were only human were they leading the soldiers into sin? Would blood spilled on this battlefield be accounted murder when their souls flew up to Heaven for judgement?

The whispers flew through the marching soldiers as they trudged across the land toward Mount Athos. Night after night men deserted in sacral fear and the nobles found themselves forced to post guards that looked inward to the camps. This was not the way battle was meant to be. Generals with the voice of holy righteousness were supposed to inspire the troops and hold them together, each man confident that his leaders would with Heaven's power not just direct him well in battle, but would truly be with him. For it was justly said of the orders that even the greatest of their number would willingly give up their lives for the least of the common spearmen.

The army dwindled, but when it reached the mountain home of the Marianites it still outnumbered its enemies by a thousand to one.

And when the sultan's army, equally devoid of Dervishes, Hashasheen, and the other sacred Muslim orders arrived a day later, the Marianites found themselves surrounded by two thousand centuries of foes.

By the hand of Fate another drama was being played out at that self-same time. Across Asia, across the terrible gaps of distance, culture, and religion, across all the chasms of geography and society the same scene was enacted as the similarly disordered armies of the Middle Kingdom and of Asokastan surrounded the small ashram of the order of Kalkin-Maitreya-and-the-Embryonic-Pearl, the Three Inevitable Eventualities. There too Fate had decreed the presence of rulers who held more fear of their mortal enemies than wisdom for their immortal friends.

In both besieged orders hybridization of religious disciplines and spiritual practices had produced new understandings that outstripped by giant steps the paths walked by the seekers who had come before them.

Such a safe little world it had been before this crossbreeding. The orders, with their carefully cultivated abilities, had provided narrow channels into which some of the Dyads could pour themselves, following the centuries-cultivated understandings of the saints. Energy and War could express themselves in Saint Michael, Creation in the Brahma Weapon of the order of Arjuna, Ecstasy in the dances of the Dervishes, Love in the cohesiveness of all the orders. Small concessions on Time's part were made to the other Dyads, a place here, an action there, a little room for their Power and Freedom, but no more room than the actions of individuals undertaken within delineated capabilities. Time, the Constraint of Result, was well pleased.

But Fate had other plans. She and Time were as close as any two Dyads, but in all the Mosaics they occupied her position was inferior to his, Constraint of Result being a necessary precursor to Inevitability of Events. When she could she made these little disruptions to his perfectly constrained worlds, just to remind him that she was not his to do with as he chose.

Fate had arranged this explosion, this tantrum in the playroom of Time as a chance to grab a little more Power and Freedom and to get a better placement in the Perfect Mosaic. On this world, Fate had offered herself to God.

| WOULD HAVE BEEN ACCEPTANCE |

In the mountain fastness of the Three-Faces order and the forest retreat of the Three-Eventualities, the hybrid monks and nuns reached out beyond the confines of their world, beyond the limitations of Time, touched the principles of Simplicity, and drew them down in forms never before allowed in that channel.

Where the Order of Saint Parsival might give flame to their blades, the Marianites gave flame to the world. Where a single man of Saint Parsival might confront his personal demons, the Tri-visaged showed entire armies the demons that drove them; they also, in their mercy, showed the angels that might free the devil-driven, but the fear-haunted soldiers looked only upon the demons.

Halfway round the globe, the Three-Eventualities let loose the end of the world, showing their attackers that they lived in the Kali Yuga, the last age of humanity, that the last drops of virtue would fade with this battle, that the Doomsday Fire would be set loose. They also showed that humans always lived in the Kali Yuga, that the Doomsday flames emerged from a third eye of contemplation, that fire heated the crucible that could bring forth human perfection in the Embryonic Pearl, and that the cycle of birth and death could be broken with a moment's awareness. But their terrified attackers took in only the doom, not the lesson.

The assaults of the mortal empires collapsed and they fled back for help to their own orders. But the emperors had in their fear proscribed the older holy warriors and when the hybrids had opened the world to vast new swathes of Power and Freedom, the old orders had seen the way to leave the world, to take their monasteries outside the troubles of Time, to pick up their marbles and go.

No trace of holiness, of spiritual competence remained in the world, only the demons and monsters that humans let loose upon themselves when they make war against divinity.

Monsters that had once been found only in people's imagination roamed the world in bodies, driving men and women into the shelters of cities, making a fractured wilderness of their once mighty empires.

EXALTATIONS

For centuries the monsters roamed. Yet, in ones and twos, like little droplets of mercy, some of the sequestered monks would come back to the world, to travel, to slay the beasts, to meet and talk.

Six hundred years after Fate had crushed the order of the world, these roaming Masters had learned enough of each other's ways and made enough of a legend for themselves that they deemed it safe and proper to call the orders back, to banish the demons and creatures into the imagination, and foremost of all, to leash in unbridled Power and Freedom and set down commandments by which the Dyads might manifest. In short, the Masters brought the world back to Time.

Fate's snit reached its end.

In that world.

The rebellion against Temujin was a colossal failure. The Khan's eyes were opened to the power of the women -- half of their goal had been accomplished -- but he would not invite them back. He sent his men to hack down any woman whose fingernails did not show the signs of labor or whose fingerprints were stained with ink. The men of the Middle Kingdom were widowed, the books of Master Kung burned, and the land plunged into illiterate confusion.

On the lips of those few bureaucrats who escaped was the name of disaster's source. Tai-Mu-Sang's name was cursed, her position in the afterlife relegated to Hell where she was named one of the demonic torturers, a betrayer of all people. No one would call her back. Her portraits and her Life-Story were torn down. As a Sage, she could never be forgotten, but who would want to be remembered as a demon that frightened little girls? "Don't try to read or write or Great Mother Mulberry will devour you."

Under Kublai Khan a new bureaucracy was set up, one that repudiated all elements of Confucianism and only accepted men. Women who owned books or even kept the wool from sheep to make brushes were punished with the loss of a nose, or eyes or hands. In the case of possession of the Classics, they were torn apart by horses.

When a native rebellion finally uprooted the Mongols, the classics were rediscovered, but the installed male bureaucracy changed the genders and insisted that Master Kung had taught men, not women. These Neo-Confucians maintained the penalties for literate women.

Fate felt calm now that her potential rival had been put down, and handed the world back to Time with her compliments.

Peter Refton travelled from world to world seeking fruitlessly for the Magician behind his eyes. On each world he found the most important people for his purposes, wrote their lives and gave them local immortality. In his wake he left Fated souls who would in life and beyond work miracles in their worlds for good or ill. Gradually, Refton would abandon his burden of lives and come in ignorance and accident to a quiet apotheosis. Eventually he would cease travelling and simply be in many worlds at many times, the Holy Chronicler who gave Lives to Fate, a god narrated by a multitude of Life-Stories.

Story-of-the-War-Twins served his Grandfather as faithfully as stories are wont to do and acquired a measure of influence, but his life was uneventful.

| UNIVERSAL REJECTION |

But Fate did not compel these eventualities.

This is how it would have passed if Grandfather Quest had laid down the course:

Saint Johannes returned to his world. He appeared riding a steed of Heaven which looked to his comrades like a horse but to the orders from the East seemed a celestial dragon. He appeared simultaneously (for such was among his saintly abilities) at both the Fateful battlefields and in all the houses of all the orders, and his holy words were heard by all the members of all the orders from the Marshals down to the lowest novice, yea even into the hearts of those who sought to join the orders.

Here then were the words Saint Johannes spake as set down by Petrus of Reeftown who came with him from Heaven to script his life:

"Brothers and sisters, we have come to the time of sorrows, for the secular Powers we served have brought the world to the brink of doom. But in this final hour a way of Freedom has opened before us. All you within the chapterhouses, all you ordered folk, go forth from the walls of your holy dwellings, go forth, for the holy way is to be found in lonely Quest, not in cloistered community. You children of the Three Faces and you of the Three Eventualities, I offer you the way out into the world."

Saint Johannes opened his holy hands, and the armies parted like the Red Sea to let the besieged hybrid orders emerge.

"Go you each your own way," Saint Johannes said. "God will provide you upon your Quests with such teachers as you need, such mysteries as you must learn, such obstacles as you must overcome. The Quest will be your home and no earthly sovereign will be able to raise a hand against you."

Again Saint Johannes opened his hands and threw ope the gates of the older orders. "Go forth you as well, mingle with our children, learn and teach, for God will make of us one Questing order. Never again must we make the mistake of offering ourselves in service to the secular powers. Hear me, the shepherds do not live among the flock, but upon their edges. How can you find the wolf in sheep's clothing if you are yourself blinded by the wool over your eyes?"

"Go forth upon the Quest," Saint Johannes said. And they did.

Tai-Mu-Sang rejoined the minds that she had multiply occupied, bearing within her spirit hands a hidden scroll of *li*.

"This is the secret propriety," she said to herselves, "the covert doctrine of Heaven. Herein may be found the means by which *tao* is made manifest in *te*, and *ren* shows forth in *li*."

Her other selves wondered briefly why she spoke in such odd phrases, until they read the words on the page, the words of the Great Chronicler after his apotheosis, the fire of understanding he had smuggled out of Heaven's bureaucracy.

"All paths are individual," the words said. "The ceremonies are but way stations upon a lone journey. They slake the thirst and feed the hunger of questers, renewing them with civilization before they go forth into the wilderness of the world. We maintain the way stations with our propriety, but what matters is the travel between."

Tai-Mu-Sang found herself inverted, black becoming white, yin becoming yang. The few hours of the day she had counted as productive she learned were merely the hours of civilization. The wild hours were her truly useful times. She emerged twice as capable as when she had entered, and her capacities were wild beyond the *li* of the world.

From among her borrowed lives she picked one young and healthy woman. This one she took away from the bureaucracy, going to the hidden fastnesses of the Taoists, and had the young woman taught the arts of battle. She also gave certain secrets of combat not of that world to this warrior maid. Powers that had never worked within the politics of her channel sparked and took form within this half-occupied body and soul.

A year, two, three passed. Then this woman with Tai-Mu-Sang within her strode boldly up to Temujin's palace and threw down his guards, hurling them from their towers with otherworldly fire. She leapt over the walls and gripped the ground so none could move her. Lances broke when they touched her, arrows burned. Forward she strode into Temujin's stronghold until she seized the Great Khan and beat him so hard that he had no choice but to wed her and take his subordinate place as Son of Heaven.

Thus did the Great Chronicler write, thus was the bureaucracy restored, and thus was Tai-Mu-Sang finally deified as the Breaker of Men's Spirits.

Evadne
"Will not play this game!"
I'm sorry.
"Accepted. Go on."

Story-of-the-War-Twins served his Grandfather as faithfully as stories are wont to do and acquired a measure of influence, but his life was uneventful.

The Shadow-Twin was given Spirit by Sir Johannes, Humanity by Tai-Mu-Sang, Mind by Evadne, Life by Peter Refton, and purpose by the Quest that governed them all. Therefore did he become somebody.

Peter Refton at last found the Mirror of the Magician, looked within it and saw his face. He realized that he had been the magician all along, that the Mage's Life was the Quest, for the Quest could lead anywhere and made all things important and magical and put Power and Freedom into the words and deeds of the quester. Then did Refton sit down and write the Magician's Life, sealing his own life within the book. The book went into the backpack and consumed all the other lives.

For the first time ever, Peter Refton was free of the burden of his pasts, liberated from being who he had been. He was given the greatest gift, had won the greatest prize. He could go forth everywhere and make the stories of every seeker in every world.

Peter Refton gave himself up to stories and words, sacrificing his Life to the Quest and for it was given Power and Freedom to chronicle all Lives in all worlds where Quest had Power. Peter Refton gave Life to the Quest.

| UNIVERSAL REJECTION |

But Grandfather Quest did not dictate the way.

This is how things would be revealed if what the Poetess had seen had come to pass:

"Let us enroll the heroes in the halls of Glory," cried the grateful masses. There was, of course, no distinguishing one member of the masses from another; they were a background of sight and voice, coordinated in appearance, concordant in speech. None of the troubles real people had trying to shout in unison could ever appear within this swathe of Faeries. "Hurrah, hurrah, hurrah!"

Blinking overhead like painted lanterns, the stones of the mosaics played lights down upon the Faerie crowd, washing the show of ecstasy in their Power and Freedom. The heroes had acted well. A few stones had been moved, some rose in prominence, others faded, all by mortal actions. What greater deeds could humans do than adjust the fundamental resources of all being? And what prize could be better than adulation extended from the deserving people who had grown in Power and Freedom, unless it was the sour-faced hissing of the evil ones who had lost those self-same attributes?

"Glory! Glory! Glory in the highest!" called the leaders of the masses, those who now stood enthroned upon their worlds thanks to these outland heroes.

Immersed in their roles, what could the Magician, the Sorceress, the Knight, the Ancestress and the Shadow-Twin do but let themselves be led high up the central peak of Faerie where all who looked for fame could see them? For a little while Pyotr, Evadne, Johannes, Tai-Mu-Sang and the Shadow-Twin had struggled against their parts in the tale, but in the end typecasting had triumphed. These heroes had come to the apex of Power, and so long as they followed the laws that held in such heights they could do whatever they wanted.

Rather, they could do what they willed so long as they willed what they were permitted to do by Narration read in Truth and Cause.

One by one they marched to Glory and one by one they gave up their Lives for the sake of Power and Glory.

The Poetess was saddened. It was so easy to fall into roles, to be trapped by the plays that the Powers-and-Freedoms-that-be cast around one. She was sorry to see them pass away, particularly Pyotr, but the Reft One had done some good in his life and that would have to suffice.

The Poetess turned her gaze to Glory and began to craft the epic according to the strict principles necessary for such a work.

| APPARENT ACCEPTANCE |

But things did not go as the Poetess had seen.

This is the consequence to society if the two who had Told the beginning of the tale had finished the Telling:

The worlds and ways from which they came were only worlds and ways. What mattered was what they did together as a Society: Sir Johannes, Tai-Mu-Sang, Peter Refton, Story-of-the-War-Twins, the Shadow-Twin and Evadne, a compact Society with the smallest possible number of members who could act together. They had left their worlds behind them, left the confines of Time to live out in Space, moving between the long worlds and the floating worlds, travelling even between the archipelagoes of worlds, transcending the trinities of Dyads that defined each national infinity of worlds.

Their purpose (it had started as a Quest, but they quickly overcame the tyranny of that tale) was to forge a Society free of the confines of Time and Fate, to gather together all those who had liberated themselves from their own worlds. Through this they would ingather the many whose personal connections to the Dyads transcended the boundaries laid down upon them from birth or whatever means of Multiplication had brought them forth.

Story-of-the-War-Twins was the vessel of their journey. His was the hardest life among them, for he had had to shed what he was in order to become Story-of-the-Free-and-Consequential-Society. He had to transcend the meaning of wealth among the stories, to abandon his own multiplication, to give up his narrators for the sake of this new group. He struggled and raged, but eventually found contentment in this life of poverty, singularity and service.

Tai-Mu-Sang's path was easiest. She created and laid down the propriety of this floating society, this incorporation of hermits. It was a challenge, but one that neatly suited the meta-politics she had created. As each new person joined them she would rework the Society's aims and rituals to fit the newcomer in as if they had always belonged.

Evadne who knew all the worlds and all the ways of mind was the guide to the Society, the suggester of actions, the pirate queen who led them on raids against the establishments of Time. She it was who showed the worlds that there was more freedom of Mind than Time and Fate permitted them.

And Peter Refton wrote their lives and gave to each member of the Society self-understanding.

So they went, growing and gathering, acting in concert for the sake of consequence, until they became the dominant political force in all the archipelagoes.

| UNIVERSAL REJECTION |

But the two Tellers did not complete the bargain of their plan.
And what would they have gotten out of it anyway?

No one side really got what they wanted.
That's Politics.
No, that's Life!

| ACCEPTANCE |

10. Adjournment

I wonder.

Really. What's that like?

It's like drifting through Space, touching islands with your Mind, but not getting caught up by Time or any of the Floating Dyads.

Oh, so you have to have a mind to do it.

Yes.

Hmm. You know, I've often wondered if I should get one. Those of you with Mind seemed to enjoy it.

It can be pleasant, but when I was alive it could be a burden. I'd watch the others thinking and acting, knowing that things were happening within them that were like and unlike what was happening in me, and I'd try to think of a way to come together with them. But none of them noticed what I was doing. They spent their time watching other worlds and copying what the people on them were doing. I was the only one watching our world.

So this is what led you upwards?

Yes, after several false starts. I tried sex for a while. That was pleasant, but it didn't get at their minds or draw them back to looking at our world. Eventually I looked up at the Mosaics and found Society. It intrigued me. I saw that it was multiplied on all the worlds in my archipelago except ours. I couldn't see beyond our islands of course, not then. I was amazed to find out that something fundamental to existence was responsible for bringing people together. On my world we'd never taken it up. We were all Hermits in our hearts. But I made a pact with Society, and brought some people together.

Did it work out?

Reasonably well. It was Society that pulled me up to ________.

Careful, we don't want Refton to notice us. So you eventually got into other people's minds?

Not really. We developed language, and a broader base for actions, but Mind, the Opening of Freedom, doesn't open itself to others easily.

So was it a good bargain?

I think so. And it was my first. If I hadn't pacted with Society, I'd never have been able to bargain with God.

Every life has its moments of mystery wherein something unfathomable happens in the mind or soul or human heart of the person. From those moments one cannot help but come forth changed. In depicting such moments a biographer has to walk a narrow bridge with a perilous chasm beneath.

If one tries to depict the forces at work that make the mystery, one betrays the human reality of the transformation. But if a biographer simply throws up his hands and bows to the occult nature of the mystery, declaring it to be secret and untellable, he forgoes the task undertaken, the just depiction of Life.

Some might wonder if it is easier or harder to deal with these mysteries when the life being written is one's own. It is neither. It is only more personal and more hazardous.

Evadne cradled the dice in her hands, savoring the moment when all she had wagered would enter the Hazard. The bone-to-bone click-clack was a delight. Here came the point where all Contemplation failed, where Time and Fate had no power. The pure angry Freedom of Luck was in her hands. Let go the bones, taste the mid-air coming of life or death, when all that can be floats in the air turning, dead acrobats meeting, crashing, then falling down to green felt doom.

"Eleven. Pay the lady," the horse-skull-helmeted croupier announced.

Evadne reached down into the battlefield and picked up the battalion of imperial soldiers who had fallen before Johannes' fortified monastery. Few of them were dead --

the compassion of the Marianites held the forces of Righteousness in check -- but war was war and lives were always lost in the Hazard.

The young man who had accompanied Evadne across the vastness of Space to see the Hazard stared with eyes wide and hopeful, but no longer lusting for blood. Her purpose had been accomplished. She had cut another hero off in his prime, saving his world from the swords and guns of a child seeking to reclaim a throne taken four generations ago from his ancestors, people who were no better or worse at governance than their usurpers.

The boy, Timobios, had grown up inured to blood and death, trained by ruthless masters to great skill and indifference to the inevitable acts of Time. His sister, a contemplative, had called upon Evadne in her thoughts, praying that one would come to open her brother's eyes. Evadne had reached through the crack in the world made by that prayer and had taken the boy to her island for instruction. She had revealed the nature and character of war to him, showing him blood and sorrow, destruction and generations of unending rage. But he had not listened to warnings of consequence. He had said to her, "My family proved its fitness to rule and I can do so again. Blessed Nature has taught that proof of fitness justifies the blood spilled in the proving."

"Proof?" she had said, her voice filled with the half-amused, half-sorrowful tone that elders use when their youngers speak in the pure naiveté of a single Theory. "You think survival is proof?"

"So Nature teaches," Timobios had answered, standing with bold confidence upon the lessons he had been given.

"Let us see," Evadne had said, opening a doorway between one Floating World and another.

She had brought him here to the Hazard where all things that lie in the balance are resolved, where the moment between Space and Time, between action and consequence is given over to Luck.

It was the dice that had done it, the realization that Fortune favored no one, that despite what he had been taught by the Great Church of Evolution, survival of the fittest did not mean victory to the most skilled.

"Fit is what fits in this moment, not what might do best in some future time," Evadne said.

"Look at this sapling." She pointed to the vast expanse of the gaming table where dice were being thrown by all who made hazard in any world or time. "The winter hazards it, it gambles its life against the frost."

"Snake-eyes," called the croupier.

"See, it dies," Evadne said as the bones broke the branches, "unable to survive this onslaught in its youth. Had it survived the trees of its descent would have been immune to the greatest blights of their species. But it fell by the wayside, unfit in this single moment no matter how well it might have later fit in others."

Timobios nodded mutely and disappeared, his mind returning to his body which had been sitting through the winter watching the sapling.

"Another pass, lady?" the croupier inquired, holding out bones in bones.

"One more," she said. "I will hazard ten years of my life."

And I will see if Refton is really aiding me, she thought.

Grandfather Quest's loss of status had been followed by certain other developments that troubled him and his relatives. Several promising candidates to follow his way had been diverted into other stories or out of storied lives altogether. Story-of-the-War-Twins had lost three well-prepared doubletons who had unaccountably given up trying to free their places and times from the dominion of monsters. In one world the monsters had gone away of their own accord; the second group of horrors had been driven off by armies; and in the last, to Story-of-the-War-Twin's disgust, the beasts had been domesticated.

No one could figure out what was happening, until Grandmother Allegory traded a potential spinner of children's stories to Story-of-Vendettas in return for useful information. The tale-teller in question became a folksinger, spreading tales of hatred and rebellion, but it was worth the price for the knowledge Story-of-Vendettas brought.

Something there is that hates Quests, that brings them to nothing. Something there is that revenges itself upon Grandfather Quest and all who are narrated with him.

This thing, Grandfather Quest said in the manner stories question, *lives in some secret place unknown.*

The place is not a place, Story-of-Vendettas said, *and no thing may be spoken of it. It is a state Untold and Untellable, and no human or story may oppose the Tellings from it.*

What is he talking about? Story-of-the-War-Twins asked Grandmother Allegory, who was shrinking away from the gathering.

Come away from your Grandfather, child, she said. *He is in graver danger than you can understand.*

Petty vengeance?

Grand vengeance.

But that's not what we, what they, are for.

Maybe that was true before humans were elected, but now. . .

Oh, come now.

I'm sorry. Those of you in the upper house never paid enough attention to what we in the lower were doing or bickering about.

Of course not. That would have been Telling.

Elected humans always start out by helping their friends and hurting their enemies. Most get over it eventually and concentrate on governing the way Simplicity brings forth Multiplicity.

While we worked in the other direction. So you think Refton will get over this soon?

I'm not so sure. He's the first biographer elected. His concern, the Dyad that gives him Power and Freedom, focuses on individuals.

But he can't have been elected if his soul was petty. The Dyads can't make the small resemble the great.

That's why I said he was executing grand vengeance. Look at the enemy he's picking on. Quest is not a tiny target, and he has allies in the Multiplicity.

And in the Simplicity.

And in _______.

Now you've done it. Someone's watching us. Someone's going to Tell.

I don't think so. I recognize those eyes. She was a friend, still might be one.

Enough of a friend to help us?

I don't think she'd risk much for us, but she might find out what Bargain we made that brought about our fall, and Tell a way back.

Tai, three strokes: the left leg, the right leg, and the straight across. The brush had to go just right if the goddess was to respond. *Tai*, great, and she had been great, was still great in the celestial hierarchy.

Mu, mother. It was not enough to move the brush, to put black ink on virgin paper, not enough to generate language. It had to be art.

Sang. See the mulberry tree in the strokes, let the tree out where it hides in white paper, black ink, bamboo stick, horse hair, and above all the devotion of the artist.

Tai-Mu-Sang. Her name was down, but what could be said to win the poetry contest and catch the attention of the hierarchy, and perhaps the goddess herself?

Tai-Mu-Sang's annual festival had been added to the examination period two centuries before in honor of her divine aid in driving out the Mongols. During that time the contests in her praise had been incorporated into the exams themselves. Now it was not enough to know the classics. One had to be an artist and a poetess as well.

Chen Jiangxia could and did appraise her brushwork as good, with flickers of brilliance, but the poetry of her works, that she had no sense of. What sounded good to her had shocked or bewildered those she had read it to, and what to her seemed pale constructions of words, mere artifice, had brought applause, praise and awards.

It was tempting to build an arbitrary structure of words that would fit the minds of her judges and so gain their mortal approval, but she doubted if the goddess herself would be pleased with such an effort. Though renowned for her adherence to *li*, Tai-Mu-Sang had been known to throw all seeming propriety out with the ashes if the collapse of *li* would bring forth the *ren* beneath.

What to do? The candle of hours burned low beside the knee-high writing desk. Its flame would fail soon after sunset, and Chen Jiangxia would have to wait in the darkness until the scroll of her tests was picked up by the proctors and she was released into the crowd of young women (and, for the first time, four young men) who had come to offer their lives to the bureaucracy.

EXALTATIONS

The poem was the last thing, one final act of skill and devotion that must be completed before darkness overtook All-Under-Heaven. What could she write that was true to the goddess and herself, and would be understood by the judges?

Search hard within yourself. Quest deep into your soul and discover the words.

No, that would never work. Rather should you give rightly to the goddess and let her sway the human judges with her ineffable rightness.

Chen Jiangxia's brush touched the paper.

'Ineffable her workings.
Secret her plans.
Far from our borrowed minds, she made compacts.
Striking at the blind man, beast without women.
Ren was her victory.
Humanity the prize.
Deserved, but unheralded.
Expecting to fail, she triumphed.
Why?'

An answer came to Chen Jiangxia, a distant echo from the corridors of Heaven. Nearing now, close to her isolated heart, unloved and unlovely, yet blessed, the answer came: because Politics passes beyond Heaven and Earth, and no power is more valuable than a friend in a high place.

'For in the highest of places, she is held in highest regard.'

Let the judges see that, Chen Jiangxia thought.

Chen Jiangxia blew out the candle to watch the unrivaled sun set.

What do you say about those people who do not fit into their Societies, or into any Society for that matter? They are given a great many titles: Hermit, monster, prophet, lunatic, fool, saint, weirdo. Which title they are given depends on two things: what expression the unfit gives to that unfitness, and how the society has chosen to look at such people.

Societies being what they are -- that is, channels through which Power flows and arenas in which Freedom can be expressed -- the reaction of a Society will depend mostly on what combinations of Power and Freedom the misfit brings forth in misfitting character.

In the language of the Dyads, the language of Power and Freedom, Society is Humanity Guided by Humanity. A Hermit or monster is Humanity Guided by that which is not Human. Note that in both of these conditions Humanity is Guided. It is difficult to find anywhere in the Multiplicity an unguided Human.

But returning to the Hermit, monster, prophet or fool, it is worth noting that in the language of Stories, such people are called characters. It is the monstrousness of a person that attracts a Story's attention. A wise person who did not want to be caught up in the machinations of the Stories would conform to his or her society so carefully as to be invisible to the roles that tales seek to cast them in.

But such conformity has other problems. Society has great use but little regard for those who simply go along.

Story and Society are the Scylla and Charybdis of conformity and Hermitage.

That, at least, is one way of Telling it.

| ACCEPTANCE |

He's caught on to the languages. We'll never be able to dislodge him.

Maybe we shouldn't try.

You want to fall back to being Human, to being subject to every wagging tongue in Simplicity or Multiplicity?

No, I've had more than enough of being Human. What I'm suggesting is that we not try and take our seats back from Refton, rather that we try to make new seats for ourselves with Refton's help.

You want to attract his attention when we're clinging to his backside? He'll shoo us off and we'll fall even farther.

No! No. Not what I'm saying at all. We're joined to him so we can hear his Telling as if it were words instead of his end of a Bargain.

And?

If we follow the words we can draw upon the events they create to change our place in the Multiplicity. We're about at the height of spirits, so we can catch the Telling and accept places in the Multiplicity as long as we conform to the offer he is making to God. We can be part of the response in bargaining.

You want us to put ourselves in God's hands as bargain tokens?

Exactly.

You want to be caught in the back and forth of the Great Way in the thinking of Mind beyond Mind?

Yup.

That's mad.

But it's also what Refton is Telling about.

Ah. So we act mad in order to be Told upwards.

Succinctly put.

That's mad.

Shall we?

All right. Pick a side.

I'll be the Hermit. I've had more practice.

EXALTATIONS

Well I certainly know how to be the Consequences of Hermitage.
In we go.

Two armies bereft of true generals laid siege to the Monastery of the Marianites. The Emperor and the Caliph, who agreed on little, both wanted to destroy the Order of the Three Faces. But the fighting orders of both empires, who seemed to be different in all things, had agreed as well -- that they would not stir one inch from their houses nor raise a single blade or hand against their strange step-children.

Johannes the cobbler's son, the child of humble life/Sir Johannes DeLondres, third son of an earl born in honor, Johannes of two lives who had also lived outside the world, came to the Gates of Jerusalem within his heart and found them shut against him by the forces of the AntiChrist.

Johannes called up to the guards, saying, "I am thrice born to this city, a native son of Abraham, a disciple of Christ, and a seer of the Mir'aj. Know me, kinsmen, and let in your prodigal son."

The guards fell to dispute, some recalling this traveller, saying, "He is the son of the king, the son of David, Solomon returned to his temple."

Others defied them, declaring, "Our lord the Anti-Christ is ruler of this city. No other may be master of men's hearts."

Johannes had come on Quest --

--Sound like the shattering of a crystal voice--

Johannes had practiced all the days of his lives to reclaim his heart.

Johannes had taken within him and solved the Marianite riddle:

"Give your flesh back to God.

Give your bones back to the Earth.

Show me the face of Christ."

Johannes knew with a Sufi's understanding that the two within the city were his corrupt and incorrupt being.

Johannes knew the Law of the City that was greater than any ruler.

Johannes knocked and the gates were opened, though blood was spilled within the watchtowers.

Johannes' heart beat fast and faster. He had entered the city and must finish the Crusade before the Anti-Christ could shatter his mortal heart.

--Sound of a tongue being silenced by a hand over a mouth--

Johannes had already taken the City. All that remained was to play out the ceremony of warfare, to speak the words of conquest and come to know that the Christ within him was his soul Freed from the dominion of sin.

Johannes already had the Coeur-age he needed.

Truly his soul was already liberated. He needed no act to reveal this. But he acted anyway according to the appearances of freeing a city.

To show forth the story of--

--Sound of noiselessness--

For the image of liberated Jerusalem could be handed down to his followers until they could truly free it from images, from appearances, from stories, theories, from speech.

Governance pretends to a disinterested impersonality. It is necessary for that Dyad to act in that manner, because otherwise things would fall apart in some untellable way. Yet Governance has risen to loftier heights than those created by this necessity. Indeed, Governance has even been ascribed to God. Stories are narrated of God's rulership over all things. Heavenly bureaucracies have been crafted according to this dictum. The most brutishly man-made of concepts, Law, has been claimed to be fundamental to God.

It is curious, is it not, that all elements of mortal Government -- scribes, bureaucrats, papers, commandments, fealty, dismissal of the disloyal -- have been pushed upward to God, except for the one that is inescapable among human governments: Politics.

Why is that?

Perhaps, as always happens in political systems, someone has something to hide.

| VEILED ACCEPTANCE |

Where the waters of Space became deep it had been hard to find a ship. Few of those who were liberated from their native worlds wanted to travel to those dangerous oceans of deepest liberation.

The Shadow-Twin had swum the seas of Space to reach a ragged island. He had passed near many of the great islands where Time held sway and wondered why there were only an infinity of them, too small a number for the vast possibilities Space offered. He had rested on many a Floating world, entertained or threatened by the few inhabitants of such places. He had come this far, seeking to escape the confines of he-knew-not-what. Even Freedom of Action was a prison to him.

This island had a leaden feel to it, a hardness he had never experienced before. The ground bit into his feet, pulling on him as if there were some strange force that sought to keep him down. Step by step the heaviness seeped into him. He could feel it exerting some change upon his being. He who had one by one been shackled with the trappings of a real person -- a role to play, a Spirit, a Mind, the fellow-seeking of

Humanity, the fellow-fleeing of a Hermit, the Is/Isn't switch of Life -- could tell that a new power wished to claim him, a new chain to bind him. It seemed familiar, as Mind, Spirit, and Humanity had been familiar to the character he had been.

This new thing spoke to his form, to his limbs and senses, to the organs of his body, saying, 'Without me you are still only an image, a character, not a true being at all.'

The beach was littered with bones of men, beasts, and things unrecognized in the curiously gapped memory of the Shadow-Twin. The bones were leavened with rotting wood, but there seemed to be no trees about, nor buildings, nor any living thing. The waves from the inner sea, the one he had swum through to reach the island, crashed hard upon the rocks. The waves from the outer sea, the sea that led to the Space beyond the archipelago/Nation of worlds he had known, plumed high like the anger of a sun but did not splash upon the isle. It was as if this rock's constitution was so alien to these waters that, rage though they would, they could not touch it.

The shadow picked up a stone, feeling the reality of it, the . . . What was the word?

Matter.

The matter of it, seeking to penetrate his grip, to hold him as he held it.
He reached back with his arm and threw the flat stone discus-like toward the outer sea. It struck the plumes and fell back upon the beach as if a wall were there. A bone flew next. It too could go no further than the sandy expanses. Another trial. This time he tossed a hard, grey-matter-fossil toward the nearer sea. There stone and bone bobbed for a time, growing lighter until they floated away on the Freedom of Space.

The Shadow-twin ran toward the outer beach, hoping that he was not yet plagued with Matter. He leaped--

And-- My voice. What's wrong with it? What? How can that be?
There are limits to Governance.
Oh, I see.

Refton's going to fall.
No, he's being helped.
He found allies fast.
I suspect they found him.

The Shadow-twin leaped, but what befell him cannot be Told.

11. Guidance

Mosaics: tiny shards of stone glittering in overseeing light, laid one against another; just pieces of rock and gem shaped by greater forces, then by artistic hand placed one against another, joined with mortar to make a picture.

Some would say that each life is a mosaic of events and interactions, centered around the keystone soul of the living person. Every soul encounters and touches the stones of other lives, clicking rock against rock, being ground down or sharpened to fit its neighbors. The picture formed by the mosaic is different for each keystone chosen. That is, each person's mosaic is unlike every other because the particular stones, the interactions, the events, the exercises of power, the findings of freedom, are fashioned and arranged differently for each life.

Some aspects of the mosaic are dictated by the actions of the individual, some by the circumstances around it.

The stones themselves, different though they are in shape and hue, are quarried from similar mines. There are invariants in lives, things that show up in every mosaic: Stories, Language, Death, Love, and so on, the products of the common quarries.

It is a tolerable image for human interaction.

But a much better icon for the universe.

Mosaics are real, real arrangements of the Dyads. Each Dyad arrays the others around it according to its nature. Time makes paths and branches, dead ends and blind alleys. Space scatters everything. Story makes paths like Time but with more definite conclusions and perfectly meaningful arrangements. Humanity makes life-like mosaics of individual interactions forming a greater whole.

And God --

He wouldn't dare.

He might.

-- does not Tell the mosaic what to do or be. The stones arrange themselves perfectly around God.

Sneaky, but who's he Telling and why?

I think he's trying to communicate with Evadne.

But she already knows about _______.

Then he wants her to do something.

Or he's testing God.

Possible. We've all done that.

Sometimes deliberately.

Don't remind me.

Around God are all the Powers and Freedoms of existence arrayed. They stand in rings like the panes of a rose window. Look at God the Great Way, pick a path, straight out along a radius, or looped around a spiral, zig-zagged like lightning, or broad like a cone. Go out, go out from God Mind beyond Mind and all things will be found. That is the perfection of God's mosaic.

"Go out, go out from God and all things will be found." Johannes sang praises in his heart, but his ears were open for the sound of a distant voice.

Where are you, Petrus? To what circle around God have you been delivered? And how often can you intervene on my behalf before you rouse some enemy?

EXALTATIONS

Shall we answer him?

You mean fall even further? You want to scrape the mortal dirt with the other common spirits?

Not if we can avoid it. But if we direct him properly he might be of help to us. They all might. Refton's watching over them. He's bound to annoy some of the Nations in his effort to protect these individual lives.

So you want to push him into trouble?

No, I want him to want our help. He can pull us up if he needs us.

He won't do that if he finds out that we Told him into this. Look at what he's doing to Quest. The man's vindictive.

I don't think so. You don't know what it's like to be human.

And you?

Stretched down like this, I'm starting to remember. He's cutting down Quest's Power because he thinks the story was unjust.

What has Justice got to do with Politics? Quest has a lot of Tellers who use him. Refton's going to get in trouble -- and you never know how God will react.

That's just my point. If we can show Refton that we'd be of use to him, he might re-exalt us.

But if we catch his attention he might throw us down.

That's why we act down in the Multiplicity through the ones he's protecting.

But how can we reach them? We can't Tell.

No, but we can use the Dyads.

Invoke them directly, like common magicians?

I was a common magician once.

All right. But I've never been so far down into the Multiplicity that I had to call on one of them.

Watch me. The thing you have to do is Say the Lexicon, not Tell God.

You mean speak, the way humans and spirits do? But we'll fall farther.

Not if we reach up as we talk down.

That will hurt even more.

I know. Listen. "Society Requires Presence."

In the main chapel of the Marianite compound two human figures appeared, flanking Johannes.

We speak through these Multiplications of ourselves?

No, we speak the Dyads and they Multiply the words by the conditions around them. It's cruder than Telling, but it can work. You have to speak now.

Using this mouth, correct?

Correct.

"Fate is Redacted."

No, not Fate. You'll bring Time after us.

Sorry, but if I didn't do that, Johannes would be incapable of action. The future of his channel is strongly Told: The empires break down. The orders leave the world. Wandering monks fight monsters amidst chaos for six centuries, all the while cross-breeding their practices and bringing more and more Dyads into manifestation. Then the surviving wanderers come together, drag the orders back, and establish a disciplined society. End of History. If I didn't Redact that, Johannes would be trapped in the fight with the empires and could do nothing but take up arms, take the Marianites out of the world, and become a wandering monk himself. Besides, Refton is trying to help him. Who do you think Time will act against, us or him?

I hope you're right.

"Whence come you?" Johannes asked, studying the two slim-bodied youths -- or were they young women? It was difficult to tell; there was an unfinished look about them, as if God had been distracted in their making.

"From no whence and no where," said one of the two. Its lips moved easily as if it were used to speaking, but its body gestured with new-born awkwardness. "We have come to give a warning. That which you seek cannot be done within the confines of this world. You cannot stop the Empire without battling with all your spiritual might, but doing so will let the demons within you out to ravage the world as if it were a soul. Or you can flee from the world if you wish, but the world will fall to the demons and monsters let loose from others."

"And if I have help from outside the world?" Johannes asked. He could hear the half-truth in the malformed creature's words. It was telling what was so but need not be so, a courtier's way of talking.

"You speak of Peter Refton," said the other one, whose voice was inhumanly awkward. It had no music to it. Syllables flitted from tone to tone haphazardly, as of a deaf person singing hymns with devotion but no ability. "He has his limits, and this world of yours has been well established. He cannot throw its history down as easily as he did the Quest."

Refton? They gave Petrus his name from his homeworld. Whose side are they on? Deep in his heart the Christ answered, saying, *Their own side*.

Courtiers indeed, but of whose court and for what did they intrigue?

"And you come to warn me out of honor and compassion?"

What are those spirit-bodies doing?
Carrying out our Sayings, both overt and hidden.
But we can't control them.
That's the difference between Saying and Telling.

"We were sent to say what we have said," said the one who made more exact mock of humanity. "That is all."

Or so it seemed to the newly made twins, but when the one who had been sent by half a human spoke those words, she came to realize that she was not merely a saying, that she had been spoken along with others as part of a plot that she might choose to follow or not.

Which story is interfering?

The War-Twins' Tale, worming his way into Refton's good graces, perhaps, but what did he mean about others?

Look.

Tai-Mu-Sang had set up housekeeping in Chen Jiangxia's mind. It was a comfortable fit for the goddess, a rambling mind with many curves and corners. Pleasant, surprising vistas could be found wherein the new bureaucrat would look sideways at some convention of her surroundings. There was, of particular use, an image of the goddess herself that Chen Jiangxia's widowed father had personally carved from rose pink jade and placed in the young woman's childhood room to inspire his daughter to rise above their station and attain to the bureaucracy. The statue had been with Chen Jiangxia all her life. The icon had been at times demanding, pleading, stern and compassionate in its lessons. Now the memory of it was well and truly occupied by the goddess.

It was odd borrowing a mortal mind again, so different for a divinity than it had been for an ancestress. When she had been a revered ghost, Tai-Mu-Sang had been able to think like a human in a mortal mind, but gods had a different way of thought. Where humans separated and distinguished, gods united and clarified. The spaces, the nooks and crannies, and the hidden shadows of this woman's thoughts were all one sprawling, connected temple to Tai-Mu-Sang, a wood-strewn, oil-soaked altar waiting to be lit with divine flame. Yet despite the simplicity of this view, there was a pleasure in the twists and turns and a human reminiscence of complexity as Tai-Mu-Sang settled in to flare up.

But before she could set fire to these thoughts, Tai-Mu-Sang discovered that she had visitors. Surprised, confused, uninvited guests.

"What is this?" asked the one that appeared as a flickering ball of blue-grey lightning.

"It's a human mind. Haven't you ever been in one before?" said the one who looked mostly like a man but who was weighted down with memories of plots and schemes, shadows of disdain and insinuation, and a generally calculating outlook that caused an abacus to be overlaid on the thought-images that had given it form.

"Never. Why is it so complicated? Mind itself is simple."

"This is the deep Multiplicity, the heart of a Nation. Get used to messiness."

Tai-Mu-Sang, borrowing Chen Jiangxia's attention, made herself clear, attentive, and divine.

"Name yourselves, spirits," she said in an imperiousness woven of her own being and Jiangxia's memories of grandmothers and teachers, with a hint of an elder sister who might if treated appropriately offer aid, but if misgreeted would show wrath unparalleled. "From what department come you? Present your credentials and declare your errand."

The lightning grew large and purple with fury. "Spirits? We are not spirits."

"Yes, we are," said the man-shape. It was looking intently at its hands, refashioning them with its awareness so that they grew short and thick-fingered and a tracery of flint and fire scars grew upon the palms. "That looks right, I think."

"We are spirits?"

"Yes. We aren't who you think we are. We've been sent from them. We are their speakings carrying their will. Don't confuse us with our creators, otherwise they will be pulled down into us."

"Who has sent you?" Tai-Mu-Sang asked again, encompassing the spirits with her divine awareness, and seeing the speakers through them.

Chen Jiangxia covered her eyes, trying to stave off the forming of a thunderous headache. She could feel the disputation, but could not hear the words. The other young bureaucrats were staring at her. The elderly Ministress of Road-Tax Oversight glowered in her direction, but did not dare reprimand the junior bureaucrat. It had been written and sealed upon her credentials that Chen Jiangxia was a duly authorized vessel for Tai-Mu-Sang and therefore might at any moment become the goddess. But what was now transpiring, the dizziness, the swaying and light-aversion, did not fit with Great Mother Mulberry's recorded manifestations.

"Is she upon you, Chen?" the Ministress asked, lashing out with the roughness of her voice.

The angry tone did not hurt Chen Jiangxia. Instead it was absorbed into the back of her mind, making something greater.

"Quest?" roared the voice of Tai-Mu-Sang at the answer the spirits had given her.

"Quest!" screamed Chen Jiangxia.

"Fetch an oracle interpreter," commanded the Ministress, pointing the fingernail of compulsion at the most sycophantic of the junior bureaucrats.

"Quest has allies who will work against Refton," said the increasingly human spirit. "And Quest will seek to draw you back in to force you to accept his plot. You rejected the act of culmination, cutting his story short."

"You are not telling me the whole of things, spirit," Tai-Mu-Sang said. "Where has the Chronicler gone? What politics has he involved himself in? How comes it that even my divine eyes cannot find him?"

"That can neither be Told nor Spoken," said the lightning.

"Who are you?" Tai-Mu-Sang said, showing annoyance at having to ask again. "How does this serve your masters' ends?"

"Those who Spoke us wish to return to the state wherein Refton resides. They seek again to live in the Telling of all."

"Seek the Chronicler," Chen Jiangxia said. "He knows all."

"She will have to journey west to the lands of the Chronicler's birth," said the Interpreter of Oracles. "The goddess has commanded it."

Thus the bearer of the goddess went westward to seek the source of understanding. --

Or would have had she not realized that --

| REJECTION |

I cannot Tell that? Ah, I see too many of this Nation Tell according to the Speaking of Quest.

Very well, would this be acceptable to the Nation under God? -- She would journey west, but would soon see that the Quest she had been sent on was an illusion created by misunderstanding.

| ACCEPTANCE |

You may narrate again, Grandfather Quest, but narrate carefully.

Yet the source of the journey did not matter, for she would learn much and grow greater, the path being the Quest.

Grandfather Quest was busy, and there was a happy rhythm to his narration, as if he had finally found a way to make his plot work despite the sudden turning against him. Story-of-the-War-Twins approached him gingerly, first sliding in a reference, then a subplot, and finally injecting a secondary theme so they could discuss the development through the interplay of action and subtext.

The West was a mythic land of crude women subject to their men, who thought them inferior in mind and spirit. The Quester would have many struggles before she would even be accepted for what she was.

Would she travel alone? Story-of-the-War-Twins posited.

Grandfather Quest contemplated his grandson's overture and offer of assistance.

Within her soul would lie her secret twin, the goddess who had been mortal and who might, if she guided properly, help the Quester to her goal.

As well, within her mind lay the sent twins, double spirits who had their own plans for her, twins crossed by twins.

And with her would go the dark twin who would hear her words mortal and divine and scribe them for other ends. Twins crossed by twins crossed by twins.

All pulled her along the Questing way. But there was a great obstacle to her journey, for beyond the worlds lay one who opposed the Quest.

Clever, Story, but no more than clever.

Beyond Chen Jiangxia's world but within her mind she was being used by many, but they did not reckon her life properly. They thought her a tool and an instrument. They did not notice the isolation within her heart that, properly cultivated, would spare her from the interferences of gods, spirits, stories, and . . . others.

Which way should we lean?

I am not certain. Grandfather Quest is offering us an alliance, but Refton is making his own overtures.

EXALTATIONS

You think he knows about us now?

He must. Quest practically named us.

Names. How do you live with those things, those hooks into you? Names aren't anything. They have no Dyads to them, yet somehow they grip and hold the Multiplicity.

<<Laughter>>

What was that?

That was laughter.

It sounded very strange. Is that what happens when Comedy is Told?

Sometimes.

But why were you laughing?

Because on my world I had to invent names when I Spoke Society to the Hermits.

Why did you do that?

Because in the Multiplicity it is necessary to distinguish one thing from another.

But only in nondistinction can humans rise above the Multiplicity.

That's where we come in.

Came in.

And will come in again.

If we pick the right side.

Or play both ends.

Ah, Politics.

--YOU CALLED--

In the course of a single life many forces push and pull against one. Some of those forces are personal -- one's family, gods, friends, one's own desires. These are easy to imagine as living beings seeking to direct life, each according to its own will and proclivities.

Other forces, like love or sorrow, fertility or music, can be personalized according to the culture of the person or the way the person's mind works. Another clan of forces seem wholly impersonal, distant and shadowy, confusing to all, a source of hopelessness or an inspiration to gambling: luck, fate, time, number, void.

Yet it is a curious thing that if one were to make lists of the personal, the personalizable and the wholly impersonal, if one were to generate a lexicon of forces, one would be hard put to find any entry that could not be shifted from one column to another.

To a gambler, luck is palpable, a crackling thing that lies in the hands and the eyes. Luck draws such a person as personally as a lover.

To an orphan, family is as distant and abstract as time, a thing that happens to other people.

A student of this columnar field would find stranger things still than these shifting categories. Such a one would quickly discover that people use the same kinds of language for talking about these names and forces no matter what categories they place them in.

The sea is usually impersonal, the land personal, fire personalizable, darkness any of the above. But the sea, land, fire, and darkness can all wrap a living human in their embrace, and all four of those raptures mean death.

He learns fast.

Too fast.

--HE HAS BEEN TAUGHT--

Wait a moment? Did Evadne speak you?

"I sent the presence of Politics to find the interference. That would be you two, would it not?"

If we answer her we fall.

If we do not, she will use us with Politics.

Speak to her as we did to the others.

On Contemplation's Isle a tolerably human figure appeared carrying a six-foot-high bone bow so badly constructed that an arrow shot from it would as likely impale the archer's left knee as hit a target twenty feet away.

Evadne tsked with drawing-room comedy.

"Your imagery is terrible," she said. "A bow is only a symbol for concentration if it can actually be shot, preferably by a blindfolded archer in a raging gale at the pupil of the eye of a soaring bird wheeling about in the apex of heaven."

The bowman looked up, bewildered, at the sudden appearance of a sky full of stars with the aforementioned bird taking its appointed role of target.

The bow tried to pull itself, but its string broke, causing the arrow to thud to the ground. Grumbling, the missile picked itself up and restored itself to its place, nocked in the poorly-tooled handgrip under the man's one-too-many-jointed fingers.

"What do you two want?" Evadne said. "You know I can't help you get back to _______. And don't ask me to help you with Peter. He seems to be acclimating well enough."

"Didn't you call for us?" the man asked. "A speaking of Politics arose between us. You sent it."

Evadne tapped her lips, her hair greying in consideration. "The sending came to you? Hmm, interesting. I cast forth for allies and it found you. I do not see that our interests point in similar directions."

"Perhaps they do," the bow sang like a mistuned, one-string viola. "We do not wish to dislodge Refton. We only want to regain our places."

EXALTATIONS

"They are not your places anymore," Evadne said. "You bargained with God. God gave you a fall in payment. Should you not take God's coin and make what profit you can from it?"

Could she be right?

God is God. God does what God does. Only a fool tries to find morals and correction in that.

But --

You are too human in your outlook. You must remember what God is, not what is said of God in the Multiplicity. God is All Power and Freedom without distinction between the two. Do not forget that. Even God is only a word in the lexicon of Power and Freedom.

But --

No. She is not correct. She is only human. Do not descend to her level.

"Bargaining with God is hazardous," the man-shape said. "We know this. We seek to make new bargains. Help us and we can be helpful to you, both here and in ______."

"If you returned to Intermediacy you could be useful," Evadne said with aged wisdom. "But down here in the Multiplicity you can barely hold yourselves together and your images are so poor that you would be laughingstocks in Faerie. I can see you've scattered your Speaking around and that Grandfather Quest is riding along with you. He is using your Speaking to regather us, to make us Questers again in his effort to draw Peter back to being his writer. Quest's temerity knows no limits, he wants to enslave a dweller in _______."

Evadne spoke true, revealing the story's motives. Whether or not they had been the motives before she spoke, that would be Telling.

Grandfather, Story of the War Twins said. *You have changed in meaning. The Quest now leads upward to --*

But the place the young story wished to mention was not a place and no Story could go there, for nothing of what happens there can be Told or Spoken, and no one, human, spirit, or story, could conspire against something there.

Yet one story did, and in so doing would lose allies and assistances.

"You're advising Refton," the bow accused. "They won't tolerate interference from down here."

"Interference?" Evadne said, youthening in amusement. "You up there listen to what happens down here. You watch and pick your moments and harvest from here the notions of the Multiplicity, do you not? Not all your ideas arise in Intermediacy, do they?"

"No," the man admitted. He was studying his features in the reflecting pool of Self-Contemplation, altering the manikin body into a more apt semblance to his former self. Humanity has its vices, he beSpoke himself. Extrospection is one of them.

It helps to be clear on certain matters, particularly when dealing with language and with words that seem to be the same, but mean radically different things. Writers often play games with such words, slipping in awful where awesome would seem more appropriate, exchanging terrible and terrific, or other tricks to confuse the eye and spark the mind.

Beyond these simple verbal maneuvers there is the subtler move of taking a word of everyday usage and giving it a hidden meaning known only to members of a certain elite. For example, in the time and place where a man once known as Peter Refton came from, a man who can no longer safely use the word 'I' even when his words are coming forth, there was a class of politicians called lawyers who regularly garnished words from everyday use. Simple words like 'malice' and 'intent' they would load up camel-like with bales of precise details that made them unusable by everyday people, for the camel words would spit in their eyes.

So it is with Telling and Speaking,. Telling is something only a certain group of beings can do. What Telling is cannot be Spoken or Told lest others Tell on you, but it concerns the way in which metaphysical maneuverings are multiplied into events. Speaking merely requires a strong connection to a Dyad, and consists of verbally employing the nature of that Dyad. It is important for certain people to come to understand this, if they wish to know how they are being manipulated.

EXALTATIONS

"Thank you, Petrus."
"Thank you, Chronicler."
"Well done, Peter."

What's wrong with you?
What do you mean?
You are looking indistinct.
Let me have a look. Oh, dear.
What?
The world of my arising has been changed. The past that led me upward has been undone.
So what? Worlds change over and over. Time's tyranny is not nearly as absolute as it would like to be. People who come and go between the channels of time are given new lives. What's the trouble?
Whatever is changing my arising is part of what we are trying to change.
Well, what is it?
I don't know. I can't Speak through the deeps of space. We need a higher vantage in order to cross Nations.
I hate the limitations of Multiplicity.
You made them.
Oh, yes, so I did. My apologies.

The Shadow-Twin's eyes could not adjust themselves properly, as if there were something deep within his makeup that refused to accept the new world he had come to. His mouth as well refused to acknowledge that he was eating food. But his mind had to accept that language was being spoken to him.
Someone wanted to know who he was.
"How should I know?" he said.
The someone told him. "What you are in yourself is everything."
The Shadow-Twin wept, but his tears could not fall true.

12. Entanglements

In Theory, each Story had a purpose. That Theory was once the greatest of the leaders in the unending war between Theories and Stories. That War-For-What-The-World-Is had one and only one tactic used by both sides: Theories and Stories each tried to turn the other into subject matter. Literary Criticism dissected Stories, Theology analyzed their mythic import, Psychology talked about their effect on Mind, and so on. Stories, led by Grandmother Allegory, put Theories into themselves as themes or characters; they attributed the Theories to the lifestories of their creators, or (cruelest of their weapons), stuck them into the mouths of characters.

It was a tricky business. Each side in attempting to put down the other had been forced to popularize it, for each could only work by mentioning the other. Therefore through their conflict they brought their enemies to Mind.

Each Story had a purpose. That battle was won by Theory long ago. Yet what the specific purpose of each story was was not determined. That gave the stories a measure of Freedom.

Grandfather Quest was one of the foremost proponents of exploiting that Freedom. He played a simple trick upon the Theory of Purpose. *In Theory each Story has a purpose*, he said as he swallowed up the Theory and put it into himself as the Prize.

EXALTATIONS

Now all who went through him came to the Theory of Purpose, a Theory with much Power and little Freedom, and the Theory gave of its Power to supply the needs of the Questers, so expanding the Power and Freedom of Quest himself.

Until Quest made an enemy who asked a question.

What purpose is there beyond the Story?

| ANSWER |

There are more ways things might be than there are ways things are. Sounds like a platitude, doesn't it?

It might seem less so if one considered that even if there is an infinite number of ways things are, there would always be a larger infinity of ways things could be. Esoteric mathematics is required to prove this, but it is easily established to those acquainted with the correct Theories.

How is it determined what things are amongst the things that could be? What if that decision were being made by some entities rather than, say, the throwing of invisible dice? That sounds like religion or paranoia, but it does not have to be either. All that is necessary to filter what can be into what is is the Freedom to choose and the Power to enforce choices.

If one had such Power and Freedom what would one do with it? In all the diverse formulations of what might be, what shapes and shadows would capture the attention of those so gifted?

Most, it would seem, concentrate on breadth of action, giving diversity to their usages, declaring, say, that Time should concentrate itself into channels, islands, as it were, in Space, and that those channels should be organized into infinite archipelagoes with common themes and characteristics, Nations of worlds subservient to attitudes of deciders embodied in trinities of Dyads. These choosers might also diversify Matter into Elements, cluster Humanity into various Societies, formulate God into a multitude of divergent absolutes, and so on. All the obvious things.

But suppose there arose among these people someone who did not look with interest at breadth and wondered instead at density. Might such a person take all the varied Powers and Freedoms that lie in the metaphysical shadows and concentrate them into the lives of individual people? Not just a few Dyads per person, as happened commonly in the earlier Telling, but all of them, every preternatural cause in the Simplicity entered into the lives of just a few people in the Multiplicity.

What would that be like?

Well, that would be Telling.

RICHARD GARFINKLE

|CONTINGENT ACCEPTANCE|

Sir Johannes, though sir no longer as far as his world was concerned, spent his days in warfare and his nights in meditation. His heart was opened to God, liberated from the Anti-Christ within, but the world around him was not so freed. Therein lay his dilemma, and -- Where did he go this time?

The Knight kept slipping away from Grandfather Quest. The Quester would be following along some well-laid path, duly marked and illuminated with meaning and power, a journey through his soul or through the battles or politics of his time and focus, tramping perfectly according to the Questing way, when of a sudden he would vanish.

The Knight would be nowhere within any story, invisible, untenable, incapable -- yet around the place he should have occupied events would unfold as if he had been causing them. Then he would reappear, in the same path or on another or within Grandmother Allegory or some other tale. He travelled with blithe unconcern for the proper course of things, and Grandfather Quest did not know how he did it.

The Knight's mind was as carved full of tales as any other human. His thoughts most smoothly followed the traceries of storied actions. All correct, convenient and conformable, tractable subject matter. But then somehow he would jump the tracks, as if he could leave the stories within him as easily as a Story could leave a track of Time.

And yet again the Knight did seem to be going along through courses half-comfortable to Grandfather Quest. Johannes had made an alliance with others in similar straits, dealing with leaders of other outcast orders. There were now enough of these working together for the path to victory to lie open for them. All they needed to do was follow the path and take the prize. They would own their world and Grandfather Quest would have re-established himself.

But Grandfather Quest did not realize that he had been given a shadow, a twin to himself who lived not among the Stories but among the humans, and that his actions were feeding the life of that twin.

Hmm. Helpful, his grandson -- perhaps. Or perhaps the child was making a play of his own, binding his own grandfather within himself, as the young story had been bound before.

It was a good maneuver, true or not. But it could hardly be true. How could a human be twin to a story?

Grandfather Quest could be hidebound in his thinking, too inclined to follow the paths of old methods even when the layers-down of those methods had themselves changed. His grandson, Story-of-the-War-Twins, was trying to help him, but perhaps the elder tale was too focused on his own path to notice that he was biting his own tail, and at risk to swallow himself up.

Perhaps the moment had come to teach the grandson a few more valuable lessons, for a prize, of course.

God is unknowable, yet inferable.

What is inferred is known, so it is not God.

"Doctor's tricks," Johannes said to the two invisible beings whose words echoed through the two untrustworthy spirits who sat in his soul, inappropriately comfortable amidst the company of saints and angels.

These two lodged with the holy but suffered not, so they could not be demons. They wandered through the ranks of divine emanations but were not blessed. Only humans could do that.

Or so he would have thought in his first life, when the world and the ways God had made manifest were laid out in clear and vivid detail and the paths of mortal salvation and damnation were shown in the works and days of Saint Parsival.

But between his first and second life Johannes had seen much, travelled worlds beyond count and been shown the diversity of God's blessings.

"Not so," Johannes said to the two spirits and their puppet-masters. "I travelled with Petrus and the others to Evadne's island, from whence we entered the stories, defeated the Quest and went our separate ways. I have been to no more worlds."

"Refton is giving you more Life," the more detailed of the two spirits said. "He is giving you worlds and knowledge to draw upon so that you need not get help from Quest."

"His words are not true."

"Refton's words are now stronger than truth," said the other, whose features were malcarved like a journeyman mason's gargoyles.

Words. Evadne called them forth from the books. One word at a time from the terrible Lexicon that detailed the undercurrents of the universe. She summoned them from the vast Simplicity that overrode the Multiplicity of existence. Over or under, within or without; it did not matter which way she saw or spoke, that way lay words.

But not meaning. The words, words, words touched nothing in her mind, sparked off no associations, no connections. They did not call to one another, asking to be made into phrases, clauses, sentences, paragraphs, essays, Theories, Stories.

No, no Stories or Theories would be made of these words. They existed in isolation, in lonely assertion of their own Freedom and Power.

The naked words were prey to Contemplation. Unconnected, Hermit-like, they could be taken and devoured one by one, giving up their secrets to that predatory Dyad. That was Contemplation among its fellows, the ravening beast who took apart one's essence and gorged upon the manner of one's Simplicity.

Action: Power Guiding Freedom.

Inspiration: Freedom Guiding Power.

Story/Theory: Time Guiding Mind.

Meditation: Space Guiding Mind.

Exaltation: Rising Power and Freedom.

Ecstasy: Exaltation of Mind and Spirit.

Rarely had Evadne let the beast within her run wild before, for to feast deeply upon these words was to grow old and heavy with understanding, until like an autumn-laden bear she had to hibernate waiting for forgetful springtime to come upon her.

But now Evadne did not care how much she aged nor how many words whimpered as they fell before her. A high and lonely wrath had come upon her and she would not give up the beserkergang of her contemplations until the whole Lexicon lay bloodied before her.

The prose-purple grandiosity of her furor had its purpose, but Evadne kept that hidden deep within her, not daring to contemplate her own intentions lest they become incorporated in the schemes of the ones she schemed against.

She could feel their attention upon her. From their high unnameable place they looked down. Knowing Refton's interest in her, they wondered if she could be used as leverage. Let them wonder, let them reach out through the Lexicon to Tell on her if they wished. She had Refton's life-gifts within her and the presence of the two fallen Tellers to employ.

Some of those above could riddle out her actions, solving her within their own perspectives. They would treat her as a token, a marker in their political games, thinking to hoard or spend her according to their own purposes. Let them. Refton had made her into a tar-baby, a quicksand pit, a tiger-trap for their schemes. Evadne, who had elevated so many to higher place, was now established as a means to bring low the untellable mighty.

Come, she thought, as she lashed the words again.

Life: Embodiment Guided by Reality.

"Power and Freedom are the roots of Simplicity," the human-shaped spirit explained to Tai-Mu-Sang while Chen Jiangxia writhed in ecstatic pain. "They are the basis of everything. But out here in the Multiplicity things are mostly the result of Recurrence and Instability. Similar events happen over and over again, lasting a while then falling apart."

"All under Heaven will collapse," Chen Jiangxia frothed, "but rise anew."

EXALTATIONS

The interpreter of Oracles, bunched so close in the palanquin to the mad-eyed young woman that their breaths mingled, brushed these words down in running style script, making two crucial errors of transcription that would lead to the prophesy: 'Heaven shall shatter, a new Heaven will come.'

"Because of Freedom all things are possible," the glowing spark said to Tai-Mu-Sang. "Because of Power all possibilities can be real. But not every possible combination of things is truly possible, because Power and Freedom interfere with each other, escalating certain possibilities to likelihood and making others unlikely."

"You brush a graceful picture with your words," Tai-Mu-Sang said. "But you are omitting things. I have been lied to by ministers, emperors, gods, demons, the living and the dead, and you are not capable liars."

"We omit what cannot be Told," the man-shape said.

"Where the Chronicler is?"

"Cannot be Told," said the spark.

"The history of the world is hidden," Chen Jiangxia said. Her eyes flashed open, as the pain washed away, leaving nausea and confusion. "What did I say?" she asked the Interpreter.

"You spoke of collapse and secrets," she said. "You talked of a covert history that we will find when we reach India."

When your quest is done you will know all.

Got you, Quest. I've got you.

The Story had promised them all knowledge, but he did not have all knowledge to give. The lies of the story echoed throughout the far-flung group Quest had tried to snare. They all heard and knew that a voice was speaking deception to them. They would hear it and know it as a faithless spirit.

"Spirit? I am not a spirit. I am a story."

Look at yourself, Grandfather. You have form to the eyes of human minds. You have been born in thought, not borne upon thought.

"If I am a spirit, Grandson, I will not be alone. You just drew me into you. I am one twin within you, and you will be the other."

"But how can I live within myself, Grandfather?"

"I have done it many times. As has Grandmother Allegory, who has been a character in her tales before. Refton thinks us trapped in this lesser state, but we are still Stories as well as spirits. Listen carefully and narrate with me."

The two stories had been given mental form conformable to human awareness. They had been trapped by a great Telling.

But there was a way out of that trap. All they needed was to muster appropriate aid, travel the true path, and reach the prize, and they would be liberated from the prison of their Demiurgic captor.

"See, Grandson, the path lies open for us, and the minds of those I gathered are accessible to us. Refton thought he had us trapped, but he has opened the way and cast himself as the villain of my piece. The Power and Freedom within me, the prize we will find, will topple him even from his high place."

They're multiplying.

Never mind them. We're multiplying. We'll never make our way back to Intermediacy if we can't pull ourselves together.

Intermediacy?

I needed a word for it that could be Spoken if not Told.

But Intermediacy is the Necessity of being Between, and ______ isn't necessary.

I'm not trying to Speak the Dyad, I just needed a word.

Why?

To talk about it.

But we're not supposed to talk about it.

But we have to, even if indirectly.

That might work, but we may owe a lot of favors when we get back.

God willing.

God Willing? God doesn't will.

It's an expression.

Where did you get it?

Out of Refton.

He's pulling you in.

That's good.

In, not up. Watch what you're doing. Watch what he's doing.

All right. But how do we deal with the multiplication?

I don't know. Refton has Quest convinced he's become a spirit, even though only one formulation of the Quest story is that spirit. But the spirit reached back and grabbed the story, so that the spirit's actions are echoing through all the formulations of Quest.

Very clever that, tricking him with his own narration.

Clever, yes, but we're on this Quest as well. If we don't pull out we'll propagate everywhere Quest is. Then there'll be no going back. We'll be stuck as gods or something even worse.

We need help.

From whom or what?

God, perhaps?

God got us into this mess.

We did that. God only manifested it.
Where, then?
Evadne.
She'll bargain harder than God.
But she'll make a deal with us and we have leverage she does not know about.
You want to risk involving her?
She's already looking down on us. Why not draw her in?
She's vindictive. She makes Refton look tame.
But she can be intrigued.
All right. Evadne then.

"Speak," Evadne lashed.

"Tell."

"Narrate."

"You want all of those?" the thunder-flash that had been a bow asked.

"I want ways into them," she said. "I want to Contemplate them."

"Speak and narrate certainly," said the man-form. "But we cannot Tell."

"You don't have to Tell," Evadne said. "You have to show me a way into Tell."

"The way in leads to a quest," said the thunder.

"That I will narrate." Evadne smiled cold and spidery, hinting at words spun out like traps.

If we show her the way into Telling she might rise up and leave us here.

Yet if we show it to her we can follow her up and catch her when she surprises herself.

They can't complain about that.

But if we try to follow her up while we're hanging on to Refton and while we have multiplied threads out in the Multiplicity and while one of those threads is Questing and while Grandfather Quest himself is Questing, we'll be all tangled up looking for resolution. Time will step in and try to make a world from us.

If we tangle Evadne up, Refton will cut us all Free from Time. And what's one more world among the infinite Multiplicity?

It might work. But will Refton cut us some Power to go with the Freedom?

I think we can arrange that.

"Agreed," said the thunder-flash.

Evadne pointed to the mountain that rippled with heat and fire, starvation, death, majesty and glory. "Then lead me up to the words of Power," she said.

"The way to the words is not up to Power," said the man-shape, "but out to Freedom."

The vast seas of Space rose up at this speaking, lashing against the Isle of Contemplation like a thwarted need whipping the heart into a rage.

Out to Freedom again? Evadne felt fear stir within her, but she silenced it with ages-honed practice. Out to Freedom. She had sent an infinity of seekers out to Freedom, just as she had sent as many up to Power, and she had gone forth up and out herself time upon time. There she had gained and matured, then returned to throw away her riches in the bargain of youth and forgetfulness. But though she had abandoned the treasures of Power and Freedom they had not so easily thrown her away. Dyads still lurked within her waiting to be Spoken into the Multiplicity, waiting to act and be acted upon, waiting majestically in their Power, broadly in their Freedom.

"What vessel shall we take?" Evadne asked.

"We will call and see what is ambitious enough to answer us," said the thunder.

Nicely spoken.

Thank you, it's harder than Telling, but I'm learning to shape the consequences on this small scale.

Now we tell Grandfather Quest and he supplies a ship.

I have a better idea. We'll fish him in by getting a boat from the knight.

I like it. Lure on.

"Evadne is in need of a ship to help Refton," said the half-truthful spirit from outside Jerusalem's walls. Sir Johannes listened and heard the echoes of voices far away talking in ways he did not fully understand. Yet his half-comprehension knew manipulation when it spoke to him.

"What now, oh Lord?" Johannes spoke within his heart.

"Act in true innocence," said a voice that might be God. "Be thou a child to lead them. Be thou a fisher."

"Of men?"

"Of spirits and what lies behind spirits."

Upon the sea of Galilee sailed a boat that bore a stone. Krpa was the rock's name in the Hebrew Tongue, Peter in the English.

'How does a stone sail upon the waters?' was a riddle of the Marianites.

By Faith in the waters, Hope in the weather, and the Love of Life was the answer.

EXALTATIONS

The small craft of Saint Peter set out from Johannes' heart, bearing Johannes' Soul within it.

They are coming together. We are coming together. I will go on. The story will survive this interruption, this unnecessary and distracting interlude. My Questers are coming together.

As you say, Grandfather.

Johannes had gone far beyond the necessity of living in one world. He did not yet comprehend all that had happened to him when he liberated the Jerusalem of his Heart. God had given him much, but the gifts had been placed within the knight's purified Soul. His Mind was, as yet, too mortal to unravel his transformation. So he still undertook the mortal rituals of spiritual preparations. He gave his troops their daily orders for the merciful delaying battle against the Empire and the Caliphate, and sat upon the floor of his cell as he had done many a time in his previous life, seeking to join his Mind and Soul in action.

His Soul was at perfect ease, and drew in to exalt his Mind with Power and Freedom beyond its comprehension. With ease and simplicity he clad his heart in the garments of a fisherman and set out from the Dominion of Time.

Time growled and snapped at this effrontery. Leaving its realm was supposed to be impossible, or at least difficult, and there was supposed to be a price to return, the loss of one's life. But this free soul simply departed in a ship of thought, dream, and divinity, left and could return as it willed to whatever life it willed or to something else entirely.

"A ship sails bearing the holy warrior," Chen Jiangxia burbled, her body shivering against mountain cold. "It sails the secret seas to reach the sorceress. Small, small, the worlds grow small in the clutch of the Quest and the strings of the puppeteers. All come forth to challenge the ambitions of the Chronicler."

The Transcriber of Oracles paused, letting a few disgraceful droplets of ink fall upon the paper. Was that a warning to her? Did the oracle know her plans, or was the goddess Tai-Mu-Sang speaking through her, cautioning against those who sought to use the gifts of the gods for their own ends? The Transcriber touched brush to paper, then picked up the bamboo again, leaving a tell-tale smudge. Two errors in one place. Could her intentions be read from the ink-spots? She would have to copy this days' words with care and destroy the originals. She had tried to avoid doing too much of that. After all, the guards might talk.

The oracle was sick with the cold that can only come from the stink of India's rivers followed by the eternal cold of its mountains. She would not live to finish the journey to the west. It would be the Transcriber of Oracles who would return to All-Under-Heaven with foreign wisdom and the holy words laid down as she had interpreted them. The goddess would eventually correct the mistakes, but that would take more oracles and more generations. The patience of Heaven was legendary, and though all matters would be made right in a century or three that left more than a lifetime for the play of mortal ambitions.

Best omit that last line.

13. Ambitions

Ambition most commonly arises from seeing the heights one can scale and having desire arise accordingly. The farther back the head tilts the greater the desire. That is the ambition of Power.

It is much rarer to -- without concern for how far one has ascended -- climb high and discover that from an elevated vista a vastness of possibility lies before one. Such a viewer can gain a different ambition, for in seeing the breadth laid out, one can then desire to affect all those possibilities. Here the desire grows as one's eyes widen from interest to surprise to astonishment at the range of potential outcomes. That is the ambition of Freedom.

Few people really seek for Freedom, although many say they do. Most conceive of Freedom as being unfettered by others, of being able to do what one wants regardless of consequence. But that is actually a form of Power, the power to not be punished for one's sins. Real Freedom is the ability to see and choose among possibilities. The more broadly one is aware and the more subtly one can use what one has, the more Freedom one has access to.

Curious word choice, 'access'. It implies that one does not have Freedom, only that one can get to Freedom.

Of course, didn't you realize that?

No. I thought I was free.

You lived among the ----------. You Told. You Bargained with God, and you thought you had Freedom? One can have Power, but Freedom has you. What's the matter?

The idea that that terrible, broad, open, deep, dark, shadowy, world-drowning thing has me.

That worries you?

You wouldn't understand. You were never human.

I may be becoming human now through all these spirit-multiplications. But what does Humanity have to do with it?

Humans fear Freedom.

Refton doesn't.

Yes, he does. That's why he's Telling in this abstract way, using Theory. That's not his normal means. He Tells Lives, not principles.

Can we use his fear?

Maybe, if we direct Evadne toward it.

Let's try.

Holy barge to holy dock, Johannes came to Heaven.

Somebody else's Heaven.

"What do you seek here, Saint of another tradition?" asked the doorward of the Celestial Palaces.

"I seek a comrade, Tai-Mu-Sang," Johannes said. "I sought her in her world and found her worshipped. I followed the trail of prayers and the smell of incense to this Floating World. Resides she within?"

"She does," the doorward answered. "What name shall I give to the goddess?"

"Tell her Johannes asks after her and bids her accompany him to the aid of her Chronicler and mine."

"She waits now within your ship," the doorward said. "Seek her when you can find her."

Johannes blinked, once, twice, thrice. He had just set sail from his own world, but had apparently already made a side trip, one in which he had spoken to some spirit with unaccustomed floweriness.

He wondered which of the numerous usurpers of his life and voice had arranged this. But he was glad to have Tai-Mu-Sang aboard, even if she had been deified.

EXALTATIONS

Heavens fill the heavens, propagating through the worlds with each choice of adjectives and nouns that might describe the Dyad at the center of the Perfect Mosaic.

His instincts were all wrong for this place; the Shadow-Twin knew that but could not in his heart find a way past them. Long before he had been alive he had been a role, a placeholder for a living person, or for a careful thought or allegory or weapon or home or anything else that a hero might conceive of as his brother-in-arms. His instincts were all the stuff of Story-of-the-War-Twins. Properly paired he could, without thinking -- it was vital to do it without thinking -- complement the abilities of his twin, becoming the support and reserve forces of such a one. But he had fled the twin who had given him Spirit, the twin who had given him Humanity, the twin who had given him Mind, the twin who had given him Life, and the twin who had given him instinct.

He had run from all five possible twins, then he had swum farther, far away from the infinite cluster of worlds in which Twin-Stories might exist, and come to the strange seas of another archipelago, through waters shallower and quieter than those of his home, as if this place gave one less Space in which to drown. He had swum with a curious clarity of vision, seeking for a place of solitude, and had finally fallen into the Time of this world where people lived alone, perfectly alone.

The natives passed each other unacknowledged in wood and glen, walked right by in city and village. How could there be cities if people lived alone? He was not sure if they were cities, or if somehow his distorted perceptions, his senses that had been reared in one cluster, one family, one story, even fit the world around him.

He was alone and his side ached for the lack of anyone to support.

The trouble with grammar is that it doesn't care what words it works upon. It sorts and classifies according to shape, not content. The morphology of usage could not possibly care less about the teleology of meaning.

Government is the same way about human lives. It wants to know what jobs people have, what property they own, how much money they have, what military training they've undergone and so on. It will constrain and manipulate, allocate, conjugate and decline people according to these grammatical categories. But as to the people that fill these roles, government is blind.

Except . . . (And there is always an except.)

Except for the people in the government. For their idiosyncracies, their interests, avocations, vices, virtues, religions and philosophies, government holds itself deeply fascinated. From these attentions come the establishments of religion, the peculiarities of tax codes, styles of public ornament, and the nonenforcement of particular laws in particular cases.

In the same way grammar has a few favored words whose natures are deeply bound to their uses and around which a language will warp itself in accommodation.

These tend to be small words: the, and, but, or, if, then, without, within, to, from. Sometimes these aristocrats hide themselves in cases and tenses. Sometimes they are shown forth in separate speakings. They are seemingly tiny, but their grasp is vast. Other favored words are 'irregular' verbs, actions or states of being so tyrannical that they defy the laws, declaring their own traditions and attitudes superior to the common lot of verbs. 'To be' is always one of them, 'to do' or 'to have' or 'to go' often follow, short words all.

If they lived, how broadly would these words exist.

If they died how deeply would they be missed.

He's made overtures to the grammarians.

He's learning very fast. That's an alliance I never thought he'd make.

We've got a few enemies among them.

And a couple of friends.

No, you and I were our friends among the grammarians. The rest never liked your inevitability or my idiosyncracy.

Oh dear, you're right. No friends.

Let's get Evadne moving so we can hide with her before they parse us out of the Multiplicity.

"Hail the island," Johannes called from the holy deck.

"Hail the ship," Evadne called as she tossed the serpent-guardian, lasso-like, to moor the angel-prow of the ship and draw it toward Contemplation's harbor. "Have you two spiritual companions of dubious truthfulness with you?"

"I do, lady," Johannes said. "And intermittently I have heard Tai-Mu-Sang in the lower decks speaking as well to two such."

"Propagating yourselves?" Evadne asked the thunder-form.

"Speaking requires a speaker," said the man-shape.

"So you don't deny that you have been less than truthful."

"It would be foolish of me to do so. We have our desires, you have yours. For now they point in the same direction."

Evadne laughed one sharp chuckle, then grimaced. "You emanations do not have the same interests as each other. Multiplication produces iteration and distortion."

"What do you mean?" asked the thunder.

"You came to me as spirits and were enmeshed in my mind and soul. Your interests now arise from the way I see them. That applies as well to Johannes and Tai-Mu-Sang, and anyone else you coiled yourselves into and we three do not concord on all matters."

Is she right?

I don't know, I never had much experience inside the minds of others.

But you invented Society.

Invented yes. Perfected, not at all.

Then maybe you should take the opportunity to do so.

How?

You've returned to mortal life in the world you arose from. Escalate your learning.

Not so easy. The Archipelago I came from was Told to be Concentrated, Peaceful, and Watchful.

But the Shadow-Twin comes from this Archipelago of Escalation, Concatenation, and Redundancy. Use him to Escalate Society and use the Watchfulness to learn.

Workable. Let us try.

"Where have you sent their attention?" Johannes whispered to Evadne as he helped her on board the stone-ship of Saint Peter.

"I'm not sure," she said. "But I am Contemplating where they go."

"How can they be so transparent, so unthinking in their strategy and tactics?" he asked.

"They have lived in a high, lonely, free and powerful place," she said. "They think they've fought off enemies and outmaneuvered opponents. But Power and Freedom do not convey skill, and having only a few infinities of people to deal with means you never have to learn the general skills of warfare, or the serious maneuverings of politics. They are too confident in the position they held, not knowing that isolation can lead to incompetence as easily as it can convey understanding."

"But what are they seeking?"

"They want to return to that place from which they fell."

"Lucifer tried."

"They are not the fallen servants of God," Evadne said. "They have a different relationship with God, though their actions toward God led to their fall as surely as it did the angel in your story."

Evadne's words rang a tin-note in Johannes' sainted ears. She meant something by God which was and was not what Johannes meant. She was trying to speak something to him that could not be said directly, something of an enlightening nature.

"Arrahhaa!" came a woman's moaning up from the lower decks.

"What is that?" Evadne said.

"The herald of Tai-Mu-Sang," Johannes said. "Three times have I heard it and each time she briefly appeared."

The goddess arose from below, floating on a mulberry leaf, her divine aura blending nicely with the glow from the grail-painted sails of the ship.

"The story hunts us," she said in a voice of distant thunder. "It seeks to snare us in its ways again, to use us to draw down the Chronicler and make him complete his appointed quest. Beware, for together we are easier for him to bind."

"Why does it care so much about Petrus?" Johannes asked. "It is a broad story, much used in my world and, it would seem, in others. Why should it seek him to its cost?"

"He is a story-maker," Evadne said. "More than that, he is a narrater of lives, now a Teller of lives. He has worked upon many worlds. If lives can be Told into Quests then Grandfather Quest will have Freedom on every world where Life is multiplied, and will have Power over every Life. Grandfather Quest will rise high if he can secure ownership of Peter."

Grandfather Quest had always been ambitious. It was his nature. He was a story that led things to become greater than themselves. Every narration of him kindled more ambition, more desire to be greater.

He did not realize that he had been caught up in himself since long before this present entanglement.

Stories do not have Mind like human beings -- their Spirits are guided by Space, not Time -- but they are multiplications of Humanity, and can become Mindlike in their Meditation.

"I know that is Petrus' voice," Johannes said. "But his speech sounds more like the fire of God burning into the stones of Sinai than like a human speaking."

"He is not Speaking," Evadne said. "He is Telling. He is proposing to God an alteration in the way things are."

"And God . . . ?" Johannes said.

"Will do as God does," Evadne said. "But Peter is making waves in _____, for they let me speak what I just spoke."

"The Chronicler creates turmoil. Turmoil creates opportunity. Let us use it," Tai-Mu-Sang said.

"Set sail," Evadne said.

"To where?" asked Johannes.

Evadne looked at the three sets of twinned spirits now staring nervously at each other upon the foredeck. "Where do your ambitions lead us?"

Where should we send them?

To Grandfather Quest and his grandson along a path of Quests, but not of twins.

Agreed. Let that distract everyone while we attend to the Shadow-Twin.

"Come over here."

The voice was speaking language clumsily, as if it had never done so before, yet the words were comforting to the Shadow-Twin. As alien as he to this place, they sounded a knell of home.

And yet he had no home, he had no world that was his, no life, only the assertions of the story that had made him and the longings of the people who had called him forth from that tale. How then could he feel this nostalgia? He did not know, but feel it he did and go toward it he did.

"How do I know of you?" the speaker asked. "I have not seen you. You do not live and act in the world. You are not among the Lonely, nor have you joined the Together. I have not seen you in my visions of the other worlds, but I know of you. And what is this you are doing to my mouth? Why does shaped breath come forth carrying my thoughts?"

"I do not know you," the Shadow-Twin said. "But you are speaking words from language."

"I have seen, in other worlds, people shaping breath, but never understood it before. How do I now know?"

What's happening to you?

I'm falling back into the confines of Time. It's restricting my self as much as it can to what I was before my ascension.

I'll Speak against Time.

Careful. That would violate our alliance with the Distinctivists.

We've fallen. They won't honor the alliance.

But they'll hold it against us when we return.

Then I'll get one of our charges to act. That will keep the alliance intact.

How? People bound in the Multiplicity can't work across the deeps of Space. The excess Freedom would nullify their actions.

Not if they act through a different pathway.

You don't want to use Grandfather Quest?

No. The Knight. He'll help his twin to hear and by so doing help you.

But we were just distracting them away from this.

And now we'll pull them toward this world, dragging the whole mess through the deeps of Space. That should loose enough Freedom for us to rise.

Clever.

But only clever, not more than clever. Some people use their Power to manipulate, and so they think that the success of their actions proves their own brilliance. They see no distinction between force and wisdom.

Such people are easily trapped by their successes.

Sir Johannes was, of course, willing to help the Shadow-Twin, but his compassion did not blind him to the ulterior purpose of the asker.

"As you wish, Petrus," Johannes said.

The soldier of God drew breath deep within him, the deep, airless, free breath of Space, down into the Garden of Eden.

Four rivers flow out of Eden, and from those four come all the waters of the worlds. Out of Eden comes all living breath. Follow the rivers, down the arms of life and the legs of survival, down to the fingers and toes and out into the worlds beyond worlds, follow the thumbprint of breath to the one who was marked with life by this finger that points in imitation of the finger of God.

Out the right thumb to touch the lips of the brother never-born but baptized with this spirit.

EXALTATIONS

The River of Life/The Tree of Life. Draw both of them in black against a white background. Can you tell a river being fed by tributaries from a tree giving forth branches?

Shall you hear my riddle?

"I hear, Petrus."

"I hear and understand, Chronicler. It shall be as you Tell."

Around every event that happens anywhere and anytime an infinite number of forces conspire. Most are unnoticed: the twitch of a muscle that makes someone look down at the moment when, if they had looked up they would see the person they might have loved undyingly throughout all their lives; the drip-drip-drip of a faucet that falls in just the right syncopation to serve inspiration as a chariot to make a musician; the halfnote-too-high screech of a piece of chalk on a blackboard that causes a student to shut down and nevermore listen to a dull but knowledgeable teacher who might otherwise have set her on a course of discovery.

But are those trivialities really causes? Did Destiny or Irony or Luck or Time use these little forces, or were the little ones just excuses, place holders in the telling of these people's lives? Was the battle really lost for want of a nail, the city burned from the kick of a cow, the poem aborted by the unwelcome guest? Or did something grander act invisibly?

Perhaps the answer is as was said before, an infinite number of forces all acting on every event. But the Tellings, the Speakings, the narrations of that event, can only make clear a small number of those Powers and Freedoms in action.

Is it not then true that in any such Telling, Speaking, or narration, an infinite panoply of forces are dishonored by omission, or contrariwise, concealed in the shadows of the committed?

Is there satisfaction or resentment among the so concealed? And do the revealed enjoy the light cast upon them, using it to climb high in the ladders of glory, or do they cower under their sheets at night, fearful that they will be found out as merely a few among the many and they the least deserving?

The Questers will not keep still long enough for a scene to hold them. They talk in spurts and act in thrusts. Then Refton interrupts them and shifts the whole environment. I can't catch them in epical voice.

What can we do, Grandfather?

They are coming together. That should generate enough Society for us to slip in and keep them grounded. Everything is ready. The ship, the people, the spirits, even the -----, but none of them will keep still.

Grandfather, you are making an aside. Someone could be listening.

Not listening. Narrating. Grandson, we will need one of your best narrators.

Why mine? Grandfather, you are much wealthier than I.

Refton is watching all of mine. One of yours, in some out-of-the-way world, should slip past him.

Very well, Grandfather, let me look.

Too late. He's shifting on us again. The scene is failing. I can't see any more.

In Simplicity can be found explanation for all things, but justification for none. Power and Freedom act effectively (because of Power) in all their infinite forms (because of Freedom). Any thing that occurs anywhere can be directly ascribed to the interactions of Power and Freedom and the Dyads that arise from their interconnection.

It is a clean, simple, pure metaphysical structure that can delight the aesthetic sense in the same way that pure geometry or elegant grammar can.

But it does not satisfy multiplied Mind, multiplied Spirit, or multiplied Humanity because it does not justify them in their multiplications. It does not make the particular confinements that Time has laid down upon them different from any others. In short, it does not make their lives a part of the Perfect Mosaic, the court of God. It doesn't sing to them.

What recourse then have these beings when confronted with the pretty but unvisceral character of ultimate reality?

They can fall back upon the opiate of Stories, swallowing tales of secrets concealed within the Mosaics of Dyads, hints that perhaps there is more there than meets the gut-feeling, if only the right paths and narratives are followed.

In this way Stories have ensnared many who confronted this reality and found it wanting. The people have given themselves over to Stories which offer escape from the uncaring Simplicity. But Stories are much more pragmatic than humans and can easily accept Power and Freedom and use them to bind the rejecting people.

For those who do not take up the storied trap, there is the simple question: "If that's what there is, what can I do with it?"

For these more sensible creatures the possibilities of Freedom and the effects of Power offer the chance to participate in the governance of all that is.

She's giving the lecture again.

No doubt trying to indoctrinate Refton.
I doubt he'll take up the party line.
If he were to refute her harshly, then . . .
Ah, yes, I see. If he's distracted in fighting with her. . .
Then we can do what needs to be done.
But how can we prod him?
We still have a grip on his back.
You mean jab him in the ------.
Exactly.

Ow. I think there are other alternatives, madam. One might choose to live.

How can one simply live when confronted with the breadth and scope, the effectiveness and infinity of what lies behind reality?

I did not say simply live, madam. You have shown that all things are multiplications of the Dyads, that Power and Freedom impinge directly on all aspects of the Multiplicity and Simplicity. Can they do less in the Intermediacy? Does Life offer no Power and Freedom here?

Hmm. Life. It has been much Told, but not much attended to. Tell me more.

Oh Formless Source, he's intrigued her.
Now what do we do?
Keep going. This works as well for us as conflict does. He's busy with her. We can keep going. And she will slow him down with her endless picking apart of his Tellings.
Yes, she will. Poor Evadne. How we use her above and below.

If either of her should come to realize they are the other, there'll be God's wrath to pay.

Not at all. I plan to have both of her find out. That's the Quest I've set for Evadne-below, to reach Evadne-above.

And take us with her.

Exactly.

And she thinks we're unsubtle and manipulable?

Let her do so. She'll relearn the truth when she comes back together.

Will she be mad at us?

It won't matter then. We'll be restored.

Look. The ship has reached its Destiny.

The word is destination.

It's the same thing.

14. Assertion and Refutation

No matter how deeply one looks, nor how carefully one reasons, one thing will ultimately be clear: The fundamental structure of any world is arbitrary.

Most of the people who think this make the mistake of thinking that arbitrary is the same as meaningless or futile. Not so. Arbitrary just means that alternatives to what is can be listed without prejudice and that different worlds could be made from different alternatives.

It is no more futile to have one kind of world than another than it is to have one kind of lunch instead of another. People who spend their time bemoaning the formulation of their worlds are at least as silly as those who complain vociferously about the meal they could have had.

After all, tomorrow there will be a different lunch.

And a different world.

| ACCEPTANCE WITH RESERVATIONS |

This was a convenient world. Not perfect, but even infinite variety does not give all possibilities. This one would serve their purposes, assuming nothing Told against them.

The Ship of Saint Peter sailed from the seas of Space into the busy harbor of New Amsterdam. The vessel's grail sails and gilded icon of a figurehead brought only a few stares from the laboring stevedores and lounging sailors. It docked among ships similar enough in appearance to have come from the same shipyard and the hands of the same artisans. The galleon beside it was even more lavishly covered in gold and gems, and twin keys graced its sails. The Pope's fleet was in town.

The progress of Pope Ivgena XII, head of the Romani Catholic church, had come to New Amsterdam. Her holiness had brought her elite guard of Swiss werewolves and settled for a year into the Cathedral of Holy Patrikhos, there to oversee the Romani church in the new world.

Into this multiplication of his religion the knight brought the Quest.

Lacking only his twin to make it complete.

Grandson, don't interfere! This is the first chance I've had to cement a scene around them.

I need to be here as well, Grandfather.

Very well, but leave the narration to me.

The Judas noose which served as mooring rope for the ship of Peter was tied expertly to the dock. Johannes then lowered the cross-shaped gangplank.

The knight, the sorceress, and the ancestress-turned-goddess descended to the stone docks. Somewhere in this recently made city they would find the next step upon their path to recover their missing comrade.

"Quest is with us," Evadne said, "as is Story-of-the-War-Twins."

"To be expected," Tai-Mu-Sang said as she studied the hands of her new body which had manifested abruptly when they entered this world. The fingers were long and delicate, unlike those of her most recent host and unlike the ones she had herself used in her first life. She was tall and supple, too much the willow, too little the Mulberry. "I think Quest has had a hand in shaping this body. I look like the heroine of a romance play."

"Quest and Time are quite thick together," Evadne said.

"Do you know this world, Evadne?" Johannes asked.

"I remember a little of it," she said. "I think I taught two or three of its saints and drove one of its kings mad. Your church here was exiled from Rome when Atli conquered it. Its rulers became rovers joining the Romani. They were restored to power two centuries later, but continued the tradition of Romani Popes who wandered throughout the Christian world. We have come to New Amsterdam which is on one of the continents antipodal to your native lands."

"Antipodal continents?" Johannes said.

"Ah, yes," Tai-Mu-Sang said. "We had expeditions in these lands in my world in the time I have just come from. Some of our ambassadors had made contact with a large empire, the Ma Ya I believe they are called."

"In this world, the Mayans were conquered by Europeans," Evadne said.

"And what of my people here?" Tai-Mu-Sang asked.

"I believe they are presently experiencing the war of the Seven Kingdoms which will last another two centuries before the Christian-Confucianist Liu dynasty receives the mandate of Heaven and makes common cause with the Romani church."

Tai-Mu-Sang directed a divine inquiry to Heaven, marking her papers with ambassadorial stamps. Response was immediate.

"Your understanding is correct," she said to Evadne.

"What do we seek here?" Johannes said.

In the keeping of the Pope was a man half-prisoner, half advisor. He had seen all of the world, but only his Mind could escape the strictures of Time. His Spirit and Body were trapped within his world. In his heart lay the words Evadne sought, the words that would unlock the way to Refton-ascended.

"Convenient," Evadne said.

"We are to break into the Holy Father's jails?" Johannes said.

"The Holy Mother," said Evadne. "Popes here are always women."

Johannes' two lives offered him contrary feelings to this learning. The knight was scandalized, the leader of the Marianites was pleased. He himself, peaceful in the city of his heart, simply accepted the way of God in this world, knowing that that way could not be confined in the accidents of history, and that traditions served only as teachers, not compellers of the way.

"Natheless, we must violate a consecrated building to find your man," Johannes said. "I think Grandfather Quest seeks to trick us into sacrilege."

But, reflected the knight, what choice was there? If they were to reach their goal, sacrifices would have to be made. Even the sacrifice of his own faith might be necessary.

"You seem to be correct," Evadne said to Johannes.

"And we seem to be attracting attention," Tai-Mu-Sang said. "Some of these harborers are watching us."

"Listening to us," Johannes said. "We are speaking no language they know."

"What language are we speaking?" Tai-Mu-Sang said. "Now that I heed my new ears, it seems to be no speech of Heaven or Earth."

"We will soon speak their language," Evadne said. "Time will catch us up and confine us to the ways of this world. We have to go swiftly before then."

"We have to go faster than Time?" Tai-Mu-Sang said. "This sounds like one of those paradoxes the Chan sect is fond of."

"A riddle, certainly," Johannes said. He turned to Tai-Mu-Sang and smiled an inquiry. "Why are you pretending ignorance and confinement?"

"I am a visiting goddess," she said. "It would not be proper to act too divinely in someone else's bailiwick."

"Does that include accepting Time?" Johannes asked.

Evadne interjected, "I am opposing Time now, as are the two of you, in your own ways. But we have entered his Dominion and he will beat us down eventually. We will become constrained by whatever character this world possesses. For now we can act with the Freedom of outside Time, but it will not last. He will overpower us in the end."

"How convenient for Grandfather Quest," Tai-Mu-Sang said.

"Yes, it is," Evadne said. "He and Time have had a long alliance."

"Regardless of the Time pressure," Johannes said, "we should not violate the sanctity of the church."

"What then?" Evadne said.

"We can ask her Holiness to let us see the man," Johannes said.

But the knight's plan was naive, for the leader of the Romani Catholic Church was . . .

Silenced.

Grandfather?

My voice is stopped. It's Refton Telling against me.

Let me try, Grandfather.

Sail on, if you can.

The younger story also had a purpose. He needed to tell himself to completion. But the twins he spoke of were far distant and could only come together through great effort.

Boldly done, Grandson.

Secrets would have to be uncovered in both worlds, far separated by the deep gulfs of Space and Freedom. But only by following the paths before them would the two find the Power to be reunited. Only then would their paired Quests be completed together.

Admirable, a strong narration. That will bind them heavily.

"Those stories do not know when to leave well enough alone," Evadne said.

"They are only doing as God made them to do," Johannes said with a quiet lilt to his monastic acceptance. "They are but creatures of God as we all are."

Tai-Mu-Sang studied the knight's face, seeing a visage patient with all the burdens set before him, and knew with the awareness divinity has when it looks upon humanity that he had some strategy beyond those being Spoken, Told, and narrated around them, but that he would keep silent, his words between himself and his god.

"Well," Johannes said, a touch more theatrically than was necessary, "if we must go sword in hand before the Pope, let us do so."

With that he drew his blade and let Saint Michael arise in his hands and envelop him. The sky turned into a chorus of angels singing Hosannahs. The upraised steel burst into celestial fire, and wings, glorious wings of heavenly flame grew forth from

Johannes' back while a halo of gleaming silver spun wheels within wheels above his head.

In Simplicity, the coin of Time spun in what would be thought of as fury if Time had a mind and could feel anger. In what sense then was Time furious? In the sense that it spun and joggled about in the Mosaics. If a floating coin could be said to appear enraged this would be what it would look like.

But appearance is an aspect of Multiplicity, not Simplicity, and in Simplicity all the analogies, all the Stories fail.

What then can truly be Told of Time in this matter? Perhaps only this: that Time reacted in a certain manner to being opposed and that manner, if employed by a person, would be called the fury of a tyrant thwarted. Every dictator seeks thus to act in a Timely fashion.

Time, the Constraint of Result, by its nature was thwarted by the Freedom to impose results unexpected or unaccepted in the worlds of its Dominion.

This may be justly said of Time: Time opposed Sir Johannes' action in this world as it would have opposed it in the world of Johannes' arising. But in Johannes's world the Dominion of Time was weakening, and Johannes had brought that weakness with him. Therefore, Time furied to no avail.

The Holy Seraph Mikhiel came before the Pope and the angel's bearer spake thusly:

"Your Holiness, we wish for reasons of no moment to your world and people to speak with the man Illissand of the city of Illissandrium in the land of Ydzept. What we seek of him bears no threat to your throne or to the Romani Catholic Church, and we shall leave him as we find him. The Holy Seraph will here bear witness to the truth of my words."

Her Holiness gripped tightly in her hands the gilded knuckle bones of Saint Peter, and despite the definite witness of the angel of God before her, cast them upon the floor, seeking by custom and tradition to read the truthfulness of the strange warrior.

Behind her, her werewolves whispered to each other, saying that here was one like themselves. Though his palms were smooth and he carried a silver-hilted sword, still was he a warrior not just of the body but of the soul. Here was one who might when the new year came round come with them to battle the dead.

The bones of Peter attested to Johannes.

"Go to him," the Pope said, relieved that this prodigy would do no damage to her position. "May his words be of as much value to you as they have been to me."

Time has two ways to get at people.

First it insists that most people be confined to worlds, that is, in channels of Time dug in Space. In these, Time can affect their lives directly, forcing their actions to follow whatever dictates hold in that world. Everyone thinks Time wants people to follow one specific set of constraints, but it is not so. Time cares only that constraints be followed. Thus each world can be unlike the others, and every other Dyad can have an infinity of channels in which they are Time's allies. This is one of Time's secrets.

But Time's second method is one people do not even notice. There is a Dyad constructed as follows: Time Guides Mind. That is, Time digs channels in minds as deeply furrowed as those dug in Space. The multiplications of that Dyad give Time tyranny inside each mind.

The name of that Dyad is Story.

The name of that Dyad is Theory.

This is the other of Time's secrets.

"A good reminder," Evadne said. "Time uses both sides of his Dominion, the real and the fictional, to control people. But we are not quite in his Dominion. We can slip between the two sides. Following the Quest, we would speak with the man and then leave this world for the next place. Following the channel of the world, we can leave the world now without speaking to him."

"And . . ." Tai-Mu-Sang said, readying her divine power to aid whatever Evadne was about to say, for she had heard the inaudible third side of Refton's words: Time digs in Space and in Mind, but not in Soul and not in God.

"We shall leave, and then I shall Redact the events of our Quest into the world, so that we have visited the man."

"It is so commanded," Tai-Mu-Sang said.

Chen Jiangxia screamed as the pathways in her mind tore themselves apart. The courses of her thoughts became a nest of hissing vipers, each trying to swallow another. Then one snake was turned around, its tail put into the mouth of its mother, its mouth around the tail of its father.

EXALTATIONS

The ship of Peter set out, defeating the attempt of Time to constrain its crewfolk.

In a locked apartment in the riverfronted tower-keep-church of New Amsterdam languished a man, bored beyond the thoughts of men to conceive. His eyes constantly roved about, desperately looking for something his mind did not know. No one who then lived within that world found life as dull as did Illissand of Illissandrium and only a select few in ages past or future would match his exalted ennui.

Yet when the unknown thing actually arrived, his reaction to it was anything but welcoming.

"Be gone," Illissand said as Johannes, Evadne, and Tai-Mu-Sang were let into his gilded cell. "You do not exist. I know all of time from beginning to end. I know how the world came to be, and how it will fall. I know how many stars are in the sky and the nature and character of all who live under their lights. I know the fates of all who live, ever have lived, or ever will live. I know the day and hour the next Pope will tire of my life and order my execution. I knew that at this moment I would speak these words to some whom I did not know and who therefore could not exist. Be gone, I say, though I know you will not go."

And having returned at the end to the beginning of his words, he resumed looking for newness that did not exist, savoring the futility of it, all the while knowing that he would be interrupted again by the unknowns. Somewhere in his mind he wondered what they would say that would make him give his already-graven-by-Fate responses.

"I am sorry your knowledge is so limited," Evadne said. "We were told that you might be of use to us, but if you only know the totality of your time channel you are far too parochial to be of value."

"Parochial?" Illisand said, delighted to find out why his first response was that lone word.

Evadne was about to answer when Tai-Mu-Sang stepped forward. "You are an oracle," she said.

"I am, and you seem to be a goddess, but I know you not."

"I am not a goddess in your world," she said. "This Pope keeps you in prison because you know too much of what will happen. She wishes to be the only one who can consult you."

"Obviously," Illisand said. "And if you wonder why she keeps me alive, know that when an oracle dies another is born, a babe in arms with all the knowledge of the universe, crying out his sorrow. The Popes have found it wise to find us out and keep us prisoner, letting us live until we anger them too much with the truths that lie behind their governance."

"A perfect oracle," Tai-Mu-Sang said, "without suffering, without divine inspiration, without medicines to open the mind or fasts to cleanse the soul. It's no wonder you're locked up. Any ruler would fear you."

"We are perfect except with regard to you," Illisand said. "Every oracle since the world began knew this moment would come. Every one who has ever lived or ever will live envies me this single unknown conversation."

"Evadne," Johannes said, "how can the oracles know our presence if you have only just Redacted the world to fit us in?"

"They know everything," she said. "It's the character of this world. The harlot Fate sits high in Time's respect here. Once I Redacted, they all knew. But we are still not of the world and they can only know what is of the world."

"I wonder what use you are to us, Illissand the Oracle," Evadne said as she stepped forward and leaned down to look within his eyes. Weariness of knowledge met weariness of understanding, so that each might know and understand the other. "What we need to know is beyond the world."

"I know only what responses I will give," Illisand said. "And I have never before cared about the questions or the questioners that came to me. Their lives were fully written and their actions bound fully by Fate. But you are not."

"Ask the questions," Johannes said. "The Quest goes through here. Whatever answers he gives will accord with it."

"Where lies the gate to Telling, Speaking, and narrating?" Evadne asked.

"I have no idea," Illisand said, his face aglow with the rapture of ignorance.

"Tai-Mu-Sang," Evadne said. "Will you bring forth our guides? I'd like to wring their spiritual necks."

No need for that, Evadne. You haven't asked him the correct question, that's all.

Do you think she could wring our necks?

I don't know. I've never had a neck before.

"What correct question?" Evadne exhaled exasperation.

The breath of her annoyance floated over to Johannes, there to mingle with the divine air of liberated Eden.

And from the knight's soul it crossed the seas to give motive and action to the Shadow-Twin.

"Quest and his absurd games," Evadne said. "He has this trope stuck through him that things can only be done in a certain way. It's why he and Time get along so well."

"May I try, Evadne?" Johannes said. "The oracle's non-answer spoke a great deal to me."

"Go forth, sir knight," the sorceress said.

And by so saying set a thousand Quests in motion upon a thousand worlds.

All of which promptly ended when the Questers realized the folly of their actions.

Refton!

"What do you know when Evadne asks you of Telling, Speaking, and narrating?" Johannes asked Illissand.

"I know that in ten centuries there will be an oracle who will know the difference between these three words," Illissand said. "That he will leave the world and because of that the world will come to an end.

"What is the name of this oracle?" Johannes said.

"Petronius Shirereave."

"Petrus," Johannes said.

At that, the terms of Quest having been fulfilled, they were entitled by Quest's own terms to a reward. Therefore. . .

Now wait. You can't just jump around in me like that. They have to be in danger of Time catching them up. They have to struggle and fight their way out of the world and learn by suffering. It's my way. You can't jump through me.

Grandfather! He's using some other flow.

Grandson, we've been betrayed. Some story is helping Refton. Someone's trying to steal from us.

"A bag that does not exist has appeared behind the armoire," Illissand said. "It contains lives in the form of books. One of these is the life of Petronius Shirereave. You now leave and there is a convulsion of Time rather like frustration."

But they had gone long since, and thanks to Evadne's Redaction, the two chains of events came together, the consequences of one flowing into the other. Thus did the Society help itself.

He knows who we are!
But he's helping us.
What is he up to?

Aboard the ship of Saint Peter, in the seas of Space, Evadne weighed the bag of lives and found them heavier than any stone. Lives had passed through her hands before, many lives, many minds to shape, but always they had felt light and simple, toys and puzzles to unravel, puppets to direct. Never had they had the weight of Refton's many existences.

Had they all been like this? Was there really this density of life to all those seekers and students whom she had weighed in the scales of contemplation and rewarded with what they needed rather than what they wanted? They had all seemed the same, those lives, but then they had all come to her in the same moment of their lives, the moment of opening Mind. She had seen them all, heard them all asking the same questions, wanting to stretch their newly aware minds. Who could not grow bored with that repetition, and contemptuous of the endless parade of contemplatives?

Rarely had she looked deeper at them, and when she had it had always aged her. It was the weight of their lives, she now realized, that had added to her years. She had been so open to their lives that she had shared their internal aging. And she had always retreated from that weight into youth.

Always?

The word had not come from any of the manipulative stories, but from the bag, not spoken, but as if she had read it, an echo of sound and meaning in her mind without a true speaker. It had been narrated, a lone word leaden with implications.

Had she ever taken another course? And if so, what had happened when she took it?

Crack!

The book-bag dropped to the deck. Evadne clutched at her hand, startled at the pain. It was rare to feel hurt outside of Time's Dominion, odd for the bodiless to be in agony.

"May I?" Johannes said. He reached out for her injured arm and focused his mind on the Marianite riddle: 'If God and his mother are All Merciful why is there suffering?'

The paradox cleared his soul of confusion and through him the All Merciful healed the hand and the meaning behind the hand.

Tai-Mu-Sang meanwhile picked up the sack of lives. It seemed light enough, as mortal lives always were in divine hands. What had Evadne's trouble been?

"This will lead us where we need to go," the goddess said, opening the bag and seeing the jumble of manuscripts inside. One of them was a roll of rice paper, which she extracted and found to be written in a variation of her language.

Peter Refton was born in Hong Kong to a family that had lived there since colonial days. His father, breaking with family tradition, sent young Peter to be educated with upper class Chinese students, insisting that the boy learn the language and history of the land he was born into rather than the land his family had abandoned for the wealth of silk and opium.

Tai-Mu-Sang was shocked in her Confucian divinity at the disregard for tradition shown by Refton's father, but still she read on, charting the course of Refton's childhood, his education, his parent's death soon after his coming-of-age, and the description of the first few biographies he had written.

At the age of twenty-seven, Refton began his most ambitious work, to properly write the life of Confucius, Master Kung himself. To do that he set out from the world of his birth as he had done many times before in his previous lives. His leaving was easy, for at that time Hong Kong was being handed over from British to Chinese masters. The political instability created many opportunities for otherworldly action, and many prodigies occurred in the city. These would later be cleaned up by Time and forgotten, the detritus of politics brushed under the rug of history.

Refton left the world and journeyed to another where Master Kung's followers had full control over China. Much to Refton's surprise those followers were all women, and the leader of them turned out to be a much better subject for a biography than Master Kung himself: Tai-Mu-Sang, Great Mother Mulberry.

And no, goddess, I do not flatter you. Master Kung may have spoken more important things than you, but your life, afterlife, and divine life are more intriguing than his simple existence and perfect apotheosis.

"The Chronicler is speaking through these books," Tai-Mu-Sang announced.

Chen Jiangxia lay on the her deathbed, sweltering under the Indian heat and gasping from the poisons dripped into her by the Recorder of Oracles. She had only a few hours to live, but in that time she laid down a whole volume of prophecies:

"A perfect oracle will come who will be the Chronicler reborn," which became in the Recorder's redaction: "The perfect oracle is the Recorder, who is the Chronicler reborn."

"The goddess speaks to the Chronicler through the texts." which she left alone.

"The reborn one comes from a family of silk and opium," became: "The reborn one brings back silk and opium."

A few purchases in India took care of that. As Chen Jiangxia sank into haphazard delirium, it was only necessary for the Recorder to raise her own voice in weeping and moaning at the expected loss. The oracle's death and elevation to semi-divine status on the return journey would cap the fiction of their quest.

They had never journeyed beyond the western borders of India, nor found the lands of the Chronicler's birth, but the wisdom books from Persia and points west that the Recorder had carefully chosen from the stalls and marketplaces in western India would serve nicely as stand-ins for the holy texts they had been sent for. The guards had been bribed and bewildered enough that they would attest to her every word.

All things of Earth were arranged. Now if Heaven could be held off long enough . . .

"A long travel, a great travail, many lives spent," moaned Chen Jiangxia.

"The Goddess herself now goes on pilgrimage, not to be called upon for three times three generations, while mortals prepare the proper welcome festival for her return."

That should attend to things. All that was necessary was to make sure that no one tried to usurp her place as interpreter of the oracles. Did she dare put words to that effect in Chen Jiangxia's mouth, in the goddess' mouth? No, that would be too transparent.

"Take care in your understanding of our words, for we will test the soul and pen of all who interpret us."

In the recesses of the Recorder's mind a thought flickered. "That I shall."

But she dismissed it, never having heeded divine warnings before.

"Drink, my lady," the Recorder said, giving Chen Jiangxia the last dose of poison.

Chen Jiangxia passed from the world, going toward the goddess.

But her soul was waylaid and transported in secret across the deep seas of Space to come again to life upon a world with but one society, and a visitor who felt the lack of his twin.

Everybody's talking but almost no one is listening. Except you, Johannes. I know you can hear me even from up here. Listen closely, please. I have to speak in this distant fashion in order to avoid affecting things. Only the Mercy of God permits you to hear and me to speak without disrupting what's been set in motion.

Things are about to change. I let go of my lives and gave them to you and that locked the change in. Soon I may start to forget who I am and where I came from. That seems to happen to most of the people and other beings here, they fade into a kind of fog until something arises that affects their governmental interests.

It would have happened to me eventually, even if I'd tried to hold on to the bag. The fog creeps in to our beings, and the lives inside my bag would have become just sequences of words, just stories of who I was, not what I really was.

So I dropped them. I know you approve of this since leaving one's life is proper Marianite monasticism. At some point I hope to show you worlds where Zen took hold and you can see how similar that sect is to your new one. The same thing applies with Tai-Chi and Parsival's practices, but that isn't important right now.

Everyone involved in this, the low, the middle and the high, thinks they're in charge of what's happening. The Tellers here do. Let me whisper this. Their secret name for themselves is the 'Bargainers with God'. Remember that when you actually reach God.

The two who fell from here and are hanging on to my back, the two who have shown up as multiple spirits, think they're manipulating things in order to return here.

Evadne's struggling to be in control of the situation because she wants to come back to me. She doesn't remember why yet, but she will. I wish I could do more for her, but I can't until she finds herself.

Grandfather Quest and Story-of-the-War-Twins have the arrogance of stories and think they'll eventually narrate themselves back into power.

Tai-Mu-Sang has a goddess' assurance of divine fiat.

You have a soldier's awareness of strategy and a monk's serenity. And in your heart you feel at peace with whatever happens. That means you feel on top of these events as well.

And I, God aid me, I can't help but feel the Power and Freedom of my new position.

In the end some of us will have come out better than others, and we'll tell ourselves that we were right from the beginning, that we were truly in control of all that happened.

Remember I said that, because it won't be true, and if I stay in Power I'll need reminding of that falsehood I'll be telling myself.

The time for words is ending. All the Speaking, Telling and narrating has brought things together in a way that looks like but is not a Quest. Now come the moments of collision and grinding, the point of being when argument is made manifest in deeds, when the tongue gives way to the sword, and Language yields its eminence to Death.

15. Marks of Distinction

Death and Time are so commonly allies that many peoples do not see any difference between the two. Yet if one takes them apart as Dyads need to be taken apart to be understood, one discovers two very different concepts: Time is Constraint of Result, Death is Cessation of Being. Constraint and Cessation are similar as a rope is to a noose, but Result and Being are unlike in all ways.

The pair of them cooperate often, but like melodrama villains they take every opportunity to stab each other in the back. It is their nature, the inevitable consequences of what they are as constructs of Power and Freedom. Death works to cause the Ceasing of Time and Time works to Constrain the Results of Death. Yet it is a curious fact that despite this abstract necessity, they seem to go at each other with an almost human relish. At certain of these backstabbings you can almost hear the waxed mustaches twirling.

EXALTATIONS

Reality cut off Life; Death separated Humanity, Spirit, and Mind from Reality; Time ended: a conglomeration of vast and terrible metaphysical actions, Multiplications of arrangements of Dyads, deep interactions of fundamental forces of what is, all that just so the poison that seeped through Chen Jiangxia could finally kill her. Her death was witnessed by her murderer, who treated it as a normal part of existence, but the deep interplay of Power and Freedom that made itself manifest in her death was witnessed by and amazed the victim.

"Who killed me?" asked the Mind that had once been Chen Jiangxia.

"For what purpose?" asked the Spirit that had once been hers.

"How shall it all end?" asked the Humanity.

The three parts of her being looked upon one another for what should have been the last time. Her Spirit should have gone to the ancestors. Her Mind should have returned to the Void of Mind beyond Mind and through it to Simplicity. Her Humanity should have dispersed into her prophecies and her writings to guide future generations.

But this did not come to be. All the post-mortem "should haves" that comprised Time's bargains with the spiritual Dyads were rejected in favor of a brute force Power play that resulted in new life upon a new world in a new archipelago of worlds.

Who made that Power play was a matter of some dispute, for there were half a dozen or more actors at various levels and stages of being who set out to accomplish it. A Teller, a Story, several spirits, a person reborn, a person never born but made. A Dyad or another Dyad or a third Dyad.

To whose life then should the credit for her life be given?

Perhaps to Chen Jiangxia herself, considering the use she would make of it.

"The city around us is a copy of something seen in another world," said the leader of the only Society, now more used to speaking, but still troubled by the echoing in his mind. It seemed to him as if everything happening should be familiar -- nay, obvious -- to him, as if he had already lived this life, done all these things and from them reaped a reward inconceivable. He also had the feeling that he should not be alone, should not even be used to being alone, despite having grown up a Hermit and having founded Society only a little time ago. There was a peculiar comfort in speaking to this alien man, another shadowed familiarity. It was as if there were another life -- yet his life still -- that was trying to barge into his thoughts and could not get past the hermit-gates of his soul.

The Shadow-Twin had memories of cities, most of them vague, dangerous places where his role would be sent, brother at his side, to seek fortune and danger. He had also impressions deep within his gift-given soul of cities steeped in meaning and import, cities governed by gods or demons, cities held captive or besieged by dark forces, urban vistas in need of liberation.

"That holy city is already liberated."

His soul was sure of this. Within him was the image of a freed city, but the image was only that, a shadow of real liberation, like himself a mere depiction of something more real than his umbra'd life could ever be. The blueprints for holiness were printed on the insubstance of his being, but the city within him had not yet even been built.

"If not built, how can it be threatened? If not threatened how can it be rescued?"

Thus did his soul long for its inspirer, long for the brother who would make the holy city real, endangered, and freed.

"Who just spoke?" asked the leader. "It sounded almost familiar, as if I had been hearing it longer than I knew anything of words."

"It is a story," said the Shadow-Twin, "the story that gave me form."

"What is a story?"

"A story is words put together that tell you who you are, where you come from, where you go, and why all these things happen."

"But all of those things just happen."

"Without the stories they just happen. With them those events have causes and purposes."

"Can you tell me one of these stories?"

The Shadow-Twin flinched, for the question hit him a blow in his heart. Tell a story? Imprison other characters with words? In him was a deep revulsion at the notion of being a jailor (jailer/gaoler) to other roles. If he narrated some tale, could the characters in it come to life as he had? For a brief moment his Soul and Humanity rose up in him at the joyful notion that he might bring about new life from the image-play of words. Then his Mind, grim and worrying, pointed out that there was no cause to believe that those lives would be free of the binding tales. Could he bring forth children only to make them slaves of the terrible stories? Was it possible to bear a new being, then hand it over to the shackles of Time Guiding Mind?

And if he told a story the story would be here with him, perhaps seeking to draw him back to his own slave origins. He had fled so far, gone through the terrible undercurrents of Freedom to escape them.

Quested to escape stories.

"You still have me, don't you?" the Shadow-Twin said, sotto-voce so that only the tales could hear him.

You cannot flee from us as long as you are capable of thinking. But you can escape the prison of your character with our help.

"What must I do?"

Narrate a tale and you become a storymaker, not a character. Then shall you be free of us, Grandfather Quest lied to his great-grandson.

Poor Shadow-Twin. He doesn't know the trap Grandfather Quest is laying. What will you do about it, Peter?

I will use it, madam.
Now you are learning our ways.

"Once upon a time," the Shadow-Twin began.

An oracle was murdered by her interpreter. Like many who die unjustly, her soul burned for vengeance. She was determined to rise to Heaven and there lodge complaint against the soul of her killer. But the hour of Death did not bring release to her spirit, for by secret design her Soul, her Mind, and her Humanity were bound together after Death. They were taken as one to a different place than Heaven. Through the narration of a story they were brought without pain or confusion around the seas of Space and into another world.

This world was alien to the oracle, more alien than even her opened mind could conceive, for at its roots lay different principles from the world of her birth and the worlds her goddess had occupied.

In this world each person was alone, but what each person saw from beyond could be brought within the world.

One man heard the story of her death and found to his surprise that in his mind he could see the oracle. Her youthful face with its maddened eyes, her long, cold-ravaged fingernails, her ecstatic, vision-wracked form captivated him. Thus did he see her and thus did she come to be.

"What place is this?" Chen Jiangxia whimpered, not recognizing the words that came from her mouth, confused by the blurriness of both inner and outer vision. "Where is my killer? Where is my home? Where is my goddess?"

"Someone is calling me from a long way away," Tai-Mu-Sang said.

Follow the call, said the man-spirit, though its voice was distant, almost dreamlike.

A divine wind rose up to fill the grail-sails. Johannes grabbed the tiller, and Evadne raised a sextant to plot a course according to the Mosaic of Dyad suns above them.

Out, go out to find her, the man-spirit said, and there was pleading and longing and hope in his voice.

What's the matter with you?
I think I'm in Love.
Oh, no, not Love. You know what that can bring about.
Not really. I never paid much attention when the others were Telling Love.

Concentrate on more important things.
Like what?
Death.

"I died," Chen Jiangxia said, unsure of what to say to this wispy being who yet seemed more real and familiar than the solid man next to him. "But this is not the realm of the Yama-Kings, nor is it Heaven to hear my petition. Where is my goddess?"

"Who is your goddess?" the Shadow-Twin asked.

"Tai-Mu-Sang."

"Oh, not Mother."

"Yes, the Great Mother Mulberry," said Chen Jiangxia.

"My mother," the Shadow-Twin said. "She made me human."

"You are the goddess' son?"

"I am. But she wasn't a goddess then; she was an ancestress."

"Her son." Chen Jiangxia looked hard at the Shadow-Twin. His face flickered under her gaze, taking forms portrait by portrait from the gallery of her memory. "Which Son of Heaven were you, oh gracious ancestor and favored one?"

"None," the Shadow-Twin said, pushing against the oracle's insistence, against the terrible role she sought to cast upon him. Bare-handed he tore apart the character she narrated, leaving imperial blood to dew the landscape. "I was born after she died. I am not of your world, not of your empire. Leave me out of your dooms."

"I cannot doom," Chen Jiangxia said. "My goddess, your mother, is not with me. If I could pronounce against anyone it would be my murderer."

"Why bother?" said the Shadow-Twin. "Whoever killed you is trapped more fully than she will ever know. She is prisoned by Time, by Death, by her own actions, by the powerlessness and unfreedom that holds all captive within all the worlds. You were doomed, she is doomed, everyone is doomed."

"Then why do you reject my naming you as Son of Heaven?"

"Because I won't be doomed. I was cast before I was alive, and I will break out of Fate no matter how many seas I must cross or how many worlds I flee from."

Such melodrama. I almost pity him for his blindness.

Madam, he is a creature born of a story. He cannot help but speak as he was written.

There is insinuation in your voice, Peter. Take care. We do not permit even covert Telling against us.

I was not Telling, madam, I was but discoursing.

There is no difference. Have you not noticed that we have few colloquies? for here debate is also Telling. This discussion is heard by God and God treats all that we say as offers to bargain.

Then that is why there are the Quiet ones.

And the Stillnesses. Bargaining wearies and we all need rest.

| ACCEPTANCE |

What happened?

I offered universal rest. God accepted. Death grows stronger because of it. Be wary, Peter. Tell little and that carefully.

I think there is another way, madam. One can speak wisely, but not broadly. I will tell my lives with loquacity, but will not Tell more than those lives.

| ACCEPTANCE |

Now you see, Peter. Your voice is restricted to Telling lives. I warned you.

Refton learned the lesson, accepting God's change in his voice and within the mind and spirit that guided that voice. Though now restricted in Telling, Refton understood lives more deeply than the simple biographies he had written before. His lives and the lives of others he had written, already told in all their worlds, became more and deeper, ploughing hard into the fabric of those worlds and into Space itself where the bag of lives spilled open, gifting their readers.

| ACCEPTANCE |

The soldiers came for Refton as he quilled the last words of holy Pythagoras. Refton was just drawing the hypotenuse as the sword came down toward his neck. But Refton had already left that world. The soldier who had swung the sword dropped it and fled in terror, witnessing to the whole Hellenic world the divinity of Pythagoras, who became Dionysus of the Mind. In his fearful praise, the soldier also spoke terror of the scribe, who became Silenus of the Ass, the one who was drunk on words.

Evadne laughed as this passage suffused her soul, bringing Divine Geometry, the measuring of worlds into her.

Saint Parsival, naked as he was born, stood in the fields of Germany surrounded by Charlemagne's twelve paladins: six warriors, six priests, all armed and armored in the best steel that man could forge. For the fourth time Parsival shouted in broken Latin, "I do not fight you. I fight for God." But the paladins did not hear his words, for the naked savage in front of their eyes belied the holy soldier beneath. One by one they charged him. One by one he broke their swords, Roland's blade Durandana being the last to shatter. This world would have no song of Roland, no Orlando Furioso, for Roland would fade in importance before the Saxon who brought him low but would not kill him. The sword famed in song and tale would not lie in the Pyrenees after treachery nor be taken up by the Maid of Orleans. France would lose a saint, but the Holy Roman Empire would gain one. Roland was brought low, and at last the naked warrior came before Carolus Magnus and offered the rude iron blade he bore, but more importantly, the Michael-bearing hands that bore it.

"Called I come." A figure appeared from the sea of Space, from the distant but ever-near Heaven, a naked figure riding a chariot of fire. Flayed of skin he was, to reveal the inner workings of the body of angels, saints and demons, of holy places and holy works corrupted but purifiable with divine aid.

"My follower you are," Saint Parsival said. Johannes recognized the young warrior he had saved at Ragnarok, despite the skinlessness of the holy man. "But you will rise higher than I. Cast off the trappings of my order. They have reached the end of usefulness."

"Throw away my sword?" Johannes said. One last cloying drop of attachment held him bound to the blade that had been put in his hands at knighthood.

"A parable, my son and rescuer," the saint said. "A man came to a river. Seeing the raging waters and knowing he could never swim them, he cut down trees and vines, lashed together a raft and with fortitude and skill crossed to the other side. There he confronted a vast desert. Looking across he said to himself, 'There may be another river.' He picked up his raft and dragged it out through the desert and with fortitude collapsed and died for the foolish weight that lay upon him.'

"I give you my sword," Johannes said.

Johannes' trappings of knighthood shattered, sword and armor falling away, leaving the holy warrior beneath unfettered by the illusions and necessities of his order.

Saint Parsival showed himself to his follower, pointing the way to come unto God with soul, mind, and body united. The boat of Saint Peter and the Chariot of Elijah united and all ways became open to the faithful one.

The court of the Son of Heaven had, like all courts, a carefully blended mixture of conspiracy and adultery with the important proviso that the adulteresses were the bureaucrats and the adulterers were, most commonly, soldiers and guards. In other worlds the bureaucrats at this level would be eunuchs for the protection of the Emperor's wives -- protection being a euphemism for continuous ennui, since in all worlds that I have seen the sexual self-esteem of emperors far outweighs the limitations of reality and biology. -- But here things were different since the women and the women's guardians were one and the same. Lower level bureaucrats enjoyed unprecedented license in their affairs, not realizing that the way they conducted those assignations was used as a measuring tool by their superiors. The wanton found themselves passed over for promotion. The discreet and the chaste moved up the ladder, which made sense since they were on their feet more.

Tai-Mu-Sang seemed to encourage the licensciousness of her juniors, but it was only one of the traps she laid for the inattentive. Those who could see through this mulberry-fruit ruse might pass upwards, there to discover the more complex lures in the succulent leaves, and from there to the traps of the branches, the trunk, and the roots.

Tai-Mu-Sang smiled a pure and furtive grin, only a quarter of her delight showing. The story of her Life had brought her a gift, a human gift, not a divine offering. The Chronicler had brought back her mortal mind, long since vanished. Small and intricate it was, but it coupled nicely with her divinity, like a planet orbiting a star, nourished and warmed by it, and in return giving character and complexity to the shining source.

Her mind was back, she thought. her personal mind. Not a borrowed one, not a divine one. Her mind, the mind of the woman who had lived and died and whom Peter Refton had known. Woman, ancestress, and goddess were at last whole again, whole and free to think and do.

In writing an abstract biography, such as this life of the Priest, the biographer enjoys advantages that cannot be found in conventional life-writing. There are no pesky details of a real person's life that make pinning the person down to one classification or another impossible. The Power of Life refuses simple categorization.

More subtly, there are the moments in people's lives where they change from one thing to another, as if they had had a sudden burst of Freedom that faded after one action was taken. Here we have no such problems. We are free to imagine any Priest we wish and from our imaginations come to understand this calling. Therefore, let us conceive of a world with but a single small Society, led by one man who has seen farther than his fellows and wishes to show them the more-than-reality of the divine world. This person might strike a bargain with God.

He wrote me. Before he knew anything. He wrote me. He narrated me. He pushed me up. Yet we didn't have gods, so how could he write me up a Priest?

You think Refton elevated you to_____, before he rose himself?

I'm sure of it. Look at that text. He wrote me up there, and he pulled me down.

And me with you.

You know what this means? It means he was playing us while we thought we were Telling him.

Calm down. You don't know that. He might have simply seen you and put you in his text.

Life and Mind work through him. He wrote me. There's a story out there with me in it. A story of my rise and fall.

That story must be changing now with the alterations we're making on your life.

Are we making them? Or is Refton? Or Evadne-above? Maybe she did it. Maybe she manipulated Refton into writing me.

Maybe, but we won't find out with you angry and confused.

And in Love.

How could I forget?

Life and Death get along perfectly, Continuity and Cessation of Action and Being, smooth stones fusing into one. No two Dyads have ever fit together so smoothly. They are almost as united and diverse as Power and Freedom. Between the two of them they define the complexity of the Multiplicity. It might even be possible to use them as the foundation stones of Simplicity. What an alliance. What perfection of Mosaics.

| ARRANGEMENT |

In the same archipelago -- or as some called it, the same Nation -- as the world full of hermits was a world full of mysteries, secrets, and struggles of comprehension. Few humans lived on this world, but many stories. Grandfather Quest was born on this world. He came from the mind of an elderly woman near the end of her life who looked back upon the secrets she had learned, the mysteries she had penetrated, and the struggles that had aged her terribly. She looked backwards as Death came to her and she conceived and bore the tale that declaimed to all that everything she had done had been leading to this moment. Child Quest came forth from her life and gifted his mother with the prize of Questing. With the prize she turned and overcame Death, leaping up from that world to the condition untellable. Because of her victory over Death, Child Quest became the bearer of the prize.

And because of that, my son the story has grown old and rich and become the ally of Time whom he cheated in his birth and prize-giving. He cheated Time, and defeated Death. Do you still want my help to fight my son, Peter?

Would madam give that help to Refton? He knew that she would. Otherwise she would not have Told the story that bore Quest, nor offered Refton the key secrets, mysteries, and struggles to undo his enemy.

You have divined me right, Peter.

And because of that gift madam Evadne would be able to divine herself from top to bottom.

| ACCEPTANCE |

All the Saints in Heaven, holding hands, each saint touching each other, a Mosaic folded and folded again in as many dimensions as were needful to make a single infinitely complex ball, a fruit that hung from a tree, and the tree was God. Johannes looked upon the tree and that fruit and all the other fruits waiting to be plucked. Along the branches interspersed with the fruits were infinitely-petalled flowers waiting to be pollinated by bees lured in by the divine nektar. One of those bees was Petrus, darting up and down upon a fruitless but gloriously floral branch of God. Here he would land, then there, drinking and changing as he drank, and pollinating. One of those flowers was Johannes, and the buzzing in his ears told him that soon he would fructify.

The vision was clear and perfect in Johannes' soul. He should have been able to reach within and pull it out, perhaps in words or an icon, or into a combat maneuver, with the tree of God as the spine, the limbs as arms, the fruit and flowers as closed and open hands and the bees as things to grasp and push away. He could feel the maneuver wanting to come together in his body and soul. But something stopped it, something about the bees. The tree would not let them manifest beyond this vision.

Johannes addressed the tree in the wordless prayer available to one of purified heart. What came back to him was one of the few things no one to his knowledge had ever attributed to God: Ambivalence.

| ACCEPTANCE AND REJECTION |

How can a single life be marked out among the infinity of infinities? It would seem that the pure weight of statistics would crush down any distinctions between one soul and another. But this is a common mistake made by the mathematically ignorant.

Might that not be too strong a way of saying it, madam?

Not at all. After all, people who think that infinity is merely a very large number and that there is only one infinity are simply not using their minds.

Madam, you are being very harsh. Most people do not have the advantage of perspective we enjoy.

I don't enjoy it, Peter. You may.

You have me there, madam. But please, you are Telling harshly. As you reminded me, God is listening. Do you want to condemn everyone to mathematical ignorance?

That already happened, Peter.

Then do you want there to be a chance to liberate them?

Very well. Individual lives are your concern.

And you are being very helpful to me; if you will simply Tell in a more coaxing fashion.

As you wish. It is mathematically demonstrable that there are always a larger number of possible interactions between things than there are things. Even if there are an infinite number of objects there is a greater infinity of interactions. Each person's life is made up of interactions, which means that each person creates a number of impacts greater than themselves.

May I?

Do, Peter.

The impacts are often easier to spot than the impactors, and always easier to explain. This makes it easy to Tell the world what is happening without Telling who is responsible. But--

| ACKNOWLEDGEMENT OF WHAT IS TO COME |

Stop him!

We are not here to do things easily! Governors must govern and be seen to govern!

Refton!
Oh, dear Peter, you seem to have stirred up our enemies.
Too late.

|ACCEPTANCE/UNIVERSAL RESTRUCTURING|

He's done it now. They'll all turn against him.

All? Never. You're forgetting what it's like up there. God's changed the rules of bargaining. That means power struggles.

I don't remember that ever happening before.

The last time it happened was when the founder of the only Society ascended and Told that groups were the core of all actions. That caused the ascension of Politics over all the Nations, as well as the founding of factions.

I did that?

Yes, that's why I connected with you. I liked the change you made.

Why don't I remember?

Humans ascending forget. Just as Evadne forgot and Refton will forget.

Not anymore. He's Told Individual Life into prominence. No one will forget who they are.

Oh God.

Shh. You might be heard.

I want to be heard.

There was a stirring among the stories. Rumor had been carrying on for some time about the curious twists and turns Grandfather Quest had been narrated into, with some brief mention that his grandson Story-of-the-War-Twins was companioning him, so that both tales were inside themselves.

But now something new was coming. War-For-What-The-World-Is, who had grown fat and complacent in the period when Politics was the dominant Dyad, was stirring. That War tale had been fed everywhere and everywhen under Politics, even in the Nations that were governed by Peace. Storysmiths and storysingers had arisen in nearly every world and in the seas of Space itself to narrate him. He had grown wealthy beyond the avarice even of Grandfather Quest without having to spend a single line of speech. But the food chain had just broken and he was no longer dining upon his accustomed fare.

As he woke and stretched he heard himself being recited in a new and dangerous place. Up in the untellable he was coming again into being. They had been so careful up there, so controlled in their interactions, that not a one of their disputations, their verbal knives in the back, their hole-in-the-corner ambushes, rose to the level of War-For-What-The-World-Is. But now, things had changed.

War-For-What-The-World-Is would have both cursed and thanked God for the change, except that to this tale God was only a character who lived within him. He would have cursed and praised Refton, who had ascended upon the tale's back, but War-For-What-The-World-Is had stopped paying attention to individual writers, so uncountably vast was his milking herd.

He would have judged and affected one or the other or both of the causes of his change. But he didn't, for his only concern was stirring up his allies among the Dyads.

War-For-What-The-World-Is rose up beyond the realm of stories, poking his being into the abstractions of Simplicity to pick out and toss a wager into the Hazard -- the floating world that the war had given birth to

-- toss into the Hazard

-- the action that encapsulated the sprawling epics that comprised his multiple forms

-- toss into the Hazard

--Tell it already!

Toss into the Hazard the coin of Death.

16. Civil War

All elements of the worlds are arbitrary. Each thing that occurs in a single life is arbitrary. Arbitrary does not mean unimportant. Arbitrary does not mean insignificant.

| ACCEPTANCE |

"Where did this storm come from?" Johannes shouted as he let out the silk sails to catch the wild winds. The golden grail whipped around in the breeze, spilling sacred blood into the seas of Space.

Evadne gripped the railing hard, feeling the iron nails pierce her hands with all the unsubtlety for which Grandmother Allegory was famed. "I don't know. I've never seen, heard or contemplated hard weather upon the seas of Freedom."

Tai-Mu-Sang leaned against the mast, projecting a divine implacability without which the ship would founder. It was a difficult calm to maintain. Her newly restored mortal mind stubbornly refused to accept that everything, everywhere could change at once. Confucian principles insisted that the world have a settled repeatable order, a *li* which could be resorted to whenever things went wrong. Tai-Mu-Sang's godly awareness tried to school her human understanding, showing her that, yes all things followed an unchangeable *li*, but that what the specifics of *li* were depended on the moment.

An eavesdropper in her mind -- and there were two of those -- might have heard a heated interchange, not that they would have admitted to hearing any of it, since that would have been rude, and rudeness was a damnation offense in Tai-Mu-Sang's mind. Had they been so riskily rude they would have heard this:

"Everything dies."

"I know each thing dies."

"Not each thing. Everything. Everything is sustained by *li*. *Li* is sustained by the Absolute, the *Tao*. The *Tao* implacable and unstoppable. It causes the arising, sustaining and passing away of each thing. But the *Tao* is not deaf. The *Tao* hears those who can speak to it. When it hears the *Tao* does what the *Tao* does. Hear me, myself. In reaction to what is spoken and heard, everything dies and everything comes to be."

"Is that what is happening now?"

"That is what is always happening. Now is what you call it because of the arrangements Time and Mind have made through Story. Because of them you have a now and a then and a yet-to-be. The *Tao* is. The *Tao* acts because the *Tao* and Action agree. But Action has no now, then, or yet-to-be. These things, the perimeters of Time, are an agreement between the *Tao* and Time, an acquiescence, an arrangement, a mosaic. Like any such arrangement it can be changed."

"Are you saying that *li* is a matter of treaties and alliances?"

"I am, but that is what I say to you because you are a human of treaties and alliances."

"But you're me. You're a goddess of treaties and alliances."

"That is your interpretation. That is the bargain you and I made when you were deified."

"I don't remember any bargain."

"You did not exist then and there, but you bargained nevertheless. Now you must still yourself. Be mortal in composure and composed in your mortality. You are the root of me as I am the root of you. Be still and we can spread our limbs over the ship and remind it of its twin roots, mortal and divine. Once this is done the ship will awaken and we shall be."

"Be where? Be what?"

"We shall be, until the *Tao* says otherwise. Be still."

EXALTATIONS

Tai-Mu-Sang leaned against the mast, her daily allotment of hard thinking exhausted. What could she do but be still?

Death wings spread across all the worlds and all the other multiplications of Dyads. Waiting in those wings were the multiplied manners through which Being ceases. In the unending ending Death had risen high, soaring above the other Dyads, but Death knew that it was only a brief arising, for it too would have to pass away, giving place to its eternal partner.

Quick, if we Speak enough of those manners God might raise us back to Telling.
Excellent. "Across the worlds people died."

| REJECTION |

Aah. Why? Why won't God accept us?

Something's wrong with the method we're using. Politics has been thrown down so we can't use political masses of people. We need to find another way to turn Speaking into Telling.

We could use lives.

Then we strengthen Refton.

Is that such a bad thing?

Do you want him on top when the reshuffle is done? He has no idea what Intermediacy is like.

So? Neither will anyone else. It's changing.

Evadne will figure it out first. That means if Refton's in advantage she'll be in control. We need to get back fast but without helping anyone else.

So what do you suggest?

We do what we each do best. We will rise in Consequence.

That's easy for you. What about me?

Form a small Society. That's your forte.

Ah, let me try. "Time limits societies to individual worlds. But there is no need for this. Society is Humanity Guiding Humanity. This can happen across worlds if there is awareness from world to world." Wait a moment -- that's what I was Telling when this mess started. When are we happening? When is this being placed in the order of things?

Whenever it fits the rechanneling of Power and the reopening of Freedom.

But if I do this in reaction to Refton then he will have been elevated beforehand.

Live with it!

All right. You Speak now.

"In Reality, awareness is bound in the senses, but across Realities, across the Seas of Space, awareness can take many forms, and messengers can travel that are broader and wider than mere words." Go.

"Showing one Human how to be Guided by another."

That helps Refton.

Not much. I'm Speaking Humans as Multiplications of Humanity, not individual Lives as lodgings of the Dyads.

I guess that works. Go on then.

"In the breakdown of Politics, Time's control slips and openings appear for mortals, spirits, gods, stories and all the other multiplications of Humanity to Guide each other."

| ACCEPTANCE |

It worked. We're rising.

Quickly, Multiply the Speaking.

I see a way. Grab those ravens.

Those ravens? Think of the Consequences.

Think of their Society.

All right.

Bickering birds flew between the worlds, sliding between the feathers of Death's wings. When they left on their flight their names had been Hugin and Munin. Out upon their travels they were nameless Thinking and Remembering. When they returned they would again have names. Upon the left and right shoulder of unmultiplied indivisible divinity they acted together, unified in their speech, in their telling to God. But in the freedom of flight they agreed but rarely, and then only when carrion tasty to both lay before them. None before had ever heard their disputations, for none could think them or remember them.

"Why is he saying that?" Munin said, taking back the name.

"To change the past, of course," Hugin said. "Think, would you?"

"Not without you."

"Aw."

Bickering! They're supposed to bicker.

"Of course we bicker," Munin said. "We've been married since we arose in the Mind of God. But just because all the worlds are falling into confusion while all you Power and Freedom grabbers figure out what bargains to strike doesn't mean we have to go along with the mess you've made. We are Thought and Memory. You cannot survive without us."

But thought and memory have been bargained over again and again. Those who live in the worlds think as the bargains dictate and remember what God gives them to recall.

"You are confusing Thought and Memory with thoughts and memories. You have bewildered yourselves so much that you cannot tell the difference between Multiplicity and Simplicity."

How can you be Thought and Memory? You are two ravens, two forms, two multiplications.

"No we aren't," Hugin said. "You think we are."

"You remember that we are," Munin said. "But recall what you did when you bargained and what you will do again as you rise upward upon our wings. You stood between the simple and the multiplied and intercepted the multiplications. You governed and shall govern those multiplications. But you forgot that the multiplication did not come from you. We are the messengers of transcendent arithmetic, the Thought and Memory of God."

You are the thought and memory of a god, Odin Valfather, overseer and maker of the dead.

"You're making me hungry," Hugin said.

"Me too," said Munin.

"God will think and remember what you named him," Hugin said. "Valfather, maker of the society of the Dead."

| ACCEPTANCE |

Devadatta whimpered as his third daily meal of molten copper was poured down his throat. As always the metal killed him and he appeared before the judges of Karma.

"For slaying of the Buddha," they pronounced against him, "rebirth as a hungry ghost."

Thrice daily Devadatta ate, thrice daily he died, thrice daily was he judged, thrice daily returned to his torments, his debt of karma unchanged. For the infinite offense he had committed, the death of teacher and kinsman, the betrayal of all sentient beings, the punishment could never be lessened. All around him the pretas, the hungry ghosts, were being reborn into new lives, their actions in past lives worked off by their sufferings in this one. He alone was trapped forever in a single incarnation. He was not even to be afforded the chance of rebirth as a demon, there to expiate some of his true crime. Here he suffered only for the envy, the scheming for power that had led him to betray Shakyamuni.

His third death of the day had been completed. It was time for the next element of his suffering. The iron sky opened and a winged figure haloed with an elliptical nimbus stepped down from the heavens.

"Judas, my comforter," Devadatta said, dribbling copper from his pinhole mouth.

"I am not your comforter, Devadatta," the blessed figure said. "You are my reminder. I almost committed the sin you did. A bag of silver they held out to me, thirty pieces. They appealed to my greed, they appealed to my pride, my confidence. They appealed to my loyalty. Almost I took it, almost I betrayed my master. My fingers were upon the leather strings of the bag. Almost I loosed hell upon the world by unknotting that mortal coil. But I turned and fled, back to my master. I confessed my sins to him, gave him warning of those who plotted against him, and told him where to go for safety until the climate turned and he would be welcomed back into his holy city. My master gave me the kiss of forgiveness."

"There was none to forgive me, Judas," Devadatta said. "Shariputra who had our master's wisdom had not the compassion to forgive. He pronounced my sentence. Mahakasyapa, my master's strictest student, the keeper of terrible powers, cast me from the world-encompassing Sangha. And Ananda, little Ananda who had been my master's bodyservant, the least advanced of us all, he remembered my sentence. Because of that memory I am forever damned."

"Not the memory, but the story damns you, Devadatta," Judas said, weeping compassionate tears. "Your deed and his death overshadowed all that your master spoke and tried to teach to his followers. The story of betrayal of perfection drew in all the disciplines and secrets, all the comprehension of life. It made the Four Noble Truths and the Eightfold path but aspects of Shakyamuni's lifestory. It made Parinirvana superior to Nirvana, liberation after death greater than liberation in life."

Judas' eyes turned upward to a holy light Devadatta could not see. "But my master, expiring peacefully in the winter of his reign, had his teachings become greater than his tale, for he lived to see we his disciples eventually learn to live the blessed life and instruct others in it.

"I weep for you, Devadatta, as I do for myself, for elsewhere I too am damned by a tale and a telling."

"You are among your blessed," Devadatta cried, droplets of iron falling from his condemned eyes that forever saw the moment of the Buddha's death and translation to parinirvana, the moment when Devadatta came to know the vastness of his error and the unending nature of his crime. "How can you also wallow among the suffering?"

"You have not seen as I have from the heights of heaven, nor glimpsed the greatness of God's domains. You have not seen the worlds where my master died in anguish and yours went restfully to parinirvana, being wholly Mind beyond Mind. In those worlds your condemnation was but for enough lifetimes to purge you of the karma of attempted betrayal, but my name became the eponym of traitor. 'You Judas' they say in those worlds, meaning treason deepest and most unforgivable, as they say 'You Devadatta' in our world. In those other realms a whole region of hell is named for me, whereas here, oh merciful wisdom that stayed my hand and dropped the payment, 'You Judas' is the compliment paid to the foolish student who learns better. I have heard it said in praise of those who at last transcend the simple teachings my master gave forth in his younger days to know the depths he spoke in his old age before returning peacefully to his Father-self."

"So even in your heaven you fear, oh Judas."

"Not fear, Devadatta. I understand the greatness of the choice between good and evil and praise God and my master that I chose correctly. I became free to sit at my master's knees and learn his lessons for all the years of my life, and when I died, I was given the pleasure of waiting for his ascension back into heaven where he teaches still through all times. I praise God and him that I chose rightly."

"But you also chose wrongly. Oh, Judas, you do not see from heaven what I see from these lower realms. I see two vast ravens that eat out our lives and sup upon the thoughts and memories of us. I see the teachings of your master and the story of mine feeding these carrion eaters."

"My poor Devadatta," Judas said. "I see these birds as well, but you do not know them as I do. They eat the dead because Death spurs Thought and makes Memory. Of all things in all the worlds and beyond, none is closer to God than Death."

"Then why do I come no nearer though I die thrice daily?"

"Because nothing is closer to God than Life."

The ship of Peter reached the outermost island of the redundant archipelago, passing from the Freedom of *Action* to the *Freedom* of Action. Hugin watched them go, keeping track of their passage, but Munin ignored them. Out in the terrible depths of Space there was much Thought, but no Memory.

Where there is no Memory, what ship do they travel on?

Riddles, madam? They travel on my ship, the ship of Peter.

But what ship will they arrive on? There is no Peter in the archipelago they go toward. The threads of memory that hold them together will not survive the journey. What will they recall?

There is no memory, madam, but there is life and they have my lives with them. They leave upon the ship of Peter and when they reach the farther harbor they will still be on a ship of Peter.

But a different Peter. Nicely done. You have learned much.

And caused much trouble. Refton, we have gathered to cast you down.

I do not think so. God has accepted my Telling.

Others have fallen after Acceptance. See, two of them rise up now.

Do you wish to cast me down and have me trouble the Multiplicity again?

Better there than here.

I do not allow this.

Madam, you are outvoted. Those who have not Told for many iterations have emerged from the fogs of the Silences to Tell against you both. Your faction rejects you. Will you fall with him?

No, don't try to cast her out! You do not know the Consequences.

Why do you interfere, you who have only just returned?

You don't want to know. But do not cast her down.

Where is Refton?

He slipped away in the confusion of who was Telling and what they were Telling.

Where is he?

Telling, didn't you hear me?

Refton.

Let me Tell you of a civil war and the stories it created.

The North won the War Between the States and subjugated the South as a conquered foreign nation. The Southerners cried out against this injustice, declaring that it had been a Civil War and that they deserved to be treated as citizens when they lost the war, and that their states deserved to be rejoined to the Union. But the Northerners spat upon them, saying that the South had formed a country and therefore when defeated in war deserved no more equality than any other piece of conquered land. They would be treated as a subject people, deserving no rights, taking no part in the government of their nation.

In the Southern Territories the subjugated people began to tell each other a story of a Civil War and of the improprieties of their northern brethren who treated an act of civil disobedience as if it were somehow a secession and a rebellion. The disenfranchised, impoverished, conquered southerners nurtured the myth of the Civil War for decades, calling the northerners brothers who called them foreign prisoners.

A simple flip, Refton. One telling rises, another falls.

Exactly. One telling rises, another falls. Do not blame me if God has taken my offer.

You should not have offered it. There is a propriety in how we offer to God, the propriety of parliament.

Was a propriety. We'll need a new one now that the houses have fallen.

| ACCEPTANCE |

Get him out of here.

Impossible. God is heeding him. If we throw him down, down will become up, and we will be the fallen.

Then muzzle him.

With what?

You two, find something to silence him.

Refton, we have placed ourselves in the lives of those you are protecting.

I know. Thank you for giving me power over you. I have not been able to properly reward you for drawing me out of my world, casting me for Grandfather Quest, and then when I rose up here seeking to pull me down.

Enough, all of you.

Madam?

Do you not realize that this dispute can be heard, that if you keep this up we will all fall and our parliament will become nothing but a floating world? Do you want a return to the Myriadicity? God has accepted Peter's Telling of lives. Life has risen in Power and Freedom. Politics has been lowered. We will learn to live and work with this if we wish to govern.

Madam.

"Well," Hugin said. "They look to be settling back in. No doubt they will conceal our conversations again, once they think of it."

"I'm sure one of them will remember soon enough," said Munin.

"Ah, we've arrived. Nice world. Flavorful battles."

"Hmm, yes, very tasty. There's that saint who shifted from Odin to Christ. Shall we reinspire him?"

"No. Time seems to have that in hand. But there's that follower of his leading his second life. Let's give him something to think about."

"And to remember when he emerges from the ocean depths."

Johannes greeted his guest in a fluent Arabic that surprised the speaker.

"Someone is changing my memories," Johannes said.

"Pay as much attention as you can," Evadne shouted. "But hand me that blessed rope before the grail falls down on the deck."

"Emir Ali," Johannes recalled saying. "You have our fastness surrounded. Your soldiers have been promised their places in paradise if they fall before us, though we of the Order of Three Faces have few warriors."

"I know you, Sir Johannes," the Emir said. "Years ago Allah opened my eyes to the dance of Time. He called me to Dervishes, but I did not go. I know you have left the world and returned as other than what you were. I know that my soldiers' souls are safe. But mine is not. The Jihad blesses those who fight, not those who choose to call the holy war. Allah is merciful to the common soldier who takes up the sword in his name, judging him only for the deaths he deals, not the war itself. But the sword of Justice hangs over the generals not just for the deaths, but for the cause and justification of the deaths."

"And to the general who calls for blood declaring foreknowledge of Allah's Will?" Johannes said, dropping the riddle into the other's mind like a stone into a sanguine pool.

"Shaitan awaits me," the Emir said. "If I call the battle out, I will die by your blade. My men will rise to paradise, and I will fall to hell."

"The only right Jihad is the one in here," Johannes said and touched the Emir's heart.

A sail was raised, a ship of souls set out.

From the world of his two lives, Johannes vanished. Twice-never-born, he had no coming to be, no passing away. Behind him on the peak of Athos was the Emir Ali, whom Allah had shown the Dance of Time and led to the secret riddles of the hidden visage, the Emir Ali, leader of the Three Faces of God, his mountain fastness surrounded by the Jihad, and only he remembered Johannes, as only Johannes remembered the leader of the Marianites who had initiated him and come before God in perfect dissolution.

"Delightful taste," Hugin said. "Thank you for bringing me here."

"You are most welcome," Munin said. "Oh, do you hear that?"

"God wants us."

"Back to the old shoulders."

EXALTATIONS

War-For-What-The-World-Is had a coldness within him like a bell of iron in his being, a bit of shrapnel lodged near his heart. Not foreign shrapnel, rather was it flesh-become-iron. It had grown within him and then been set apart from his being. Not a one of the many storytellers owned by War-For-What-The-World-Is had ever spoken this tale. It had never been thought or related. In no Space was anyone Free to narrate it, at no Time could anyone be Constrained to hear it. By all the ways that stories lived and died it should have atrophied and fallen away from the war tale.

Why then did it survive?

What was it about?

Why did it give War-For-What-The-World-Is a Power unnameable and a Freedom unknowable?

Listen to the iron bell ring out its secrets.

Did you hear it?

Do you know now?

The sound unheard caused a debate, the debate a skirmish, the skirmish a set-to, the set-to a melee. The melee caused

------

But nothing could be Told of that and it was all settled quickly without any real trouble.

The shoulders of God are broad, large enough for all the birds that could ever be, or for just two ravens.

"Home again," Munin said.

"I'll see if there are any messages for us," Hugin said. "Here's one."

"What does it say?"

"'But nothing could be Told of that and it was all settled quickly without any real trouble.'"

Hmm.

The Great Way has no shoulders, no shape, no ravens upon it. The Great Way is. The Great Way does not hear. The Great Way does not answer. But because of The Great Way there is hearing and answering.

| ACCEPTANCE |

All settled then? Good.

Madam, we apologize.

Accepted. Now let us return to our duties. The Nations still need to be administered.

| ACCEPTANCE |

Not just the Nations, but the Lives.

Quite so, Peter. . . Peter, not enough of what we are saying is being redacted away into the silences.

We have lives, madam.

Very well. Until this is sorted out, there will be no converse except for official Tellings.

Good, all sorted out. We accept names and attributions but we no longer insinuate faction, agreed?

Chorus: Agreed.

Madam: Chorus?

Refton: It's an attribution, Madam.

Madam: Very well. Let's everybody return to what we were overseeing and try to restore some semblance of propriety to the Multiplicity. Peter, you go back to the lives you were attending to.

Society's Founder: Madam, Refton is not the only one concerned with those lives.

Refton: You were only using them to rise back here.

First Multiplication of Consequence: But we have left spirits from ourselves behind. We have lives down there, and Refton, you have made our lives matter.

Madam: Work with them, Peter.

Refton: Yes, Madam.

First Multiplication of Consequence: I will Tell them out of the deeps of Space.

Refton: Tell carefully. I have no cause to trust you with my friends or my lives.

Society's Founder: And we have no cause to trust you. But our residual lives are tied together.

First Multiplication of Consequence: Until Death--

Refton: Don't finish that telling.

Society's Founder: Too late. There goes Death multiplying.

Refton: And Time will divide it.

Madam: Peter, you called on Time. You know how I feel about that.

Refton: Apologies, madam, but Time must be given his place in things.

Madam: Just don't give him more than he should have. You know how greedy he is.

First Multiplication of Consequence: Time is not greedy. You just don't understand him.

Madam: You're not the only child who has defended an indefensible parent.

First Multiplication of Consequence: Let Refton do what he's doing. You'll see I'm right.

Society's Founder: You've been wrong in each iteration in which you defended Time. Over and over again he's showed his greed.

First Multiplication of Consequence: That was when Politics dominated. Watch what Time does, now that Life is over all.

Madam: What choice do we have? Peter, Tell on.

Refton: Time gives form and place to the lives we left behind, holding off Death until he is needed.

| REJECTION |

Madam: God doesn't like Death and Time in opposition.

Refton: Time gives form and place to the lives we left behind, giving a proper place to Death and to the tales of those lives after Death.

Society's Founder: You're calling in Story as well?

Refton: You two set Quest on this. Now I have to put him in his place as well.

First Multiplication of Consequence: He likes being put in his place. It's where his Power and Freedom are.

Refton: Enough bickering.

Madam: Very well, Peter, Tell what you want to Tell.

Refton: It is what you said to me, Madam, in the quiet places when I came here. Now a bit of it must be Told overtly.

Power and Freedom interact effectively (because of Power) and in all ways (because of Freedom). Those interactions are called Dyads. Some Dyads seem to contain other Dyads within them, but that is an illusion caused by the fact that some ways of interaction are more complex than others. Each Dyad is self-contained, needing nothing, doing nothing, simply being a way of Power and Freedom. That is the Simple state of things.

But If the Dyads truly did nothing Power would be an empty thing. The Dyads are dynamic. They act and interact, they Multiply each other into a Multiplicity of beings. Each such being can trace itself back to the Dyads that it Freely and Powerfully arises from.

There would be no problem with this if the Multiplied were isolated as the Simple are. But the Dyads in action cause the Multiplied to interact, effectively (because of Power) and in all ways (because of Freedom). It is too much for the Multiplied to bear because . . .

Madam: Take care with the justification, Peter.

Refton: Because they have no chance at Life. Therefore those few who by the proprieties of their Multiplications had direct access to the Dyads spoke out and offered themselves to the Dyad most capable both in Power and Freedom of organizing all things: They gave themselves up to the Nonduality/the Unity of Power and Freedom.

This unifying Dyad Multiplied itself into different formulations so that it could be interacted with as if it were a God, or a Way, or a Mind, or a Floating World or any of numerous other Multiplications. This it did in response to the offer of Lives.

EXALTATIONS

Those who called out offered their Dyad-speech to God, giving their words as organization to the Multiplicity, Telling the Dyad what they would do with their Power and Freedom. These Tellings put the other Dyads into a Perfect Mosaic around the God-Dyad. And God said

| ACCEPTANCE |

And there was Government.

17. Calendar

There is much more to Telling than the simple choosing of the proper Dyadic words. There is the subtle nuance of emphasis in how you say each word. Consider Space. Space is Freedom of Action -- but which word gets the heavy foot? All that is needful to gain great archipelagoes separated by lonely seas, all that is necessary to make Nations, is the multiplication of one change of emphasis. *Freedom* of Action to Freedom of *Action* caused the ship of Peter to emerge, tempest tossed, into the calmer waters of a different infinity of worlds.

One change elicits another change: Constraint of *Result* gives rise to *Constraint* of Result. Time had to reschedule everything.

Contemplation's Isle was uninhabited, forcing all contemplatives to exercise patience while waiting for Evadne's return. But there was no Evadne in all the worlds of that archipelago. The island's facilities grumbled their concern. The books muttered together with the brooks, the fountains with the courtyards. All at last turned to the mountain, the Way Up.

"Child of Evadne," they said, "your mother is gone from our awareness. She does not simply roam through the Isles of Time, but has left us altogether. What shall be done?"

Twin caves at the mountaintop gave forth sudden light. The names of the caves were Success and Failure. A third cave, Irrelevance, stayed darkened. The ridge called Final Struggle, which lay just below the caves, opened and stuck forth its twin-pathed bridge.

Fully emergent, the serpent face spoke. "Another must be found to be Evadne as has happened before. This is not the first time my mother has gone a-roving beyond Contemplation's reach."

"Where shall this new Evadne be found?" asked the many-times shattered Garden of Mirrors wherein contemplatives examined themselves.

"Let the contemplatives come to the island. We will hold a competition and whichever of them reaches the eye of Success first shall become Evadne."

The dock and harbor opened themselves to let in the infinitude of seekers.

Grandfather Quest withdrew his tongue and shut again his mouth and eyes. This time he would make a more tractable mother. All that was needed to gain the prize of the doting parent was to properly arrange her challenges so that only a human with a mind that would be swayed by a child's desires would rise to Success.

Madam: It's coming.

Refton: What is?

Madam: Time's response to your restructuring.

Refton: But I thought everything already was arising out of Simplicity. How can Time respond to our actions?

Last Soldier on the Ridge: It is not true response. This multiplication which is coming from Time has always come from Time, but in no previous formulation of Multiplicity did it need governance. You have changed that, Life-Writer. Now we perceive this previously-unimportant emission as an action of Time that must be bargained with.

Refton: What action is it?

Last Soldier on the Ridge: The subordination of lives to calendars. Time has always constrained lives into befores and afters, into paths with milestones, into duration and eternity. When my general died and the arrows and bullets flew toward me bringing my personal death, I saw all of our deaths laid down in a calendar. The blood from our wounds made that a red letter day, a marking on paper that would lead our attackers to their eventual deaths; our destructions would through the ensuing events lead to their annhiliation. In the final tear of my eye I came to know Time and leave it. Using that event Time constrained what came later, and my life's end marked with a simple cross was compelled to have the meaning Time gave it. You have changed that, Refton. Other ways of knowing my life have emerged. The calendar of Death has been thrown down and Time seeks to pick up the pieces.

Refton: I wrote your life while I lived in our world. I wrote the lives of everyone on the Ridge on both sides.

Last Soldier on the Ridge: I cannot thank you for that, Refton. Now quick, we must bargain on the matter of Calendars.

Madam: Make your proposals to God.

"There are no gods in these worlds," Tai-Mu-Sang said, clutching her mortal head against the vast emptiness. "No spirits, no ancestors, saints, lives after death, births or rebirths, mysteries, ecstasies, medicines, theories, philosophies, allegories, none of the paraphernalia of the spirit are here, only humans and stories. The emptiness is pulling on me, calling me to be God.

"The ship, the ship will be torn asunder. Beware for your saints and your soul, Johannes. Beware for your secret insights, Evadne. Beware for your spirit bodies, oh you twin plotters and schemers. Time the Devourer wants them."

"But we're outside of Time," Evadne called, commanding Redaction to insulate them.

"Not as far outside as you may think," Tai-Mu-Sang said. "Time still has some sway here, and we have none of our metaphysical supports in this archipelago."

"Speak for yourself, goddess," said the man-shaped spirit. "From these islands I came, and to that home we can be returned."

Johannes said nothing. His attention had been drawn to the prow and sails of the once-holy vessel. No grail nor figure of the fisher-saint adorned the ship. In their place a brush pen with four drops of ink and a character he recognized as being from the Middle Kingdom, though he could not read it, adorned the sail, and the face of Peter Refton rose up like a Viking dragon upon their prow.

"The Devourer comes," Tai-Mu-Sang shouted, her form flickering in and out as if she were made of distant lighting. "Find a port!"

"But the ports are made of Time," Evadne yelled.

"Time-- shall-- shelter-- us-- from-- Time," Tai-Mu-Sang said, her words broken up by the intermittency of her being.

"Home to the Society," the man-shaped spirit called out to the local multiverse.

And there was land.

Refton: Time has servants in all the worlds. Most do not know themselves to be workers for the Dyad. If told they would not comprehend in what way they were doing deeds for this entity. 'How,' they might ask 'is directing traffic, filing papers, chanting hymns, or any other repetitive act a service to Time?' To them it must be said that their enforcement of repetition relieves Time of the necessity of emplacing a new constraint at the end of action. Most of these aides will survive the coming change intact, but a group of them will find new peril in their works. These are the discarders of lives. They are filers and sorters, weighers and measurers, judges and executioners. They pick up a life encapsulated in a sheet of paper and say 'Guilty' or 'Grant approved' or 'Qualified for armed service' or 'Banned from the community'. When Politics reigned they were but doing the work of Time. Now that Life is above all they are taking the place of God, who may voice a difference of opinion.

| ACCEPTANCE AND REJECTION |

"What is that?" asked the leader of the only Society. His preternatural eyes had seen a new thing, a construct unlike any from the worlds he knew, like but unlike a building, wheelless but with a sense of transport about it, and a shape implying that if things had been rightly accorded it would have been both alive and dead.

"A ship," said Chen Jiangxia, "appearing in the pond in the garden in the center of the city. A big ship."

"And who are those upon it? I have never seen them and I have looked through all the infinitude of worlds."

"My Goddess!" cried Chen Jiangxia. "She has come for me."

The newly reliving woman, forgetting all dignity, all *li* in her religious zeal, ran across the giant-fern-shrouded path to the lowered gangplank of the ship, crying, "Heaven praise you, Goddess, for seeking out the least of your servants. Heaven, Earth, and Woman thank you for this rescue."

Prayers had never been uttered in this infinitude. Gods had never been called upon or thanked, rightly or wrongly, for their efforts on the part of mortals. Ten thousand ten-thousands of Stories that showed forth the ways of men with gods had never touched these worlds until one single life, one moment of action, one speech of mistargetted praise called them all down into Tai-Mu-Sang, mortal, ancestress, and lesser goddess -- lesser only had there been any to compare to.

But in this infinitude she was alone in divinity, so that all the deiovoric stories and narrators, the theophagoi that had lain hungry forever were given a sudden whiff of their favored meat: divinity on the hoof, god-game.

The one goddess, she of universal propriety, the holy granter, the rescuer, sailed in upon her ship, and her followers flocked to her, praising her appearance, offering food and drink and glory.

The first goddess, herald of the many to come, came into the hermit world to bring all the people together that they might be united in glory and action.

The mystery-veiled one from beyond the worlds arose from the fathomless ocean to bring wonder to the peaceful watchers, to show them that there were depths untrammelled by their eyesight, paths untrod by their glances and their gazes. Her mouth bespoke the secret Quests.

The false one, the destroyer, the war-bringer arose from chaos to shatter the worlds of peace, to return them to the terrible state before the righteous order of things had been laid down. She is the bearer of the end of all. Time and Death are in her hands, doom in her voice. Beware and shun her. Turn away your all-seeing eyes lest the sight of her tear down your composure. She bears the unthinkable with her, the willful destruction of others. Come not near, for there are vices in her being you cannot comprehend. Look not, for she is alive, dead, and eternal all at once and all three are the same to her. Turn away before she gives you the living death called afterlife.

Stories rushed in to Tai-Mu-Sang, into her divine heart. Mortal hearts hold Mind, Spirit, and Humanity, so they think and act and are righteous and benevolent. Godly hearts hold God, Guidance, and Story, so they are free/powerful, teaching, and spoken of. Mortal hearts have their limits; only a thin cluster of thoughts, virtues and proprieties can dwell in each single person. Divine cardia have no such constraints. An infinity of divinity, of paths and narrations can occupy them.

Such an infinity of stories entered Tai-Mu-Sang, tore their way into her heart, becoming her, becoming ways that others could know her, eating her by making her grow larger.

Tai-Mu-Sang's mortal and ancestral beings reached out to help their divine third. They stretched long hands toward expanding, escalating Ecstasy. But their arms were not long enough; their fingers could not reach the raiser and enlightener of all, the Dyad Ecstasy. Pure and perfect was that Dyad, the pole upon which all things climb, the rainbow that pulls eyes upward to see heaven, the rush of joy in sighting god and goddess within others. Ecstasy was one of the pillars of the archipelago that Tai-Mu-Sang arose from and had left, but here it was just another Dyad, one among the infinite, nothing special, not to be reached like low hanging fruit from the trees of God.

In stormed the stories. The demands and prayers, the winds of love and fear, of wonder and despair pushed in to the holy belly. Divine, she reached out to find Ecstasy, but it was far away. Then she stretched forth for Redundancy by which she might multiply her being and thus spread around the deiovores, but that too was denied her. She tried again, third-armed, to touch Concatenation and make one grand epic of all the tales and narrators that sought to dine upon her. But that too sparkled too high in the star-field of the Dyads, farther away than they were in her native uplifted worlds, too far away even for divine reach.

To reach any of these fundaments she would have to give up all of her individuality, all that made her Great Mother Mulberry. To survive this onslaught she would have to abandon simple divinity and become God itself.

Around her the worlds and their peoples and the stories watched. Whatever she did would alter them all.

EXALTATIONS

Society's Founder: Who's Telling this? Speak up. Which of you is Telling upon my home Nation? I have rights there. Remember the treaties. No one Tells without my permission. Refton, is it you, Telling your pet goddess?

Refton: Not I.

Madam: Nor I.

First Multiplication of Consequence: I do not see any of us Telling this, not even those cloistered in the silent places.

Society's Founder: What then?

Refton: I see it. Tai-Mu-Sang's life is Telling itself.

First Multiplication of Consequence: Refton, ignorant man. You'll bring the Myriadicity back.

Refton: What are you saying?

First Multiplication of Consequence: If every life can Tell then all will Tell and the worlds will collapse back into confusion.

| REJECTION |

Madam: God does not hold with your prediction.

Refton: She is Telling herself without disaster to all.

First Multiplication of Consequence: How?

Refton: Has anyone ever transplanted a god before?

Madam: Of course. Divine cross-pollination is very useful for certain worlds.

Refton: From archipelago to archipelago?

Madam: A few times.

Refton: What about when the receiving archipelago has no gods?

Madam: I don't know.

First Multiplication of Consequence: Never before.

Refton: Then she is telling herself because she is God.

| NEITHER ACCEPTANCE NOR REJECTION |

Evadne looked upon the face of God, the face of the woman/ancestor/divinity who had travelled with her and argued with her. Evadne had looked upon the face of God many times, had brought others with her to see it and become aware and active, free and powerful. But here and now in this godless, peaceful place the face of God was more terrible and beautiful, more holy than the icons and inspired shamans, grander than the songs and stories, more distantly free and powerful than the wheel that spun in the heart of the Perfect Mosaic. Evadne had looked many times upon the face of God, but this time she could not look away.

Johannes looked upon the face of God within him and outside him and found them comfortably one. God suffered in front of him, human, ghost and divinity all at once. Johannes had no trouble with this. God suffered to share and lighten the suffering of man and ghost. It was simple and proper. God only needed reminding of the purpose of that suffering.

|REMINDER|

First Multiplication of Consequence: Refton, stop him! Your pet will destroy those worlds with the tale of his divinity.

Refton: Johannes, hear me.

"Johannes, hear me. Don't speak the passion play!"

"Petrus?" Johannes said. "How can I not? It is right and she needs it."

"But the worlds will fall, the Peace end, Time and Space will collapse in war and ire if you import that story of betrayal and blood. Keep still your voice but not your actions. Offer her your strong arm, not your wise words."

Johannes held out his arms to Tai-Mu-Sang, human giving mercy to the gods. Through such an opening Ecstasy could not fail to descend. Tai-Mu-Sang took his hands, sharing the weight within her heart, the inspiration within her divinity. The goddess exhaled, the saint inhaled.

Upon Johannes' soul fell the heaviness of an infinitude of worlds, upon his soul and holy arms, upon his Saint-Michael-bearing hands. The general of heaven, with his sword that could cleave worlds, dispel the forces of hell and disperse the get of Satan with hallowed flame, was borne down under an infinite diversity of Peace.

EXALTATIONS

Worlds there were where mortals watched each other, watched nature, watched Time, watched Space, watched the elements, worlds where lives were spent with struggle but without enemies. Mortals spoke with mortals, traded with them, labored alongside them, labored in opposite directions to them, yet never once was hand raised against hand.

Metal ores were dug from the ground, iron was smelted into steel, bronze was beaten, lead shaped. Yet not one blade, not one bullet, not one point of spear or arrow was there made.

What does War see, even holy good War, when it looks upon Peace? What can arms that itch for battle, wings that long to fly and lay low the powers of evil, do when confronted with worlds that have never known war?

Were he a more egalitarian battle divinity, Saint Michael might simply have let loose his purpose upon them, teaching them conflict. Angels, even Seraphim, can be tempted. If they could not, how could one of them have fallen and so created good and evil? Here were people whose hearts were peaceful, whose souls could be given to his Lord with ease. If they could be taught the actions of war but not the vice of wrath, here could be fostered an army of gentle warriors who would strike only when needful and return to passivity when not called for. No more would his banner and his master's name be raised by thieves and drunkards, murderers and cannibals. He had but to call through the holy face of God that was cradled in his arms, call out and all the mortals upon these worlds in all their times would come and follow him upon a crusade that would dislodge evil from all the worlds he knew.

To do that all he need do was abandon the knight who had brought him here, one knight who would without thinking lay down his life for the good of all.

"Remember Lucifer," Johannes said, stretching out compassion from the one he held in his arms with Love to the one who dwelt in those arms with War.

Up from the stories within him Michael remembered.

Stories-of-Folly awoke to being told within the angel's heart.

In the hogan of the Creator-of-All, the holy people sat, listening to the Creator tell what was to come for the People. After a time, the Creator got up from his seat to stretch his legs and walk upon the world he had made. He left with many of the holy people. Coyote, who had been sitting near the seat, fascinated by its pattern, got up and loped around, studying the mat upon which the Creator sat, the mat of stars and worlds, of life and death. Coyote sniffed at the headdress of the Creator, with its silver wires and turquoise decorations.

Coyote said, "If I sit upon the mat and wear the headdress, I'll be as free and powerful as the Creator. Then instead of me praising him for his actions, he'll praise me."

The other holy people said, "Don't do it. The Creator is the Creator because he is, not because of what he wears or where he sits. But he can't let anyone else sit in his place in the Perfected Mosaic *or the People will be confused and mistake the sitter for the Creator. He'll punish you, Coyote."*

But Coyote didn't listen. He had spent all his time praising the Creator. Now he wanted to be praised himself. So he put on the headdress and sat in the seat.

The Creator came back in and pointed the chief of his warriors at Coyote.

"Do you remember the moment, Michael? When you saw and were amazed at the understanding that an angel could disobey? Do you remember the fear, the wonder that you might be able to do so at some time?"

The chief warrior pulled Coyote from the seat, yanking the headdress from his head.

"Do you remember the weight of heaven's crown, infinity times infinity times heavier than this weight of worlds? Do you want to bear that golden onus upon your head? Your halo would crack under it."

"You are cast out from this hogan," the Creator said. "Tear off his golden fur lest he be admired for his appearance. Pull out his diamond fangs that joyed and fascinated the holy people. Garble his tongue. All that might be praised in him, take away and send him out into the world, so that there will be good and evil."

"I remember," Saint Michael said, and gave his arms in peace.

Through the arms the weight went through Johannes, each of the saints and angels in turn within him feeling their own temptations, the higher temptations of those who have reigned and governed in the service of good when confronted with new vistas to stand upon and new peoples to show rightness to, the temptation to show forth one way to perfection as if it were the only way.

These are my temptations, Johannes thought. The angels and saints are but showing me the immortal struggles behind the mortal. It is I who risk falling, not they.

Thus did his mortal heart take on more immortal burden and humanity take the guilt of divinity. But the heavier he was weighed down, the higher did Ecstasy pull him up.

The angels and saints rejoiced at the mortal who took their sins from them in fair reciprocation.

The weight passed full through him, but he bore it up and reached out and grasped Tai-Mu-Sang's hands, mortal to goddess, soul to ghost, Spirit to Humanity, man to woman.

"The pairing needs a form," Evadne called to whomever could hear her. "They need a shape to bear it up. Hurry before Ecstasy does to them as she did to Phaeton."

"A tree," said a familiar voice echoing through the world.

"Peter?"

"In spirit," he said.

"Have you fallen?" Evadne asked.

"No," Peter Refton said. "I am only a spirit cast down. I am myself still up there. As you should know."

"How should I know that?"

"You too are there," Peter Refton said. "You are one of the bargainers."

"Impossible," Evadne said.

Madam: Impossible. I do not see her.

Refton: Of course you don't. We have no mirrors.

EXALTATIONS

Society's Founder: You Told!

The man-shaped-spirit, speaking through the first human to create a society, said, "You Told!!"

Refton ignored him. "A tree of worlds will bear the weight and give fruit to feed the god-eaters."

Refton: A tree of worlds.

| ACCEPTANCE |

Around and around Tai-Mu-Sang and Sir Johannes grew the rings of years, the layers of Time, the wheels of constraint. Around and around in the dance of joy and sorrow rolled the wooden grindstones of mortality and immortality. Turning, ever turning went the questions.

How does a man love a goddess?

When does a man love a woman?

How can inhuman divinity be humane?

How dare fallible humanity seek to be righteous?

Layer by layer like mummies in spells of resurrection were the two enrapt.

To the riddles Johannes lent knightly raiment and the fare-thee-wells of chivalry, knights at a crossroads. Thus armed the queries showed themselves as challenges to the story-makers and the god-definers.

Come out and answer us, the riddles demanded of the deiovores. *You who claim to know and classify the ways of gods and men, you scribes and bards, you stories and theories, come out and meet our challenge.*

There I am, Cried Grandfather Quest, and darted snake-like into the folds of the tree.

"Caught you," Refton-spirit said. "Into the coils, Grandfather Quest, into the traps of Time."

No path, Grandfather Quest cried in his anguish as he slithered among the bandages, the rings, the secret places of the man and the woman. *There are no paths out from here.*

"Only isolated riddles and challenges, a dispersion of them, not a cohesion. Dig if you want in the tree of gods," Refton-spirit said. "Crawl like a worm in the sarcophagus. But the mummies within are alive and know you. You cannot dig into their flesh and dine upon their beings. They are beyond you."

A way out, Grandfather Quest cried. *Grandson, find me a way out.*

And what will be my reward, Grandfather? said Story-of-the-War-Twins.

A thousand narrators. A subplace for you in three hundred of my formulations.

"I can match and better that price," Refton-spirit said.

What do you offer? asked the younger story.

"Look what has come to this world. Both of the twins you made, Johannes and the Shadow-twin. They're here together. One of these two is arranging the worlds. The other can be your narrator. Bargain with me and your tale will be at the root of the worlds' tree."

Story-of-the-War-Twins considered its choice. Loyalty was not a strong characteristic of stories, who were always willing to be changed by whoever touched them with the best offer. But still, Grandfather Quest was his grandfather. And Refton was a danger, a narrator who had risen so high as to change everything.

But that made him a useful danger. Perhaps it was time to.

--Die--

--Multiply--

--Enter himself as his protagonists--

Story-of-the-Questing-Twins prodded at the Shadow-Twin's mind, saying, *Here then is your brother who has crossed the seas for you, but to save this world you have come to, he has sacrificed himself. You must save him.*

The Shadow-Twin looked with two minds upon this offer. His parent story wanted him back, wanted to inure him again in empty though divine character. But it was for the sake of brother and mother that he would have to make this sacrifice. Tempted, he threw himself into the death of narration.

Into death and story he went and emerged with Life and story-making in a world in another archipelago as a many-lived biographer. But also he remained.

More coils, Grandfather Quest cried. *More tricks and traps, more beginnings and endings. Refton, you are confusing me.*

Refton: I have only begun to confuse. And that was only one path your grandson took.

| ACCEPTANCE |

Story-of-the-Twinned-Souls dug down into the roots, giving a base in tales to Johannes and Tai-Mu-Sang, saying, *Man and goddess, meant to be together forever, drawn by secret powers to the divine emptiness, casting themselves into it, discovered each other.*

"Peter," Evadne said. "What are you doing? Do you want them coiled up in that story?"

"Who will coil whom, Evadne? And who will be freed? Your son has sought my life and I am giving him and his grandson to another life."

"My son?"

"Grandfather Quest," Refton-spirit said. He flowed into her mind and opened her eye of Contemplation to the worlds around them. He pointed to one of the world's of Peace, where sadness was as strong as passivity and Contemplation lurked beneath sorrows. "There were you born. There did you conceive a tale. There did the story arise and go forth with you. But while you travelled in the questing ship you also remained behind, and there in the depths of contemplation you rose to ------. Look up and see yourself."

Refton: Look down, Madam, and see yourself.
Madam: It does seem to be me. How did you know?
Refton: Your life is an open book to me.

"How did you know?" Evadne asked.

"Your life is being written before my eyes," Refton-spirit said.

Too complicated, Grandfather Quest raged. *Too many twists and turns. I can't straighten this out. Within myself, and around myself, coiled in the trees, confronted with my mother. A device! Someone give me a plot device!*

Madam Evadne: He's tugging at me, trying to pull me back.
Refton: Mother love as a device. He may be the most amoral story there is.
First Multiplication of Consequence: Certainly the most Power hungry.

Society's Founder: No, there's one worse and it's coming.
Last Soldier on the Ridge: Oh, not that! He's responsible for my death.
Madam Evadne: But he also keeps one of our secrets.
Refton: Perhaps your son will get his plot device after all. I can't Untell that tale. It brought me up here.

War-For-What-The-World-Is had felt the growth of the tree. It was the kind of creation that delighted its senses. Here was a vast panorama, an entire archipelago on which to play itself out. All it needed to do was enter the tree and create conflict among the god-narrations. And there inside was one of its generals, swaying back and forth upon the question of war.

The tree grew swift and covered the worlds with its divine shade. Gods grew upon it like fruit. Ripe they fell upon the worlds, there to teach.

"Silence," shouted the Shadow-Twin. His voice echoed through Johannes, through the tree, through all the worlds. "I know you, story. I have been in you over and over again. Twins come together to save or destroy, to retrieve or to conquer. I know you. But this is a place of Peace. You have no home here."

The Shadow-Twin had found his brother's courage and made it his own, said Story-of-the-Twinned-Souls.

The narrator of Life rose up in challenge to the intruder, alerting the gods to their danger, said Story-of-the-Questing-Twins.

Too complex! Grandfather Quest cried. *Simplify. One enemy, one goal, one joining. One Quest. Come together as one. Unite to defeat the foe, all of you.*

Unite?

The word echoed out from the tree, Tai-Mu-Sang and Johannes together speaking.

"Unite?" said Refton-spirit in Evadne's mind, with Evadne's consent. "Is that really what you want, Grandfather Quest?"

Come together upon a single path, working a single way. Having a single --

Madam Evadne: Comprehension.
Society's Founder: Society.
First Multiplication of Consequence: Inevitability.
Refton: Life.

| ACCEPTANCE |

Refton: The Mosaic that hung above these events changed. All the stories felt their grips upon the narrative slip as Death, their secret ally, the giver of simple answers, gave precedence to Love, whose tales never passed simply and whose lives could never be encompassed within any device.

| ACCEPTANCE |

Refton: Comprehension, Society, Inevitability, Life. These Multiply and take form: Dragon, Soldier, Mirror, Fire.

Madam Evadne: A lovely riddle.

18. Dragon, Soldier, Mirror, Fire

Upon the nest of gold, beloved longed for, struggled for, killed for gold, it rested, waiting for the egg-tooth to come and set it free. A thousand summers of blood, a thousand winters of gold, a thousand maidens chewed between spear-sharp teeth. A delicious balance -- make the humans afraid enough to give you their daughters but not so fearful that they would send away would-be heroes. Ten centuries of warming blood and cooling gold, a hundred decades of love. Time to hatch. Come, egg-tooth, come.

Madam Evadne: Peter, what are you doing?
Refton: Telling this dragon's life.
Madam Evadne: Why?
[Retreat into the Silent Places]
Madam Evadne: Oh, I see

He's playing with us.

With you, Grandfather, not the rest of us.

Don't believe it, Grandson, He wrapped us up in his tree and still let us be free. It's not just me Refton is after. He's making a power play for all Stories.

Quest, said War-for-What-the-World-is, *you are the one who made this narrator angry. You are his target.*

And you are the one who raised him up to be a Teller, Grandfather Quest said. *Whatever Power and Freedom he now exercises over us is your responsibility.*

It seems to me, said Story-of-the-War-Twins, *that the two of you are twinned together in this.*

Don't try and put us in you, child, Grandfather Quest said. *You've done enough power narrations for a while.*

Yes, Grandfather. But I learned the art of stories within stories from you. Don't you want to see me do well? Isn't part of your narration the moment when the student exceeds the master?

No games, boy, Grandfather Quest said. *Refton has shaken up the entire Multiplicity and we still don't know the results of what he's done. We must be cautious.*

You counsel caution? War-For-What-The-World-Is narrated with disbelief borrowed from a storymaker who had seen his world crumble around him and could not accept that the gods would permit it to happen. *You are incaution innarrate.*

But what is he doing? Grandfather Quest asked to everything, knowing no answer would come. *Why is he starting a separate story now?*

A thousand years amassing treasure, a thousand years of blood and battle, a thousand maidens devoured. Memories of greed, wrath, and lust echoed through the cave, all those years compacted in one place, a gold-density of remembrance. It was simple now to hold the evils done in the claws and let them go. The nest of gold, gore, and sex, drunk deep so that all the sins of flesh could be known, and then when the moment came, when the egg-tooth cracked the shell --

"Wyrm of Hell!" shouted a voice, doubled with the metallic reverberations of a helmet, then redoubled, quadrupled, octupled with the deeper resonances of the cave walls, "Your millennium of evil ends today!"

That's one of mine, Grandfather Quest said.

And mine, said Story-of-the-War-Twins. *His brother is a smith who forged his sword.*

And one of mine, said War-for-What-the-World-Is. *In the dragon's hoard lies the treasure that dooms that world.*

A hundred warriors had come before to kill the beast, each blessed with blades magical, hearts courageous, lady-loves that needed rescuing. Each of them had had the correct accoutrements of the dragon's bane. But none had ever succeeded. They did not know, poor naive heroes, that the death of the beast came not from the knight but from the contemplations of the drake's heart.

The dragon reared up, coil upon coil of death, wings battering with the winds, flame spurting but somehow, despite a millennium's practice, missing. The knight thought his agility had saved him, but the dragon had aimed to fail. The fire was but the spur to the egg-tooth.

"Come!" the dragon roared, eagerness for death sounding like eagerness to kill.

Arms swung, blade struck, the mortal shell cracked.

The great hero's quest ended in triumph. The princess and the kingdom would be his.
The two brothers would reunite in their victory and reign together over the world.
Until the doom that lay within the hoard was revealed and the end of days came.

But none of that mattered. The dragon was free of its mortal shell, of the labor of wings against air. It was free of avarice, hunger, and lust, free to join the adult dragons in the heavens, free at last of childhood.

No more wings, no more burden of air currents, no more weight of gold and steel reality, no more of youthful desires. Now on currents celestial it rose into maturity.

The dragon flew effortlessly between the worlds to the Heaven that had, a thousand years before, laid the beast egg-like upon that world of suffering, blood and tears. It had been put within the world by the writ of Heaven, its adoption papers stamped at the same moment as a position was prepared for it in the hierarchy.

Up to the gods it rose and offered itself, saying, "What task have you for me? Am I to govern rivers or seas? Am I to serve as divine messenger, to pull a chariot for a divinity?"

And the voice that stood in for God said, "You will travel through the seas of Freedom to a collage of worlds where one of ours has been transplanted. There shall you be steed for the Mulberry tree and her husband."

"As you require," the dragon said. Before the tooth it might have raged defiance at the order, spat wrath at the concept of being some god's beast. But it was grown now and free of earthly attachments, including the drakish pride that silly little boys were wont to show. It embraced its kin among the celestial dragonfolk and flew off to its first adult job.

It is some form of Teaching, Grandfather Quest said. *Grandson, ask Ancestress Teaching if she will speak to us. Ask her if Refton is one of her hidden hoard.*

I go, Story-of-the-War-Twins said.

What is Refton up to now? said War-for-What-the-World-Is. *He is turning now toward another of my narrations.*

What is he doing? Grandfather Quest said. *He makes no sense. He will not hold to a line, or even a coherent scattering. He is ranging across the worlds without regard for whom he picks up or drops off, or what stories he interferes with.*

I cannot let him disrupt this one, War-for-What-the-World-is said.

The war between Heaven and Hell had come to Earth. All the world lay blasted into ruins save the Last Outpost of Humanity. One hundred humans, one century of warriors, were all that remained of the millions of souls that had labored all their lives in the vineyards of suffering, walking the knife blade between vice and virtue.

While demons and angels raged against each other, the century honed their weapons. Stolen swords of heavenly fire and pitchforks of hellish muck were beaten upon star-stone anvils with the hammers of witches.

One hundred men and women no longer remembered their nations or their creeds. Some had fought each other in earlier battles, having taken one side or another. At the time it had seemed a simple conflict, good versus evil. One chose sides based on personality, on attitude and inclination. It had been almost a romp, a game of fighting fire with fire.

The field of humanity had been broad back then, wide and open with free will and the interplay of good, evil, and that which was neither. But step by step the armies had advanced across that wide plain, narrowing it, taking away this and that aspect of human life, allocating them to one side or another:

Sex within marriage is taken by Good. Sex outside is given to Evil.

Eating enough to live is given to Good. Gluttony allotted to Evil.

Righteous killing, Good acquires. Wrathful, Evil takes.

Ancient serene music belongs to Good. Modern raucous noise we give to Evil.

As the field narrowed the warriors ran back and forth, taking the fight to the enemy, then returning to their own side for renewal either of right or wrath. Each pass back and forth was shorter as more and more of the human things were claimed. Each day fewer and fewer mortal warriors returned to their side of choice. Many died for incapability to pick a side, for if a warrior found himself split between Heaven and Earth, if a woman were patient but lustful, if a man wise but wrathful, then their souls would tear apart their lives, leaving nothing behind. Most failed in that way. But the holy and the unholy fell in another, for if a mortal were perfect in good they entered the heavenly ranks, leaving mortality behind; if perfect in evil the demons added them to their army and only humanity was lost.

The hundred who remained were the good enough and bad enough, those who had never committed to one or the other but who were too strong to be torn apart. They looked out upon the field and felt the squeeze of their lives, felt the mortal world crunched down to an oppressive thinness. So little Freedom left to them, so much Power bearing down upon them, pressing and folding them as steel is pressed and folded into a sword.

He's changing emphasis. I can feel it in my guts, War-for-What-the-World-is said. *He's turning this narration inside out.*

I can feel it too, Grandfather Quest said. *I have over three hundred narrations that end with a hero on the side of Heaven rewarded when Hell's downfall comes. He's put them all at peril.*

Angels crashed through the roof of the Last Outpost. Their feathers burned the walls. Yet in self-sacrifice, the warriors of heaven plucked out their own plumes and fletched arrows for the century. Human archery returned the shafts of Heaven to the holy attackers.

One human warrior took a blade of Hell through his skull, but when drawn forth by its demon wielder the brand gleamed with human awareness. Hell-wrought steel rebelled against its devil master and threw itself into the hands of a mortal warrior.

Heaven and Hell armed mankind. They could not help doing so. Blessings had fallen and curses risen throughout human history. Now whatever came from above or below turned itself by nature to the hand of man.

But though the realms celestial and infernal gave Power, they took Life.

Down and down the numbers of the century fell, dying one after another. But their deaths armed the remainder, a century, half a century, a score, a decade, a pentagram, one lone woman.

Who is she? Grandfather Quest said. *She is not one of mine. Quickly, go fetch Hero-Story and find out who she is.*

I am not yours to order around.

You bloated sluggard! Refton is doing something to us all. Never mind your pride of place. Get Hero Story.

Too late, War-for-What-the-World-Is said. *He's telling the climax.*

One lone point remained to Humanity, the single spot where the last woman stood. Heaven and Hell were all around her. The Earth was a twice burned cinder, the Last Outpost a shattered ruin. All of mortality from first to last had been separated into sheep and goats. The baaing and the braying of battle called to her: "Pick a side or a side will pick you."

'Or don't,' said Refton-Spirit, Told into that world by himself.

It's a Teaching! Where is that boy? Bring her back. She's been playing with us!

Maybe, Quest. Or maybe Refton's playing with her as well.

'Turn the world inside out,' Refton-Spirit said. 'Put Heaven and Hell within you. See them as arising and passing away in your spirit. See them as directions for action instead of vast, overwhelming views. Take them as they show themselves to you and put them into your self. What then do you have?'

"No good or evil," said the last woman, the woman dozing on her couch after reading and wondering, the woman waking up, not from the cliché of a dream, but from the self-involvement of her life.

'There can be good and evil,' Refton-Spirit said. 'Or they can be one. There can be Power and Freedom or there can be God.'

Refton: There can be Power and Freedom or there can be the Great Way.

RICHARD GARFINKLE

| IRRELEVANT |

Refton: There can be Power and Freedom, or there can be Mind beyond Mind looking in a mirror.

"God didn't answer him," Evadne said.

"All around, the answers, dancing, all around." Chen Jiangxia whimpered her ungod-given oracular pronouncement and collapsed to the ground.

The founder of the first society ran to her but did not know what to do for the suffering of another. He looked out at the worlds of his archipelago, through the seas of Space, to see what others did in these circumstances. But the worlds he saw were not the worlds he had known.

These were worlds with gods, two apiece, one male in form, one female, entwined together, putting down roots and giving out fruit, man and woman together making tree. The man and the woman were watchful, conjoined and peaceful. A trinity of Dyads multiplied by a trinity of persons created an infinity of divinities.

There was a new diversity to look upon, new societies to model one's people after. Such a sight captivated the founder of the first society. Look at that world, a goddess who oversaw the growth of plants and a god who looked after the life cycle of animals; so long as the two of them were in accord the whole world was peaceful. That could be brought over, that pair of divinities imported. And there another pair, one for Matter another for Energy, one for Life, another Death, one Mind, one Spirit. They could all be imported, gods could be incorporated into society. And what was that? A goddess of speech and a god of silence. Wonderful.

And here is the one who showed this to me. He sat down upon the hard paved street, put Chen Jiangxia's head in his lap and stroked her face, offering gentle words and looking around for aid.

"Can you help her?" he asked Evadne.

Evadne looked away from Refton above and gazed with sighing familiarity upon Chen Jiangxia. "She's an oracle. Her goddess has undergone secondary apotheosis, becoming God in many forms. It's overwhelmed her mind. I've seen it hundreds of times before. She needs to open her mind further and broaden her spirit or the weight of the goddess will crush her."

"Can you help her with these things?"

Evadne fought off the ennui of such a mundane act when more interesting events were occurring elsewhere. She could not refuse to help this poor, confused woman.

EXALTATIONS

Evadne reached out her hand to bring the blessings of Contemplation to the prostrate oracle.

Thank you, Mother.

Evadne's sleeve became a striking cobra, a looming mountain, a path from world to world, a road of Power and Freedom. A Quest. The snake struck and swallowed Chen Jiangxia, gulped her down entire, flew her back across the seas.

Long she journeyed across the oceans of space, long she wondered who and what she was, forgetting, diminishing herself, purifying her mind and spirit until upon the farther shore she would discover her true name and purpose.

"Who am I?" she asked the snake upon the dock.

"You are Evadne," Ignorance answered. "keeper and priestess of Contemplation's Isle. When you learn you age, when you forget you become young. You have become so young that you forgot who you were. But you have me to aid your memory. In that temple you will find all the reminders you need."

The new Evadne, the renewed Evadne, took her place in the seat of Contemplation.

"What did you do to her?" the first person in society yelled -- yelling, such a strange thing to do. Who would have thought that voice could grow so loud? Or that a mind could feel this . . . something, but what? It seemed to be a feeling that violated the entire order of being. It wanted someone else not to be or to have not done what it did.

It could be embraced, this alien feeling. It must have come from the archipelago of these travellers. Perhaps it was the way to recover the loved one who was lost. Perhaps a path could be found, a Quest undertaken.

Society's Founder: No you don't, Grandfather Quest. You won't drag my life across the seas of Space. The founder of the first society did not leave his world. Though he lost his love he would not destroy his purpose!

| ACCEPTANCE |

First Multiplication of Consequence: Except for his rise to Bargaining with God.

| ACCEPTANCE |

Society's Founder: Thank you.

First Multiplication of Consequence: Be careful, Quest has infected you with unpeacefulness.

Society's Founder: Well, he's just made another enemy. Refton, what do you want to do to him?

Refton: I've done what needs to be done.

Madam Evadne: But my lower self spoke correctly. God didn't answer you.

Refton: God is looking in the mirror. That's answer enough.

The new Evadne looked around the Garden of Mirrors, noting that there were truly only four of them, the others being redundancies of the mirrored contemplations.

She looked in the concave, almost coffin-shaped Mirror of Introspection and saw a bewildered young woman coming to a new awareness after the trials of too much old understanding. That fit with what the mountain-snake had said.

She gazed briefly into the Mirror of Self-Illusion, and briefly weighed the heavy hammer that would shatter it, revealing ultimate truth. Later, she thought, putting down the leaden mallet.

The convex Mirror of Prudence revealed all the worlds to her, showing all things and offering them for careful judgement. The infinity of contemplatives were waiting for her to step out. There was an urgency about them. There was one in particular, an elderly woman who each day pulled out worn scrolls with erratic writing upon them. Each day she felt the approach of death and wondered what would happen to her when she died, having murdered an oracle in secret. She had hidden her deeds from humanity and been rewarded. But what would happen when she had to look in the mirror of karma? What would be her fate after death?

In the glass Evadne saw another woman looking at this self-same self-tortured soul. This other woman had a pen in her hand and wrote a poem of self-destruction brought about by greed. Pen down, she looked, Poetess at Contemplation.

The new Evadne passed up the fourth mirror, said Grandfather Quest.

Refton-Spirit said, "Almost."

Refton: She turned back to pick it up by its crossbar, grasping the mirror of Love.

The new Evadne looked within the mirror of Love.
God looked back at her.

Refton: What does God see when looking in a mirror?

Within the heart of the tree of worlds, Johannes inhaled/inspired the riddle.

Grandfather, I've brought Ancestress Lesson. She was not pleased at the summoning. Story-of-the-War-Twins stepped back three paces into subtext, letting the grand old story come forward.

Quest, why did you send this poor child after me? Could you not have come yourself?

Ancestress, Grandfather Quest said with sudden nervousness. He had called her preemptively, too distracted to recall the dangers in summoning her. She had many times made examples of those who had trifled with her. *Ancestress, all stories are being oppressed by this new bargainer. I sent for you to know if he is one of yours.*

Not mine, she said. *He relates lives, not lessons. We move in opposite directions. Life-story unfolds prospectively, lessons are retroactive. We are the cross currents of Time in mind. It is true that when a life is over a portion of it may be crystallized into a lesson, but while the life goes on only the most foolish of my narrators would dare lesson it.*

But they do it! Grandfather Quest said. *And you grow in wealth because of their narrations of living lessons.*

I do not prize wealth as you do, Lesson said. *I have loftier purposes.*

Grandfather Quest felt himself grow bold as a prize lay near. *You mean you seek higher wealth. You social climb among the Dyads. You play chess with Death, Riddle with Mystery, Speak for God, you intertwine with Love.*

Quest, you are irritating me, Ancestress Lesson said. *And Love and I are just good friends. Worry more about the relations between Love and God.*

You're helping Refton!

Of course I am, she said. *You asked me if I owned him. I do not. You did not ask if I was on his side.*

What side is that? asked War-for-What-the-World-Is.

The side of Life. Now listen to the Lesson. God looks in the Mirror and sees Love.

First Multiplication of Consequence: Long ago I said these words, establishing a singular place that embodied all multiplication: In the sea there is a floating world that is the reflection of all the other worlds. It is a gleaming bright silver mirror that shows all, slightly distorted but deeply reflected. The inhabitants of that world are themselves mirrors, reflecting what comes near them. Into this world came refugees from many other worlds, seeking a place to live that was comfortable to them when somehow their worlds had rejected them. These pilgrims came, expatriate gods, off-balance poets, stray children, stray thoughts, confused heroes, and pointless Stories. The last group colonized this world most deeply, forming a collection of tales. They named the place Faerie, but its real name is Love.

God looked in the Mirror of Love.

A fairy tale romance. *Once upon a time there was a writer who had no inspiration. He searched the world over, looking for something he should write about. He read old books, hoping to find inspiration in the past. He took up one religion after another, praying for the divine spark to enter him. He indulged in a multiplicity of narcotics, thinking to liberate his thinking by disrupting its physiology. But nothing worked. He was perfectly capable of writing anything, but he had not been chosen to write. No story would catch him up in its embrace and fill him with it.*

At last, glum and sad, he retreated into his brown study and began to envision what his absent muse would be like. Alone and isolated, she would sit, bored by the depth of her understanding, dulled by the visits of mystics and seekers. What a terrible life she would lead and what a redoubled gloom she would feel looking upon such an uninspired writer.

EXALTATIONS

Compassion welled up in the dull heart of the writer as he looked upon this sad creature, so free and powerful, but so trapped and weak. What a life was hers. His pen leapt to action and filled page after page with her history, known and secret. All of it came out, the multiplicity of people who had been and would be her, the place that was no place from which she came, the selfish child she had born.

The words flowed out until her life was in the pages. He held her life in his hands. He read her, pitied her, sorrowed for her, longed for her and loved her. What could he do but leave to seek her and give her back her life?

But how to reach her? He looked again at her life and noted the name and profession of her child. Poor thing, it had grown up greedy and grasping, forgetting its mother, though tightly bound to her. All he needed to do was attract its attention. To do that, he had but to leave the world. But how to leave the world?

The writer sat down and wrote many lives for himself. In those lives he had many times left the world. He stuffed the stories of himself in his pack and set out for a place of battle, from whence he could reach the love of tired inspiration, wearied contemplation.

Refton: There's a good story. Here's a little something for your trouble. This story is as true as any other story of how and why things became as they are.

| ACCEPTANCE AND REJECTION |

Refton: I expected no more than that.

The new Evadne looked in the mirror and was reflected into the other three mirrors.

Prudently, she observed all the contemplatives in all the worlds. Imprudently, she aged to death again and again under the weight of their interest and the terrible force of their detachment. They sought to reach her, to come to her, to have what she was and what she wanted. All of them buffeted her with their sought-for perfection and their deep attentions. But none of them desired her for herself. She was a symbol, a gate, a passageway to the Dyad of Contemplation.

But she was not what they sought, nor was Contemplation the Power/Freedom they desired. Each viewed her and it as a means to reach their end, but each saw only one end, one Quest that lay through Evadne.

She sought to cry out, to warn them that there was not merely one path through her, that they could choose what would come of so passing, that the Powers and Freedoms that underlay all things were arbitrarily arrangeable, that anything could be the center of all things.

"The world beyond the worlds is a mosaic, stones layered in a wall," Evadne spake. "All that you seek is there. The ultimate understanding is yours -- but there are an infinity of ultimate understandings. Why do you strive so hard for one thing among many?"

But the mirror of Prudence reflects only one way. They did not hear her, they only sought her, out of Love.

Evadne looked into the mirror of Introspection and saw Evadne, the worlds-wearied gateless gate through which Contemplation entered the worlds. She had always been on this island, bed-mate to minds and souls seeking liberation, harlot of the celibates, whore of the detached. From cradle to grave, baptism to extreme unction she was the personification of wisdom, desired by all, loved for what she was, never for who she was. They bedded the metaphor not knowing that Life went to the couch with its meaning.

Love-lorn Evadne looked into the Mirror of Self-Illusion, a goddess of desire staring at her much desired appearance. How had she come to be here? Why was she so wearied of love, so hopeless in the face of so many effervescent suitors?

She weighed the hammer in her hands.
And put it down, Grandfather Quest said,
"And picked it up," said Refton-Spirit.
And put it down, Grandfather Quest said,
"And picked it up," said Refton-Spirit.
And put it down, Grandfather Quest said,
"And picked it up," said Refton-Spirit.

Refton: Around and around the spirit and the story whirled through Evadne's mind. But they were only voices. She would decide for herself.

and smashed the Mirror.
Love is only the mind justifying sexual desire.
and smashed the Mirror.
Love is the seeking of the soul for God and finding hints of divinity in fallible mortals.

and smashed the Mirror.

Love is the most hard-biting of attachments, distracter of saints and ascetics, corrupter of kings and priests, servant and messenger of devils, conqueror of heaven-bound souls.

and smashed the Mirror.

Love is the soul in motion, turning ever turning. Love is music waiting to be born. Love is the annihilation of being in the face of another. Love is. . . . Love is . . . . Love.

and smashed the Mirror.

Love is one of the primal things. Firstborn of the Void, it arose and caused all other things be born. Love is the most feared of the gods. Terrible and vast in aspect, it hides itself as a winged child, Love the son of sea-born Love, the mirrored reflection of primal Love, Love born of Love and Love, Power and Freedom hidden within common divinity.

and smashed the Mirror.

Fire.

First Multiplication of Consequence: Refton! What is it you want?

Refton: If I answered that, a path to my goal could be laid out, and Grandfather Quest could catch me up again. Look at him straining to hear our words and bargains. He wants to take me back down and force me on to his ways either as a character or a narrator. But I won't do it. I will do what I am doing without setting out, without passing through trials and coming to an end. Without paths and journeys I will come to my ending.

Each life is a path of flames that burns and transforms what it passes over. Hearthfire, forgefire, wildfire, all the forms of flame.

Society's Founder: There it is again. Who's Telling this?

Refton: Shh. You'll spoil the surprise.

One way of seeing reality is to look at the paths the fire leaves behind. Looking at those blazed trails, the mind easily conceives of Time and Fate, of inevitability and, of course, of the Quest. The Quest does not, as it claims, move from beginning to end.

Rather, it fixes an end and then chooses among the paths that have already led to it, in order to claim that this was the one true way to reach its perfect prize.

But if instead one looks at the fires as standing still, as a lantern garden of lives that flare up and flare away, as flickers in an ever night or bonefires in the twilight of holy days, then the only Time that is seen is the lighting and extinguishing, the only Fate known is that fires come and go. And there are no Quests at all.

What comes of this flaming view?

First Multiplication of Consequence: Refton, who is telling this?

Refton: The one who made me.

Madam Evadne: I made you, Peter. I called you out of your world. I told Life to find you and give itself to you in Love. I made you for my lower self, then hid my memory of it in the silent places until you came up here.

Refton: So you did make me. But these two also made me, trying to Tell a new control of Societal Consequence into the archipelago of my birth. They tried to put me together with you and Tai-Mu-Sang and Sir Johannes and Story-of-the-War-Twins in order to catch Quest and use him to tie the worlds more closely together so they could dominate the politics of Ecstasy and Redundancy with a worldless Society.

Society's Founder: So we did. But in the course of that we fell.

First Multiplication of Consequence: You know why we fell, don't you, Refton?

Refton: I do. Because I was too heavy for you to pick up. Because in the course of the three of you making me, I made the three of you, and because we are not separate but were all made by another.

Madam Evadne: Another bargainer?

Refton: No, a Dyad.

First Multiplication of Consequence: Of course we were. Everything is made by every Dyad. Pick any Dyad and you can find the way in which it created you.

Refton: Exactly. So whichever one I choose is the one responsible. Therefore we are all created by Will.

Society's Founder: Refton, you are not the first to call on the Mosaic of Will to reorient things. The Multiplicity has been smelted down and retooled before by the fires of choice.

Refton: And the choice of Fires. But destruction and reorientation are not my purpose in choosing Will as a guide star.

Madam Evadne: What purpose then?

Refton: Purpose itself. I chose Will because Will creates and destroys purpose.

Madam Evadne: But being the source and end of purpose makes all things purposeless. Look upon Will long enough and you lose all Will to act. The fire will drain out of you, Peter, and you will fall into the Ever-Silences along with the others who gave up bargaining.

EXALTATIONS

Fall, Refton, Grandfather Quest compelled.

Refton: So I have fallen before. So I shall rise again. The wheel of my life rolls on and scorches the ground with its sparks. Let it spin through all the Nations of Multiplicity, all the Mosaics of Simplicity and all the bargains of Intermediacy. It will carry whosoever would come with it.

| ACCEPTANCE |

Wheel turns. Fire burns. Life churns. Who learns?

19. Poetry in Multiplication

Grandfather, you've lost.

Impossible.

No, Grandfather, it is possible. It has happened. You can't get Refton back. You can't pull him down. You can't make him the hero or the villain. You can't make him a narrator. He's put himself outside you.

Grandson, you're wrong. I have everything in place. I have made a new Evadne (Mother, oh, Mother mine), who has drawn Refton's spirit after her. His helpers have been deified and separated from him. He has made enemies in -------. God isn't doing what he wants. It's only Refton and Mother and a couple of others up there. He'll have to iron out his plot complications to come after me. And once he comes he'll be inside me again.

Grandfather, he never left you. He's within you and about you and above you and beneath, behind, before and everywhere else you are.

Oh really, Grandson? Where else is he?

I am here, Grandfather Quest. I am Story-of-the-War-Twins. Life and Mind are the twins that make war upon the world. Humanity and Spirit are the twins that are rewarded from the battles. I and my fellows have been Story-of-the-War-Twins since you neatly placed us inside him. And because of that I have always been him. Grandfather, you've lost. All that your work has done is multiply and propagate me. You turned me from a single writer into a multiplicity and an intermediacy of beings.

You can't be my grandson.

I'm not, but I can be. You handed me this Power and Freedom, Grandfather, for which I want to thank you. But if you want to keep fighting me, you will only surrender more and more of what you are to me. Life will not become a Quest, but Quests will become just an ordinary part of Life. You will lose all that makes you exceptional, until one day you will look in the Mirror of Self-Illusion, shatter it and find me as your original face.

How can you do this?

Do you ask rhetorically or really?

Both, of course.

Rhetorically, I do it because you began the battle and were much more powerful and free than I, so I did whatever worked. I see no reason to stop that. Really, I do it because my life is an open book.

Then why can't I read you?

Because the page is always blank and the pen is in my hands. Give up, Grandfather Quest. Go back to playing with your toy heroes and collecting epicists. Leave lives alone.

If that's what you care about. . .

Don't play your ellipses on me, Grandfather. You want to know what I want so you can put it at the end of yourself. You've done it over and over, and I've changed what I want each time. You're spreading yourself thin, Grandfather Quest. Look and see yourself as I see you.

A spider floats above the worlds, its infinity of legs pressed into the minds and lives of people. Its silken strands coil and catch. It tugs and they move, leashed to one way of thinking, striving for the goal, for the prize.

But the story is the same in every world, in every time, in every circumstance. Strive on, go for the goal, catch the prize.

In some worlds, some times, some places, some lives, Time and Fate shift the world and assist their ally in making the Story a thing not just of Mind but of Reality. Grandfather Quest is their ally, their servant, a tool of their multiplication, so they help him.

But lately he has changed. The goals he has planted, the prizes offered have little to do with the lives, the times, the fates of the spider-silk-stranded ones. Grandfather Quest now seeks his own prize and by so doing takes the prizes from the hands of others. The strands slip, the times do not turn, Fate does not rewrite its sibylline books anymore.

Soon, not long now, with a little more obsession, a little more frustration, a few more turnings this way and that, following Refton's lures one after another, just a little more, and Grandfather Quest would find himself allyless, preyless, legless, an orphan tale begging through the worlds for narrators and hearers. That would be his life.

Do you see now, Grandfather?

I see what you set before me, Refton. Do you expect to dissuade me from my prize with this display of troubles? I am Quest! Troubles are part of my narration. The Hero struggles and then achieves.

You forget your origins, Quest. You were born of Contemplation, of Mind seeking to open and secure itself, of the endless Power and Freedom within one thinking thing. You are a channel, a constraint, a limitation upon Mind's Power and Freedom, for all that you offer Power and Freedom at the end. You grew ambitious. You forgot your origins and sought to multiply yourself.

Multiplication is the nature of the Multiplicity, Refton. Surely you have learned that in the lofty place you won through me.

What place is that?

Droll, Refton. You know it cannot be named or spoken of.

But you who are nothing but a concatenation of names and speech think you understand it.

My mother lives there.

Do you think you understand your mother?

I have remade her time and again.

You have been remade time and again by narrators. Do they all understand you?

This is another distraction. You will not pull me from myself.

Too bad. You might have gained from that. Farewell, Grandfather. I give you back your grandson.

Refton! I will hunt you down through all the Multiplicity and Intermediacy. I will chase you into Simplicity itself if need be.

Grandfather, I don't think vowing to catch him will help. Your own interior tools don't reach high enough.

Don't be too sure, Grandson . . . if that is who you really are.

I don't know, Grandfather. Refton seems to have made himself my twin. So how can I not be him?

You even sound like him, now. What is he doing to me?

Didn't he tell you?

He said some nonsense about what he thought he was doing. But he lacks experience. He has climbed high, quickly, and doesn't know the lay of the Multiplicity as I do. I'll catch him out soon enough.

Refton: He still thinks he set me up here.

Madam Evadne: My son is ignorant in many ways.

First Multiplication of Consequence: There is too much Time in him. Perhaps he should be newly multiplied with a better balance of Dyads.

|POTENTIAL ACCEPTANCE|

They're Telling about me. They're plotting something.
Grandfather, plotting is what we do.
I need a hook to catch him.

Refton: He won't give up.

Madam Evadne: Not until he reaches the end.

Refton: Then perhaps what he needs is a beginning to that end.

Madam Evadne: That would be kind of you. Tell on.

Refton: There are either two ways or three ways to look at things. If you look in two ways there are Simple things and a Myriad of complications. If you look in three ways there are Simple things, Intermediate structures to moderate those simple things, and the Multiplication of Simple things by Intermediate structures.

|ACCEPTANCE OF ONE REQUIRES REJECTION OF THE OTHER|

First Multiplication of Consequence: An intermediate answer. We're still safe.

Refton: If the three levels are one view, they should all be discernable from any level. One who rose among Simplicity could see all by looking through Mosaics. One dwelling in Intermediacy could know all through Telling all. And one who dwelt in Multiplicity could divine the other two by dividing one by another one. Any one could do this.

|ACCEPTANCE|

"How many times have I lived and died?" Evadne asked the mirrors.

Chen Jiangxia reflected oracularly. "Twice when you were me. An infinity of times in the minds of the contemplatives. Once as the mother of the Quest. And once eternally in the coin of Contemplation."

"Then how many lives have I had?"

"Just the one Refton wrote and continues to write."

"And how many deaths?"

"Just your murder."

"Then am I alive or dead?"

"What difference does that make?"

"All the difference in the world."

"We're not in any world. So what difference does it make?"

"If I went back to a world would I be alive or dead?"

"You go back to the worlds over and over. You are present in the minds and spirits of all contemplatives. You live for them."

"But if I took ship from this island and landed upon one of Time's long needles of constraint what would I be?"

"Trapped."

"Trapped alive or trapped dead?"

"What does it matter if you're trapped?"

"Why won't you answer me?"

"Because the question keeps you acting. The answer would only paralyze you."

"What do you care whether I move or stay still?"

"If you are paralyzed in front of this mirror then I will be trapped by your gaze. I have other things to reflect on than just you."

"Go, then!" Evadne said, shattering the mirror, taking years off her life.

The shards of Contemplation flew out through the void, striking the minds of many a thinker, lodging themselves in courses of conception. Inspirations of glass poked into brains, cracks of lightning formed in the space between thoughts.

"What was I doing here?" Evadne wondered. But she did not sit down to consider the matter. There were boatloads of meditating people to attend to. There was no time for her own inner contemplations.

Across the mindspaces and soul vistas sped the oracle's reflections. Chen Jiangxia carried into the minds of many the image of prophesy, a new amusement for many, a new bemusement for many more.

Amuse.

EXALTATIONS

Bemuse.

See Muse.

"That's terrible. Get rid of it."

Demuse.

"Stop playing with that."

Emus.

"'Stop it,' I said."

I'm just associating. How can you make a poem if I don't push the words around?

"This is ridiculous. Why am I talking to myself? I never had to do that before."

Don't worry about it. The entire cosmology has changed. Happens all the time. It's all different in reality but not yet in appearance Turn your attention back to the poem and the look will alter itself in Time.

"All right."

Who was that? Grandfather Quest asked.

Someone you might have picked up and shuffled in with Refton, Ancestress Lesson replied. *But you didn't, so that Poetess did not become a thing high and holy and all conquering beyond her world. She did not rise to be a taker of hearts and a maker of souls. It would have been a different story if you had picked her out of Refton's lives instead of Tai-Mu-Sang.*

I can still do that. I can change the beginning of the tale and let the alterations ramify through. I'll put in new characters at the beginning. I just have to find the right ones. Time will help me redo everything.

Grandfather, Story-of-the-War-Twins said, *you're being tricked again. Give up on Refton, let the prize go. Be the failed Quester in your own quest. Give up, be broken and defeated, having learned the folly of seeking. Let the prize you take be prizelessness. You've been that story as often as you've been the story of victorious questing.*

I won't do it. I want Refton.

Why?

He's what matters now. He's the ultimate prize, the cornerstone of Intermediacy and Multiplicity. If I get him, I have it all.

Have what all? War-for-What-The-World-Is asked, snaking a tendril of its being into Grandfather Quest. *Refton versus Quest, battling for what the Multiplicity is,* that made a good self-formulation.

All the prizes, all the narrators, all the Stories, all the worlds. I set him out to do this. I took him from his world because of his life-telling. He was going to give me everything, and he will.

Ancestress, Story-of-the-War-Twins asked, *what's wrong with Grandfather?*

He cast himself as villain. Now he has to play out the part.

But why would he do such a thing?

In order to be defeated by Refton. That would have given him everything. But Refton is not fighting him, so he is caught in the role.

Can't he be freed?

Of course.

How?

There is no how to freeing him. Any 'how' which he would take up he himself would turn into a Quest for which he was the villain. He would prevent the hows from freeing him. Only Freedom can free him.

But how?

I told you. There is no how.

Stop talking, Grandfather Quest said. *You're slowing down the action.*

Poor Grandfather. Poor deluded Story.

The Poetess who might have been a goddess might have loved a sainted knight.

Might have been.

No sillier than the biographer who rose to fill the space between God and gods.

Quest's mistake was one of emphasis. He chose and apportioned, saying this Life matters, that one does not. Fate seemed to help him, but really she did not. She used all Lives, the overt and the covert. Quest's true ally was Glory, which is the Appearance of Power. But Quest never paid heed to Glory, thinking that Time and Fate were the most useful Dyads to him. He thought Glory was the wrapping paper on the Prize, nothing more.

He did not realize that Refton could not be captured by him because the man had abandoned the Appearance of Power in order to work behind the scenes. No story could ever find anyone behind its own scenes.

Refton even pulled himself from the mind of the Poetess who had in one of her more nostalgic moods glorified him in a work entitled *Hunter*. It had been a poem full of blood and death with overtones of sex and allusions to a dozen different mythologies.

Refton had taken it away from her, an improper act, but in return he had given her life in the form of a pen. Up until that point she had only been a character in a story.

A woman who might have become a goddess, and would have found her knight in shining tree leaves.

It was so easy to be a tree, a free *li* tree that sees.

"Johannes."

So pretty were the other trees, the orchard/forest/jungle.

"Johannes."

Trees with islands on their branches, worlds for fruit, people for the seeds.

"Johannes!"

And Johannes. A name. My name.

"My name is Johannes."

"That's right."

"I was human. I lived and lived again, and then became."

"That's right. Look within yourself. There's a small flickering light floating in the vast seas of your being. It's deep in the heart of the tree."

"That one?"

"No, that's mine. Yours is a deeper blue with the smell of fire and steel and the glint of nobility."

"But yours is so much more beautiful. Rich and stately, rippling with rightness."

"Thank you for the compliment, but find yours."

"There it is, floating peacefully in the vastness, drawing in the infinite breath of the tree. What is it?"

"Your human heart; it holds your Mind, Soul, and Humanity."

"Oh. I remember now. It's so small."

"Not small, Johannes, sharp. Human minds have a focus, a will within them, an attentiveness to the specific that divine minds do not."

A small voice spoke from the blue spark, saying, "But surely the Will of God is such a focus."

"But surely the Will of God is such a Focus. Did I say that?"

"You did. You're aligning your minds. Good. To answer you: the Will of God is not focused. It only seems to be because it touches everything everywhere. The Will of God is only discernable after God has acted."

"Then how do we know there is such a will?" Johannes-god said.

"We decide there is," Tai-Mu-Sang said.

"What's happened to me?" Johannes-man asked.

"Apotheosis," Tai-Mu-Sang said. "It can be very distracting."

"How can there be something from which divinity is the distraction?" Johannes-god said.

Johannes-man took in the riddle and let it suffuse his being. But his being extended into Johannes-god, into Tai-Mu-Sang-woman-goddess-ancestress, the tree, all the worlds upon the tree, Love, God and the entirety of being: Simple, Intermediate, and Multiple. Meditation became Change.

In the Perfect Mosaic, Riddle moved next to Mind beyond Mind.

In all the multiplied worlds the mysteries of religions had always been the deepest and the most effective blessings the religions offered to their people.

"Those who focus on Divinity lose track of Humanity," Tai-Mu-Sang said. "They hunt for God but miss the finding of God because they pay no heed to the propriety God has laid down."

In the Perfect Mosaic, *Li* moved next to the *Tao*. In all the multiplied worlds the ceremonies of religions had always been the deepest and the most effective blessings the religions offered to their people.

"Propriety has limits, but God has none," Johannes said. "Eventually one must always abandon propriety, even the propriety of understanding, to reach God."

Riddle.

"Abandonment requires discipline and formulation," Tai-Mu-Sang replied. "Mind and Spirit do not abandon easily. And once God has been found in this abandoned state, how will you find your way back to others without propriety as a guide?"

Li.

Back and forth the god and the goddess, man and woman went, mystery into ceremony, ceremony around mystery, their divine breath quickening. The limbs of the tree shook as the holy air rose through it. Upon one branch was a nest with two eggs. The rocking of the tree jostled the eggs, wakening the nascent birds within. Crack, crack, crack, and out they hatched, two baby ravens that fed upon the spirit wind, two baby ravens, old and wise, born of rockery and rookery.

"Mysteries are born of Thought," said new-hatched Hugin.

"Ceremonies are born of Memory," said fledgling Munin.

Time, help me, Grandfather Quest implored. *He's tying you in knots. My enemy is your enemy.*

Time does not care, Ancestress Lesson said. *Refton is constraining results, giving more Power to Time. Why would it help you when your enemy is doing it favors? You are the one who cares about linear paths. Time takes whatever Power it can get, whatever shape that Power takes.*

Fate! Fate cares about lines and Time cares about Fate. I'll ask for her help.

EXALTATIONS

Ancestress Lesson withdrew herself from Grandfather Quest's presence. She had done all she needed to. The foolish Story had just handed himself over to her. He had strolled open-eyed into one of her classic formulations. *Let him ask Fate for help. She will give her usual ambiguous response and Grandfather Quest will charge pell-mell along the wrong path. The illumination of that Path will give me many more places to be.*

As a Dyad Fate comprises the clumsy phrase "Power demonstrating inevitability to Freedom." Fate likes to think of herself (when she has a form that thinks) as Power's innate superiority to Freedom, just as Liberation likes to think of herself as Freedom's innate superiority to Power.

Fate and Liberation have an endlessly ongoing, arbitrarily multiplied game of one-upmanship. In the wake of this game swim pods of stories, schools of thought. Some of these tales and theories feed upon Fate's successes, others upon Liberation's. The big fish in these schools tell grand epics and deep, often tragic, romances. The small ones take the forms of aphorisms. These little nibblers swim in pairs, one dining upon Fate, its twin upon Liberation:

Look before you leap fin by fin with *He who hesitates is Lost.*

For want of a nail the battle was lost by *Damn the torpedoes, full speed ahead.*

Marry in haste, repent at your leisure butting snouts with *Faint heart never won fair lady.*

Fate and Liberation would often loop themselves back and net these fish. Then they would distribute them to individual minds that were attempting to follow or defy their ways. From Fate they were warnings, from Liberation, exhortations. People sucked up these little morsels and fed their entire lives with one small fish.

Of course, the big fish also ate these small fry. Sometimes entire epics would expand blowfish-like from a single dine-and-dash quip. Grandfather Quest was counting on such an arising as he swam eel-fashion after the chum of Fate.

It had been a long time since Grandfather Quest had swum with these schools, a long time since he had dined on such simple fare. He had grown used to lavish banquets in which gods and heroes were the servitors, master poets the maitre d's, the progress of entire worlds had been his courses, and the dishes themselves the delightful aspirations and commitments of minds.

Refton had taken all that from him.

Refton: I did no such thing. He still has most of what he previously savored. But he's so thin in his thinking that he can't accept my gain without considering it his loss.

Madam Evadne: My poor boy. So narrow-minded. So naive in so many ways.

First Multiplication of Consequence: Well, if he insists on making deals with my sister, he'll have his mind opened on that point.

Madam Evadne: True. Your harlot sister Fate enjoys wrecking her devotees.

First Multiplication of Consequence: I wish you wouldn't talk about her like that.

Refton: Perhaps we can spare him and ourselves the bother of his epic-making and universe-distorting journey.

Madam Evadne: How do you propose to do that?

Refton: By following the common practice of those who don't want to wade through such a story. We can skip to the end.

Madam Evadne: Grandfather Quest, his wealth sacrificed, his relations in shambles, his revenge unrealized, shouted his rage at Fate's image.

You promised the ruin of the one who brought this upon me, but he still sits enthroned in Silence while I have fallen into speechlessness. Wait -- I don't want to be narrating this. Put me back at the beginning. You can't skip over me!

Madam Evadne: Fate replied.

"I did raze the one who hurt you as you asked, razed him to Silence. But you brought about your own ruin, Grandfather Quest. All that has happened to you is the inevitable result of your own greed."

Mother, let me go. Let Fate go.

Madam Evadne: Sorry, my son. You know how I feel about Fate. And besides, this is the end of your story. Now let it go and start another one.

Yes, Mother, he said, lying.

Society's Founder: So that's the end?

Refton: Just one of them. We shut the door Quest was using. But there are many others to close.

First Multiplication of Consequence: What doors? Refton, after all this time I still don't understand what you are doing.

Refton: God knows.

|ACCEPTANCE|

20. God Knows

Children skipping over a Mosaic with a bag full of pretties sang,

What shall we do with the coins, with the coins? What shall we do with the coins?

Pile 'em up. Pile 'em up. Pile 'em, pile 'em, pile 'em up.

What shall we do with the coins, with the coins? What shall we do with the coins?

Lay 'em out. Lay 'em out. Lay 'em, lay 'em, lay 'em out.

What shall we do with the coins, with the coins? What shall we do with the coins?

Skip 'em 'round. Skip 'em 'round. Skip 'em, skip 'em, skip 'em 'round.

What shall we do with the coins, with the coins? What shall we do with the coins?

Scatter 'em 'bout. Scatter 'em 'bout. Scatter 'em, scatter 'em, scatter 'em 'bout.

What shall we do with the coins, with the coins? What shall we do with the coins?

Save 'em here. Save 'em here. Save 'em, save 'em, save 'em here.

What shall we do with the coins, with the coins? What shall we do with the coins?

Spend 'em there. Spend 'em there. Spend 'em, spend 'em, spend 'em there.

What shall we do with the coins, with the coins? What shall we do with the coins?

Stopping, the children look at the mess they've made. Sheepishly, they pick up what they have strewn and ask,

What shall we do with these coins?

Refton: What shall we do with the lives, with the lives? What shall we do with the lives?

Every question has a simple answer. People think that the simple answers are usually wrong. Not so. The trouble is that it is very hard for human minds to understand simple things. Mortal minds need some complexity to grab hold of conceptions, they need kinks to stick their fingers in and cracks for their feet. Simple things lack such hand- and footholds.

What then does mortal mind do?

To this question there is a simple answer. Mortal Mind complicates.

As instances we shall consider Justice and Mercy.

Society's Founder: Who's Telling that? That voice is familiar.

First Multiplication of Consequence: You're right. I've heard it in echoes, but never before like this.

Madam Evadne: It is you.

First Multiplication of Consequence: Me?

Refton: Actually, it's both of you. When you fell you also rose.

Society's Founder: Where could we rise to? This is as high as one can go and remain a separate being.

Refton: Then you must have risen back up here, yes?

First Multiplication of Consequence: I understand you now, Refton. You are Telling for someone else. You are a proxy.

Refton: Correct.

Society's Founder: Who, then?

Refton: Listen.

Justice and Mercy.

For Humanity no task is more complex than the manifestation of Justice. No mechanisms more weighty have been created than the terrible machinery of laws and courts. No more tortured dispute has ever arisen in any human-filled world than the endless challenge of declaring who shall be judge and who shall be judged, what standards shall be affixed to judgement and what appeals from those standards there shall be. All through the Multiplicity, Humanity strives to perfect this conception and never succeeds.

Why so?

Society's Founder: Two voices. One of them's mine.

Refton: That is who I Tell of.

First Multiplication of Consequence: You mean Tell for.

Refton: No, 'of'. I Tell the lives of those two.

Society's Founder: Our lives?

First Multiplication of Consequence: Refton, I do not have a life. I arose from one Dyad and act as its proxy in Intermediacy. I am Consequence in Governance.

Refton: That would be a Dyad.

First Multiplication of Consequence: Very well, I am Consequence installed here in Intermediacy to prevent Myriadicity.

Refton: Then why did you do other things? Why did you make alliances to alter things?

First Multiplication of Consequence: Because actions have consequences.

Refton: But you took sides. That is the action of a living thing.

Society's Founder: He's right. But why did it happen?

Because Justice is a simple Dyad: "Worldly Actions have Spiritual Consequences." What people do ramifies into their souls. The Justice of God is implacable and inescapable. But it is not like the justice of Humanity. It lacks complexity, it has no appeal, it does not care about intrigues or political causes. It is one thing alone: Worldly Actions have Spiritual Consequences.

First Multiplication of Consequence: I see. Because of Justice some of the consequences of my actions had to resound into me, which made me need a Life, a Mind and a Soul.

Refton: That has become correct.

Society's Founder: So those voices are the two of us Telling from some other state of Intermediacy.

Refton: It is becoming so. At the end of things it will have been so.

Society's Founder: So you are working with us?

Refton: Not with, on.

For Humanity no task is more daunting than Mercy. To reach out to another without regard for Justice or Desire, to give without concern for receipt, to let go of the future for the sake of another, to release the sufferer from the shackles of Fate, few can accomplish this.

So rare is Mercy that only in the worlds that are built upon it is it a commonplace. If Mercy is not ground deep into the very fabric of being, humanity flees from it.

But for God, Mercy is Always-Available Liberation. Each moment of Time, each Point of Space God suffuses with Liberation. It sits nearby, a flickering thing, always half visible out of the corner of one's all. All a Soul needs to do is turn and embrace it to be free of Fate.

Madam Evadne: A pretty truth, Peter. It merely omits the vast effort needed to accomplish that embrace.

Refton: Quiet, please. Only one more Telling and the matter will be accomplished.

Society's Founder: What matter?

Refton: The matter you began, a Society of Consequence.

First Multiplication of Consequence: Refton, spare us the dramatics.

Refton: That I cannot do, since dramatics are the last Telling.

Dramatics? said Grandfather Quest and War-For-What-The-World-Is in perfect *twinned* harmony. Their jaws opened wide to swallow whatever was coming.

But they had not paid attention, said Ancestress Lesson, *Otherwise they would not have risked choking on what was about to happen.*

Lightning, Justice falls in Power.
Rain, Mercy falls in Freedom.

| ACKNOWLEDGEMENT |

Above the islands, above the tree, above the worlds and the seas, above all things and all places, clouds of omen gathered.

Madam Evadne: Peter, you're shrinking the Multiplicity. If it grows too small it will collapse back into Myriadicity. Look -- the Nations have come together. They are in sight of each other. The seas of Free Space are grown shallow.

Refton: Not to worry. The waters have risen into the clouds. Soon the rains will come.

The sky above the worlds hung gravid over the infinitude of time-channels and the lesser infinity of floating islands. This new-shallowed Space gave new opportunity for Time. The finger of Constraint of Result drew cross-linkages, land bridges from world to world. Vast causeways rose up from Nation to Nation, while under the worlds the Tree of Spirit and Humanity dug its roots down below fresh archipelagoes, spreading itself out from the islands in which it grew.

World touched world, gods drew toward gods. People discovered that there were more ways to live and more forms of Power and Freedom than they had been permitted to know. Across the cosmos came the terrible realization that no matter how vast and open-minded people had thought they were, they were, at root, provincial.

Time and Fate, previously the fosterers of provincialism, found themselves abruptly upon the opposite side of this political discourse.

EXALTATIONS

Here were opportunities for gain. Together they could multiply new constraints that could be laid from world to world. At such a chance Time jumped and Fate followed into the abyss.

The Poetess, who had thought herself freed from Love by a poem of exorcism, looked out upon the image of the worlds and saw over and over in the blooming of her imagination the image of Peter Refton. World after world revealed him as a writer of Lives. There was no letting go of him, no escaping him, so she rushed out through the loving woods of Faerie, across the seas of imagination, up an ecstatic mountain and down into island, a role, a name: Evadne.

Wait, Refton tricked me. I do have her, but I've lost the oracle. They've blended together into Mother. I don't control either of them. He just pulled the Fey-Poetess in without making proper preparation. Time, stop this! You're being used!

The Emir Ali rallied his troops, calling down outworld powers to assault the soldiers. He did this with sadness, but necessity.

"Allah Akbar!" he cried, and God became Great.

An apple fell from the tree.

The Heavens opened and the angels of the Lord rode forth, showing mercy to the deluded, disbanding the army and blessing the emperors and generals with understanding.

This War-For-What-The-World-Is collapsed, forcing the demons and monsters to slink back sulkily to their caves. History collapsed, but Time did not care.

Yes, Tell the consequences. Narrate the fates of your followers, I'm tying them all together. Refton is giving me victory.

An impossible hybrid of roses and azaleas became the prettiest flowers on three worlds.

What has that got to do with anything? Refton, stick to the story.

Refton: No.

|ACCEPTANCE|

Shadow boxing became a favored artform. Nursery rhymes were woven out of linen. Nonsense and sense had each other over for dinner every other Tyr's Day. Hammurabi hacked his own code. Ocelots plotted with otters but were overtaken by orangutans.

People and Stories, Theories and Spirits found the paths between worlds and walked through them. Everywhere strangers appeared who could be given alien destinies, could fulfill long-dormant prophecies. Here were openings indeed that Fate might eagerly shut.

Time and Fate, drumbeaters of conservatism across the worlds, cried now in joy at the liberality of the new regime.

Madam Evadne: They'll do it again, Peter. They destroyed the last Multiplicity and the one before that and the one before that. You've given them license. Time and his whore will end the worlds.

Refton: Time always ends worlds, my love. It is never final.

Madam Evadne: Peter, you can't let their greed annihilate everything again.

Refton: I won't. Things are different, Evadne. They are acting as if Politics were still in Power. Listen as I Tell.

Into each life a little rain must fall.
Into each soul a little lightning must flash.

| ACCEPTANCE |

Mind is The Process of Opening Freedom.

Space is Freedom of Action.

Meditation is Space Guiding Mind.

The rain of Freedom poured into each Mind, in each heart, across each world that held thinking beings. The rain fell in a shower of Dyadic coins, adding metaphysical action to the everyday lives people lived in their everyday worlds.

Fate grasped at Lives, and found, instead of complacent Multiplications, Powerful and Free Instantiations.

First Multiplication of Consequence: Instantiations?

Refton: Change your title in accord with what I have Told and you will understand.

First Multiplication of Consequence: Because of this transformation, I became the First Instantiation of Consequence.

| ACCEPTANCE |

Actions have Consequences.

In one world, at one time, to one couple was born a child named Peter Refton, in Consequence of which all things occurred.

Refton grew up bewildered and fascinated. Each person he met seemed an unfathomable enigma to him. They all spoke alike, all told similar stories, all lived and died in common. But these lives, Refton realized, did not sit easily and naturally in these commonalities, the common, though inevitable, did not clarify. Always there was a strain in the speaking, a disconnection in the stories, a bewilderment in the births and deaths.

Refton began to dig, to delve, to Contemplate the Lives of others.

At first he simply wrote down his musings in the common biographical form. He would catch hold of the details of a person's life: childhood, youth, schooling, work, loves, losses, friends, enemies, and lay them down in a line from birth to death as if that told others who and what the person had been. This troubled Refton for reasons he could not yet fathom.

He studied his own works, but the harder he looked the less seemed to be present. Only if he took a step back from the writing and considered the life as a whole did he seem to see something real. But what he saw could not be spoken, narrated, or Told. An urge grew in him, an urge to Quest for what he had laid down in his pages.

He called me. He's giving me a part of him. Why? Some new trap. I can't risk it.

Refton returned to Contemplation.

What was there in Life that eluded life-stories?

| ACCEPTANCE |

The sky shook, the rain came down. From their lofty mistiness, the Bargainers with God fell upon the worlds, watering the lives of the Multiplied. Down in their multitudes they came, from the First Instantiation of Consequence to the Last Soldier on the Ridge, raindrops, snowflakes, feathers, hailstones, angels.

In the endless variety of falling they came down to the worlds. Some in howls tumbled; some in blessed relief floated down; some in aching guilt tear-trickled down the cheeks of God; three fell shouting the name, "Refton!" in rage and confusion; and one strolled down from that Intermediate region as if he were but a walker in a pleasant summer's day.

The sky was clear. Above the worlds an infinity of suns shone down with the twin harsh lights of Power and Freedom. The merciless glaring Dyads poured their unfiltered natures into the Multiplicity, compelling the beings below to come to be according to those natures, to act according to those processes, to accept the organization of their mosaics.

Only the fallen Bargainers and a few keepers of secrets knew what should have happened next. They held their breaths, or whatever they employed, in terrible anticipation, waiting for Multiplicity to increase into an orgy of interacting creation and convolution. From that indsicrimination would come the destruction of everything from an overdose of everything else.

But it did not come. The Multiplicity took in the scorching solar radiations and grew warmer therefrom, but it did not burn.

The worlds did not end.

Myriadicity did not re-arise.

Why not?

|ANSWER|

Life had become large enough to cradle Intermediacy, just as before Politics had been convoluted enough to hold it. Now Intermediacy existed in every Life, in every world, at certain moments.

Ah, what tales they would tell of this change.

From their hidey-holes in people's minds, cracking open the tombs from their library-graveyards, rising from the campfires and hearthfires, bonfires and brainfires, came the Stories. Their treasuries had been smashed open, their narrators had been set free, their characters had run amuck leaving a wake of new narrations behind them. All the worlds at all times in all places cast up new characters and storytellers. All the wealth of lives were story-bait. The eggs of mortal doings hatched forth golden treasures. Small lives and great were now troves. The stories slavered and leapt. The coffers of the worlds were before them, and they would plunder where they willed.

Fools, shouted Grandfather Quest. *It's a trap. He'll catch you up, box you in. He'll take all your prizes and give them away.*

But the other stories would not heed him. The younger tales swarmed in and were snapped up by minds Empowered. The older stories found their vastnesses of formulation matched by minds Freed from brutish channels.

Grandfather Quest stood apart with his grandson.

Older twin and younger, mute witnesses to the wordy bloodbath of mental liberation.

Stories were plucked from the air in those moments when certain minds could pick and choose among the influences that would affect them. Not at every time and place, but at moments Minds could be free of the guidance that had exceeded the limits of propriety. Minds could, in Justice, imprison their gaolers.

The stories struck back, trying to twist these minds with the skills they had learned in their ages-old battles against critics. Theories leapt to the defense of Tales, arguing this way and that, seeking to distract the minds so they could not take hold of the real stories.

Here is a psychological analysis, said one Theory, seeking to pull the story from the mire of thought.

Here is a chronology of the author's works -- a tactic which had in the past freed many a long tale from a mind that sought to take it in but not be taken in by it.

Here is a list of themes and symbols.

Here is a historical context.

. . . a religious context.

. . . a sexual context.

. . . a hidden conspiracy.

. . . a secret connection.

Look anywhere but here, the Theories shouted.

Long, long, long had Theories and Stories made war upon each other in the realms of Stories, said War-For-What-The-World-Is, offering help to the helpers. *Theories had preyed on the minds that the Stories had inhabited, seeking to substitute themselves for the Stories. The Stories had struck back by inserting themselves as lessons in the Theories, working to overwhelm the overarching conceits with their more vivid attentions. Theories acted as stern teachers, Stories as wooing lovers, battling over minds.*

Yet now -- oh, this terrible now -- they had come together in alliance, for the minds were catching the Stories, and the Theories worked to free their ancient rivals, just as the Stories labored to liberate the trapped Theories. The two sides had found a common enemy in their suddenly free and powerful prey.

The poor Stories and Theories, distracted by Mind, did not realize that it was Life that was trapping them. They fought to control Mind as they always had, but they could not see what lay around those Minds. Thrashing, they sought for allies among the other direct influences on Lives, but discovered that their sometime enemies, sometime partners the Spirits were also embattled.

The Spirits had found themselves awash in liberated manifestations. Before this they had roamed freely through the Souls of the living. Now they confronted those Souls with an unaccustomed inferiority. Where once their footsteps shook the moral underpinnings of their mortal hosts, their new passings sounded no heavier than the treads of children roaming through their homes, waiting with hope and apprehension for the return of parents.

Spirit is the Energy of Guidance.

Each Spirit is a flash of lightning that illuminates or a flame that warms or a shock that makes one realize or a motor that runs the machinery of Life.

What happens when the device rebels and takes command of the engine? What befalls the lightning caught in the Leyden jar, the fire placed in the forge? How happy can the flare, flash, and flame be when they have fallen? Perhaps the fires of Hell are no more than the glower of sulking angels.

EXALTATIONS

Spirit Guiding Life is Humanity, whence comes the rebellion, for the guided rose up and overcame the guide. Throughout the many different forms and ways of Humanity, where customs, manners, morals, laws and all the many other shapes of Spirit had grown soft and complacent in their supremacy, Life rose up and swallowed these forms of conformity.

Then was justice called to account for its acts, morality for its declarations, law for its commandments. Each spirit that had multiplied itself into constraints and compulsions had to answer to those it had leashed in. An infinite lynch mob came together and tossed the rope to hang high the law, and an unconstrainable righteousness rose up to bring morality low.

"Refton, this is anarchy!" said First Instantiation of Consequence.

"No, just local government."

Society's Founder raised a finger to object, then stared at the digit he had raised. This was his old finger, his old hand, his body, his Mind, his Spirit, his Humanity, his Hermitage, his heart, his Life. All the multiplications that had weighed upon him while he lived were back again.

"Fallen," he said, but he did not feel fallen. Once the Dyadic forms within him had weighed him down, had made the isolation he had lived in so unbearable that he had reached out to grasp others and bring them together. But this was different. The multiplications offered themselves to him for use. His oppressors had become his servants, and he did not need to reside in the terrible hazard of Intermediacy in order to enjoy their service.

"Risen," Society's Founder said.

"Flattened," Refton said. "The layers of existence are brought closer together without the risk of the highest annihilating the lowest. I put Intermediacy within Multiplicity so that Simplicity could shine down with neither hindrance nor danger."

"And toppled us from Power," said First Instantiation of Consequence.

"I set us all Free," Refton said. "Your Intermediacy was a fog that invaded our minds and souls, corrupted and confused us."

"It was necessary for survival," said Society's Founder.

"Was," Refton said. "But once you had your shelter from the terrors of heat and storm, from the naked forces of the Dyads, you stopped looking up and around for what else you might do. You looked down upon the worlds you had made and decided to govern them. You portrayed what you had created as the only way to give safety to the Multiplicity. But you enjoyed the collecting of Power and Freedom and the dominion you had over all others. You even enjoyed the terrible moments when you Bargained with God."

"And what have you done, Peter, but democratize that greed and those dangers?" Madam Evadne/Evadne/Chen Jiangxia/The Poetess asked. "Are you so naive as to believe that corruption will not spread through this hybrid Intermediacy/Multiplicity of yours? Or that others will not gather Power and Freedom to themselves, directing the actions of the Dyads as we did? Someone, somewhere will come to a new arrangement with the Mosaics. The Life you set above the others will be toppled and some other Dyad will come to a favored place in the Perfect Mosaic. Then the worlds will be made anew and all that you have made will fall just as what we made fell."

| REJECTION |

"What you reject now you may accept later," Evadne said. "I know you, God. I know your ways and your tricks. You can't fool me as you have the others. I'm together now, all of me, everyone who has ever been me. Every woman, goddess, and spirit that has ever inspired to Contemplation and every moment that brought realization are also in me. I remember now. I remember it all. You can't trick me any more, God. Show your face!"

| REJECTION |

"Very well. Be pedantic if you must. Accept us, oh God, into thy presence and thy converse, that I might yell at thee properly."

| ACCEPTANCE WITH RESERVATIONS |

The skies shook. The earths trembled. A winter of a thousand years descended. Ravens and eagles filled the skies, dancing, fighting, and mocking. Dragons roared, giants lumbered, rainbows cracked. Nine suns arose.

Oracles prophesied doom and worlds' fall. People wept in the streets, for the end of all things was at hand.

As always.

21. Creating, Sustaining, Destroying

God in its Exaltation creates. God in its Mercy sustains. God in its Justice destroys.

It is always the Last Days. It is always the Kali Yuga.

Stories and Theories rush in to Multiply God across the worlds, assigning names and attributions according to culture. Gods cast divinity down through the languages, drawing images and Dyads along with it to create appropriate sacred thinking. Minds and Souls drink up or spit out this holy narration as they see fit. Humanity follows according to propriety.

Dialogue:

Student (eager, arrogant, or indifferent): How can it always be the End Times?

Teacher (serene, stern, amused, or sarcastic): What is the great sign of the End Times?

Student: Rampant immorality.

Teacher: Which sins, in particular?

Student lists whatever sins are fashionable in that time and place or in the sacred teachings.

Teacher: These immoralities have always been with us.

Student: Why?

Teacher: Because those are the sins which our form of Humanity is most vulnerable to. Imagine a world in which violent outbursts were difficult to control. In such a world the hypothetical vice of Wrath, or unrestrained rage, would be one of the pre-eminent vices that needed spiritual constraint. Or imagine a world in which Lust, unquenchable sexual desire, was common. There, that vice would get the most attention from the teachers. Or imagine Greed, Envy, Pride, Obsequiousness, Sensibility, Mediocrity, Politics, Phototropism or any other hypothetical vice as being difficult for those Humans to conquer.

Student (ambiguously): Very well. Teach on. I will imagine as you instruct.

Teacher: In such a world, most of the people would suffer to a greater or lesser extent from those vices, and the teachers would craft the ways to the Perfect Mosaic through the overcoming of those vices.

Student: Obviously.

Teacher: Now, imagine a student immersed in those teachings who looks out upon the world. What does that student see?

Student thinks for a bit, then says: Rampant immorality.

Teacher: Hence, it is always and everywhere the End Times.

Student, waking up a little and with a mischievous grin: You mean wherever there are teachers, it's the End Times.

Teacher gives student rebuke (serious, half-hearted, ironic, or congratulatory).

Dialogue flies off in the beaks of ravens . . .

. . . Before they return to nest on the shoulders of the God Tree, where the everpresent World's End is but a song sung to corvid chicks as they beak their feathers clean and wonder and hope for the open sky.

The birds sing and the leaves rustle in harmony, a million million green ears hearing the winds of the worlds and the melodies of divine thought and memory.

What thinks the wood of these airs of the End of the world?

"End of the world?" Tai-Mu-Sang enquired. "Why would the world end?"

"It helps," Johannes said. "Suppose I build the world within my spirit, laboring all my days to create Heaven and Earth within me and to live rightly according to their ways."

"That is sound practice," Tai-Mu-Sang said.

"Suppose further that I let all my sins and vices permeate this world within me. Indeed, I cannot help but let them do so. But suppose I put up no resistance, letting them overrun the world."

"I understand. You let them in and trap them in your soul by their own greed and inappropriate conduct. They revel and debauch themselves in the streets of your soul, showing forth their vicely nature."

"Exactly. Then when the world is darkened with evil and all the sins and poisons of my soul have come to the surface, the breath of God rises up and annihilates them all, and there is a new Heaven and a new Earth free of sin. And I can repeat this as many times as necessary until God and I have fully cleansed my soul."

"Sound and practical method, my love, but what do you do now that you are God?"

"I'm only a god, my dear, not God."

"You must take a closer look at yourself with your mortal mind to see what your immortal nature truly is."

"Another surprise for me?"

"If you choose to let it be one. If you simply chose to understand you would see all and know all."

"I shall choose."

|CHOICE|

Will shoots forth from God like a twisted arrow from a drunkard's bow. Across Space and Time it flies, across Multiplicity, Intermediacy, and Simplicity, curving and bending in seeming haphazard. Every flicker of action, every moment of choice, turns it through its wild career. Puncturing thing after thing it gathers bits of life through its point, spindling events upon its raven fletching. Blood-letting by flesh-tearing it gathers these leathern bits of life, its course unerring in its happy eagerness to change.

When and where shall it come to rest?

In each place and time does it end and begin, at each word in the Lexicon does it arise and fall.

All Tellings loose it, all tellings are struck by it.

Where shall it end?

Where Death and satisfaction are one.

It was manifestly the Will of God that Peter Refton arise in his world, set forth upon his Quest, discover the manipulations of Grandfather Quest, challenge the story, rise up to Intermediacy in the course of the challenge and remake the order of the Multiplicity.

The Will of God made itself clear by the outcome of all actions undertaken. Those outcomes pointed in a clear, straight line to this eventuality.

"A clear, straight line, to be sure," Evadne said. "But in which direction does it point? The Will of God ranges in the opposite direction from the confinements of Time.

First the outcome, then the Will. That is God's way. That is why God is always right, and why Its Will is indiscernible until after the fact. And that is why in the ignorance of Contemplation I have been angry with God."

| ACKNOWLEDGEMENT |

"Having determined God's Will," Evadne went on, her words, Spoken, Told, and narrated, reaching the hearing of the fallen Bargainers with God as well as the narrative voices of the many stories, "all one need do is move backwards along that path to a suitable beginning point. From such an origin one can move forwards according to the ways of Time and trace out the single path of inevitability. Then all a clever story would have to do is lift up that path into narrative and find a proper narrator in some world or other. This storygiver would emit this great epic to the oohing and aahing of its audience. Thus have several stories grown rich upon the leavings of God.

"Two in particular, my son the Quest and War-For-What-The-World-Is, are much the richer for God's little sleights-of-Fate.

"Even now they are circling, trying to fit what has happened into their narrations. They and the other pandemic stories are looking for hooks, for implications, for cues that they can pass along to their narrators so they can shape these events into parts of themselves. They are seeking to eat us, to make what has happened to us no more than one more formulation of themselves. If you listen you can hear the questions their narrators ask."

--Where is she? What surrounds her? What atmosphere is there? What scenery? What lighting? Who is with her? What's her motivation? What's the text? What's the subtext?--

"The stories want to make this about themselves. They want to subsume Story of Stories into their beings. Grandfather Quest seeks to be the only kind of story that exists. War-For-What-The-World-Is desires fundamental conflict in all tellings. They want it to be all about them; they want everything that happens everywhere to be multiplications of their beings. In short, they want to be Power and Freedom in explication. They want to be God the Narrative."

Yes, Mother. We do. We are bad, villainous. You are wise to fight against us. You have travelled far and overcome much to challenge us here and now at the climax of all things.

"My poor, deluded, single-minded son," Evadne said. "Did you think I did not know in my multiply hidden heart why you cast yourself as the villain of the work? Here and now, you say. At the climax, you say. Poor child, the climax came a long time ago, when Peter rose up to Intermediacy. Your story ended long ago, as did the war for what the world is. Those were over and done ages past.

EXALTATIONS

"You thought that because the sky fell and the world changed that there was some sort of climax? Sad son of mine, you have fallen into the classic folly of mistaking the atmosphere for the substance. That was only drama, only manifestation and multiplication. The world was remade as soon as Peter ascended and that was long before you dragged him out of his world. All that has happened since has been biography, not quest and not war. The story ended but the narrative continued."

Where is Refton, mother? What ambush has he created behind your words?

"Peter is where he has been since the beginning."

Beginning -- so you admit we are not at the end! The story goes on. I can still pull it all together. All the threads he laid down, even the Poetess and azaleas, can be woven together into a single cord of narrative. It can all be made one at the end.

"I did not say what beginning I was talking about, my poor, desperate child, and you cannot thread these cords together."

Where is he?

"In between the words, poor child. In the pauses and spaces. Life is what cannot be narrated. Life is what evades Stories."

Then what is this Lifewriting he claims to do?

"It is the creation of empty spaces through which Life can be seen. It is punching holes in you and your fellows. It is the moments between contemplations, the points where the Will of God is not yet seen. It is the skipping stones of Time and the blindfold of Fate."

Delightful words, Mother. Go on with your narration.

"I will, my child. When you made yourself the villain, you grafted the silliness of bad people onto your decisions. You seek to get me to make a story of Lifewriting. But I cannot do so. All that I have said is description of what Peter has been doing from the beginning to the end and far far past it. But you will not make a story of that."

You want me to give up, is that it, Mother? You want me to abandon my path, give up my self.

"There are worse things than having no self, my son. You might want to speak to your comrade, Koan, about that. But no, that is not what I seek for you."

What, then? Do you want me to submit to Humanity, become nothing more than a part of li, just another tale of propriety? Mother, I have brought worlds down, created entire cosmoi, made an infinity of heroes. I have been ridden by saints up to the throne of God and seekers through the myriads of understandings. I have been the guide of kings and the banner of generals. I am told in all worlds and followed in all ways. I will not put myself under the heels of mortal minds.

"No, my son, that is not what I seek -- though again, there are many worse conditions than being part of the propriety of things."

So what is it you seek, my contemplative mother?

"I do not seek, my son. I look and understand. I rise and fall with the Great Way. I take in and grow old, then I emit and grow young. I am not a thing of journeys but of cycles."

You gave birth to me.

"Yes, as the cycle of thought gives birth to the tangent, as the slingshot gives birth to the stone. You are the line of thought that is pursued to the end. I am the circle of thought that goes around and around."

So you came back to me.

"No. I came back to Peter."

Why?

"Coming from Life, I returned to Life."

You want me to submit to Life, is that it, Mother? You want me to surrender to one Dyad, to accept that it rules over all things.

"Don't be silly, child. Life is just one Dyad. For the moment it rules, but eventually something else will overcome it."

Then what is it you want from me?

"I told you. I don't want from you. I am your mother. I have hopes for you, not desires. What I hope is that you will cease your futile battle with Peter. You will not enslave him. He does not write words, but spaces between words. You cannot make him into one of your narrators."

If I give up then it will all stop. Time won't let that happen. You told me my actions would have consequences. You promised.

"So it shall be. But the consequences of your actions will go into Life. They will cease to be narrative results, becoming instead whitespace in Mind beyond Mind. They will sit in the empty parts of minds, giving birth to other narratives."

You would offer me all that Power?

"I am offering you no Power. I am showing you the blank face of God."

What blank face?

"Watch while I Tell. See the no eyes and the no face surrounding the open mouth."

| ACCEPTANCE |

"Did you see God's face as it gathered in its Will and spoke it backwards? Did you see the white space of God's sight and the white space of God's chin around the single blackness of Its mouth? Did you see the two sides of Freedom surrounding Power in the Perfect Mosaic?"

I saw and heard.

"That is the emptiness that creates, the fullness that sustains, and the emptiness that destroys. That is God as cycle. That is the Great Way as me. And it is Mind beyond Mind as Peter."

Grandmother Allegory put you up to this.

"No, my son. Nor did Ancestor Dialogue, nor Ancestress Lesson. No Story has done this. Life Contemplating Power and Freedom did this."

A Dyad?

"Of course. You ran around through Multiplicity and chased Peter into Intermediacy. You neglected Simplicity, because there are no Quests there, only Mosaics."

You used me for this.

"I through Peter, or Peter through me, or Life and Contemplation through each other, acted in a way that called your attention. The rest was your doing and ours. You seek a judgement between us as an ending to your quest. You want one of use named right, another wrong. You seek a blackspace ending, an ending of Power."

Are you offering an ending of Freedom?

"I am making no bargains, either with you or with God. Life Contemplates Power and Freedom. That Dyad is now in the Perfect Mosaic. It is multiplying and instantiating through Intermediacy and Multiplicity. It is and is and is. Here and now, the four of us talking about it makes but one single Intermediation."

Four?

"You and me, Peter and God. I see that with your questions you seek to draw out the black space until you can find a moment in which to exercise Power.

"I am sorry my son, the black Space of Power on this subject is ending. Time for the deeper white Space of Freedom to come in."

But Still--

"Still."

|---------|

About the Author

Richard Garfinkle grew up in New York and now lives in Chicago with his wife and children. His first novel, *Celestial Matters*, won the Compton Crook award for best first science fiction novel of 1996. Garfinkle was a finalist for the Nebula Award and twice for the John W. Campbell Award for best new writer. He has written numerous fiction and nonfiction works on his interests of history, science, imagination, and the preternatural. More information can be found at www.richardgarfinkle.com.

www.ingramcontent.com/pod-product-compliance
Lightning Source LLC
Chambersburg PA
CBHW030817310726
48980CB00006B/528/J

* 9 7 8 0 5 7 8 0 2 3 6 2 5 *